The Dazzling Universe
of Helen Fox

by

Tom Richards

Storylines
Entertainment Ltd

About The Dazzling Universe of Helen Fox

"Is there life on other planets?" Helen Fox asks her husband Doug Masters. He can't answer. He's not sure what's out there. And right now, none of us are. Yet there are signals coming from the centre of the Centauri Galaxy. Could that be life? In this author's opinion, the answer is 'Yes'. This book takes course over many generations as humankind attempts to conquer our Solar System.

It starts in 1976. Doug Masters, a young pilot, is flying a Lear Jet to an Alaskan airport. When he encounters a strange object that almost destroys his jet and realizes it's a UFO, he vows never to tell anyone. Yet, when he begins to dream about a young woman he'll meet someday, and a silent voice whispers in his head about a future of both happiness and global tragedy, Doug at first thinks he's insane. What follows is an encounter not only with the young woman of his dreams but also an experience that makes him realize that his dream was reality not fiction—one which takes him, as well as the woman, on a voyage to outer space.

Years later, Helen Fox, a thirty-two-year-old Irish woman, becomes pregnant in Ireland and is simultaneously operated on for cancer, resulting in the horrific stillbirth of her infant. Fleeing Ireland, she flies to New York City. Onboard that airplane, she meets Doug Martin, a co-pilot for United Airlines. They fall in love and, after only a few days, Doug asks her to marry him. Following a horrific accident during which Doug is the pilot-in-command of a stricken passenger aircraft, half the passengers die and half survive. Suffering from life-threatening injuries due to the violent crash, he experiences nightmares and related symptoms due to Post Traumatic Stress Disorder. Helen visits him in the hospital and realizes that his symptoms are not only the result of the accident but also due to a woman she also had heard whisper silently in her head, just like Doug.

Both of them soon experience the inexplicable. First that silent voice, then a Lady who is much more than a woman, visits them both in their dreams. But it turns out that the dreams are actually reality. They find themselves aboard a NASA space vehicle near the Centauri Galaxy. Alone and without oxygen, food or water, an alien intergalactic spaceship rescues them. Soon, Helen and Doug learn that the beings who saved them are from the planet Gaia near the Centauri Galaxy.

The Royal Queen and her Consort take them to that planet. There, Helen and Doug are married. But they learn that when the Queen dies Helen will become the next Royal Queen of the planet Gaia. It is up to Helen and Doug to save the Earth from annihilation.

The Dazzling Universe of Helen Fox is a story first about space travel to a distant galaxy—and a dystopian view of what the world might turn into if humankind lets it.

✝ Denotes Feature Films or Television Series of these Novels
Soon in Production

** Denotes Novels in development

Dedication

This novel has been written for

Jackie Harrington,

a glittering friend from Rolling Meadows High School

&

Will Arnold, RMHS Class of 1974 and still
my Best Buddy in the USA

Children feared when we were children

The nightmare of the nuclear flames

Now the world's gone mad again

The bang, the whimper, the slaughter

But have faith in God's eternal whisper

The lesson that His Son spoke aloud

"Treat others as you would want to be treated"

The world has been blessed and cannot end

But we are responsible to protect it

— Lawrence Wilson

Behold, he cometh with clouds; and every eye shall see him, and they also which pierced him: and all kindreds of the earth shall wail because of him.

Even so, Amen.

— Revelation 1:7 The Holy Bible, King James Version

Maps, Artists' Renditions, and Photographs of Planets and Solar Systems in this Novel

Figure 1 GAIA, named after the Royal Ruler of that Distant Planet

Figure 2: Earth's Moon

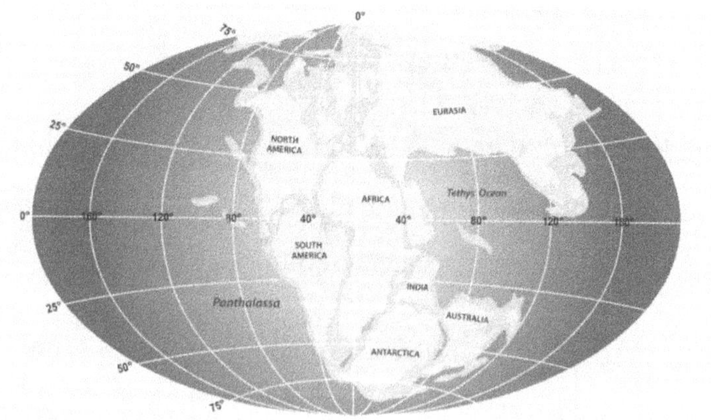

Figure 3: NEW EARTH - which looks much like Earth did Millions of Years Ago

Figure 4 Location of Alpha Centauri Galaxy viewed from the Southern Hemisphere

Figure 5 Black Hole including its Event Horizon and Singularity

Figure 6: Milky Way Galaxy

Figure 7: On the surface of Alpha Centauri b

Table Of Contents

Prologue:

Unexplained Encounters

Chapter One

YEAR: 1976

PLACE: NORAD, CHEYANNE U.S. DEFENSE COMMAND CENTER

Buried three hundred feet below the Cheyanne mountains in the state of Colorado, in a hanger-like cement bunker protecting it from nuclear destruction, radar operator Sargent Will Johnson looked down at his glowing monitor. But the radar readout which came from a satellite in geocentric orbit over the United States showed nothing except commercial airliners and other objects miles below the U.S. Air Force spy satellite.

He stretched and looked around. Other military personnel were sitting at their radar monitors, on the phone, or talking to their superior officers. Will looked up at the giant screen bolted to a nearby wall which displayed the North American continent. At the bottom of the screen that was over one-hundred feet wide and fifty feet tall, a printed display stated that the country was at DEFCON TWO, which was usual with no dangerous conflicts anywhere in the world. Turning around in his swivel chair, he looked behind him at the towering office block that had been built into the rocky cave of the mountain. He noticed a Colonel with some invited guests from China as he took them on a tour of NORAD's most important command center. Thirty minutes ago, Will had been ordered by the Captain of his unit to hide anything secret that the Chinese delegation might see. The few secret documents that he had were locked in his desk drawer.

The door to a ground floor office opened. Major General Bud Gleeson, in charge of the NORAD command post, walked out. He stood by his Colonel and an American woman from the State Department who could translate from English to Chinese and back again. One of the Chinese delegation took out a camera and pointed toward the giant display board. The State Department official nodded and the delegate took ten pictures then all shook hands. The American officers strode toward Will as the delegates and the State Department representative walked out of the huge cavern.

"Goddam Chinese!" the Major General snarled. "What the hell does the State Department mean by bringing them here? This is the most critical center of our global defense systems. If I was the president, I'd fire whoever allowed them in."

"Damned right, Sir," replied the Colonel. "If I had my way, I'd boil those bastards in a Chinese Wok then have my dogs eat 'em. You can't trust the Chinese any more than you can trust the Russians."

"Yeah, but that's not what the president thinks. It's nineteen seventy-six, after all. Two hundred years after our nation was founded. But the current peanut farmer who's in office doesn't believe his Joint Chiefs of Staff. They understand that the Commies are still a threat. The Russians have God alone knows how many nuclear weapons and the Chinese capability is growing fast. If we're not careful, they'll fire when we're not looking and wipe us off the face of the Earth."

"You're right, General. Thank God we can leave most of it to the politicians. All we have to do is make sure that nothing gets into our airspace. If it looks like a threat, then I guess all we have to do…"

"Is fire! That's right, Colonel. It's standard operating procedure. If we see something that looks threatening to our country, we fire first to shoot it down and ask questions later. Now come on. It's early but what about a shot of Scotch? I have a bottle in my office."

As the two officers walked back to the Major General's office, Will looked to the radar operator sitting next to him. Private Genny Volker, one of the first black women to be assigned to duty in NORAD, glanced to Will and smiled.

"Oh, wouldn't you love to be an officer? Can you imagine sharing a bottle of Scotch this early in the day? Officers in the military have balls of brass, or so the tradition says. They must have livers made of steel, too."

Will grinned back, stretching, because he'd been on duty since midnight.

"That's mighty true, Genny. Balls of brass. Don't know about you, but I'll be glad to get off duty. You know my wife, Susan, is expecting any day now."

"Our unit Captain gave you time off, right?"

"Two weeks leave. When I get off his shift I'm homeward bound."

"You live in Colorado Springs?"

"Yep, that's a surety. Two weeks of vacation time with just me, Susan and my kid if she gives birth while I'm with her."

Will's phone rang. Picking it up, he listened to his Captain. As his unit commander talked, Will turned on his speaker so Genny could listen, too.

"Yes, Sir, I heard you," Will said into the speaker phone. "Where'd you say it was headed?"

"Toward Alaska," the Captain replied. "We think it's a standard private jet aircraft but we are having trouble getting through to the pilot. For now, consider it a target. We'll call it Bogey One."

"Got that sir. You've told the Major General?"

"Are you shitting me? He's having a drink with the Colonel. If the aircraft does anything suspicious, then I'll call our commanding officer. Capiche, Sargent?"

"You got it, sir. We'll find it and let you know if Bogey One does anything suspicious."

Genny looked up from her radar monitor. "I got Bogey One, Will. It's just coming into our quadrant."

Will looked down at his own screen. "I see it. Tracking due west. Can't say it appears much of a threat. It's like the Captain told us. Bet the poor fella is just off course or has hit some winds he wasn't expecting. See? He's already over the Juan de Fucca straights just west-north-west of Seattle, Washington. Genny, you call the NORAD base out there. They can help us keep an eye on it."

As Private Volker lifted her phone, Will shook his head. "If that guy doesn't radio in soon, he might well be a dead man."

✈ ✈ ✈

Over two thousand miles from the Cheyanne Mountain NORAD Complex, Doug Martin, twenty-six years old, looked down from his Lear jet cockpit at the desolate Alaskan landscape below him. Flying in clear skies, and from an altitude of thirty-two thousand feet, all he could see were green forests, lakes, and a group of inlets that led out to the deep blue of the Pacific Ocean. In the distance to the west was Mount McKinley, the tallest mountain in North America, rising from the wilderness like a snow-capped island. He looked up and to his left. Pinned just below the cockpit window was a birthday card from his parents. He picked it up, opening it again, and read his mother's neat handwriting.

October 4 1982

To our dearest son,

May you have many safe hours of flying in your long career. Enclosed, please find a twenty-dollar bill. Have a few beers on us when you have some time.

With all our love, Mom and Dad

He'd have to make a point to drive out to his parent's house on Long Island, New York, when he got back from this trip. He'd been so busy flying that he hadn't seen his folks in over a year. Doug closed the card and placed it back beneath the window. Then he stretched, rolled his neck, and checked his position again on the Jeppesen map that he's placed in the co-pilot's seat to his right.

Having flown the Lear from Chicago, and with a final destination of Juneau, Doug had piloted the jet alone with no co-pilot onboard, which was standard practice when ferrying that type of aircraft to pick up passengers. Having received clearance to descend from forty-thousand feet to his present altitude by Anchorage Air Traffic Control, he had been told to contact Juneau Approach Control who would now be responsible for his final approach to the airport. Doug glanced out the window one more time then keyed his mic.

"Juneau Approach Control, this is Lear November Four Hundred Quebec Bravo. I'm fifty miles east of Hobart Bay and would like clearance to descend for landing at Juneau. Do you read me, over?"

As he waited for the response, he thought about how lucky he had been to land this job. A year earlier, with America entering recession and pilots all over the States being given their pink slips, he had been hired by a large U.S. corporation to fly its company jets, which Doug realized was a great way to build up flying time. After the interview, the company's chief pilot had shaken his hand. "Doug, you're the youngest pilot we've ever hired. You've so many hours flying jets and various other aircraft in your brief career, and assuming you work hard over the next few months, I'll promote you to Captain to fly our Lear and Gulfstream jets. Congratulations!"

For Doug, it was a huge step up on the ladder leading to a professional career in aviation. His ambition was to fly for United Airlines just like his father did before he retired. He realized that if he built up enough hours in various kinds of jets his dream of becoming a United pilot would come true. This trip to Alaska would add another five hours to his log book. When he picked up the company's Chief Executive Officer and some members of the board of directors the next morning, Doug would fly them direct to London, which would add another ten hours to his total flying time. With any luck, in another year he would have a grand total of almost four thousand hours, more than enough to apply for a job at United.

Having received no response from Juneau Approach Control, Doug keyed his mic again. "Juneau approach, this is November Four Hundred Quebec Bravo. Do you read me, over?"

Doug adjusted the headset that covered his ears and listened for Juneau Approach but all he heard was static. Reaching to the radio on the instrument panel in front of him, he turned up the volume but the static in his headset only grew louder. Then he heard a short 'bleep' followed by what sounded like Morse Code beating into his ears. "Ta—ta— ta –da, ta—ta—ta—da, ta—ta—ta—da," repeated itself over and over again.

He reached to the primary radio, turning it off, convinced there was a problem with it. Then he flipped a switch and tried the alternate radio. But the same thing happened. All he heard through his headset was a transmission that sounded like Morse, so he tuned that radio to other frequencies but all he heard was the strange pattern of code. Frustrated, he turned off the alternate radio. Like most pilots, Doug had learned how to read Morse Code but this sequence of 'ta's' and 'da's' made no sense to him. Now worried that he would have no radio at all to contact any air traffic controller, he started to plan how he would safely make his approach to Juneau. As he held the Lear's altitude at thirty-two thousand feet, knowing he could not go lower until he received clearance from Juneau Approach, he made a handwritten note on a pad of paper to report the fault and have the company mechanics fix it. He also realized that if they could not repair the problem in Juneau, the company would have to fly in another aircraft or cancel the trip to London.

As Doug again began to think of how he could make a safe landing without any radio, he glanced out the forward windshield. Lights as bright as ten suns filled the horizon, suddenly blinding him. Shielding his eyes and face from the glare that suddenly felt red-hot, he grimaced in pain and shouted: "What in Almighty God is that!"

In the NORAD Command Center, Will and Genny both jumped up from their screens at the same time.

"Do you see those?" Will shouted as Genny reached for her phone.

"Captain, Will and I both have the same thing on our radars. Yes sir, we're still tracking Bogey One. He's on approach to Juneau Airport right now but I've talked to the airport's Approach Control supervisor and they haven't been able to raise the pilot of Bogey One. Sir, it's a Lear jet piloted by a Doug Martin. We've pulled his files. He's twenty-six years old and has quite a few flying hours." She paused as the Captain said something back to her. "But this call is relevant, Sir. Will and I also have ten other Bogeys on our scopes. We contacted Chicago ATC. Mr Masters filed a flight plan before he left Chicago. That Bogey One is him, all right. As to the other bogeys?" She glanced again at Will who nodded to her. "Sir, we're classifying them as Unidentified Flying Objects." Again, she looked at Will. "The Captain says he wants to talk to you, too. I'll put him on speaker."

"What the hell do you mean you have ten UFOs on your radar?" the Captain shouted. "Ten? That's impossible. NORAD in Alaska is showing nothing but Bogey One."

"Sir, that's what we're showing," Will said to his senior officer. "It's on Private Volker's radar, too."

"Balls, Sargent! The scope is fucked up. I'll be right down with a technician."

Will looked at Genny and she looked back at him as she pointed to her screen. "That's what it shows, isn't it?"

"Yep, it sure does. So does mine."

Both of them looked back at their radar screens, watching as one blip peeled off from the others and raced toward the Lear jet.

"Fuckin' A! Look at that Bogey go!"

"I see it, Will. I'm guessing it's at about one-hundred and fifty thousand feet and descending toward the Lear. I make its speed at Mach ten or more. Is that what you think?"

"You know it. I wouldn't want to be in that pilot's shoes right now. Would you?"

"You kiddin' me? I don't like to fly anyway."

They both watched as the blip which they had now classified as Bogey Two moved in on the Lear jet.

In his cockpit, Doug still shielded his face with both hands. The Lear buffeted in turbulence which, Doug knew, was possible at his present altitude and in the current clear weather conditions but was also very rare. When he finally felt the heat on his arms and hands begin to cool, he lowered them from his face and opened his eyes. A mile in front of him was some kind of aircraft heading directly toward him.

"What the hell…?"

It was traveling at high speed and looked more like a kite or a flying box than any airplane he had ever seen in his life. As it speeded toward him, the anti-avoidance warning system in the Lear's cockpit began to wail. Grabbing the wheel, he banked the jet more than he knew he should at such an altitude and airspeed. Behind him, through the door that led to the passenger cabin, he heard glasses shatter as they fell from their shelves. Looking out the windshield again, Doug saw nothing but empty skies. But then the strange vehicle was right in front of him again. Knowing he had to perform another steep bank because otherwise he would hit it, he started the turn. The unidentifiable object made a ninety-degree change in course, as if on a dime, then stopped in mid-air just in front of the Lear. This time, it backed away from the nose of his aircraft, keeping in front of him at a safe distance. Doug looked at the jet's airspeed indicator. He was flying at three hundred and seventy-five knots and the craft in front of him was still traveling backwards at that same airspeed.

"Christ, that's impossible!" he shouted to himself as he gawked at it through the window. "Not even an advanced Air Force jet like the Blackbird SR-71 can perform those sorts of maneuvers at this height and airspeed."

As the advanced vehicle pirouetted in front of Doug's Lear, the bright light again lit the skies. Doug watched, now terrified, as his jet's forward windshield warped and cracked. He was convinced it would soon shatter and knew that if that happened, he would be helpless. But the windshield somehow held together. Clutching the aircraft's steering wheel tight with both hands, he was unable to see clearly outside which made flying almost impossible except by instruments. Then the Lear shuddered again and, as he heard an explosion behind him, he lost power in the right engine. Doug shut down that engine and compensated by pushing hard on the left rudder peddle.

Looking out the unbroken side window of the windshield and peering forward, he noted that the light had disappeared. But now the weird vehicle was only yards from the Lear, flying on its left-hand side. This time he had a closer view of the bizarre object. He noted that it was square and built like a sort of box with stubby wings on each side and what appeared to be standard aircraft engines hanging beneath them like any modern aircraft. It had no windshield so he couldn't see the pilot. The strange craft paced alongside his left window as if whoever was inside wanted Doug to see how proud they were of their silver vehicle.

'Maybe it's the Chinese or the Russians,' Doug thought. 'I'm not that far from Siberia and both countries have a whole lot of military airports all along the east side of their continent. Maybe this is an advanced enemy prototype. If it is, the US Air Force doesn't stand a chance in the air anymore. I wish I had a rocket. I'd shoot down the damned bastard. That would stop the Communist threat in its tracks.'

"My child…"

Doug automatically keyed his radio mic. "Sir, can you repeat that? Juneau Approach, do you read me?"

"Do not be afraid. We come to you now to tell you that very soon, we shall come again."

"Juneau Approach! Do you read!"

"The approach control cannot hear you. But I am always here with you. After all, I am your mother."

Doug looked up at the radio speaker. "Mom? Is that you?"

Then he heard a whisper again and realized it came from inside his head. "You have many, many mothers, my dear son. But I am the most important one."

He thought he had gone crazy. He looked down at his hands. They were shaking. At that point, he wanted to be anywhere else but in the cockpit of the jet and worried that if anyone found out he was nuts he'd no longer be able to fly anything, much less have a career with United Airlines. But as if reading his negative thoughts, the object took off, this time straight up. Then the Lear began to climb behind it though Doug had not pulled back the wheel of the aircraft to ascend to a new altitude. Doug glanced at the jet's altimeter. He was at thirty-four thousand feet and climbing like a bat out of hell, which he knew was impossible with only one engine. Pulling the throttle lever closed for the working left engine, he grasped the control wheel tight with both hands and tried to pull the Lear out of its climb. Worried the plane would stall from lack of speed, he looked at the airspeed indicator. His jet was climbing at five-hundred and seventy knots, a speed Doug knew the Lear was not designed for nor capable of doing. Yet the jet held together as, with another blinding flash, the box-like vehicle appeared again right beside Doug's side window. Then it disappeared leaving nothing but blue empty sky where it had been just a second before.

There was another flash of light. When Doug looked up, it was as if a ground crew had replaced the shattered front windshield. It didn't have a scratch on it.

He blinked, then blinked again, disbelieving what his own eyes told him. What he saw in front of the Lear could only be Juneau Airport's main runway. Somehow, he was on final approach to land which was also impossible. He glanced again at his altimeter. Rather than thirty-four thousand feet, it now read two-thousand feet and descending on the runway's glidepath.

The primary radio came to life even though he had not touched it since turning it off.

"Unidentified aircraft on final approach, this is Juneau Airport," Doug heard the controller state clearly. "What the hell do you think you're doing? You never asked for clearance to land!"

Doug keyed his mic. "Pan, pan, pan. Juneau Approach, I'm declaring an emergency. This is Lear Four Hundred Quebec Bravo. I've lost an engine and, until now, my radio. Am having trouble controlling the aircraft. Can you alert emergency services? There's only one soul onboard."

"Roger Quebec Bravo. Sir, you're on short final with no landing gear or flaps down. I recommend you do a go-around then we'll vector you back to the runway. Do you read, Lear QB? Come in, over."

✈ ✈ ✈

"Get the hell away from your desks!" the Captain shouted at Will and Genny. As they stepped away, a technician ran up to Will's desk. He carried a tool box and, pulling out a screwdriver, starting taking apart the radar monitor.

"Captain, there's nothing wrong with my radar," Will said. "The Private and me, we both ran standard troubleshooting measures on both sets. It came back in the green even though we ran it three times."

The Captain stepped up to Genny's radar. Looking down, his finger pointed at the screen.

"Okay, we have ten blips again, Private. The one that was near the Lear has joined the others. What about the Learjet?"

"We got a call a minute ago from Juneau Approach Control. The Lear is on final and should be landing in less than five minutes."

"Captain, look at that!" Will said in a hushed voice. "See that blip? It's descending again at Mach ten right toward Juneau Airport."

"Holy God Almighty!" the Captain shouted, and turned to the radar technician. "Put that radar back together right now! Private, call NORAD in Juneau. Tell them to scramble their jets immediately. Make sure they're armed with Sparrows. Get the Major General down here, Sargent."

The Captain picked up the mic to the NORAD Command Center PA. As he did, he pressed a red button. A Claxon began to wail.

"Attention! This is not a drill. We're going to DEFCOM four right now! All staff, man your stations." Then he picked up another phone. "Pete, this is Johnny over at the Mountain. Yep, that's what we see, too. Ten of 'em and one diving on Juneau. We got all sorts of nuclear weapons and missiles stored there. Yeah, I just ordered DEFCOM four. The Major General is coming in to authorize my order. If I were you, I'd get the B-52s ready to roll and crank up your Minutemen missiles all over North America. Looks like it could be a first strike. If they bomb us we'll take out every city in their country." Will and Genny saw the Captain listen to his friend located in a Wyoming NORAD Air Force base. "Which country do you target? Hell, I'd target all of 'em. China and Russia are always in cahoots with each other." The Captain looked up. The Major General was jogging toward him. "Okay, here comes the commanding officer. I'll call you right back."

When the Major General strode up to the desks, all of them saluted.

"Captain, what the hell is going on here?" the Major General barked. "Can't a guy have a nap?"

"Sir, I've just ordered DEFCOM four. Juneau is under attack."

"You're sure?"

"Positive sir."

Will looked toward the office block. The Chinese delegation and the State Department representative walked out a steel door and toward the desks. As they came closer the General exploded in rage.

"Get those people out of here!" He looked at the Captain. "Get the Secretary of State on the line. Tell him what's happening in Alaska. Tell him I've ordered DEFCON four and if it's necessary, we're gonna have to take out Peking and Moscow as well as all their major cities."

"But General, we don't know that the Chinese or Russians are doing this," Will interjected. "Shouldn't we wait until we make a positive identification?"

"Who the hell do you think you are, Sargent?" the General snapped. "Make that Private. You've just been demoted."

A Chinese delegate stepped forward and bowed slightly. "Major General, I am General Wong. Yes, I wear civilian clothes when I am with my delegation in America. Did I hear you say you plan to bomb Beijing?"

"Listen, you Chinese idiot. Get out of here! This is now top secret and I will not discuss any of this with you. Take it up with your ambassador."

Will watched as the Chinese General's face turned red. "You make large large mistake, Major General. It is your country who will pay the price if you bomb us first. I will call my Premier. We will prepare to strike you with every nuclear weapon we have."

"Which won't be enough! We'll wipe you Communists off the planet."

The State Department official stepped in between the two men. "Gentlemen, may I suggest that we let the U.S. president and Chinese Premier resolve this? They have talked many times to ease tensions between east and west."

"Fine!" the General shouted. "But I'm not going back to DEFCOM Two until the president orders me to. You got that, Mr Chinese General? You're messing with the wrong country!"

The Major General turned on his heel and marched back to the office block. The Captain took a seat at the monitor.

"I hope you are more reasonable than your Commanding officer," the Chinese General said to the Captain. "We have never planned a first strike on any country. We are a peace-loving people."

"Sure you are, General," the Captain said and turned to an Air Force MP that stood next to them. "Private, escort the General out of here. Right now, do you hear me?"

"What do we do now, Captain?" Genny asked as the Chinese General was marched out of the facility.

"What do we do? We wait, that's what. Let's do what the Sargent suggested. When we have positive identification, we'll figure out what we do next." He looked again to Will. "Where's that speeding Bogey now, Sargent?"

Will looked up from his monitor which had just started working again. "Sir, it's screaming toward Juneau Airport like a bat out of hell."

"Lear November Four Hundred Quebec Bravo! Go around now. You still haven't extended your landing gear."

In the Learjet cockpit, Doug keyed his radio mic again.

"No, sir, I can't go around. I need to land immediately. To repeat, I've lost all power in the right engine. The left engine is beginning to overheat. I need to continue my straight-in approach. I'm now lowering flaps and landing gear."

"I got that, Quebec Bravo. Emergency Services will be waiting for you on the runway."

Doug glanced again at the working left engine's temperature. The single white needle had moved into the red danger arc. He pulled the throttle back to one-quarter thrust, then lowered the flaps to twenty degrees and extended the landing gear. Seeing three green lights which informed him that the gear was fully extended, Doug pulled back the throttle to zero thrust. Now over the threshold, he hauled back hard on the control wheel.

As the plane's tires touched the concrete surface of the runway, the box-like unidentified object suddenly appeared again, zipping past the left-hand side of his aircraft, traveling at what must have been supersonic speed down the long runway. Its immense wake toppled over a fire truck speeding down a taxi strip as it moved at an incredible velocity toward the end of the airport. Then the strange thing climbed straight up. Performing a Split-S, the flying object swiveled sharply then descended at speed and shot right by the airport control tower. Doug watched as its sonic boom broke all of the tower's windows, showering the tarmac and ramp personnel standing below it with glass. Then the object shot vertically into the afternoon skies, disappearing from sight.

"What the hell was that?" a Juneau Ground Controller broadcast on her radio to anyone who was listening. "Air Alaska Seven Nineteen, did you see what just screamed down the runway and right by us?"

"Tower, this is Air Alaska Seven Nineteen," the pilot of the 737 answered. "See what? We're parked at the ramp and can't see the runway from here. All we saw was the glass exploding in the tower. Are you folks all right up there?"

"Yeah, we're all fine, Nineteen. Some of us have been cut up a little and all of us are in a state of shock. But we'll survive." The Controller cleared her throat then called, "Air Force Tango Oscar. How about you? Did you see that?"

"Ah, yes Ma'am, Tango Oscar did see that," the Air Force C-130 pilot called back, his voice hesitating. "Can't say I know what to do about it. We tracked it on our radar. It disappeared clean up into the stratosphere and we are no longer able to detect it. Ma'am, can you still see it on your radar?"

"No sir, Tango Oscar. All our radar are out. Lear Four Hundred Quebec Bravo, do you want to report what you've seen?"

Inside his jet, as he taxied toward the terminal, Doug hesitated then keyed his radio mic. "I don't think so, Juneau. No one would believe it if I did. I'll report this as a standard mechanical incident to the FAA and my company. Air Force Tango Oscar, are you going to report that weird thing as a UFO sighting?"

"Not in a Mississippi million years of hell I will. My commanding officer would think I was crazy or high on drugs. Nor will my co-pilot. Nope, not a word from us two."

"How about you, Tower?" Doug enquired. "Are you going to report it?"

"Not on your life, Quebec Bravo. I agree with Tango Oscar's opinion. The FAA would think we were all nuts if we reported a UFO. Anyway, I think what we all saw was a large moose on the runway, trying to get out of the way of your jet. Isn't that what you saw?"

"Moose?" Doug said and laughed. "If that's what it was, it was the fastest moose I've ever seen."

As the Tower Ground Controller laughed back, Doug taxied off the runway. Parking the Lear on the ramp near a hangar, he let the left engine wind down then deplaned the aircraft. Walking around the Lear with a local aircraft mechanic, the first thing they both saw was exposed metal where the white paint and company logo had been burned off most of the fuselage.

"Good Lord Almighty!" the mechanic said. "Look at that! It's like God's burning finger touched it. I've never seen paint burned off like that! What did you fly through? A furnace?"

As they approached the shattered right engine, Doug bent down and picked up a piece of titanium fan blade. Then he looked inside what remained of the engine cowling. The entire fan blade had destroyed. "My Lord God, thanks for being there," he whispered, his eyes never leaving the engine. "I'm a lucky man to be alive."

"Bet you crapped in your pants, didn't you kid, when that engine shattered. I bet you prayed all the way down for God Himself to be in the right seat to help you fly this thing in."

"Crap in my pants?" Doug replied. "Put it this way, when I take my shower I'm going to throw away my shorts. As for prayer—I was so damned focused on getting that Lear down in one piece, I completely forgot to do it. If that shattered fan had penetrated the fuselage, I would have lost all hydraulics. Then I really would have been in a jam."

Reaching up, he patted the pitted, burned metal of the aircraft fuselage near the right engine with his hand. "See? It's just pitted where some of the pieces of titanium hit it."

"Yep, you're a lucky man," the mechanic said, slapping Doug's arm and grinning. "I would'a drunk a bottle of scotch on the way down just to keep myself from throwing up."

Later, when Doug went into the terminal, the mechanic examined the jet engine alone. He scratched his beard as he looked at what remained of the turbine. "Absolutely impossible. Look how that damned blade shattered. Must have been some scary ride for that young kid." He looked up at the hanger ceiling. "Whatever saved that

young fella was much more than simple luck. It was an act of God."

Two weeks later, the top brass from NORAD met with the Joint Chiefs of Staff at the Pentagon Building. As they gathered around the long walnut table sipping coffee, a civilian secretary passed around some papers. An Admiral, holding a copy high, sat near the top of the table.

"Gentlemen and ladies, can you please take your seats. What we have here is a standard incident report from the Lear jet pilot, Doug Masters. The first page gives you the basics. Name, address, date of birth, names of parents, grades in school, number of flight hours and so forth. As you can see, he's had a good career for someone so young. I'm sure this young fella will eventually end up with a commercial airline. Damn but I wish he'd consider the Navy. He'd make a great aircraft carrier pilot."

An Army Major sitting across from the General stood up.

"Sir, I am a psychologist based in Texas. I've read Doug's report and talked to his boss at the young man's company. He says that Masters is one of the best pilots they have. He also stated that, having been contacted by our NORAD research team, Masters had already filled in the standard incident report but he point-blank refused to make any sort of statement about the UFO sighting. He said it was, and I quote his commanding officer, 'None of our damned business what he experienced'. But when Doug Masters was pressed by an official at NORAD he agreed to make this short statement."

"I see," the Admiral responded. "Well, this is all we have to go on. To be honest, it's a standard UFO report that anyone who had seen such an unexplained flying object would have written. God alone knows I wouldn't want to make a report on one of those things."

"May I make a point, Admiral?" The five-star general from the Joint Chiefs of Staff, sitting next to his fellow officer, looked over his glasses as he scanned the report. "This strange thing flew in a way no one has seen before. And it came within how close to the Lear?…let's see now, what does he say?. within fifty feet of his aircraft. That's a close encounter if I've ever heard of one. And that's pretty much all this kid has to say?"

"Yes sir," the Admiral replied. "He doesn't go into much detail at all. We have the forensic evidence of our team that examined the aircraft. As you can read, the fuselage was scorched and the right-hand engine failed. But other than that, it's really a report for the NTSB and the FAA."

"And NASA, too," a woman said as she stood up. "Gentlemen, my name is Gloria Stern. We've received some data from a telescope observatory in Australia. I've read the NORAD report about ten UFOs being sighted by their radar operators. The Australian NASA team, who all have top secret clearances, were listening in to the Cheyanne Mountain radio traffic. They tracked those ten targets back to a large object which they believe is in orbit around the Sun."

"You're kidding?" the five-star General growled. "But that can't be. No one has the technology to do that. Not us. Not the Russkies nor the Chinese. No one."

"Ten-hut!" a Marine Lieutenant standing at the door shouted. The door opened. The President of the United States walked into the room. He smiled and then, sweeping his graying light brown hair off his forehead, sat at the head of the table.

"Ladies and gentlemen, let's not stand on ceremony," the President said. "I have a meeting with my cabinet in five minutes so we'll make this quick. Admiral?"

"Yes, Sir."

"I've read the reports. Seems to me you've got yourself a tiger by the tail. What the heck is going on, any idea?"

"No, Sir. Not yet, anyway."

"That's what I thought." Carter put his elbow on the table, holding his chin in the palm of his hand. "Well, this president has an opinion on the matter, if it's okay with you-all. See, I've always believed we're not exactly alone and I'm not talking about God. That large unidentified object which NASA and the Australians state is revolving around old Sol was put there for a reason. I'd suggest that we allocate some budget to launch a satellite to fly by it. If we can get there before it leaves, we can monitor that thing for signs of life. Son, let me see that."

Carter's five-star General handed the President a copy of Doug's report. Jimmy Carter put on his glasses and flipped to the last page. He re-read it then looked up. "If it was hostile or a threat, we'd know about it already. They would'a blasted Juneau and maybe the rest of the state of Alaska off the face of the Earth. Maybe that kid flying this Lear was right as was that mechanic who examined the aircraft." The President stood up, placing both palms on the table. "Maybe, just maybe, it really was the finger of God Himself or something just as powerful. Perhaps it's a new capability built by the Russians. Or maybe it was some form of life we know nothing about yet. Whatever it was and is, file this all as Top Secret. We need to know more. And I'd also suggest you contact the SETI researchers to monitor what's orbiting around the Sun. Is that clear to y'all?"

"Yes, Mr President," the officials said as they stood up.

"Good. Now if you'll excuse me…"

He turned and walked out of the room. The Admiral sat down and took a deep breath.

"That Carter's no fool. He won't win the next election but maybe this one time he's got something right." The Admiral turned to the four-star General. "Well, I guess we gotta do what Jimmy says we gotta do."

"That's for certain."

The General stood. "Okay, people. You heard him. Carry out the President's orders ASAP. And that's an order."

Chapter Two

The silver and black spacecraft floated between planets as, onboard, its crew viewed the Earth's sun and the surrounding Solar System with the type of advanced instruments that humankind would not create for the next thousand years. It had taken generations for this race of people to develop what the three Gaian officers were crewing that day. As the Captain of the vehicle watched through a window, his second-in-command slowly passed by his field of vision as she continued her spacewalk. Holding up a gloved hand, Gaian Lieutenant Berg Larmieso waved at him. She held up a long silver cylinder and, as Captain Joyis Mexcopio watched, he could see her concentrate through the invisible helmet she wore. Her face seemed to contract into itself, so much was her focus, and as Mexcopio looked on, the cylinder extended into space, eventually reaching thousands of kilometers in length. As the Captain watched, he saw Larmieso stretch then pull back. On an infrared monitor, he saw a large vial at the end of what was now a pole dip into the sun's core as his second-in-command controlled it. Finished, she looked back through the window and nodded.

"You have the sample, Lieutenant?" he asked in a silent whisper.

"I do, Sir. If you make the analysis now, I'll let the sample go back into the sun," she replied with silent Gaian telepathy.

The Captain also concentrated. As he did, the large screen beside him glowed with white numbers.

"It is as our Royal Queen Gaia suspected. This sun will last another few billion years or much more. But there is a sign of trouble in the near future. It will begin putting out vast solar flares which will affect the gravitation field and the core of the planet that our Queen just visited. According to my interpretation of this data, I assume that what the human race calls Earth will destroy itself within the next few thousand of their years. I will transmit this data to the scientists on our home planet and let them analyze it further. Come on in now, Lieutenant. We are finished with this part of our mission."

When he heard the airlock open, the Captain made his way aft to help his second-in-command off with her spacesuit. He hugged her and she hugged him back.

"When we're finished with this mission," Joyis Mexcopio said in perfect English, "I'd like us to be married."

"Married?" Berg Larmieso replied, also in English. She smiled at him. "Yes, perhaps it is finally time. We have been together for what seems like forever. When we return to our home planet, let's ask the Queen for some leave for the two of us. I'm sure she'll agree. It's been a successful mission. Where's Pierre? Is he in the cafeteria?"

"No, our Earth-born Frenchman is in the laboratory looking at the samples our Queen brought to us from Earth."

When Joyis had also stripped off his spacesuit, the pair held hands and descended into the living quarters of the Codeq Two space vehicle. They found Pierre in the laboratory.

"Bonne journée," Berg said, greeting the scientist. Pierre looked over from the live sample that was swimming in a glass aquarium. "What is that you have there? It looks just like a Pleimiot on our planet."

The Frenchman smiled. "Yes, this is the same fish as we have in Gaia but it goes by a different name on Earth. In English it is called a

Barreleye, found in some of the deepest seas on the planet. There are many fish that live in deep water. Some of them glow in the dark to attract their mates." He looked back and forth between the couple. "Like you two, perhaps?"

At that, Berg blushed. Joyis watched as her entire body lit up like the green phosphorescence of the oceans on their home planet.

"Perhaps," Berg said, shrugging her naked shoulders. "When I put on my nightwear, not even Pierre will see me blush."

The scientist laughed. "Tell that to Joyis. I know what you two do when you go to sleep. And I do not think either of you are blushing. You want children, yes?"

"Yes," Joyis replied. "We're asking the Queen when we get home if we can have leave to get married."

The Frenchman clapped his hands. "Toutes nos félicitations! May God and Queen Gaia bless you with many children!"

"We hope so, Pierre," Berg replied. "Are you almost done with your analysis?"

"Yes, I am finished. I want to eat a baguette and then I, too, will sleep." He smiled at them. "When I was called by the Queen in my dreams so many, many years ago, I did not realize her message meant that I would live on a different planet. While I miss my home in France, Gaia has promised me that someday soon I too will get leave to visit again Paris."

A short whistle echoed through the laboratory.

"Captain and Lieutenant," the ship's computer said in English. "I have received new instructions from our home planet. The two of you are to immediately board the remaining Rescue craft, the one that our Queen did not use when meeting Douglas Masters, her son. You are to use Stardrive when you leave this spacecraft and, upon landing, you will meet the Queen who has already given you a month of leave to be married. That is the end of the Space Command transmission."

"So I am to be left behind on my own?" Pierre said, a frown on his face. "But I will be lonely here on the Codeq Two."

"The Queen has made special arrangements for you, Monsieur," the Codeq Two computer stated in her computerized voice. "You will orbit this sun for another week in Earth time. As you do, you will test the Code Repeater we have placed onboard. Space Command and our Queen wants to make certain that the code, which currently originates in the Pegasus constellation, is transmitted to the various SETI instruments so that the Earth scientists will hear it."

"A week on my own," Pierre said forlornly, "with nothing to do but make tests?"

"But then," the computer replied, "you are to board the escape pod and leave this spacecraft. It will take you back to Paris where you can again visit your many relatives. There, you will live for as long as you want. When you desire to come back again to the Centauri Galaxy, simply think it. We shall then send that pod to pick you up and return you to our planet. The Queen asks if that is acceptable to her great friend, Pierre."

"Of course, it is acceptable. Please send her my thanks."

"She already knows how you pine for your family and want to be married again. She is still so sorry that your wife and only child died in the fire in your Paris apartment so many years ago. She also tells you that as a special reward for your hard work you will see them both again when you land."

Pierre's mouth hung open. "I shall see my Rebecca and Lauri? But that is not possible! I buried them both in a cemetery near the Seine many years ago."

"Pierre, this is your Queen, and it is true what I have now promised you," the Earth scientist heard whisper in his head. "My great French friend will see his family again when you return to your home planet."

"Did you hear that?" Pierre said to the Captain and Lieutenant. "Once again, she talks in my head."

"Yes, we did," Berg replied. "If our Queen promises you a gift like that, then it will come true."

"Une bénédiction!" he said and tears came into his eyes. "It is a miracle! Thank you so much, my Queen. I am speechless."

Joyis turned to Berg. "We must make ready for the transition to the Rescue craft. When you are ready to go, call me. I have some final preparations to make for Pierre in the command module then I'll join you and we shall leave the Codeq Two."

An hour later, the two Gaian officers were ready for the great leap to the nearby galaxy then onward to their home planet. Pierre stayed in the command module to help them navigate out of the large Rescue vehicle hanger.

"Pierre, this is the Captain," Joyis said on his radio mic. "Please open the outer doors."

In the control room of the spherical command module, Pierre pushed a button. On an overhead monitor he watched as the bay doors open. Beyond, all he could see was stars.

"Captain, this is Pierre. Shall I extend the bay arms to take the Rescue craft outside the airlock?"

In the Rescue vehicle, Joyis smiled at Berg who sat in the command seats beside him.

"Berg, let us give that Frenchman one last surprise, okay?"

She winked at him. "Mon dieu if I've ever heard one!"

Joyis again keyed his mic. "Pierre, that is a negative regarding the arms. I'll take it from here." Again, he looked at Berg. *"Ready?"*

"On my mark. Two, one…"

They both concentrated, focusing on the Stardrive.

"Launch."

Back in the command module, Pierre looked at the monitor. "But where is the ship! It is gone!"

The monitor showed nothing but an empty bay hanger and the open bay doors. Beyond that he could see a shooting star heading past the sun.

"Bon chance!" he said in his head. "I shall see you again when I come back to our home planet which is also called Gaia, named after our Royal Queen."

In the Rescue vehicle, Joyis set course for the center of the Milky Way Galaxy.

"Berg, do you want to go home the fast way or the slow way. It's been a long time since we had a chance to visit what humans call the M51 and the Orion Constellation."

She laughed. "The fast way. Joyis, I want to go home."

"That is perfect. Setting course for the center of the Milky Way and its Black Hole. Let's push the speed up a step or three."

Again, they both concentrated and could immediately feel the acceleration of the small spacecraft increase as they were pushed into their seats. When Berg looked up at her monitor, she saw that their spacecraft was already at the center of the Milky Way. Its Black Hole glittered with a bright spiral ring caused by the Event Horizon as it warped incoming starlight that fell into it.

"Ready?" Joyis asked her. He put out a hand and she held it.

"Ready!"

Their ship tore through the dust near the darkness of the hole.

At a monitor in the Codeq Two, Pierre intercepted a signal from a Gaian satellite that revolved well beyond the Event Horizon. As he watched, the bright meteor caused by the Rescue craft's Stardrive rippled as it moved into the singularity of the Black Hole. Then, the vehicle disappeared from sight.

"How they can do that I'll never understand nor will any human," Pierre said to no one as he scratched his beard. "Maybe, if someone on Earth interprets the Gaian code correctly then humans will also be able to fly faster than the speed of light."

Chapter Three

Following the submission of his short report to the team of investigators at Cheyanne Mountain, Doug refused to talk to anyone about the strange encounter he'd had in Juneau. But one afternoon, a week after he'd landed a job with Eagle Airways, a subsidiary of United Airlines, which hired him based on his performance to land his Lear following the unexplained turbulence, he received a phone call from NASA.

As he walked into the Eagle Airways Crew Desk having flown as co-pilot from Charlotte, North Carolina, to Chicago's Midway Field, the supervisor motioned him to the counter and handed him a phone.

"Call for you, Doug. Lady says she's from NASA," George O'Mahony said. "I asked if the caller was kidding but she said she was absolutely serious."

When Doug took the phone he found himself talking to the lead manager of the Space Agency's new division investigating UFO sightings.

"Is this Mr Martin?

"Sure is. Can I help you?"

"Doug, my name is Gloria Stern. I don't have much time so I'll come straight to the point. A few months ago, we heard about an encounter you had in Alaska. We impounded your Lear's Black Box and have fully analyzed the aircraft's inflight data as well as the radio recordings and observations you made. We did that at the direct order of the President of the United States."

"President Carter?"

"The President wants to know if you have anything to add."

Doug glanced at George and frowned, putting his hand over the telephone receiver. "The lady says she's from NASA all right and tells me she's calling on behalf of the President Carter. I think it's some sort of prank. She's talking about an incident I had months ago in Alaska. Everyone who saw that weird thing in the sky agreed not to report it to anyone. When NORAD put pressure on me I had to make a short statement."

"Incident?" George asked. "What the hell are you talking about? Finish the conversation then tell me about it."

"I'm sorry, Ma'am," Doug said into the handset. "Can you give me your name again?"

"Gloria Stern. I'm the lead investigator with the new UFO division."

"You impounded the Lear's Black Box?"

"Yes, we did. Doug, as I said I don't have much time. I'm flying to Ireland to investigate another reported sighting off that country's west coast. My flight is leaving right now. All I wanted to ask was this. Would you be willing to serve on our investigation team or at least testify to our panel of investigators about what you saw? We don't pay much if you join the team but because you have a background in flying as well as an interest in astrophysics, we thought you'd be a perfect addition to the division."

Doug didn't even have to think about it. "Ms Stern, I don't mind testifying at some point particularly if the President wants me to but

I just got a job with Eagle Airways. I need to focus on that, okay? But thank you for the invitation. When do you want me to testify?"

"In a week, as soon as we can organize it with your employer. I gave my phone number to the supervisor. I'll give you a call in a week. The President thanks you for your cooperation."

When she hung up, all that Doug could do was stare at the handset.

"Doug, you okay?" George asked as he took the phone. "You look like a lion ate you for lunch. What's wrong?"

"I don't believe it. That sure was NASA. The woman just asked me to join their UFO investigation team but I turned her down. President Carter has requested me to testify before them."

"The president asked you to testify? About what?"

Doug gave him a quick rundown of the Juneau incident. When he was finished, the Crew Desk supervisor laughed.

"Are you crazy? Look, it's none of my business but if word got out to airline management about this it might not go down too well. I thought you said that everyone who saw that thing agreed not to talk about it. If I were you, I'd drop it. The President *requested* you to testify, he didn't order you to." George turned to a print out of the latest forecast for the east coast of the United States which rested on the counter. "Let's get back to businesses. Here's the weather for Scranton, Pennsylvania. You better file the flight plan for your Captain and get out to the aircraft."

When Doug finally dead-headed home to John F. Kennedy Airport after the flight to Scranton, he was bushed. He took a cab out to his apartment in New York City. There, he changed out of his uniform and put on his pajamas. He was too tired to eat, so sat up and watched a film for an hour. Then he went to bed.

For hours he tossed and turned, not able to get to sleep. When he finally did, he slept soundly but woke up a few hours later. He went to the kitchen to get a glass of milk and, as he sat at the table, he realized what had woken him was a dream he'd had about a woman.

"Who the hell was that?" he asked himself as he remembered the auburn-haired woman of his dream. "She seemed so real. Almost like I've known her all my life."

When he finished, he switched off the lights and climbed back into bed. As he fell asleep, he could have sworn he heard someone calling him.

"Doug? Doug.... Doug, my son."

He sat bolt upright, staring into the darkness. "Who said that?"

"It is me, my child. It is your mother."

He waited for the voice to say something else but all he heard was silence. Exhausted and knowing he was dreaming again, he laid back down. "You can't be my mother," he mumbled sadly as he pulled up the blanket. "My mother is dead."

"Yes, she is gone from your sight but I am also your mother. My name is Gaia. And I have a surprise. Do you remember the young woman you dreamed of earlier?"

Doug rubbed his eyes. He leaned over, turning on the nightstand lamp, then scanned the bedroom but found it was empty.

"Who is this?" He climbed out of bed, putting on his robe. "I asked you, who is this?"

"I talked to you before, don't you remember my child?"

Doug blinked in the semi-darkness. He knew exactly what the voice in his head was talking about.

"Juneau," he whispered. "It was you, wasn't it."

"Yes," the voice whispered. "My son, get back into bed. Tonight, you will dream again of one who will become important to you for the rest of your life."

"You mean the woman?"

"You will recognize her name the moment you see her. For months, she will come to you in your dreams because it is a time of preparation for you. But soon you will meet her and that I promise you."

Light hit his bedroom as if it was noon, not three o'clock in the morning. The lightbulbs in the room shattered. Broken glass littered the carpeting. Then the bright light disappeared. The bedside lamp lit again. The floor was no longer covered with glass. He walked about the room looking for an intruder but no one was in the room.

Not knowing what else to do, Doug took off his robe and climbed back into bed. "What the hell just happened? I know I wasn't dreaming. I'm wide awake." He again turned off the bedside lamp then rolled over and put his arm under the pillow. "I know I'm not nuts. I can't be. What the hell's going on? What just happened was as strange as the Alaskan encounter."

When he finally fell asleep he again dreamed of the auburn-haired woman as a voice kept whispering "Helen" over and over again.

PART ONE:

DEPARTURES

Chapter Four

When Helen Fox climbed out of bed on an early autumn Irish morning, she felt a distinct chill in the air. As she closed the window of her bedroom, she noticed that a wicked wind was blowing the red and yellow roses almost flat in the front garden of her parent's home in the town of Trim, County Meath, Ireland, located thirty miles north of Dublin. As she watched, rose petals flew across the yard. Feeling a cramp in her stomach, she walked to the small bathroom in the back of the house, hoping that her period had come. But her pad was still clean, and she felt her stomach drop as she remembered she had not had a period in over seven months.

Only thirty-two-years-old, the young woman with no children had married whom she had thought was her best male friend, Geoffrey Johnston. He lived in the country not far from her parent's cottage and owned a small farm. He had promised her everything when he had fallen on one knee to propose to her in marriage."

"Sure, you've no one else to marry," Geoff said. "You've dated so many men around Trim and no one has won your heart. All you do is say the rosary and go to Lourdes to take care of invalids on their pilgrimages. Helen, how can you think that's fun? It's time to start living!"

In spite of the foreboding she had felt in her stomach, a sickness she hadn't yet identified, Helen let herself be swayed by this man because she honestly thought he was a friend. Now, eight months after their marriage, she realised she was pregnant by him.

As Helen sat down on the toilet, she examined her leg. There, she saw a strange looking wart on her right inner thigh. When she told her mother, Josie, about it, her mam had asked Helen's father, Tommy, a local poet and short-story writer, to take her to the local hospital. When the doctors examined her they immediately referred her to Saint Luke's, a cancer hospital in Dublin City. There, Helen was subjected to a variety of tests and scans which discovered she was suffering from a melanoma, a highly virulent form of cancer. The doctors informed her that many people died from such a malignant tumor.

"It's caused by the sun," a young female surgeon from India told her. "You love the sun, don't you, Helen?"

She admitted that she loved the sun so much, she'd sit out all day in her father's back garden without putting any sunscreen on.

"That's dangerous," replied the kind doctor. "That's why you have a melanoma. You're not only fair skinned but you also have freckles. Many people of your coloring die due to such a cancer."

But Helen was lucky because the surgeon was highly skilled. Later that day, she found herself in theater. When she was anaesthetized, the medical team performed the surgery. They cut out not only the small wart but also tracked the cancer up her right leg, removing the lymph glands there and on the right-hand side of her crotch. Helen was told by the nurses that she would not only limp but would also have to wear a surgical stocking. This would counter her lymphoedema by keeping pressure on her leg, keeping the blood flow to her heart almost normal.

As she lay in the hospital bed recovering, the doctor from India entered her cubicle in the public ward, sitting down next to her.

As Helen opened her eyes, the doctor held out a black and white picture. Helen took the photograph and carefully examined it.

"Do you know what that is?" the doctor asked.

Helen, not certain what the photo showed, only shook her head.

"That's a fetus. So it's good news. You're almost eight months along, well into your third trimester."

Helen felt her stomach drop and her heart began to race.

"But that's impossible," Helen said, her voice shaking. "I've had to buy new jeans a size larger because I've gained some weight. But I'm not getting morning sickness, though I can feel quite ill when I get out of bed at the start of the day."

"That's more good news," the doctor said taking Helen's hand in hers. "Not all pregnant women get morning sickness or look like they're pregnant. Some women have flat stomachs even right before giving birth. And don't worry, your tummy will show very soon. Before long, nothing will fit at all. Your husband will have to buy you an entire new wardrobe. You like to shop for new clothes, don't you?"

"Not particularly," Helen said. "My husband says I shop like a man. I know what will fit, so all I do is grab what I need and don't even bother trying them on."

When the doctor left the room, Helen began to cry uncontrollably. She wished she had thought to take birth control pills. She never wanted to get pregnant by Geoff. While she loved children, and hoped to someday have more than one, she realised she never loved this man who many people, including her best friend Paula, called a gobshite and rightly so.

Still laying in her hospital bed she remembered the conversation she'd had with her friend a month after her marriage. Paula had said that her husband had been fooling around behind Helen's back. She had also been informed that Geoff had at least two other children, one each from two different women. "In fact," Paula had whispered to Helen when they sat drinking a glass of lager in a local pub, "I saw Geoff Johnston with yet another woman only yesterday. She was wearing a sort of tent dress and I know feckin' well she was at least four months gone."

At first, Helen couldn't believe it. Then, over a few months' time, she had noticed that their joint savings account was smaller than she had expected. Helen knew damned well when she married him that Geoff had a gambling problem, or so her mother Josie had told her. Geoff loved to go to the racecourse to bet a majority of his wages on a horse that was always last coming in and that was, Helen knew, still running. For that reason, the couple had to live on the sole weekly wages Helen made at a dry cleaner.

Still resting in the hospital bed, she remembered that things had only gotten worse over time. While Geoff had stopped drinking, and though he occasionally attended Alcoholics Anonymous, she realised he was now a dry drunk. When they argued he sometimes beat her, striking her in the stomach so she wouldn't have any bruises on her face or arms For that reason, she never had any proof that Geoff could beat her senseless. Helen never said a word to anyone about what her husband was doing to her, not even to her best friend.

A week later and still recovering in hospital, with Geoff never bothering to visit or phone to check on his wife, Helen was in the toilet when she felt a huge pain in her abdomen. When she shrieked for help, a nurse opened the door to find her on the floor, blood streaming from her crotch.

Shouting for assistance, the nurse helped her out of the toilet and onto a gurney. Quickly, with two other nurses, they wheeled her into a maternity room. To ease the pain that Helen was suffering, the maternity doctor gave her gas but it was never enough to put Helen out or make her unconscious. As if dreaming, she felt pressure on her stomach as the doctor pressed down.

Within moments, the doctor held a tiny bundle in both hands. "I'm sorry," the doctor said with finality, turning to her as he handed the eight-month-old infant to a nurse. "We rarely understand why some babies don't survive. Do you want to know the sex of your child and name it before we take it to the hospital mortuary? Would you like to hold it?"

Helen knew exactly what to do. She took the baby from a nurse. With the miscarried wee thing wrapped in a blanket, the young mother held it as if she could never let go. Then she opened the blanket and trying hard not to cry, Helen looked first at her child then up at the young doctor.

"Please call a priest. I want her baptized before I have to bury her. Tell him what happened and that the baby's name is Josie, after my mother."

A nurse took the miscarried infant from her and, when everyone was out of the room, Helen broke down again. The next morning the priest baptized the baby and promised to bury it in the family plot in Trim right next to the church when Helen was released from hospital.

Throughout all that time and her suffering, Geoff never once bothered showing up at the hospital or phoning his wife.

The day after her wee Josie had been born, Helen got undressed with the help of her maternity nurse. "I know you're still not well after your surgery and stillbirth. You ate nothing tonight. Helen, are you sure I can't at least bring you a cup of tea?"

Helen shook her head, tears still in her eyes. "No thank you, Sister. All I want to do is go to sleep."

The nurse helped her into the hospital bed and to make Helen more comfortable opened the window. Outside, the wind had got up and they could see tree limbs tremble in the darkness. When the nurse turned off the lights, Helen closed her eyes and tried to sleep. But all she could do was cry.

"I can't stand this!" she said to the darkness. "My wee little gersha is dead. I'll never get married again and I'll never have another child with any other man." Once again, she began sobbing. Then clasping her hands together, she sat up in bed and looked at the dark ceiling.

"Oh Mary, mother of Jesus, please pray for my dead child. Now and forever. Amen." Then she crossed herself three times and tried to sleep again. But as she lay her head back on the pillow she heard a voice whisper to her.

"My daughter, why are you crying? Is it because of the wee one who I now cradle in my arms?"

Helen opened her eyes again. She looked around the room but no one was there. In the nightlight that had been left on, all that she could see was the sink where the nurse had washed her before helping her slip on her nightgown.

"Who is that?" Helen whispered back. Then, against the windowpane, she heard the sound of branches tapping as if calling her name. 'Tap-tap-tap' it went, then repeated itself.

"I must be crazy because of the death of my child but I could swear that branch was calling my name."

"And so all living things will tap your name and the name of your deceased baby, in honor of your strength," the whisper said to Helen. "Now is the time to sleep, my child, before you get ill again. You need to rest and when you do, you will dream of a handsome young American man who will come to you soon."

"An American will come to me? What do you mean? Who are you?"

"I am but an unseen voice crying in your wilderness. But I am also your mother. Call me Gaia. And as for the man? He flies an airplane for a living and very soon you shall be with him. You will recognize his name the moment you see him and together you shall have many, many other children. You shall see, sweet young one. The promise I make is not one I make lightly. And as for the dead infant, that one will be with you tonight so you can hold and kiss her before she is called back to me. That I promise on this night of endless miracles and suffering."

When the whispered voice stopped talking, she eased herself from the bed and closed the window. She turned on the overhead light and looked around but no one was in the room. She thought of calling the nurse but realized that the woman was busy with other patients. Stepping into the middle of the room, she again looked up at the ceiling, not expecting to hear an answer.

"But I already have a mother. Her name is Josephine and she lives not thirty miles from here."

"Yes, and she is blessed like all good mothers who have children that are as wonderful as you. But at least for tonight, pretend that you have not one mother but two. On this night of miracles, call me Mother, too."

Helen thought for a moment. Yes, like most Catholics, she believed in miracles. She also believed in the seen and the unseen, ghosts and the Mother of her Lord whom she had prayed to moments ago. Deciding, she said with a tentative voice: "Mother?"

"Yes, my daughter."

"Are you the Mother of Our Lord?"

"If that makes you more comfortable, then yes, I am."

"And will I really see my child tonight? And will a man truly marry me and give me more children?"

"A promise is a promise, is it not, Helen? Yes, all of those things will come true over time and many more as well. Now get back into bed and sleep. Soon, your child will come to say goodnight to you. You shall see that Josie is no longer a tiny infant but is actually three."

"She's already three years old?"

"In a place you call Heaven, time does not pass as it does with those still living on Earth. Go now, daughter. You have said your prayers already so sleep. Will you not mind what your Mother tells you to do this night?"

Helen smiled because the voice, which she thought had come through the window with the tapping of branches but which now talked silently in her head, also told her what to do like her own mother, Josephine. When Helen crawled into bed, having switched the lights off, she waited. After a while she thought that nothing would happen and the promises she had heard were all a dream. But then the door cracked open and in a stream of light from the outside hallway, a small girl with an elfin face, long red hair tied in a ponytail and wearing a dress of white, ran in laughing.

"Mammy!" she said and jumped on the bed.

"I thought that promise was only a dream," Helen said and started to cry. "I thought I'd never see you again. My, Josie, but how you've grown!"

"I'm three now," the little girl said, holding up three fingers. "Tomorrow, Grandnanny says that I'll be four! Isn't that fun! Where I live now, we have birthday parties every day!"

"Isn't that wonderful, Josie. I wish I could come to your next birthday party."

"But you will! Grandnanny says you can visit me anytime in your dreams. And you know what?"

"What? Tell me."

"I had a dream about a man last night who lives in a place called America. Did you know that he's my real Daddy? That's what my Grandnanny promised."

"She did, did she?" said Helen. She dried her eyes, picked up her child and gave her a big hug. "What else did she say?"

"That I'll have a whole lot of brothers and sisters! And that Christmas's will be huge!"

"Well, that's true, isn't it? If you have many brothers and sisters, I'll have to get a big Christmas tree for you all and lots of presents."

Then little Josie yawned, stretching. "Mammy, I'm tired. Can I sleep beside you?"

"Of course, you can." Helen pulled up the blanket and the girl snuggled in beside her. She turned, facing her mother. "Mammy, I love you. And I always miss you."

"I love you too, sweetie. And I'll always miss you too. But if your Grandnanny promises that we can visit each other in our dreams, then we'll only have to miss each other during the daytime, won't we?"

Josie's eyes began to close. "Goodnight, Mam. See you tomorrow night if I'm not busy."

"Don't worry, little Josie. Now that I know we can see each other, I won't mind if you're busy. Go to sleep now. I'll see you in the morning."

Then the little girl reached into a pocket stitched onto the side of her dress. From it, she pulled out two single roses, one white and one red, and gave them to Helen. "These are for you. I found them in Heaven."

"Did you now?" Helen said as she took them. She put them to her nose. Their fragrance was unlike anything she had ever smelled before. "You found these in Heaven?"

The little girl nodded. "Yes. An angel with long wings gave them to me to give to you. Her name was Gaia and she looked like my Grandnanny only much younger."

Helen smiled in the darkness. Turning, she placed the two roses on the side locker. "Isn't that wonderful!" she said. "Now go to sleep and we'll talk in the morning."

When Helen woke, sun still streamed through the open window. She pulled up her bedclothes, looking for her young daughter but the bed was empty beside her. All she saw was an indent where a small warm body had once been. But turning, she saw that the two roses, one white and one red, had been placed into a glass of water. Both were in full bloom. Beside it was a Valentine's Day card. She reached out, picking it up and opened it. In childish handwriting, the note inside read:

Dear Mammy,

I am already ~~four~~ five years old and am ~~lrnng~~ learning to write. Grandnanny is helping. So I hope you can ~~red~~ read this note. I hope you love the roses as much as we do. Please take care of my Daddy when you ~~met~~ meet him because you'll fall in luv with him, or so my ~~nGany~~ Grandnanny promises because, as I told you, he's my real loving Dad not that other man. I'll see you in our ~~DRems~~ dreams. Love my Mammy so so so much! xoxoxoxox

Helen held the card to her breast, one that she would keep forever. "My little girl truly is alive in Heaven. Thank you, My Lady, for giving me the promise of never-ending love." Then, still half-asleep, Helen rolled over and closed her eyes. Behind her, the two roses glowed like the feathers of angels' wings.

A week later, Helen was well enough to go home. But having been given more strength from the nightly dreams of her child, she made a final decision that would change her life. Back in Trim and still forced to live in the family house because she could not afford to rent anything else, Helen decided to tell Geoff that she wanted a divorce. Standing in their living room, Helen waited until her husband walked in through the front door at seven-thirty in the morning.

"So you've been out all night again?" Helen said in a determined voice. "Geoff, I want a divorce. I know it's impossible for us to get one in Ireland right now because of the current laws. You're a proud man and the last thing you'd want is for anyone to find out I'm demanding a divorce from you. If you don't agree to my demand I'll let everyone in Trim know that you're a sniveling coward. This means that there's only one option left to you. We'll go to England and get divorced there."

"They'll think you're a liar," Geoff replied, thumping the kitchen table with a closed fist. "If you don't calm down I'm gonna beat you within an inch of your life."

"Do it! Go on, hit me again!" Helen stated. "But if you do, this time I'll call the Gards. I'll testify at your trial and they'll throw you in jail for attempted murder. With any luck, you'll be sentenced to thirty years or more in Mountjoy Prison. How would you like that, Mr Johnston? To spend the rest of your life in jail? Now get out of my house before I call the cops and have you arrested."

"Where's the proof that I've ever beaten you up, sweetie?" he sneered. "You don't have any, do you? Besides, this is our house!"

All that Helen did was smile.

"It's mine. I'm paying the mortgage, not you. And I warn you, don't call me *sweetie*. When I miscarried I told the doctors what you had done, and how you had beaten me most every day of our marriage. They told me that that's why I miscarried. They promised they'd testify against you in court when the trial date is set."

"You bitch!" Geoff shouted.

"Call me what you want. I'm done with you. Now get out."

She stood in the living room as he went back to their bedroom. She could hear him opening drawers and the closet, yelling obscenities about her but she wouldn't listen. Then he came back holding a large black plastic bag in his hand.

"Take the house, you horrible woman. I'll make sure you pay for what you're doing to me for the rest of your life."

"You don't scare me anymore, Geoff. Now go on. Get out of my home!"

When he left, slamming the door behind him, Helen started organizing the divorce. She called her boss, Paul, at her place of work. Because they were good friends, she told him everything. Later in the day, she went into town to see him. After Paul lent her the money, she walked to the travel agent and booked a return trip for two people to London on the Dublin ferry. Two days later, the Irish ferry *Avalon* took the unhappy married couple from Dublin Port to Wales and onward by bus to London.

Having found a London solicitor who had already organized a court date, a week later Geoff Johnston and Helen Johnston were officially divorced. With the divorce papers in hand, she went directly back to Dublin then took a bus to Trim. Seeing her family solicitor, she showed him the divorce papers and asked him to change her last name back to her maiden name.

Two weeks later, sitting at her home's kitchen table and drinking a cup of tea, she held both the divorce decree and the change of name certificate in one hand. In the other, she held the Valentine's Day card she had received from her daughter, Josie. 'Now it's time for a complete change of life,' she thought to herself. 'Now that I'm Helen

Fox again, I'll learn to love myself and do what's best for me and my future children.'

But then, a week later, she learned the hard way that once again bad things happen to good people. A Garda Sergeant called to her home together with Paula, her best friend. When Helen looked into Paula's eyes, she realized it was terrible news that had visited her door.

"It's Mam and Dad, isn't it Paula?"

Her friend nodded her head, then started crying. "They've both been killed in a horrible car accident on the way home from Dublin. Oh, Helen. I'm so sorry. I don't know what to say." Then they were holding each other as the Garda stood beside them.

Three days later, Helen buried her parents next to Josie. But as they were laid to rest in the pouring rain of the local Trim cemetery, she touched with a finger the secret smile that had formed on her lips. As the priest once again intoned the final prayers for the dead, Helen thought to herself: 'Just like Josie, Mam and Dad are alive in Heaven. I'll be able to visit them in my dreams, soon, or at least I hope I will.'

A week after the funeral, Helen packed a bag and using all of her savings except a few Irish pounds and some dollars, Helen booked a flight to New York City. As she took the bus to Dublin Airport, she remembered that she'd never been out of her native country except to

England. Smiling again, she realized that her future was like a pot of gold waiting to be discovered. All she needed was a solid, loving partner to help her find it.

Chapter Five

As Helen checked in her luggage at Dublin Airport, she realized that this was her very first flight on any type of airplane. Suddenly nervous, she decided to think about something else. Then, looking at the date on the boarding ticket that the United Airlines Customer Service Agent had handed to her, Helen realized that it was Wednesday the 26th of November, the eve of Thanksgiving Day, one of her father's favourite American holidays. But because Ireland never celebrated that holiday, she couldn't be sure.

"Thanks for everything," Helen said as she folded her ticket and placed it in her bag with her passport. "I know you're busy but could you answer one question? Is tomorrow Thanksgiving Day in America?"

"Of course, it is," the American agent replied in her flat mid-western accent and smiled. "When I get home from work tomorrow afternoon, we'll have turkey and all the trimmings."

"Then Happy Thanksgiving!" Helen replied with genuine enthusiasm. "Can you tell me where I go to get on the airplane?"

"Up the escalator and to your right. Then, when you're through security and after the airport Duty Free, find Gate B27. The flight will leave on-time, so you'd better hurry. There are many Irish people traveling to the States to be with their families on Thanksgiving so it'll take you almost an hour to get through the security area."

When Helen made it through security and past Duty Free to the gate, her flight was being called. She looked up at the Departures sign and saw that the agent was right. Her trip to JFK International Airport was leaving from Gate B27. Walking to the gate, she presented her Irish passport and ticket to another United agent, then hurried down the enclosed jetway past a few ramp agents wearing bright yellow safety jackets. Pulling her carry-on bag by the handle, she climbed onboard the airliner behind a line of other passengers. As she handed her ticket to a flight attendant, she spotted a young man in an airline uniform, complete with a dark blue jacket, tie, white shirt and a peaked hat. His jacket had three stripes on the bottom of each sleeve. He stood near a tall, narrow door that was open. Behind him she could see a small room with many levers, instruments, lights and knobs in front of an older man that she assumed to be the young pilot's boss. Behind her and to her right, she could also see what she assumed to be the toilet and a small galley. Then she noticed that the uniformed young pilot was talking to the flight attendant. As he finished chatting, he turned to Helen, his eyes moving up and down her slim body then settling on her hazel eyes. He smiled and said, "Welcome aboard, Miss. Can I help you find your seat?"

She handed him her ticket and he read it carefully. "That's in economy, Ms Fox, in the back of the aircraft. Let me take your carry-on and I'll help you stow it in an overhead bin."

"Before you help me find my seat can I use the toilet, Mr Pilot?"

He laughed at her use of the term and put out a hand. "My name is Doug Martin. And while, yes, I'm a pilot, the proper term to use is 'Co-pilot'."

Helen stepped back on hearing his name. "Did you say Doug Martin?"

"That's right."

"So, what do I call you?" Helen asked, his name reverberating through her head as she remembered what the Lady had said to her. "Mr Co-pilot Doug Martin? Your name sounds familiar."

"There are a lot of Martins in America, Miss. Just call me Doug," he said, glancing again at her ticket. "What do I call you? Ms Fox or Helen?"

"Helen is just fine. It's what all my friends and relatives call me."

"Your full name is Helen Fox?" he asked as his eyes narrowed. Then he remembered how the voice he had heard in his head a number of months ago had told him that a woman's name would sound very familiar to him. "I know we've not met before but your name sounds familiar to me, too. You're Irish, aren't you? I'm from New York City. Long Island, to be exact."

"My ex-husband is now living somewhere in Boston," Helen said. "That's not too near New York, is it? I looked it up on a map and I guess it's at least four hours away by car."

"That's right. Are you flying out to see him? Why didn't you fly direct to Boston?"

"See who? My Ex?" she said and laughed. "I don't want to see him ever again."

"Oh, I'm sorry. I shouldn't have said anything."

"You can say anything you want about that man. I've already forgotten him. Mr Martin, is Long Island close to New York City?"

"Only an hour or so if you take the Long Island Railway."

"That's not too far, is it." She looked up at him. "Mr Martin, how long will it take to get to New York?"

"I'm guessing about five or six hours but when we get the winds aloft over the Atlantic Ocean we'll be able to calculate our actual estimated time of arrival."

"The Atlantic Ocean? I didn't know we'd have to fly over an ocean."

From the tone of Helen's voice, Doug realized she was nervous. He watched as she looked back toward the open door of the aircraft and began to believe she wanted to get off.

The he looked again at the attractive young woman. He noticed how her freckled face was snow white, and when he saw her hands shaking, he made an obvious guess. "Is this the first time you've flown, Helen?"

She nodded and it was then that he saw the fear in her eyes.

"Look, there's nothing to be afraid of. I'll take you to your seat but first let me show you how to use the toilet. It's not complicated but very different from a bathroom toilet in a house."

"We're in Ireland now, Doug. In Ireland, we call it a *loo*."

"A loo? What's a loo? Does it rhyme with 'kangaroo'?" he said laughing.

"That's exactly right," Helen smiled and he saw her beginning to relax. "If you're male, it's also called a *Fir* in the Irish. If you're a female, it's called a *Mna*."

"*Fir* and *Mna*? That sounds crazy. I'll never remember that."

"I tell you what. If you have any kind of break at all during our flight, come back and find me and I'll teach you a few words of Gaelic."

"Gaelic? Like Scots? I'm Scots by descent but I don't have any Irish blood in me at all."

"What other heritage do you have?" Helen asked, and though she didn't know it her hands had stopped shaking as she talked to this good-looking man. "I'm only Irish, not anything else."

"But Fox isn't Irish, is it? I thought Fox was English."

"English! How dare you, Mr Co-Pilot. You obviously don't know your Gaelic from your English. In Ireland, we have many people with the surname of Fox. As I said, I'm Irish!"

"No you're not," Doug laughed. "You're English."

"I'm Irish!" Helen replied, also laughing.

"English."

"Irish!"

A man wearing four stripes on each sleeve stepped out of the open narrow door at the front of the passenger cabin and made his way toward them.

"Doug, have you finished your walk-around? It's almost time to close up the aircraft. The last passengers have already boarded. I'm expecting ATC clearance any moment now. With a bit of luck, we'll push-back from the gate well ahead of schedule."

"Yes, we're ready to go, Captain Pryde. Sir, can I introduce you to Helen Fox? She's Irish, though her last name is decidedly English."

Captain Pride shook hands with Helen. "Welcome aboard, Ms Fox. We'll be arriving at JFK an hour early by the look of things. I just received the weather report. The forecast is for smooth weather all the way to our destination. I'm sure you'll have a pleasant flight."

"Captain, I'm just going to show Helen how to use the Blue Room. Sir, I'll be right with you."

"No problem Doug." Then the Captain went back forward and through the small door.

"Is that where you fly the plane from?" Helen asked. "I saw a bit of it. It looked like the inside of a complicated car."

"It's called a cockpit."

"Cockpit?" Helen asked not sure what he meant. "It sounds like a cockfight."

"A 'cockfight' is very different from a cockpit." Doug replied, trying to sound as if he was serious. "Mind you, we have many fights in the cockpit."

"You do? Honestly, Doug? What happens when you have a fight?"

Doug shrugged. "The Captain throws me out the window and I have to walk all the way to JFK or swim to New York."

The flight attendant who Doug had been talking with had been listening to their conversation and couldn't help but laugh.

"Don't take Doug seriously, Helen. He's always getting the crew and passengers to laugh."

"So I can tell," Helen said and pointed to the toilet. "Doug, you call this a Blue Room? But it's not blue at all. That said, blue is my favourite color."

"Mine, too. Now let me show you, then I have to go to work."

It only took Doug a few moments to show her what to do. First he pointed at the outer door and showed her that when the sign was red it meant it was occupied. When it was green, it was free. "When you go in, just shut the door and slide the lever. The lights will come on. Then you'll know that no one will disturb you."

He let Helen step into the small cubicle first and, as Doug leaned over her, he could smell her perfume, a moment which he already knew he would never forget. He studied her auburn red hair, elfin cheeks and button nose and decided on the spot that when they landed at John F. Kennedy International Airport, he'd invite her into the cockpit to show her all the bells and whistles. Then, if he could work up the courage, he'd ask her out for dinner and maybe take her to a show on New York's Time Square.

He showed her how the toilet flushed and, because it was in Business Class, it had shampoo, razers, mouthwash, and extra napkins. "While you're not a Business Class passenger, and because we have some empty seats, I'll ask the senior flight attendant, Ms Marple, the woman we were talking to, if she'll reseat you up here."

"Thank you, Doug. But I honestly can't afford something so expensive."

He smiled again. "What do they say if you're a bartender serving a great customer? 'Why, Helen, it's on the house!' If Ms Marple can reseat you, it's all free. Now I have to get to work. Have a great flight. You'll be safe because Captain Pryde has over twenty-five-thousand hours flying aircraft. He's a very experienced pilot."

Then he left her to use the Blue Room and, when he stepped into the cockpit, closed the small door. After Helen used the loo and found her seat in the economy section, she sat down and looked for her carry-on bag.

"Doug put it in a bin in Business Class," a male flight attendant explained to her. "We had a message that when we reach cruising altitude we'll be reseating you. We also understand that this is your first flight. Just sit back and relax and if you need anything at all, just press this button above your head." He showed her the flight attendant call button. He smiled and walked back to the very end of the airplane. That's when Helen looked forward, over the other seats, toward the Business Class section and saw Doug open the drapes and stroll toward her.

"I only have a minute, Helen," Doug said, smiling again. "Captain Pryde gave me permission to come back aft and reassure you once more. We received clearance to push back within the next few minutes and if we're that quick we'll be number two to take the runway for takeoff. But there's time to let me show you a few things."

He reached around her waist to make sure Helen had her seatbelt tightened fast. But he quickly discovered that she wasn't wearing a seatbelt at all.

"Here, let me show you how to do this. First, pull the buckle back, making sure that the strap is lose. See, like this." He uncinched the tight seatbelt strap and put both ends around her waist. "Now fasten the seatbelt by raising this end of the buckle and insert the other end of the seatbelt into the narrow part. You'll hear it snap. Then pull it tight and that's it. Helen, it's almost like a car seatbelt. It's that quick and simple to strap yourself in."

She looked up at his smile and thought back on how he had looked at her so carefully in what he had called the Blue Room.

"We're scheduled for a smooth flight, as Captain Pryde told you," Doug continued. "It'll be a little bumpy when we lift off and as soon as we're airborne, you'll hear two distinct thumps. That's the landing gear coming up and nothing to worry about. If you need anything else, let your flight attendant know. I'll tell him where you're sitting."

"Thanks, Doug. He already told me how to call him," she said, pointing at the button above her. "Thanks to you and Captain Pryde, I don't think I'm too nervous anymore."

Finally, Doug took leave of her and went back to work. As the aircraft rolled onto the runway, Helen sat in the aisle seat clutching the arm rests with both hands. But just as Doug had promised, when the airplane took off she felt as safe as houses. And when they had climbed to cruising altitude, and right after the sign had lit above her seat stating that it was safe to unbuckle her seatbelt, she was escorted by Ms Marple into Business Class. There, she was made to feel comfortable in a big, wide seat right next to the window. A few minutes later, another flight attendant gave her a glass of Prosecco mixed with orange juice.

"Have one of these," the Purser said as he placed the glass down on Helen's large pullout tray. Next to the glass, the man placed a menu card. "In a few minutes we'll be serving dinner. Now what would you like, Helen? In economy, the choice is chicken or pasta. But in

Business Class, you get a larger choice. Today, for dinner, you can have filet mignon, fresh salmon, or a Cesar Salad. Dessert is here," he said, turning the menu over. "Chocolate cake with cream or ice-cream. of your choice. A cheese board or tiramisu. Have a think about it. For breakfast, I'll bring you a separate menu. By the way, with dinner you can either have champagne, or a choice of red or white wine. I'll give you a minute and you can let me know what you want. How's that?"

"It all sounds wonderful but it's too expensive," said Helen, embarrassed. "All I have with me is a few hundred dollars plus a hundred euro in Irish notes. I have to use that to survive until I get a job somewhere in New York."

"Helen, as Doug said, it's all on the house. It's free when you fly Business Class. So just sip your drink and enjoy the flight and I'll see you in a few minutes."

Helen sat back and did exactly what the flight attendant had suggested. As the airplane skimmed over a sea of white she looked out, seeing a streak that looked like the grey shadow of a rocket trail on the bright clouds below her. She suspected it was the dark silhouette of her airplane. Then the sun set, turning that sea to a brilliant red as if the hand of God had painted it.

"I wish life could be as wonderful as this is, all the time," she whispered to herself, then laughed. "But would I want that? Life isn't half-bad now. Not when I'm sitting here, looking out a window that's high in the sky, drinking a glass of Prosecco mixed with orange juice, and watching the sunset over a sea of white clouds."

Then later, after dinner and dessert, Helen slept for a few minutes. When she woke up, Doug was looking down at her.

"Hey, you're finally awake. Are you having a good flight?"

"I'm having a wonderful flight," she said, peering up at him in the darkness. "I feel like I'm dreaming."

"This is no dream, Helen. This is perfect, don't you think?"

Doug looked around the Business Class section and saw that most of the passengers were fast asleep. The flight attendants were busy in the galley.

"Helen, I have a question for you," he asked, and she could tell by the hesitant sound of his voice that he was embarrassed.

"Go on, Mr Co-Pilot. What's your question?"

He cleared his throat and looked down on her with his deep blue eyes.

"Ms Fox, would you mind if I kissed you?"

Helen looked around the cabin, too, and saw a flight attendant step out of the galley to bring another passenger a cup of coffee. "But what if someone sees us? Won't you get fired?"

"No one will see us. The lights are dimmed. See how dark it is? You don't have to if you don't want to. But it's just that…"

"Doug, would you please be quiet? I'd like to kiss you, too."

Then she grabbed his tie and pulled him toward her. For a long moment, their lips touched in what would turn out to be the first kiss of a million, million kisses and hugs. For years to come, Helen and Doug would tell the story to their children and great-grandchildren of how fate had allowed them to meet in the skies above the Atlantic, and how they were able to seal their love with a simple kiss aboard an aircraft bound for New York City and a lucky encounter.

Five-hundred thousand feet about the United Airlines jetliner, in a

space station that was invisible to Earth's many radar systems, an astronaut working for Queen Gaia smiled. He relaxed his freckled celadon-green face and let the images of Doug and Helen fade from his mind. Knowing that His Lady would want to know as soon as possible about this critical event, and realizing that she would be too busy to hear him in her mind, he keyed his mic and instead called Gaian Space Command.

"Command, this is Gongril. Can you pass this message on to the Queen. The two humans she asked me to monitor have now found each other. They're future relationship, as the Earth people would put it, has been 'sealed with a kiss'."

The Gaian officer's speaker hissed for a moment. "Got that, Gongril. I'll let the Queen know as soon as she comes out of a meeting with her husband and Royal Consort Amendus. You are instructed to maintain your observations."

"Understood, Command. If I see any disruption to what our Queen has planned I'll contact you. But so far, it seems that they are moving well into the first phase of a longer-termed relationship."

"One other instruction from Our Lady, Gongril. If they need anything to move that relationship along, do it. Use the powers that you have to help them but by no means make yourself known to them or any other human being."

"That is clear, Sir. I will do what I can do to help but nothing to let our secret out. Space Station Gaia will leave the transmitter open."

The Gaian space station commander rested his large feet upon the command desk and smiled to himself. "It is going just as planned," he said to his brother officer who sat next to him. "The future of Earth might be at stake depending on the outcome of this new human relationship. But, all over the Universe, many races know what love smells like and on that aircraft far below us, love is in the air."

Chapter Six

When Doug walked back into Business Class toward the end of the flight, he found Helen sleeping again. He looked down on her lovely face and was so very glad they had met each other. The lights came on throughout the entire aircraft and the flight attendants started serving breakfast. When Helen woke up, she stretched and, seeing Doug, smiled up at him.

"Do you know, you're beautiful when you're sleeping," Doug murmured.

"Really? I'm not beautiful at all. Pretty, maybe. That's what my mother always said."

"Your mother was right but I'd go farther than that. I wouldn't call you just beautiful. You're unique in a wonderful kind of way. That's what your mother should have said about you."

When Helen was fully awake, Doug showed her where to find the small headset and how to turn on the entertainment system.

"See?" Doug said and, as Helen pulled on the headset, he explained the controls that were stored in the seat's chair near the tray table. "Push this button and you can see a whole variety of movies or TV shows or even local news. Push that one, and you can hear all sorts of music. You can even see a map of where our aircraft is over the Atlantic and how much time there's left until we get to New York." He clicked his way to the map and showed her. "Or, maybe you'd like this. It's an innovation that United is testing." He clicked another button. The image of the flight deck came into view, Captain Pryde still in the left seat and at the controls. "You've met our Captain already. As I mentioned, he has thousands of hours flying various types of airplanes. I only have a few thousand hours in many types of aircraft, including the DC-10. But with Captain Pryde as pilot-in-command, you're more than safe, okay? You're in great hands."

She smiled at him again and picked up a silver fork. "This might sound strange but I hate eating with plastic. That's what I was going to get with my meals back in economy. Is this really a silver fork?"

He bent over as he laughed at her comment. "Sure it is. In Business Class, all of our cutlery is made of silver plate. In economy, our passengers get steel cutlery not plastic." Then he laughed again. "What's the problem? Are you allergic to plastic?"

"What's so funny. Lots of people hate plastic."

"What else do you hate?"

"Lead pencils," she admitted. "I'll only use a pen to write."

Again, he laughed. "I usually use a pen to write but sometimes I use a pencil. If you ever need to write, I'll make sure you have a pen around." Then he glanced toward the cockpit door. "Helen, I'm afraid I have to go back to work again. We're getting close to the final stretch of our flight. The Captain's estimated time of arrival was a little bit off. It turns out we'll be landing an hour and a half early."

As Doug walked back into the cockpit, Helen ate her breakfast of scrambled eggs mixed with smoked salmon, as well as hash brown potatoes, a buttered roll, orange juice, a Danish roll and coffee. Because she had been asleep, Doug had chosen her breakfast from the extensive menu.

'How does he do that!' Helen thought to herself as she ate. 'I usually have tea with most meals but I always have coffee for breakfast. And scrambled eggs? Mam makes great scrambled eggs and these are as good as hers. But smoked salmon in them? I've never had anything that tasted so wonderful.'

When the flight attendant came by with an orange juice with Prosecco for her, Helen refused. "No thank you," she said to Ms Marple. "One glass of wine or anything at all this early in the morning and I get half drunk."

"Good for you, Helen," Ms Marple said. "And do call me Pat. Not having alcohol as we approach our final destination will help you get over the jetlag quicker. I just heard from the cockpit. Doug says we're about an hour from JFK and about to begin our descent."

Pat took away Helen's breakfast tray. Then the PA crackled and when Helen heard the sound of Doug's voice, she discovered that she was suddenly very proud of him.

"Folks, this is Doug Martin, your co-pilot for this flight. We hope you had a pleasant sleep and breakfast. We've started our descent into JFK International. I'm delighted to tell you that we'll be an hour and a half early. The weather in New York is typical for this time of year. They have broken clouds at two-thousand feet and a chance of rain with some frost later this morning. The temperature is currently twenty-two degrees Fahrenheit and is scheduled to rise to thirty-three degrees later this afternoon. Fortunately, for the Macy's Thanksgiving Parade balloons and their carriers, New York City will have no wind for the next few days. When we're on the ground I'll give you any update I receive."

When the aircraft landed and was about to pull up to the gate, Doug looked back at the Flight Engineer who sat in a seat behind the him and winked. As the Flight Engineer grinned and winked back, Doug turned to the Captain and asked him if he could show Helen around the cockpit.

"That's no problem, Doug," Captain Pryde said, grinning at him. "Pat told me on the sly that she saw you kiss that wonderful woman. Don't worry. She also told me that nobody else had seen it. Let me ask you something, Doug. Are wedding bells in the offing or are you too smart to get caught in a trap set by that Irish fox?"

Doug grinned back. "If it's a trap, Captain, that's fine by me. I've never met such a beautiful woman."

When the DC-10 had pulled up to the jetway and the engines were shut down, the cockpit crew waited until most of the passengers had deplaned. When Doug opened the cockpit door, he found Helen waiting with Pat.

"Thanks, Pat. I sure appreciate it. Are you flying anywhere tomorrow?"

"No way!" Pat replied. "I finally have enough seniority to take Thanksgiving Day off. Were you able to take the holiday weekend off or do you have to work?"

"I got lucky. I managed to get a few days off. Good thing, too," he said with a twinkle in his eye as he put an arm around Helen's shoulders. "I don't want to spend Thanksgiving Day alone."

"It looks like you won't have to," Captain Pryde said from the cockpit. "Now come in here, you fine Irish woman, and we'll show you why you should never be frightened of flying again." The Captain climbed out of his seat and motioned Helen forward. "Helen, sit here. Doug will sit in his usual seat. See that old man behind you? That's Flight Engineer Cleve Spring. He was a Captain on this type of aircraft but as he got older, United management asked if he'd fly in that back seat. Doug, Cleve knew your dad when they were both based in San Francisco."

"So I gather," Doug said, then turned to face Cleve. "Dad always thought highly of you, Cleve. Thank you for also showing up at the funeral."

"That's never a problem. Not when your father flew West. I still miss the guy but, hell, he lived a great long life." Cleve stood up and picked up his leather flight bag. "Now if you'll excuse us, let's let Doug show this Irish girl around the cockpit."

Once the two airline pilots had left, Helen sat down in the pilot-in-command's seat and Doug strapped her in as if they were about to take the aircraft on a trip back to Ireland.

"Okay, you're all set, Helen," he said, buckling the seatbelt and the two shoulder harnesses around him. "If you were flying the plane, you'd have to wear these. We'll pretend we'll have thunderstorms all the way to Dublin, and the aircraft will hit major turbulence."

Then he pretended to get on the radio and said, "JFK Ground Control, this is United two-eight-six. We're ready for pushback, Sir."

With that, he changed the radio frequency. "Don't worry, Helen. The radio's off." He keyed the mic and said, "New York Air Traffic Control, this is United Flight two-eight-six. Can you activate our flight plan, Ma'am?" Again, pretending to listen, he wrote down some numbers. "Thank you. Two-eight-six out." Doug picked up the pad and showed her. "See, Helen? She not only gave us our flight airway—which is sort of a highway leading to Ireland—but also our departure heading and changes of altitude as we climb to level flight.

ATC, which means Air Traffic Control, also gave us the weather enroute. This is fiction but it helps you to understand how we ensure that we keep the passengers as comfortable as we can." Doug read out his notes to her. "If we stayed on the compass heading I originally requested from ATC when I filed our flight plan, we'd find it more turbulent than it has to be. So ATC gave us a new heading. We'll head directly west then turn northeast. When we get to Labrador, just north of Prince Edward Island, Canada, the weather should be as smooth as silk."

Helen leaned over, examining the scrawl he'd made in pen. "Those notes say that? Doug, I can't even read it!"

"It's like Morse Code in a way." He pointed his pen at the first notation which read 35000ft. "That means the altitude. The next one," he said, moving his pen across the page, "is the cloud cover and then the wind direction. And the final notation gives us the chance of bad weather and temperature. We want to make sure we encounter as little ice as we can. If we do, we flick this switch," he said, pointing to a control above his head. "That turns the de-icing system in the wings, vertical and horizontal stabilizers on. That makes sure we can fly even when the weather conditions get really bad. But let's say we did encounter ice and the airplane was in danger of stalling. 'Stalling' means the aircraft can no longer fly. Go on. Hold the wheel in both hands and feel what happens."

Doug reached down and pushed a button. Immediately, the wheel started shaking and a loud bell sounded. The racket in the cockpit scared Helen half to death. "See how all that grabs your attention?" he said, grinning at her. "The shaking is called a 'stick shaker', which shakes what pilots call the 'yoke', which is the wheel that you're holding. The horn and bell are our anti-stall warning system. All together, they tell the crew that we should immediately descend to an altitude that is warmer and where no ice can form at all."

Then Doug asked Helen to imagine that they were approaching the Irish west coast.

"If the weather were clear, we could see all the way to Athlone from thirty-five thousand feet. But now let's pretend that we're ten miles away from Shannon Airport. At this point we'd be descending for the last twenty minutes."

Again pretending to key the mic, he said: "Shannon Air Traffic Control, this is United two-eight-six. We're descending through thirty-thousand feet. Roger that. We'll contact Dublin Approach Control in ten minutes. Did you read me, Sir?"

Then he again pretended to be an air traffic controller but this time tried his best to sound like an Irishman. "Hey-ho, United. We sure hear ye! By all means, make that call when ye get closer to Dublin Airport."

All that Helen did was laugh. "Doug, that doesn't sound like an Irish accent at all! To me it sounds like something between a southern accent and one from Scotland. Didn't you ever see any Irish films? My favorites are Irish films my father, Tommy, bought at a boot sale."

"What's a boot sale?" Doug asked. "Is it a sale where they sell only boots?"

"No, you silly crater. People gather together in parking lots and sell used things, like household items or old toys or even old videos from their car boots."

"But cars don't wear boot," Doug answered, now clearly puzzled. "How could cars ever wear boots? We have boots but we wear them on our feet."

"No, Doug. Boots! I said *boots*! Like the opposite of a bonnet."

"But a bonnet is something that women wear on their heads."

"That's a hat, you silly man. A boot is the thing that's in the back of a car. You raise it and place things in it. Underneath the bonnet is where the engine is."

"Ah-hah! Now I've got it. In the States, we call a 'boot' a trunk and a 'bonnet' a hood!"

When they finished laughing, Doug decided it was time to conclude his lesson in aircraft fundamentals. "Okay, Helen, let's say we're getting very close to Dublin Airport. We've already contacted the airport's approach control and have asked them to vector us in due to the bad weather we're still experiencing. Now, we'll pretend we're out over the Irish Sea, flying over Howth which is on our left, and if you look carefully you can see Gaye Byrne's lovely home."

"You know who Gaye Byrne is? I didn't think any Americans would know who that TV and radio personality was."

"I heard he was a fine man with many talents. If I remember right, he's the longest-serving TV presenter in history. What a great man, as you say." Doug looked up, pretending to see the runway. "Okay, Helen, now we're on close final approach and if we were really flying, we'd be down to under one-thousand feet by now. We'd be beneath the clouds and could see the runway lights."

Doug reached out and pulled back the three throttle levers. "Okay, we've decreased power to final approach speed. Right now, we'd be flying at one-hundred and sixty knots. Just under two-hundred miles an hour or so. Then, if I was the Captain, I'd call to my co-pilot, 'Flaps twenty degrees'. Helen, pull back that lever there by two notches."

Helen did as she was asked and pulled them back. Then a horn went off again and Doug laughed as Helen jumped in her seat. "That's the landing gear warning," he explained. "If I don't put the gear down when we're under one-thousand feet, that horn will go off to remind the crew to do it. Now, pull that lever down," he told Helen and she reached out with her left hand to do it. "If this were a real flight, you'd see three green lights right below the lever. That means that all of our landing gear are down and locked. Now, Helen, why don't you take over and make the landing."

She grasped the wheel with both hands just as she had seen Doug do.

"Now we're getting close to the runway. Pull the yoke back, that's right. Further. A little more. More! Even more!" He smiled as he said, "Touch down! And that's the end of our flight. We're an hour and a half late due to the weather but we got here just the same. There! We made it. Did you enjoy it?"

"It was…different. It's not like flying a car, is it?"

"No, but if I were teaching you to fly in a very small airplane, you'd be surprised at how much like a car an aircraft is to drive." Doug reached over the throttles and took her hand. "Now I have a question for you. I don't like eating Thanksgiving Dinner on my own. If you're not doing anything else, would you have dinner with me tomorrow afternoon? If you come to my hotel room in the morning, we can watch the Macy's Thanksgiving Parade together. Please don't say no. It's a real special holiday."

"I don't know anyone in New York City. I was supposed to stay with my aunt but she's in Florida with her extended family." Helen looked at his hand holding hers and squeezed it. "I'd love to spend Thanksgiving with you Doug."

"Do you promise you'll be with me?" he asked.

"It's a promise."

Chapter Seven

Finished with Helen's flying lesson, Doug grabbed his leather brain-bag holding his Jeppesen charts of the Atlantic, and the various navigation tools including his late father's protractor and plastic flight computer he always brought with him on a trip. Then he picked up his uniform jacket and cap and led Helen out of the cockpit. Lifting her carry-on bag out of the bin in Business Class, he carried it off the aircraft.

"Don't forget, Helen, you promised me we'd have Thanksgiving Day dinner later. I own an apartment right on the Macy's Thanksgiving Day parade route, in the same hotel you're staying in. After I help check you into the hotel, why not take a nap and get changed. Then I'll phone you and we'll get together. Is that okay with you?"

"You know I can't afford an expensive hotel room. I already booked a bed at a low priced hotel in Brooklyn. My Ex wanted me to come to Boston to stay with him as I told you. But I'll be damned if I'll ever spend another night in the same house as he's in. I'm glad I've divorced that no-good man," Helen said furiously. "I'll just have to stay in Brooklyn."

That was the first time Doug had heard Helen talk about how much she hated her ex-husband. He saw tears coursing down her freckled cheeks.

"Didn't I mention it before? The hotel room comes free with Business Class on United Airlines. I thought I told you that, when you fly United, you get many extras including a free hotel room in New York City."

"But Doug, the only reason I flew Business Class is you asked the Captain and flight attendant if I could."

"And weren't we both happy that it happened?" Doug winked at her. "Now we have to get off the aircraft so the ground crew can clean it."

Deplaning, he took her into the International Terminal and then to Immigration. As they stood in the long line, Helen saw that the hallways were filled with American flags, as well as the flags of many other countries. As they finally approached what Helen thought to be a toll box she looked up to see a photograph of President Ronald Reagan.

"I didn't vote for him in the last election, though I guess he's a pretty good president," Doug remarked. "He's doing his best to negotiate with the Russian and Chinese governments."

"My father didn't like the man at all, Doug," Helen replied. "He loved John F. Kennedy, Ireland's favorite son."

The official in the Immigration booth looked up at Doug. The pilot walked toward him and presented his U.S. passport.

"Welcome home, Mr Martin. I gather you've nothing to declare because you're only carrying your flight bag and that one piece of luggage. If so then you can go right out of the Terminal. The other flight crew from your United flight already cleared customs and I know they're waiting outside with a taxi to take you to your hotel."

"Would you mind if I wait just over here while Ms Fox goes through customs? It's the first time she's flown anywhere and while Helen may not say so I suspect she'll be nervous."

"She's an Irish citizen? Has she ever been to the United States before?"

"As I say, she's never flown anywhere. She's spent her whole life in Ireland."

The Customs Agent waved Helen forward and she stepped up, presenting her Irish passport.

"This is a rather special occasion," Doug told the immigration officer. "This will also be Ms Fox's first Thanksgiving in America."

"Really?" the man said, smiling. "Then welcome to the United States of America, Ms Fox." He stamped her passport and smiled again. "Welcome to the good ol' U. S. of A!"

After they picked up Helen's luggage in the baggage claims area, they walked out of the International Terminal. The first thing Helen saw was the impressive TWA building across the street, and Doug explained that Trans World Airlines was one of the first airlines to operate in the world.

"See that building, Helen?" Doug said, pointing to the huge terminal built in the architecture of futurist design though it had opened in 1962. "That's the original Flight Center for Trans World Airlines. It's one of the best terminal buildings in America."

Helen marveled at the wonderful building then stretched her arms high into the air.

"I can't believe I actually did it, Doug! I traveled all the way to New York all by myself. Of course, I had a lot of help, didn't I?" she said, and he saw how her eyes twinkled at him.

"Not really. I knew you'd be fine. Some Irish women are brave flyers. Now let me hail a cab for us," Doug said and, walking to the curb, he held up an arm. A Yellow Cab screeched to a stop. A cabbie from New York City climbed out, opened the trunk and grabbed the couple's luggage. He threw them in, closed it, then opened the passenger door. Doug insisted that Helen climb in first.

"Sit on the right-hand side of the cab, Helen," Doug said. "You'll have a better view of the skyline of New York as well as Times Square."

As they drove toward the city, Doug soon realized how determined Helen was to get a job somewhere in Long Island. "My aunt says she'll find me a job on the island. I plan to rent an apartment in the Bronx or Queens. Is Long Island really that far from there?"

"Far enough," Doug stated, now worried for her. "You'll have to take at least one or two trains to get to Long Island. It all depends on where you end up getting a job. Too, remember you'll need a U.S. work permit if you're going to be employed in the States. Look," he continued, "as you know, I'm a pilot. I have a long career ahead of me. I'm not married. I lease a three-bedroom apartment in the same hotel where you'll be staying tonight. Why not stay in the apartment until you get on your feet? You'll have your own room so there's nothing to worry about."

Helen still wasn't sure of Doug's intentions despite the fact she now more than liked this man: she realized she was falling in love with him. "That's a nice offer, Doug. But just so you know, I'm not the type to sleep around. I never have. And Doug, I don't care if you're rich. And you should know that I've always paid my own way. As I've already said, I have a few hundred dollars and euro in my wallet which is more than enough to see me through until I can get a job. I applied for my work permit months ago before I divorced Geoff, and a few days before I left Ireland I received it in the post. Remember, this isn't a holiday for me. I've come to live here."

"Okay, but just so you know I'm not the type to sleep around either. In fact, I've only had a few girlfriends in my whole life. Honestly, I'd never want you to do anything you didn't want to do, okay? But I do hope you'll take me up on my offer. When I'm on a trip with United, the apartment is empty. Why not save some money?"

"Let's talk about it later, okay Doug?" she replied. Smiling at him, she took his hand and sat back in the wide back seat of the cab. When they crossed the Hudson Bridge, New York City came into close view. From the window she could see the magnificence of that great city and Doug pointed out the tallest buildings.

"That's the World Trade Center, the tallest buildings in New York. North of them, see that big impressive building? That's the Empire State Building made famous by any number of films including *An Affair to Remember*. Then that one there?" he continued, leaning over Helen's lap, "that one is the Chrysler Building designed in an art deco style. I always thought that was the prettiest building in the city."

Helen was Amazed by all the buildings she saw, much taller than anything constructed in Ireland. And she couldn't believe all the cars on the steel suspension bridge. Her country didn't have that either. Then the cab took a turn and descended into a tunnel and Helen opened the window beside her, putting out her hand. She stretched her fingers, feeling the cool moist air hit her palm. When the taxi popped back out into the light, she found herself smack in the middle of the city. She stretched up her head, trying to take in the astounding view.

"It's so big and the buildings are so tall!" she exclaimed as they drove on into Manhattan.

Turning left, Doug said, "This is Times Square. Wait till you see it tonight. When the lights come on the town is painted in bright reds, blues and white and the square is lit up like a Christmas tree."

Then the taxi turned again and came to a stop in front of their hotel. Doug hopped out, grabbing his flight bag and suitcase. Strapping them together, he opened Helen's door and put out his hand. She took it and, as she did, felt his firm grip as he helped her from the cab.

"Here we are," Doug said and, as he let go of her hand, he realized he wanted to hold onto the small fingers forever. "See? We're at the Ritz Carlton. As I said, I lease an apartment here and we're not far from where I want to take you to dinner tonight."

"You really lease an apartment here?" Helen said with wide eyes as she looked up at the tall building. "And you want to take me out to dinner? Where did you want to go?"

"It's a surprise," Doug replied, trying to hide his laughter as he looked at her suspicious eyes.

"Oh go on, ya fecker. Don't keep it a secret. It's just dinner, fer God sakes."

"Is that really how the Irish speak?" Doug asked, now breaking into laughter.

"Sometimes," Helen replied. "I'll teach you how the Irish drink and curse and always love the craíc."

"What's craíc? Isn't that an illegal drug you put up your nose?"

"Not at all," Helen said, laughing again. "Why ya ignorant Yank! You just wait till I teach you to talk like a real Irishman." She looked at him again, their eyes holding each other's for a long moment. "You never told me where we're going to dinner. Is it expensive?"

"More expensive than most," Doug admitted. "You see, my dad passed on last year and Mom died years ago. After we held Dad's funeral Mass and he was buried, I sat down with the lawyer who read his will. I'm the only child, you see. Dad invested wisely and he had a platinum health insurance policy and airline pension. He was also a United pilot. When he passed away due to dementia, I inherited quite a bit. No, I'm not a zillionaire but I have more cash than most people."

"Then the dinner is on you," she said soberly. "You mentioned a funeral Mass. Are you Catholic?"

He nodded. "Dad was French Canadian and English. Mom was mostly Scots and English. So we have mostly Catholic heritage. Which means, if we ever get married, we can go to Mass together."

"Married, Mr Martin? Aren't you pushing things just a little? We've only just met and I've just divorced, remember?"

"I'm teasing, of course. But you never know what might happen when two strangers meet on their way to New York City."

She held out her arm and, as Doug took her by the elbow, they climbed the steps into the hotel. Walking together through the front door held open by a porter dressed in the hotel's uniform and wearing a black stove pipe hat, Doug helped Helen check in.

"Her room is on United Airlines," Doug said, winking at the receptionist as he gave her his credit card. "I'd like the best room you have available. Helen, can you give the receptionist your passport? That's all she needs to check you in."

When Helen was handed her room keys, Doug took her to the elevator. As the doors opened, six other people as well as Doug and Helen entered the large elevator car. Pressing one of the top buttons, they stood together as one person after another stepped out to their room. Alone except for one other businessman, the door finally opened on Floor Thirty-Three. When they found her room, Doug opened the door and helped Helen inside. She walked to the large window.

"Look at that view!" Helen cried. "I've never seen anything so beautiful! Doug, what park is that?"

"That's Central Park. You're in one of the most famous hotels in the world. Isn't that view something?"

As they stood together, Doug put his arm around her shoulder. She looked up at him, then her eyes moved to the wide double bed.

"I'm pretty tired," Helen said. "Can I nap for a while before we have dinner?"

He smiled down on her. "It's only noon, Helen. We've hours until we go to dinner. My apartment isn't too far from your room. Go to sleep, have a shower and I'll phone you an hour before the taxi picks us up."

Looking up at him, she gave him a kiss on the cheek. "Thank you. You're so sweet."

He walked to the door and as he opened it, turned to look back at her. "You know what? I'm the luckiest guy in the world. If I haven't said it, and I think I have, I thought I'd be eating Thanksgiving Dinner alone again."

"I'll see you later, sweetie."

"You know it."

He stepped through the door, closing it. Alone, Helen realized just how lucky she was, too. If not for Doug, she'd be alone and homeless in a city she didn't know at all.

Chapter Eight

Four suns revolved not only around each other but also around a pin-wheel of stars named the Centauri Galaxy by scientists on Earth. Near the second sun, known by humankind as Proxima Centauri B, four planets lay in the Goldilocks region which provided two of the planets with all that was necessary for life.

On the second one, which Earth's scientists had not yet detected, a planet that looked much like Earth was named Gaia by the race of beings that lived on it, after that advanced civilization's ruler. The only difference between Earth and Proxima Centauri B was that the latter planet was one third larger in circumference with a mass that resulted in a higher rotational speed. For that reason, the humans who already lived there because they had been called by the Queen to their new home planet had to become used to the effect of higher gravity which could make their legs feel like lead.

Approaching the star Alpha Centauri B, an interstellar spaceship—The Leoni V— made a return to Gaia. The sleek craft looked nothing like the Rescue vehicle that Doug Masters had seen in Juneau. Instead, it was silver and white and glistened in the sunlight of a nearby star. At the front was a large globular module that held the Command deck. The long center section revolved slowly to create artificial gravity. At the rear, a separate section contained the plasma and gravitational field that drove the ship's Stardrive engine. The ship bristled with aerials, radar, and other communications and navigational antennae. The vehicle, a Royal spacecraft, seemed to move slowly to anyone who could see it, but this far from Earth no one could detect it except the controllers on planet Gaia.

The craft was decelerating from well over lightspeed. On the Control Deck, the Captain looked up at his instruments and decided to make an adjustment. Frowning, he turned to his second-in-command.

"We are still traveling too quickly, Ensign. What will happen if we do not slow down further?" he asked silently to his fellow officer in Gaian telepathy.

In the seat beside the Captain, the young Gaian officer thought hard. "We will slingshot around our planet and head toward our sun. Then we will have to come back again. Is that not right, Captain?"

"You have been studying, haven't you Ensign? Yes, now please communicate with our ship's computer," he ordered his second-in-command with another silent thought, "and slow the craft down."

The Ensign thought hard about the command. As he looked up at the instrumentation after thinking the order, he saw that the ship was already decelerating.

"Good, Ensign," the Captain said silently. "You have the Con. Now that we will be safely in orbit, I'm going back to the ship's cafeteria to eat. If you need me, I'll be there."

As the Captain floated aft into the ship's living quarters, he passed Selomasin, their Queen's Lady-in-Waiting. He knew that his Royal Lady, having been away from her subjects for some time, had locked herself into her quarters. As he passed the Queen's servant, he looked at the older woman and smiled.

"We will be entering orbit around Gaia as scheduled. Can you tell the Queen when you see her?"

"I will, Captain," the Gaian woman said silently, smiling back. "She'll be delighted to be home."

As the Captain walked toward the cafeteria, Selomasin looked down at her monitor in the Royal Starship which held an image of the Royal bedroom. She saw that her Queen was floating high above an immense bed even though the living quarters had gravity. Selomasin smiled.

"My Queen looks happy," she said silently as the Royal Consort Amendus, the Queen's husband, walked by her. *"Are you going to your quarters, my Lord?"*

"No, not yet. When she has finished her meditation and chat with this Helen, only then will I visit my wife. And she does look happy, doesn't she?" Amendus said, leaning over the Lady's shoulder to look at the monitor.

"So she is and shall be so long as that Earth couple Doug and Helen are wed soon. I will bring in her breakfast now. She is done speaking with Helen who sleeps on a bed in that Earth city, New York."

Picking up a tray holding a pot of hot tea and cups, Selomasin walked down the hall then knocked on the door to the Royal couple's quarters. When no one answered she let herself in. Placing the tea on a table in the expansive living room, the Lady-in-Waiting strode to the bedroom and tapped on the door.

"My Queen, if you are ready I have tea for you."

"Come in, my dear," the Queen answered silently.

Selomasin opened the door. The Queen still floated high above her, almost touching the ceiling. The Queen turned her head, looking down on her longtime friend.

"You looked pleased, my Queen."

"And so I should be. Selo, you must address me as Gaia, not my Queen. How long have we been friends? I gave you birth, remember?"

"So you did my friend and mother. What's happening to the couple on Earth? Can you tell me anything?"

"It goes well, this plan of ours," replied Gaia. She smiled again then began slowly descending to her bed. "Helen is perfect. As perfect as a human being can be for the job she may one day receive. There are few like her though we've tried to find women of her kind so many times throughout human history. She will make a perfect mother."

Behind Selo, the door opened and a tall teenager ran in. "Grandnanny!" the teenaged woman said in English. "How are you? Were you talking to Mam?"

As the Queen's feet touched the floor, she opened her arms "And so I was, my Josie," she replied in English. "It was your birthday again yesterday. How old are you now?"

"Thirty-five Earth years. But I want my mam to see me this way—as a young adult of fifteen. She would be frightened if she saw me any older."

"And you are right, my Josie. Did you see her last night in your dreams of her?"

"No, she was tired from taking the aircraft to America and meeting the man who you tell me is my true father. I'll talk to her later in the day. Did you talk to her just now?"

"I did and we are now finished. She is as excited as a school girl and though she suspects it, she's already fallen in love with your father, Douglas Masters."

"Granny, is it true what you promised? Is Doug my real Dad?"

"So he is. I with my husband helped to bring both Doug and Helen into their world. We need them to marry so their children can help us to protect the Earth and all that is important to humankind. You ask if Douglas Masters is your father? That was written in our ancient unknown Bible many years before even I was born. An unknown God with No Name wrote it and it was written in stone. Doug Masters thinks that he's human but he and Helen will eventually find out that they are both much more than that! So says our Bible in its first Book. Your birth was also necessary not only for the survival of Earth but the survival of all peoples in all of our eventual Universes. At some point, you will look older no matter what you do to hide your true self. Your hair color will change from red to blonde, for that is also written in our first Book of our Bible. In that you do not want to frighten Helen, when you look older that Book says that you shall call yourself Sally Simpson, not Josie Fox. We will tell your mother that Sally, too, is from Earth but like you, were also brought to my planet in my arms when Sally was just an infant. So it is written and therefore so it shall be, and so shall your mother, Helen, believe it."

Selo curtsied to her Queen. "So that is the true interpretation of that first Book of the Unknown Bible?" she said in English so Josie could also understand. "The human race and our Gaian race are one anyway. We were all born on Earth as you know, at least those of our generation and age."

"Yes, and now the two civilizations shall eventually become one again. But before that, much will happen to Earth's many peoples and its planet. It is far too early to tell exactly what, but that is part of what I shall soon give to all of humankind in our code and with our many gifts. Then, someday, we shall know if humankind is ready for their transition."

"Granny, when can I *really* see my Mam in the flesh?" Josie asked. "Will I have to wait until I am called Sally Simpson?"

"Soon enough, child. Do not be impatient like your father, Douglas. Learn to wait. In the time it takes for your home planet to revolve around its sun perhaps only five to ten more times, you shall see your mother and father. Now give me a hug and let me talk to Selo."

The teenager was swept into Gaia's arms, then left the room. With Selo, the Queen walked into the living room and poured a cup of tea for both of them.

"Will this Doug and Helen bear children?" Selo asked, deciding to continue practicing her English.

"Yes, but not right now. It is important for them to wait. They must be ready and Doug must go through many things to understand what and who he really is. Then, and only then, will they be ready to bear children."

The ladies sat, sipping their tea. When she had finished, Selo walked up to a series of instruments. Touching a button on a glowing screen, she opened the outer sliding door that protected the immense window.

"Home!" Selo cried.

The Queen stood up, looking down at her planet. "It looks so much like Earth. No wonder we came here when we were forced to do so by the ancient accident that destroyed most life and much of our original home."

Spinning below them was a planet with vast oceans of blue, deserts of yellow, mountains with snow on their peaks, massive continents of brown, yellow and green, and a glistening polar cap. White clouds floated above the continents.

"They will call this planet, when they eventually find it, Alpha Centauri B. We, of course, call it Gaia. Why my people insist on that is still a mystery to me. What the humans don't know is that they will also find Alpha Centauri C, which we call Amendus named after my husband and Royal Consort. Already, as you know, we have populated it with more millions of people that have joined us from

Earth and well beyond that planet." The Queen turned back to her Lady-in-Waiting. "Now, Selo, let me get dressed and join my husband. Together, we must plan what will come next."

When the taxi came to collect them for dinner, Helen and Doug sat in the back and she instinctively took his hand. He squeezed it once and she held on tight. When they arrived in Midtown New York she again gazed up, this time at another tall building all ablaze in lights. As the Yellow Cab pulled up to the entrance, Helen couldn't help but guess at the reason for this amazing destination.

✈ ✈ ✈

"You're taking me to dinner in there?" Helen asked, astonished again. "What is this? The Empire State Building?"

"No, Helen. This is the renowned Porcelain Room of the Golden Arches. Just ask our driver if that's not true."

The Yellow Cab driver turned around in his seat and looked back. "Yes, Ma'am," the driver said, smiling wickedly at her and then Doug. "The restaurant doesn't have any golden arches because it's fancier than that. By the way," he said, reaching back and shaking

126

Helen's hand, "my name is Simon Gowran and I've been driving taxis in New York for over fifteen years. I know all the sites of this wonderful city and let me tell you, that's the best restaurant in all of New York. It's well regarded for its menu which features, among many other things, a very tall entrée they call The Double Beef McD Bonanza. It comes with a choice of sides including flaming chips with an assortment of sauces and your choice of drinks."

"Honestly?" Helen asked the driver. "The Porcelain Room of the Golden Arches? We don't have anything like that in Ireland."

Then the driver, who was trying his best to keep a straight face, broke down in laughter. Doug couldn't help but laugh, too. "Dad used to tease Mom when he first started flying and they were dead broke. We're talking about McDonald's Restaurant, made famous internationally for its Big Mac."

Helen started laughing too. "Okay, you two. So go on, tell me I'm an Irish fool. I'll have to remember that joke. My father would have loved it. Ireland doesn't have a McDonald's yet but we're told they'll be coming to us soon. Now, come on. Tell me what this building really is? No joking this time."

"That's the famous Rockefeller Center," Doug replied. "Movie stars and stage stars often come here. Who knows? We might see a lead actor from the live musical, *Jesus Christ Superstar*, which has opened again on Times Square. Do you like musical theatre?"

"I love it," Helen replied. "I've seen musicals on television but never live on stage."

"Then it's time you saw a live musical. Now come on. We don't want to be late and we're already twenty minutes behind schedule."

The driver climbed out of the taxi and, opening Helen's door, helped her out. Then Doug, having paid him, placed a hand on the small of Helen's back. When he did, she thought she had never felt anything so comfortable or safe. As the taxi sped away, Doug led her up the Center's concrete stairs, past the doorman wearing a tall silken hat and red uniform jacket, and into the busy front concourse of the building.

When he helped Helen out of her light brown full-length wool coat in the crowded Concourse area of Rockefeller Center he couldn't help but notice that his date was wearing a long, flowered gown. The front of the dress was cut quite high but the rear of her dress was cut very low. Again, placing his hand on the small of her back, he could feel the warmth of her smooth skin. He looked down, seeing her curling auburn hair and, smelling the sweet fragrance of her perfume, couldn't help but saying, "You know how beautiful you look, don't you?"

"No I don't," Helen replied, clearly embarrassed.

"Yes you do."

"No I don't."

"You do!"

"No I don't!" Helen replied again then, looking up at him, she noticed how handsome he looked in his black dinner jacket and red tie. She smiled, her face all dimples and high cheekbones.

When Doug saw her smile up at him, his stomach turned over. He realized that he was falling in love with this rural Irish girl.

The Concourse had cleared out and was now empty. As Doug walked Helen to the elevator, his hand moved to her right arm and gently squeezed it. She turned into him and they suddenly found themselves embracing. As Helen held on tight, Doug lifted her sweet face to his. Without saying a word, Helen raised her lips to his. Then they kissed. Not once, but a dozen times. To both of them, it seemed like the earth was shaking.

Then they heard the chime of the elevator. Entering the car, Helen kissed him again, this time a kiss of endearment. As the elevator rose, their long-lasting kiss seemed as if their two bodies had become one. When the elevator doors opened, they were both breathing hard.

"Let me wipe the lipstick off your lips," Helen breathed. "You don't want to look like a lush, do you?"

"I'm not the lush. You are," he said smiling.

Then, before they could get out, the doors slid closed again and they were back in each other's arms The couple went up and down in the elevator three more times and to both of them it seemed like a lifetime of romance. For the rest of their lives, they would both remember it as their eternal 'elevator kiss'.

When they finally walked into the Rockefeller Center's Le Rock

Restaurant, they were led to their window table by a waiter dressed in black trousers and a white coast. Then a sommelier in a black tuxedo, long skirt and bow tie strode up to them, holding out a thick wine menu for the restaurant. Doug took the menu from her and placed it on the table.

"Thank you for this but I've already ordered champagne in an iced bucket when I made reservations. Can you please bring it out with two chilled glasses?"

Helen didn't blink, pretending she drank champagne all the time. But as the sommelier came back to their seats, placing the bucket and glasses on the table, Helen couldn't help but say, "I've never tasted champagne."

"You haven't?" Doug asked. "Wait until you try it. It's meant only for special occasions and is truly delicious."

Helen watched as the sommelier untwisted a wire which held the cork tight into the bottle. Then the woman popped the cork with a wine clothe placed carefully over the top. The woman didn't want to spill even one single drop because her customer knew that this single bottle of Dom Perignon cost over six-hundred dollars. As she poured it, the bubbles glistened with the soft lights of the restaurant as well as the brilliance of the glittering lights of New York City, outside the window.

Doug winked at Helen, pretending to be Humphrey Bogart.

"Here's looking at you, kid," he said, and both of them lifted their glasses. Then they toasted and took a single sip. The sommelier looked down at him.

"Does that meet your expectations, sir, or shall I bring you something else?"

"No, this is wonderful," said Doug. "Thank you, Ma'am. May I ask what your name is?"

"It's Tony, sir. Short for Antoinette."

"A French name, I'm sure. No wonder you know so much about champagne."

"With Dom Perignon, there's not much to know. It's always excellent. Sir, if you need anything else ask the Head Waiter to get me."

When the sommelier left, Doug looked across the table at Helen. "Mademoiselle Fox, what do you think?"

"This is brilliant!" Helen said, having tasted the wine for the first time. "It's sort of like Prosecco."

"Do you like Prosecco?" asked Doug, smiling. "I'll buy you a case of it when we go home. And flowers, too. You must like flowers, don't you?"

"No one has ever bought me flowers."

"No one?" he asked again, elbows now on the table. "But why? You're beautiful. Didn't I tell you that?"

"And I told you, I'm not."

"You are so."

"I am not."

"Yes you are."

Helen started laughing again. "Don't you start again, Doug. Enough!"

Doug leaned back in his seat, taking another sip of wine. "I've told you a lot about me. But what about you? Let me ask you something. Did you ever go to college?"

She shook her head. "I never even graduated from Secondary School. I guess you call that High School. But I was taught by the nuns in a Trim elementary school until I was fifteen. Most of them gave us a great education."

"Nuns? I had nuns when I was younger, too. I'm sure they gave you a great foundation in all of your subjects."

"Doug, how long have you been a pilot?"

"Since I was a kid. Dad started teaching me to fly when I was thirteen years old. But enough of me. What about you?" He leaned in toward her again. "Helen, this is personal so don't answer if you don't want to. But every now and then I notice that you limp."

"When we walked up the stairs to the Rockefeller Centre, you noticed, didn't you? I had cancer."

"You did?"

She nodded. "I had surgery for a melanoma which is why I limp sometimes. You can't see what I'm wearing beneath my dress. It's a black surgical stocking."

Doug pulled in closer to her. "No one can see what's under your dress. Your leg's beneath the table. Do you want to show me?"

She hiked her dress up to her thigh. Leaning down to look underneath the table, Doug could see the compression stocking. "It looks just like any old stocking. Maybe a winter stocking. So what are you embarrassed about?"

She looked him right in the eye. "When they found out I had cancer, they had to give me radiation therapy and chemo. I didn't know it but I was pregnant. I lost my baby." And with that, she started crying, her face hidden by her long auburn hair.

His hand went to her knee after she pulled down the dress to hide the stocking. "Helen, you're still young. You have time to have another baby."

"I love children but I can't lose another baby. What happens if the cancer comes back?"

"When did you have the surgery."

"A few months ago."

"Okay," he said, leaning back in his chair again. He pulled a handkerchief from his back pocket and, reaching out, dried her eyes. "Come on, Helen. Everything's going to be all right. You have time to remarry and have another child."

"Do you think so?" she said, still crying. "What if no man ever wants me?"

"You're not giving yourself a chance. I keep telling you you're beautiful. You're strong and you have a heart like no one else I've ever met. Don't you get it? I'm in love with you. Someday soon, I'm going to ask you to marry me."

"I don't believe you," Helen responded. Doug again picked up his glass.

"You should. So here's to our future, if you'll have me. And I promise you, it's gonna be a good one."

She picked up her glass, too, and touched his. "To our future," she replied, and he could sense doubt in her words. But as they drank, they looked out the window together. Helen could see the full moon rise over the Empire State Building.

"Look at that moon! It's beautiful."

"Just like you. You should see it in Miami, Florida. It seems twice as big there." He considered her for a moment. She really did look as beautiful as the moon, and all the stars, too. Her hair glistened as if stardust had fallen on it. "Helen, if we get married, when would you like to do it?"

"We'll never get married. You'll never want me."

"And I say I do."

Helen blushed. "I do? That's what you say at the wedding ceremony."

"We both say it at our wedding ceremony. So when?"

She looked into his eyes. "Next year?"

"Not next year. Next week."

"But don't we need to plan the wedding and send out invitations to friends and family?"

"We don't need any of that," Doug said, taking her hand again. "Why not just me and you and two witnesses. In New York, all we need is a blood test. You're divorced, so we won't be able to be married in the Church."

"You really mean next week? That's much too early. But are you really proposing to me, Doug?"

He shook his head. "Yes, but I need to buy an engagement ring. We can get that on the way back to the hotel, too. Most retailers stay open late and if we're lucky, we'll find one with a wonderful collection of rings."

With that, the waiter brough up their dinner: a cart was laden with food and a silver lid covered a single golden dish.

"What's that?" Helen wanted to know. "It smells like a combination of a bakery and a butcher's shop."

"Chateaubriand for two," Doug said. "I ordered that when I made the reservation. I've never had it before, either. It's the first time for both of us."

As the waiter carved the beef covered in pastry, poured rich gravy over it, and added potatoes and vegetables, Helen said to him, "Can you give me more vegetables please? I love vegetables."

"You love life, don't you, Helen," Doug replied instead of the waiter.

"I love my veg," Helen said to his question, "as well as life."

"I love life, too," he replied and raised his glass of Champagne, toasting her. "To a future of happiness for both of us."

With that, the waiter laid the large plates on their table and they both tucked in.

Chapter Nine

After finishing dinner as well as a desert of flaming cherries jubilee, the couple sat back with a dessert wine that, this time, Doug allowed the sommelier to choose. When they finished, he paid for the meal in cash and heavily tipped the staff for a fantastic dinner.

As they entered the elevator for the second time, Helen laughed at the memory of their first elevator kiss as Doug, who'd been given a piece of mistletoe by the Head Waiter, held it up over her head.

"It's time for some entertainment," he said after he kissed her. "Do you remember I mentioned *Jesus Christ Superstar* was playing? I have another surprise right here." And he tapped his head.

"What, you have tickets in your head?" Helen smiled. "You might be a magician but that one is impossible."

"Maybe I have a rabbit in my head."

"Still impossible, you American fecker."

"So, keep looking."

Helen looked him up and down as the elevator doors closed. She patted his bottom jacket pocket, then reached inside his coat, looking for the tickets. When she couldn't find them, she looked up at him.

"Okay, Joker. Where did you hide them? We're not really going, are we?"

"Have you ever seen *Get Smart*, the TV spy series?" Doug asked, laughing at her confused eyes. "Where does Max hide his phone?"

Helen thought back, remembering how much her father, Tommy, loved sitting her on his lap when she was small. She remembered the black and white TV flicker at night in their tiny front sitting room, and how it cast shadows on the ceiling. Thinking more, she said, "Ah-hah! I have it, Chief," she replied in a lousy American accent as she imitated Maxwell Smart. "In your shoe!"

"Exactly, Max. But you don't look like Max."

With that, Doug took off his right shoe and pulled two tickets from it.

When they came out of the elevator car, they walked again through the main concourse, then down the front steps of the Rockefeller Center, hand-in-hand. They found a taxi waiting. The taxi driver, dressed in a leather jacket and black hat, a yellow band running just above the brim, got out of the car and opened the door for them.

"Ladies first," Doug said, stepping aside so Helen could get in.

"This time, it's co-pilots first. After all, occasionally they deserve some respect, too."

Then the driver closed the door, got back into the cab, and took off into the New York traffic. A moment later, they found themselves in the City Theatre District. When the taxi stopped, Helen looked up: a white neon sign with tall red Capital letters shouted, JESUS CHRST SUPERSTAR DIRECT TO NEW YORK FROM LONDON!

After they entered the large theater, Doug led the way up the five flights of stairs. They found themselves on the Upper Circle of the large auditorium. As they sat down in adjoining seats, Doug leaned over to Helen. "It may seem like we're sitting in Heaven but these are the best seats in the house. From here we can see all of the action and hear all of the singing. You're going to love this."

Helen held up a black and yellow play bill, one that Doug had bought them when they first entered the theatre, studying it. "Is this cast really from London? And Doug, who are these two?"

He looked at the pictures of the two London stage stars. "That's Paul Nicholas who played Jesus Christ in the first London opening back in 1972 and Danna Gillespie who played Mary Magdalene in the same opening. They both have voices that are still terrific! Wait until you hear them sing, Helen."

Then the house lights dimmed and the orchestra began to play the opening themes. "Do you hear that guitar riff? Don't you love it, Helen?"

"That electric guitar sounds like something Jimmy Hendrix would play. You're right, Doug. This is going to be much more than terrific."

About a third of the way into the musical, Mary Magdalene began to sing *Everything's Alright*. As she sang, Doug and Helen couldn't help but hum along to the music. When Danna, the actress, sang that everything was all right, Helen started to sing quietly along.

"What a beautiful song," she said when the actress finished singing, and the audience stood up giving her a loud applause. Then Helen glanced at Doug and noticed how sad he looked. "What's wrong, Doug? I thought you loved this song."

"I do love it, Helen. It's just that…well…some people believe that Mary Magdalene was the wife of Jesus. In only a few days' time, she'll lose him to a horrible crucifixion. They've only just met each other but some scholars think she was Christ's head disciple. Just out of curiosity, have you ever seen *The Last Supper*, the painting by Leonardo da Vinci?"

"Sure I have. We have a copy of that painting in our Parish Church."

"Do you remember the man that da Vinci painted to Jesus's left? Many think that was one of the male disciples. But as I said, some scholars think that's not a man but a woman. And the woman is…"

"Mary Magdalene," Helen finished.

Then the last song was played for the first half of the musical and the house lights came up for Intermission. They went down for a drink in the crowded lobby, then when the lobby lights blinked, went back to their seats to finish the musical.

After the show, Doug hailed another taxi but all of them were full due to the large crowd that had left the theater. All of them were shouting "Taxi! Over here!"

Instead of trying to catch a cab, Helen and Doug held hands as he looked down at his watch.

"It's late. Let's walk up the street. Most of the retailers are still open. Let's do some window shopping and we'll get a cab a few blocks from here."

As it started to drizzle and get even colder, Doug ran across the street to a small shop. He soon came hurrying back, giving Helen a big red and white umbrella to keep the rain off her coat and hair. As they continued their way toward Mid-Town, Helen soon found that Doug was right: many retailers were still open, as were some bars and cafés, even though it was well after 11P.M.

"Do you know what tomorrow is?" he asked, again taking her hand.

"Of course, I do."

"So tell me," he asked.

"It's Christmas Eve," she joked.

"No it is not! It's still a month until Christmas."

"It's Thanksgiving Day," she snorted, laughing again and squeezed his hand. "The Irish aren't that ignorant, you know. I told you my father taught me about all the things that were American, including Thanksgiving dinner. We have a similar meal on Christmas Day: turkey, ham and all the trimmings."

"Remember, you promised you'd have Thanksgiving dinner with me after the Parade. My apartment in the hotel has a view of one of the streets that's a big part of their route. I'll show you when you get there, but that location is near the start of the parade. We can hear the big brass bands play before they turn the corner to march toward my apartment and see all of the big balloons as well."

"You mean it'll be just like *Miracle on Thirty-Fourth Street*? That film?"

"Just like it. Well, almost, anyway. The only difference is the Parade and Santa won't be in a feature film shot in the nineteen forties! Nor will it star Maureen O'Hara."

As they walked down the street, Helen spied an exclusive jewelry shop with rings, necklaces, earrings and expensive watches still displayed in the lit shop window.

"I'd love to see them up close," she said, walking to the window. "We're window shopping, right? Doug, please don't buy me an engagement ring. As I've mentioned at least a dozen times, we've only just met and besides," she continued, seeing some of the price labels on the assortment of rings, "they're incredibly expensive."

"I promise we'll just look, okay? Let's go inside to see what's in the jewelry cases."

Helen tried opening the front door but it was locked. Doug stepped up and rapped on the window. But when he realized no one was in the shop, he looked over to her again.

"Looks like it's no engagement ring, at least not for tonight. Come on, let's try to find that cab." Then he took her hand again and, together, they started to cross the street.

Still orbiting high above the Earth, the Captain looked down from a television monitor and grinned to his second-in-command.

"Ensign, what were we told by our Queen via the controller back on our home planet? 'Don't make yourself known to anyone, but help if you can'. Seems to me we have the opportunity."

"Are you going down, Sir?" the Ensign asked in English.

"Sure, that's why I'm practicing their language. I won't be long and you've got command until I'm back."

The Captain went to the space station's living quarters and changed out of his spacesuit. From a closet, he chose an appropriate disguise. Putting it on, he looked at himself in the mirror.

"Perfect! They'll never know my true identity."

His green and gold-flecked Gaian face was gone, replaced by an older man with a greying beard and mustache. His hands were no longer too long and instead of a thumb and five fingers, his hands both looked exactly like those of human beings. He opened and closed them, testing each finger.

"The metamorphosis is already over," the Captain said to himself. He snapped his fingers. "Just like that! Just as my Queen would have wanted."

Then he made his way to the transportation room. Now ready, he said to the speaker near the complicated equipment, "Ensign, power up the transportation system. Aim for the inside of that jewelry shop we saw in our television monitor, the one with the door the couple tried to open. Make sure the shop's alarm system is off. We don't want to frighten our targets."

"Yes, Sir," the Ensign said over the speaker. "Powering up now."

There was a faint hum and, just as the Captain began saying "Jackie Robinson!" he disappeared.

Still trying to get across the street because it was blocked with late night traffic, Doug took Helen's hand. "Let's walk further up the street, Helen. We're sure to find a cab there."

"Sir, wait! I hear you knocking."

The front door of the jewelry shop was open and lights went on inside. A man hurried out, dressed in an overcoat, dark suit and tie.

"I thought you were closed," Doug said as the owner pushed the front door wide open.

"I will always open for a beautiful woman," he answered. He bowed to Helen then took her arm and brought her into the warm shop as Doug followed. There on the counter, he had already placed several ring boxes, their lids already open. Inside each one, a diamond the size of what seemed to Helen to be an ostrich egg sparkled in the soft light.

"Why not try one on?" the owner asked. "Just to see what fits on that wonderful finger of yours."

"How did you know that we wanted to look at engagement rings?"

He tapped his large nose. "The nose knows as does every experienced jeweler. Such a pretty woman and handsome man. Why would you not want to be engaged, mon cheri Ms Fox?"

Helen was surprised that he knew her name, as was Doug.

"Sir, we've never met before. How did you know her last name?"

"Ah, but she wears it inside her coat. See?"

The jeweler pulled back Helen's wool coat. Inside the collar, Doug could see where her name had been stitched by hand.

"Just in case I ever lose it," Helen said then looked at the shop owner again. "But how could you see my collar when I have my coat closed?"

"Ah, yes, it is a small question you ask. I am from Paris and I am also a renowned magician. My audiences all ask me how I can read their minds. The answer? Simple! It's just a matter of telepathy."

Helen and Doug both laughed as, with shaking hands, she selected the one with the smallest diamond. But Doug wouldn't have it. He picked out a middle sized one.

"Try this on for size," Doug said. He took her hand and slipped the ring on her wedding finger. It flashed like a star as Helen looked at it, stupefied. She searched for the price but the label had been removed.

"How much does it cost?" Helen whispered. "It has to cost as much as my family's house."

"It's much less expensive than you would be, Helen, if someone put you up for sale," Doug told her. "You're worth your weight in gold. I'd pay as much for you as for a ride in a rocket to see all the stars that sparkle just like your dazzling eyes."

She looked up at him and saw that he wasn't kidding. Then he kissed her check and took her hand. "Helen, this is a perfect two-caret diamond. Two carets: one for each of your eyes."

Then he kissed her again and she slipped off the ring.

"When are you getting married?" the jeweler asked.

"We're not sure. Maybe next year."

"I wanted to get married this Christmas," Doug said, "but this time it seems that Helen has won. She wants to wait until sometime next year."

"Women always win," the jeweler said, smiling. "Now, shall I wrap the ring so you can take it home?"

"Let me pay for it now, sir, but can we keep it here until we we're ready to pick it up? I'd rather have it in your shop, under lock and key, then in a hotel room or in our luggage."

"Of course, sir. Can I call you Doug Martin? You see, I know your name, too. Doug, call here anytime and you can pick it up."

After Doug paid for the ring, the Parisian jeweler escorted the couple back out onto the street. As the owner locked up the shop and turned off the lights, he saw Doug hail an empty taxi. When the couple had driven away, the jeweler-in-disguise looked up, smiling softly into the New York City lights.

"They did not know who I really am," the Captain said silently to his Queen. *"I like zis accent, my Majesty. If I can play ze jeweler again, by all means ask me!"* Then he placed the cash that Doug had given him in an envelope with a note for the real jewelry shop owner.

Dear   Sir   or   Madam.,
My name is Francois Genoble, and am your new friend. I am also a jeweler from Paris, where I live. Your shop door was open and a couple walked into it. They were looking to purchase a diamond engagement ring, so I took the liberty of selling it to them on your behalf. Inside this envelop is the cash that Mr Douglas Masters paid for your diamond ring. The couple live not far away. He will come to collect it—I have given him a receipt for payment which includes appropriate taxes—when that couple have set the date of their happy wedding. I will now turn on the alarm, turn out the lights and lock the door. Your front door key is where you left it."

Then he signed the note with a flourish. "Oh, I love being a Frenchman or any human being on Earth! Perhaps my Queen will someday let me be an Englishman or Irishman."

In the taxi, and as they drove back to their hotel, Doug saw an open wine shop. He tapped on the window between the passenger's and driver's compartment, motioning for the driver to stop.

"I'll just be a minute," Doug said to Helen, then he hurried into the wine shop as Helen waited in the cab. When he came out, he was lugging a big heavy box.

"What's that," Helen asked when she rolled down the window.

"A box of Prosecco. Remember? I promised you that, too. Now let's drive back to the hotel and get some sleep."

The driver hurried out from behind his wheel and took the box from Doug, placing it in the trunk. Then the taxi sped away into the night. In the back seat of the cab, Helen dozed, resting her head against the shoulder of the man she'd found and would soon discover she would never have to be without again.

"Do you know, Helen. I'm not sure about that jeweler."

"What about him?" Helen said drowsily.

"He knew my full name. But I don't have a label sewn into the inside of my coat like you do."

Helen smiled again. "He said he was also a magician, that's what it is. And he made it a perfectly magical night."

✈ ✈ ✈

When they walked back to her hotel room and Doug put down the Prosecco box outside the door, it wasn't Doug who kissed Helen. This time it was Helen who kissed Doug. Neither of them wanted to go into their rooms or sleep. All they wanted to do was stand in the deserted hallway, learning to love each other. When they at last moved apart, Doug unlocked the door and opened it.

"I'd like you to come in and spend the night with me," Helen said, then looked down at her feet as she blushed. "But you know how things can turn out. You may find you don't want me, and besides…"

"… you're not that type of girl, are you?" he replied, finishing her sentence as if he'd read her mind. "I'll wait forever until you're ready. When that happens, and we're married, then we can make love for the first time."

154

Then he brought the box of Prosecco inside. After he put it down on the floor near a coffee table, he stepped out the door again. The couple hugged and kissed once more, and Doug murmured his goodnight into her ear as he held her. Then he went to his room and thought about Helen all night. Little did he know that Helen was thinking about him all night, too. Both of them little sleep and when they woke up it was Thanksgiving Day morning.

In the Royal Spaceship, the Queen smiled to Selo.

✈ ✈ ✈

"Congratulate that Captain," the Queen said to her Lady-in-Waiting. "See that he's allowed to come home soon. Or send him on another assignment on Earth because he was so good at it and liked it. If he comes back to our home planet, he'll need a replacement because that Ensign isn't ready for more responsibility, not quite yet. But if the Ensign had a co-officer and some guidance from Space Command, then we could send…"

"Josie?"

"Yes, exactly. Selo, can you call her for me?"

A few minutes later, the teenager who now looked like a young woman, walked into the Queen's living room with a smile on her face.

"So, I didn't have to wait even a few years to go home?" she guessed because of the smile on her Grandma's face.

"No, my dear," the Queen answered. "It is time for you to go home now. You will report for duty onboard the Earth Space Station. When you do, you will introduce yourself to everyone you will eventually meet, even your mother and father, as Ensign Sally Simpson. For now, you and your co-Ensign will take orders from Gaian Space Command. Do you understand me, granddaughter?"

"Yes, my Queen," the woman said, and bowed. When she looked up, she saw her face reflected in a mirror. "My hair! It was long and auburn this morning. But now it's short and blonde! And look at the uniform I'm wearing. Are those Ensign's insignia's on my collar?"

Sela smiled, looking her up and down. "Yes, and you look so smart in that new Gaian uniform. And your blonde hair is a perfect match for what you're wearing."

"It's short," Josie, who from now on would be known as Sally, said as she stroked her soft new hair. "It'll fit in any kind of helmet.

I would have had to jam that long red hair of mine into a helmet. It would have been uncomfortable."

"Go now, Ensign Simpson. Your orders are waiting for you onboard the Space Station. Our Captain will organize quick transport for you back to your home planet."

"Granny, when will I see you next?"

The Queen stroked her granddaughter's face. "Every day, and not in your dreams, either. From now on I bequeath to you a great gift from the Gaian race. From this day forth, you too shall have the gift of telepathy. When you need me, call my name and I shall answer."

Ensign Sally Simpson bowed before her Queen and then saluted with military precision. Turning on her toe and heel, she marched out of the Queen's living room.

"She will make a wonderful Captain, someday, My Lady," Selo said.

"So she shall, Selo, and many higher ranks. In her hands, heart and soul also rests the fate of the human race though she does not know it yet. And I will not tell her until it is time.

PART TWO:

ARRIVALS

Chapter Ten

The next morning, the sun shone down brightly on Central Park. Helen woke up in her huge King-sized bed and threw back the down blanket. Propping herself up on both of the large pillows, she gazed out the window at the sunny New York autumn day. Then she heard a knock at the front door. Getting out of bed, she put on her robe and answered it. At the door stood a waiter pushing a cart with a number of plates on it, each covered with a silver top.

"Excuse me, Ms Fox. Mr Martin asked that we bring you breakfast. Can I take the cart into the living area?"

"Of course. Can I ask what you brought me for breakfast?"

The waiter lifted one of the silver tops. "Scrambled eggs, bacon and hash browns. Under here," he said, pointing, "is a selection of bread including white and brown toast, brown bread and soda bread. And, of course, there's a large pot of tea, milk and sugar as well as a glass of orange juice."

As he pushed the cart into the living room, he turned his head asking, "Miss, would you like a Mimosa? While it's not alcohol free, it is a light drink."

As the waiter popped the cork of the small bottle of champagne and added the glass of orange juice to the tall wine flute, Helen sat down at a table while the waiter served her breakfast. After pouring a cup of tea, he left the room.

Helen was just finishing breakfast when the telephone on the table next to her rang. Picking up the receiver, she wasn't surprised to hear Doug's voice on the other end.

"Good morning, sweetheart. How's your breakfast?" he asked.

"It's wonderful. I can't eat another bite. Did you have breakfast, too?"

"I sure did and I just finished. How about if I give you a half an hour to do what you need to do, then come up to my room. I'm just above you. The Thanksgiving Parade will be starting then and we'll watch it together."

"Give me a few minutes and I'll be straight up."

As Helen showered, she couldn't help but think of the wonderful time they had yesterday evening. As she washed her hair she started humming some of the tunes she had heard at *Jesus Christ Superstar*. Then, when she was finished showering, she put on the only pair of dress trousers she had brought to America with her, as well as a pair of low heels. Her gown from last night was dirty as was her underwear and she put them into a white hotel bag which she had found in a closet just as the someone rang the doorbell. Answering it, she found the waiter again and he asked if he could take away her breakfast trolly.

"Ms Fox, do you need anything else?" Then he saw the full white bag sitting on the living room sofa and picked it up. "If these clothes are dirty, we'll have them washed, dried and pressed, and back to your room within the hour."

"You offer that service, too?"

"Of course, we do, madam," he said, smiling. "It's a five-star hotel, isn't it? That's why many of our guests come back, because of the service."

When she offered to tip him, he refused. "Mr Martin will tip all of us when you check out. So please, don't worry about it."

As he started to leave with the cart, Helen asked him how to find Mr Master's apartment.

"Take the elevator right there," he said, pointing across the hallway, "up to the next floor. Mr Martin's door is right across the hallway from it."

Ten minutes later, Helen was ready to meet Doug. When she entered the elevator, she again sprayed perfume onto her neck and a bit all over her body. Then the elevator chimed and opened, and she saw the door across the hallway that was already pushed ajar for her arrival.

✈ ✈ ✈

"The parade is just starting!" Doug called out as Helen brought in two cups of hot coffee from the kitchen's coffee machine. She sat down beside him on the window seat. As they drank they could hear the trumpets and bass drums of a marching band.

"That's the University of Michigan Marching Band. Wait 'til you see them. They have really colorful uniforms and the drum major tosses his baton into the air like a rocket."

"I can't wait," Helen replied, leaning out the window to get a better view. At that moment the marching band came around the corner. "I see them! They're here!"

They sat back to watch the entire parade. Behind the first marching band came the older balloons, their ropes held by men and women against the wind. Helen shrieked when she saw Superman, then laughed when Snoopy appeared astride his dog house, waving a fist in the air at the Red Baron, who circled high above the city in his three-winged German fighter.

Over thirty other balloons and more marching bands came down the street. First up were the Benedict College Marching Tiger Band of Distinction from Columbia, South Carolina. Right behind them was Ronald McDonald sitting on his Big Red Shoe Car and then the Macy's Starlets dancing their legs off. Then Sinclair's *The Dino* came around the corner, a green brontosaurus that made both Doug and Helen laugh. Toward the end of the parade, the Macy's Singing Christmas Tree sang *"Santa Clause is Coming to Town!"* and the happy couple still sitting on the window seat could see the parents lining the parade route around Central Park lean toward their children, because the kids wanted to know where Saint Nick was.

"Is it almost the end?" Helen asked, snuggling toward Doug.

"Almost. Santa Claus on his sleigh with his reindeer, surrounded by elves, comes next. Do you believe in Santa?" he asked.

"What do you think," she said with a grin. "How do Christmas presents get under the tree?"

"Parents buy them from the shop," Doug said, confidently. "That's what I think, anyway. Years ago, a kid in fourth grade told me that Santa Claus was all a big fake."

"Fake?" Helen gasped. "Santa is not a fake! He brought me many things over the years that my parents couldn't afford. Like a new blue bike with a pink basket and pink tassels at the end of both handlebars."

"Did you have a front light powered by a generator?"

She punched him in the arm. "I already told you. We never got modern things when I was a child growing up in Ireland. A simple torch was all I had, and Dad insisted that I light it up every time I rode my bike at night. Like I said last night to you, I believe in Santa. Don't laugh at me, I dream of my dead daughter Josie every night and talk to her. The dream isn't fake."

"I would never laugh at you, Helen. Many things in this world and Universe can't be explained, particularly dreams. Sometimes, I dream of Mom and Dad but I can't talk to them."

"I talk to Josie. So said the Lady when she came to me after my only child passed on."

"You mean, the Virgin Mary? Odd, isn't it. I heard her a few times. The first time was when I experienced something I couldn't explain during a flight to Alaska. It was a few years ago. Every now and then, I hear the same whisper in my head."

"That's how she talked to me, too. In a whisper."

The pair sat at the window as the parade continued to pass by. "Helen," Doug said, "you asked me if I believe in miracles. The answer is: yes, I do. Somewhere up above us are angels, like your daughter Josie and your parents and my Mom and Dad. I pray for all of them every night and know they pray for us, too."

"I know they do. I hear Josie pray for me every night when I see her in my dreams. She wants to communicate to me from Heaven and I know that when she talks she's right next to me in bed."

They heard the blast of trumpets and a final fanfare. Around the corner came the Saint Nicholas Band, some of the band members holding the ropes to a Santa Claus balloon. The wind was whipping up, and Helen and Doug could see that they had to hang on tight.

"Hold on," Doug called out the window, "or that balloon will end up at the end of Long Island."

As the wind abated again, the trumpets blared louder. Santa Claus appeared in his red sleigh and the couple could hear the kids roar as the parents applauded. Just like Doug had told her, the man in the red suit and white beard snapped his long whip at eight giant reindeer. The elves, dressed in elf costumes, threw candy at the kids who scrambled through the crowded street to grab their favourite chocolates.

"That's it," said Doug as Santa and his elves disappeared around the far corner. "Did you enjoy it?"

"I loved it! It was fantastic. As good as a trip to Disneyland."

Then they kissed and Helen went to her hotel room to change again, because Doug had promised her that they'd have Thanksgiving Day dinner next. When the waiter rolled his dinner cart into Doug's room, Helen could see that he was right in his description. It was just like the dinner they all had in Ireland on Christmas Day: there were shrimp in a glass bowl sitting on a bed of lettuce as an appetizer and for dinner, turkey, ham., vegetables, gravy, stuffing and cranberry sauce. The waiter, who had served Helen breakfast, made a big deal about opening a bottle of white wine, and placed it carefully in a silver bucket. When he was gone, Doug poured Helen a glass of Pinot Grigio, then one for himself. Raising his own glass, he said, "Here's to your first Thanksgiving not only in America but anywhere else in the world! Congratulations, Helen, and I hope we'll have many more Thanksgivings together."

They touched glasses and drank. When they were finished with that first Thanksgiving dinner together, eating so much they nearly burst, Doug asked Helen if she'd like him to order a slice of hot apple pie and cream. But Helen rubbed her belly and told him she couldn't eat another thing.

Then they sat down on the couch together and took a long nap. When Helen woke, she looked at Doug, still sleeping beside her.

"I really love you," she whispered, not wanting to wake him. "And I want to marry you. Are you sure in a few months you'll still want me?" Then she covered him with a woolen throw that she found on the back of the couch and crept out the front door, then down to her room where she sat on the couch waiting for him to wake up.

Chapter Eleven

An hour later, Doug called Helen, asking her to come back to his apartment. When she did, they sat together on the living room couch as he stretched, then laid his head down on her lap. Looking up at her, he gazed into her dazzling eyes. Then she looked around the room and frowned.

"Doug, it will be Christmas in a month. I'd like to take you up on your offer and live with you. As you promised, I can have a separate bedroom. But we don't have a fireplace here. I'd love to have that. Over there," she said, pointing to the far wall, "it would be lovely to have an open fire like we do back in Ireland. I can see how the logs would burn so bright on Christmas Eve with two stockings—maybe three someday—hanging from a big mantle. Without a fireplace and a chimney, how would Santa ever find us?"

"I don't think the hotel management would ever let us build a fireplace in here," he said, grinning. "But we could always leave the window open, couldn't we?"

"He'll never find us! Okay, we both believe in Saint Nicholas but let's face it, Christmas is just for kids."

"You don't really believe that, do you?" Then he sat up and took an envelope out of his trousers pocket. Handing it to her, he said, "I betcha, someday when you least expect it, Santa brings you a Christmas gift with a chimney in it."

Opening the envelope, she took out a letter and a piece of paper cut from a local newspaper.

"Look at the advertisement first," Doug suggested. "Then read the letter."

She unfolded it, studying a full-color display ad with a picture of a three-story house. "It looks as cute as a doll's house," Helen said, not understanding what she was holding in her hand. "Is that what it is?"

"Nope, guess again."

"A house we could buy someday in the future?"

"Close but still not right."

"Then what is it, Doug? I want to know now."

"My God, you're as impatient as I am," he said, laughing. "I said you were close. It's a house in the country. A home with a big fireplace and a front and backyard with lots of trees and shrubs. It even has a built-in garage for two cars. It seems that Santa has a Christmas present in mind for you this year."

"But why would you need two places to live, Doug? You already have the apartment."

"I lease it, remember? I guess good old Saint Nick thinks we need a big house for our future family."

Helen looked at the ad again. "It has a two-car garage? That's no reason to buy it. After all, you're the only one to have a car. I don't even drive."

"Not yet, you don't. But you never know. Santa might bring you driving lessons, and leave another surprise in the garage. Then we'd really need a two-car garage. If you could have any car at all, what kind of car would you like Santa to bring you?"

"A little car," Helen said. "One that doesn't go too fast."

"Would you one where the top goes back?"

"I'd love it, Doug! We could take it out in good weather when you're home from your airline trips."

"Done!" he laughed.

"But it isn't Christmas yet."

"Then it'll be a surprise on Christmas Day. Here's another gift you can read and re-read until I get back from my next trip. Now open the letter." When she opened it, the first thing she spied was a big red bow and the words, *Merry Christmas, Helen!*

"What's this?"

"I don't know. I found it in the mail box this morning. The envelope had been half-eaten. I could even see large teeth marks on it. Maybe they were made by Santa's reindeer. Don't you see the bites on the letter?"

Helen looked at the letter again and saw the marks of big teeth. She giggled, then read the short letter.

Dear Helen,

I understand from Saint Nick that you put a letter up your parent's chimney many years ago, when you were only six years old. In that letter, you asked for a bigger house for your family. You lived with a family of seven, in a small home in Ireland. You also asked for a new car for your father. But you never asked for one single thing for yourself.

I know it's been so many Christmases since you posted that magic letter. All I can do is make sure that this Christmas, your wishes come true. So go to sleep early on Christmas Eve. You may not find this Big Present under your Christmas Tree. But you never know what miracles can occur when you send a letter to Santa, even one written when you were a little girl.

Many blessings to you and your entire family,

Doug

Helen looked up from the letter.

"Doug, how did you know about that letter I sent to Santa? No one knew about it, not even my parents."

"Do you really want to know? You believe in Santa like I do. I always sent letters to him before Christmas, so I knew you would've, too. I thought Saint Nickolas would have promised that

someday you would get everything you ever wanted for Christmas."
He took her hand. "When Santa says he's going to bring something
for Christmas, he always does. He never tells one single lie." Then he
looked up at her and winked. "I guess he's made a down-payment on
a house maybe in a rural area on the very western tip of Long Island.
I bet he's also building a brand-new car for you right now."

"What kind is it? Please Doug. It won't spoil my Christmas."

"I have no idea. I guess you'll just have to wait to find out."

Later in the day, he ordered a taxi to take them to the western
end of Long Island. As they passed over the 54th Street Bridge, Doug
pointed out the Statue of Liberty to Helen.

"Oh say can you see…" she sang as she leaned against him to
see out the window.

"Are you already getting ready for your citizenship exam
already?" Doug asked.

"Not really. But I'll study hard over the next coming months."

Then the car went into a tunnel and Helen couldn't see much
until they emerged into the sunlight. As their car passed a green and
white sign, she saw that it listed a number of towns along their route,
with Point Jefferson as the last exit on the highway.

"Where are we going? To Oyster Bay? Isn't that the location of President Teddy Roosevelt's old home?"

"Nope, but you're really prepared for that exam already, aren't you? Helen, we already passed the turnoff to Oyster Bay. We're heading to Port Jefferson. We've about an hour or so to go."

When at last they turned off the freeway, Doug made Helen close her eyes.

"Why do you want me to close my eyes?" she asked.

"You don't want to ruin Santa's big surprise, do you?"

When at last the taxi stopped, Doug helped her out of the car. With her eyes closed, he took her hand and she could feel something soft beneath her feet.

"Be careful of the grass," Doug said. "You don't want to slip."

"Grass? Did Santa really bring us a house for Christmas?"

"Okay, sweetheart, you can open your eyes now."

In front of her was a magnificent three-story house. It had a number of pointed eves on the third floor built over five windows. The house had a long, sheltered porch where they could sit in the summer and look at the snow in the winter. The yard was huge even by American standards. Tall fir trees stood in the front garden and a long hedge lined the driveway. A two-car garage was built to the left of the house and as they walked toward the closed garage doors, Doug handed her the garage door opener.

"Just press that button and see what happens."

She did as she was instructed and inside was a small dark blue car, just as Doug had promised.

"Is that really mine?" Helen asked, with eyes as wide as saucers.

"It sure is," Doug replied, handing her a set of keys. "Why don't you sit into it to see how it fits?"

When she did, she found the car fit her as well as a pair of gloves. "What kind of car is it?"

"It's a good used Porche. It's very safe and fun to drive but not very expensive."

Then Doug handed her another pair of keys as he helped her out of her Christmas gift.

"The brass key is for the front door. The other one is for the back door."

As he gave them to her she saw they hung on a blue colored keyring. A small white dog was stamped on it. "Oh Doug, I love it."

"I know we both love dogs. And because the keyring is bright blue you'll probably never lose them. I've made you two copies of each key, with separate key rings, one of which you can hide in the house." He reached into his trousers and took out the other set of keys.

"Oh, sweetie," she said with tears in her eyes. "Thank you for our home."

"You said, 'our'," Doug responded. "And you're right. It's not mine. It's ours."

He lifted her in his arms and, giggled, Helen kicked her legs as he climbed up the steps. "Okay, unlock the door with your new key."

When she did, Doug carried Helen over the threshold into their new home.

"Sweetheart, you have to pick out the furnishings and work with the architect to furnish all the rooms I'm sure you want to take a look around."

She took his hand and led him around the house. First, they walked up the central grand stairway and down the first floor with its wide hallway, and she looked into every room she found. Four large guest rooms, each complete with their own bathrooms, were as big as any two bedrooms put together in Helen's Irish family home. Then she led him by the hand into the expansive Master bedroom.

"We can put the bed here," Helen said, looking out the window. "And look! We can see the ocean here, too. What's that body of water, Doug?"

"That's Long Island Sound. See that peninsula way over there? And the two-story wooden house? That's the museum to Teddy Roosevelt."

Helen took her time wandering around the large bedroom. She entered the Master bathroom and saw its perfect finish. It was complete with a double sink, huge mirror, side table where she could put on her makeup and polish her nails, an expansive shower with an immense shower head and six separate units to shower her torso, arms, legs and feet. And to top it off, there was a toilet with what appeared to be a solid gold seat.

"That's not real gold, is it?"

"No," he laughed. "That's brass."

When they finished, he lifted her, carrying her down the stairway and through the large family room and open-plan dining room. "See?" Doug said proudly. "We've enough room for a dozen kids."

"Who said I want any kids at all?"

"I thought you said you did."

"No I didn't."

"Yes you did."

"No I…"

"Don't start that again."

And both of them howled with laughter.

Then Doug carried Helen toward a pair of double doors. Kicking them open with his foot, he set her down. She gazed out the picture window of the living room to the sea beyond. "This is amazing."

"Just like you."

She walked up to the window and studied it. "We can put our Christmas tree here," she said and looked up at the twenty-foot ceilings. "Where will we buy such an enormous tree?"

"I know a fellow up in Connecticut. He grows them in a Christmas tree farm. A few years ago, one of his trees was picked up by a truck, and the driver dressed as Santa Claus. He drove all over the United States, and ended back in Washington D.C. They put the tree up in front of the White House, with enough Christmas lights and ornaments to light New York City. Then, the President and First Lady turned on the lights."

"It must have been beautiful. I'd love to see that."

"Maybe we can. It happens every year."

Then Helen turned around, noticing the huge fireplace with its solid oak mantel. "That has enough space to hold a dozen Christmas stockings."

She walked to the fireplace, measuring it with her eye. Then she looked above the fireplace. "What's that? It looks like an American license plate. Is that from your car?"

"No, it isn't," Doug stated sadly as he walked toward her, looking up at the rectangular piece of metal. "That's a California license plate. Dad had it on one of the cars he owned then. See the big blue letters? Do you know what they mean?"

"Mean? Why nothing. It's only letters and a number."

"Helen, read them out. I nailed it above the wall to the fireplace the day Santa told me his Elves had built the house for us. Eventually, I'll nail it to a wall in a tool shed I'd like to build in the back yard."

Helen studied the plate again and read out the numbers and letter, "WD6J. So what, Doug? They don't mean anything to me."

"Oh, they do to me. That was Dad's ham radio handle. A 'handle' is a sort of code, something like Morse Code."

"You use Morse when you fly, isn't that what you told me?"

Doug nodded. "If you add up the letters, one by one, they all add up to twenty-four."

"Twenty-four? But how?"

"Okay, let me add them up. 'W' is the twenty-second letter of the alphabet. And two plus two is equal to four. 'D' is easy. That's also four. So add four to four and you get eight. The next is the easiest of all. That's six. Add six to eight and that's fourteen. Then add the 'J', the final letter. That's a ..."

"Ten," cried Helen, seeing how Doug's explanation worked. "So the final answer, if you add it all together, is twenty-four! That's my age right now. Doug, I wonder what we'll be doing four years from now?"

"God knows, Helen but I'd like to think we'll have a couple of kids by then. My father always told my mom that there was something special about me when I was born. He said to her when she was still in hospital, and when he first saw me, 'Mary, that guy is going to be a clever son. The day of his birthday is October fourth, and I've always considered four a lucky number'. So, if I want to be really clever, multiply five times two, which is Helen and Doug, then subtract it from thirty-two, my age. And what do you get? Twenty-four, which is your age now! It's as if Mom and Dad knew that before we were even born, we were meant to be married to each other."

"Are you saying that we were meant to be married even before the dawn of everything?"

He grinned, looking at her puzzled face. "I'm not into numerology. That's for crazy people. I'm a pilot, remember, and so was Dad. Mom was as practical as they come but, and I'll admit, somewhat prescient in that she claimed to see things. I'm teasing, sweetie, but I do think that in Heaven, all of our parents planned for us to meet on that airplane, fall in love, get married and have kids."

"I think that's what my parents would have wanted, too. They'd all want us to be happy."

"And they're all right. I'm sure of it."

Helen glanced at Doug. She was silent for a moment. "Doug, do you know that before I ever met you, I dreamed of Our Lady in Heaven? She whispered to me in my waking dream that I'd meet an American who flew for a living and he'd make me happy for the rest of my life by marrying me."

"That's odd too, Helen. I had a similar dream to that. Our Lady came to me during a strange incident that I had in Juneau, Alaska. She saved my life. Then she came to me on the night before I met you. She also told me that I'd meet an Irish woman who would make me happy for the rest of my life. She also whispered in my head that I would recognize your name when I heard it."

Helen took Doug's hand. "Doug, that's what she told me, too. When I first heard your name, I thought you were a man I knew for all of my life. Which is impossible."

"Yes, it is."

He looked at her and squeezed Helen's hand. "It's a miracle."

"This entire time together has been a miracle. Just look at this house? Where did you find the ad for it?"

Doug thought for a moment. "I found it in the New York Times real estate section. I didn't even see the ad. I threw the entire newspaper in the garbage can right before I took the trip to Ireland to meet you. But, when we got to the hotel and I came into my apartment, I found that the ad had been ripped out of that section and left on the kitchen table."

"See? It's all been a miracle. How we met, the fact that you decided to take care of a woman you didn't even know, the quick decision I made to come to New York…"

"And the fact that we both found out that we needed each other, that I proposed to you and that you accepted."

Doug and Helen stood up from the couch. They both looked to the ceiling.

"Thank you, Holy Mother," Helen prayed, "for giving both of us this blessing." Then they walked out the door hand-in-hand and took a taxi back to the City.

Chapter Twelve

Amendus, the Queen's Consort, found his wife in the Rescue vehicle hanger at their planet's spaceport. He walked in through the open doors, wearing his General's uniform. When he saw his wife with Sally Simpson, he approached the spacecraft they were examining.

"So my granddaughter," he heard Gaia say to Sally, "I understand that this is your new command. You have passed all your examinations and, because we require new senior officers, I have asked our Space Fleet Admiral to make you a Lieutenant with all speed."

"Thank you, Granny," Amendus heard Sally reply. "As you know, I took a Rescue vehicle to planet Mars to help our local geologists land there and do even more research. My Captain on that flight told me that I had obeyed and correctly executed every order he gave to me. On the return flight, and though I was an Ensign, he honored me by letting me fly home in the Captain's seat."

"You did well, my grand-daughter," Gaia replied. Then she turned and saw her husband. "Amendus, why are you wearing your uniform? As far as I am aware, there is no formal occasion today that requires one."

The Royal Consort bowed low to his wife. "My Queen and wife, I am sure you are aware of many signals coming from the other side of our Centauri Galaxy. We have intercepted them and decoded them. It is *them*, my wife."

"Them?" Sally asked. "May I ask my Lord, who is *them*?"

"It is a civilization which requires no name," Amendus said. "They have a name but I'd rather not utter it not even once."

Gaia laughed. "Pay no attention to my husband, Sally. *Them* is a race of creatures descended from the dust of many planets. They are our eternal enemies. *Them* is the name many Gaians give to the Smarmi race. They look nothing like us. Instead, they look like creatures you've never seen before, not even in your worst nightmares. We have defeated them many times in the past. But on one occasion, when we were not expecting their surprise attack, they defeated us in battle and almost destroyed our planet."

"Yes, they did, but they were not successful in the end," Amendus explained to the new Lieutenant. "After many more pitched battles, and even fighting in hand-to-hand combat on the surface of Gaia, we drove those beasts back to their corner of their Galaxy. But we always knew that, given the chance, they would strike again. Which, it appears, they are now planning to do."

"Then we must prepare ourselves," the Queen said. "I have, as you know my husband, already sensed our Galaxy quiver with a coming battle. But I have also seen our future and we shall win this single battle though it will cost our civilization many lives and the Smarmi race their entire planet."

"Queen, is there nothing we can do to prevent these horrific losses?" Sally asked. "An entire planet? Surely, there must be some other way than destroy it. I didn't realize that in this Universe such power existed."

"Such power does exist, Lieutenant," Amendus replied. "And we have learned to harness it though we rarely use it."

"No, we shall not be the ones to destroy their planet," Gaia interjected. "Instead, they will destroy their own planet. That is why they are after ours. They have already used all of the resources on their planet of Zanichost which is why they want to steal Gaia."

Sally looked down at her Ensign uniform. "Ma'am, may I fight in this war? If these beasts are after Gaia, and should they win, then they will someday try to overwhelm Earth."

Gaia looked down on her. "Yes, my child. You too must fight. Have a new uniform issued to you. But you shall not fight as a Lieutenant. Instead, you will be promoted to Captain. Tell those that issue uniforms that I have already done so to you. Also tell the payroll soldiers that you shall receive an increase in salary commensurate with your new rank."

The new Captain bowed. "I understand, your Royal Highness. I will gather my new uniform then prepare my Rescue vehicle for battle."

Amendus looked from his Queen to Sally and down at his own General's uniform. "I shall also do battle with you, Captain Simpson. But we will not take your older Rescue vehicle. I have a new Starship battleship waiting. It's already orbiting our planet. I will sit in the left seat when we begin our flight. When we engage that ugly race in battle, you can command our fighting teams placed in our other spacecraft and coordinate our defensive attack."

"I thank you, my Lord and General. I shall now change and get a ship to take me to your spaceship."

As Sally left, Gaia looked to her husband. "Do not let anything happen to that young one, my Amendus. Too much of the future rests in her hands. Nor can you have anything happen to you or your spacecraft."

"It is I who usually worry, not you, my wife. We won't be too long. We're already tracking their incoming craft. Twelve hundred have already decelerated into our Solar System. We have trained our warheads on these inferior craft and they shall be loosed at them any moment. When they are finished, only a handful of the enemy targets will have survived. Then, it will only be a mopping up operation."

He gave his wife an enormous hug and began walking out of the hanger.

"Be careful, Amendus. Come back to me," the Queen called after him. "While you and my granddaughter are gone, I shall be in touch with Helen and Doug to make certain that at least they are safe."

When her husband had disappeared out the hanger doors, Gaia looked to the Heavens and bowed her head. "Oh my Unknown Lord with no name whatsoever. Please protect my husband and all of my family, wherever they may roam. Let us destroy our enemies and, if we can, take prisoners. Then we shall teach them your Holy Way and help them start a civilization again on a new planet which they shall learn to protect, not destroy."

For the next few days, Doug and Helen not only planned for their wedding but also the children that they would one day have. The couple talked to Doug's real estate agent and, because he was paying cash for their new home, they quickly had the keys to the property. Following that, they moved out of Doug's leased apartment. When he explained to the hotel owners about their engagement and pending marriage, the finance director told them she would break the lease for the happy couple.

Doug hired a truck and moved his furniture into the new house, though both of them knew that they would soon need much more to furnish the large country residence. They had enough of Doug's furniture to fit out most of the downstairs and also two bedrooms Helen and Doug slept in separate rooms, as was their promise to each other, and she picked out one bedroom that would be her infant's room when, someday, their first child came along. She and Doug visited a number of stores in the nearby town where Helen bought wallpaper, paint and brushes and purchased a child's bed. She also bought a large number of toys and stuffed animals including a Teddy Bear that held a big felt heart stitched with the words, *I Love My Mommy & Daddy*. As a last purchase, Doug took Helen to a local furniture store where he bought her a white rocking chair.

"We can put this in your bedroom so, when the child wakes and needs to be fed, you can rock him or her back to sleep again," Doug said. "Mind you, I don't mind doing it if you start to bottle feed the infant. You can rest while I rock our baby to sleep."

When they had paid for the rocking chair, a store clerk helped him load it on top of his SUV. Once it was tied down, they went back to their new home and Doug carried the chair up the stairs and into Helen's room so she could try it.

"Darling, it's perfect," she said as she rocked in the chair. "Now you try it."

"Let's try it together. Helen, move over and we'll try rocking as if our baby is already here."

When they finished with the chair, and after a quick lunch of hot beef stew and bread, the couple started wallpapering the child's room. As she unrolled the paper on a piece of plywood held up by two sawhorses, Doug admired it. "That's another great choice, Helen.

Giraffes, zebras, butterflies, red, yellow and blue balloons, hippos and more. Why it'll be a regular zoo in here when you're finished."

Helen started hanging the first strip of wallpaper as Doug went to the kitchen to make dinner. When she was half finished, she came down to join him. As they ate spaghetti and meat sauce, Doug took a sip of wine and, looking up at her, shook his head.

"Helen, I'm sorry but I have a trip to fly to Atlanta in a few days. I pulled the short straw because I'm junior on the seniority totem pole. I leave on the twenty-second of December but I'll be back on Christmas Day. That's a promise, Helen. We're not spending our first Christmas apart."

"I understand," she said as she took the dirty plates to the sink. "It's your job. And you've told me what seniority means. Someday, when you're a senior pilot, we can spend all of our Christmases together."

"You know it. Next Christmas we'll be together and, if we're lucky, we'll have our first child with us as we decorate our Christmas tree."

She smiled over her shoulder at him. "Not next Christmas, idiot. We won't be married for another few months so can't sleep together until then. But the Christmas after?" Helen dried her hands on a towel. "Maybe we'll have two children watching us decorate that tree."

They hugged each other and Doug kissed her. "I promised you we wouldn't make love before we were married. But maybe, just once?"

She shook her head then smiled. "Maybe, honey. Besides, in my dreams I've already made love to you."

"And so have I."

In the personal quarters on her home planet, Queen Gaia stopped concentrating as she floated down from a point near her bedroom ceiling to the floor. She smiled to herself again. *'It goes well, doesn't it Helen?'* she communicated to her daughter. *'And yes, you have already made love and already have children though you don't know it yet. But soon, you shall know more happiness than you have ever known before. However, I detect many more ripples in your galaxy that you and your future husband must overcome before you are married and have children. However, daughter, do not worry. Amendus and I, with your daughter, shall work to overcome anything that might harm you or those you love.'*

Gaia looked into her mind and could see her daughter laying on a couch with Doug. They were both smiling yet Gaia could only frown and shake her head.

"She has no idea what I or any Gaian look like and neither does her fiancé," the Queen said as Selo strode into the room with a tray filled with food. "In only a few months by her time I shall be forced to reveal myself."

Selo put down the tray on a bedside table and looked toward her Queen as Gaia touched the floor with her feet. "Is there a problem on her planet? Why, as you say, will you be *forced* to show yourself?"

"My friend, you know not the ways of humans. In only a few years by our time, and within only forty years by Earth time, that planet shall undergo the start of a conflagration never known by humankind before. Even now, they work to destroy each other."

"Are humans that cruel?"

"I'm afraid they are as well as many other civilized races. I will never understand it. We are, as you know, part human. We were born on that planet, as you reminded me recently. Yet, they have powers already harnessed that they could use to wipe their civilization off their world." Gaia raised up a hand and started counting the Earth's past and future disasters off on her fingers. "One. Forty years ago by their time, they first used nuclear weapons on their own peoples. Hundreds of thousands were killed outright. Many more died later due to radiation poisoning." She dropped her second finger. "Two. They keep having unjustified wars on each other. While what they continue to call World War Two may have been justified due to the army of the Nazi's and their inhuman treatment of many people, what they do not yet understand is that no war is ever justified. It can only be tolerated and they must work together to ensure that such wars never happen again. Yet since that great war, there have been many other wars and conflicts that have resulted in millions of deaths. It seems that this race can never learn the lessons that they have been given. Three." Again, she lowered a finger. "A few months ago, the current president of a country they call the United States of America which, I might add, has never had a united people, made war on a small island they call Grenada. They invaded it to protect and save teachers and students from certain death. Yet they could have done the same thing by negotiating, and if that did not work, with justified threats. They have concluded that they were justified in invading Grenada but many have died and many more will die." Gaia lowered her fourth finger. "Other island called the Falklands by some, at least, were almost blown to pieces by the woman War Lord they call Thatcher who is also a prime minister of her country. This was a war that could never, ever be justified. Hundreds of people on both sides of this bloody conflict died and were horrifically injured by so-called modern technologies that both sides used." Gaia lowered her fifth finger as well as her thumb. "And five and six, Selo? That is both what is happening in the next few years and what will happen to Earth in the future. Even now, two major countries point their many nuclear warheads at each other, creating more tension on a planet ready to destroy itself. Other countries also plan to get their share of what is left when, someday, they all fire nuclear weapons at each other. Already, there is a man named Putin, a young man with high ambitions. He is watching as his own country, the Soviet Union, falls apart. Soon, he will gather together those who think just like him and they will plot to take over what remains of their country and plan on how to rebuild what is left. That," Gaia said, finally sitting in a chair near to her Lady-in-Waiting, "is what their future holds. It holds much more but I am too tired and upset to think about all of the death and destruction humankind will soon rain down on their own planet."

Selo blinked at her Queen's forecast then lifted a pot and poured tea for both of them. As she looked out the window, she saw on the horizon a streak of light as a Gaian Battleship empowered its Stardrive.

"What about us?" she asked her Queen as Selo's eyes followed the bright object across the darkening sky. "Will we someday also destroy ourselves?"

"No, Selo. It will never come to that. We have spent generations learning from our own mistakes about how to treat each other and those who are unlike us. Soon, we shall help to rebuild our current enemy's planet or help them find a new home. Then we will turn to other issues and problems that face us. Now, if you don't mind, my dear, your Queen would like to sleep."

Selo carried the tray and the food, which had not been touched, out of the Queen's quarters. As she was washing up in the kitchen, she heard radio chatter come over the quarter's speakers.

"X-Ray Delta One, this is Space Command. We have the enemy on our radars. They are getting ready to open fire."

"Space Command, this is Battleship X-Ray Delta One. We have an opportunity to fire on their remaining spacecraft." Selo could hear the intermittent buzz as a frequency was turned by the woman who had spoken on the radio. "All Gaian ships, this is your Captain, Sally Simpson. Prepare to engage the enemy. On my command, open fire!"

Again, Selo heard the buzz of nothing except the silence of space. Then she heard the Queen's Granddaughter order: "Open fire!"

Selo closed her eyes, imagining the battle that was taking place thousands of miles above her. She again looked out a window, seeing an orange and golden light as if a small sun had exploded. "Target down! Target down!" Sally's voice called over the speaker. "Bravo Two-four, fire on that space cruiser that is attempting to escape! Don't hit it. Detonate your weapon near enough to it so that it will be disabled. Do you understand, Lieutenant?"

"I do, Captain Simpson. Bravo two-four will comply. Can I ask you why we cannot hit it?"

"That ship contains the leader of their military. We must negotiate a truce so that we can take these survivor's back to their home planet to see if we can still save it."

"I understand, Captain. I am ready to receive your transmissions when you have something more to communicate."

Selo kept looking out the window as another small dawn filled the sky.

The radio speaker hissed again. "That's a detonation! Captain Simpson, we have disabled the spacecraft. We shall take the enemy troops onboard a Rescue vehicle and send them over to you."

Selo turned down the volume on the speaker system and slowly breathed out. "Gaia is right. We have learned too much to destroy even our own enemies. We only destroy those who threaten us, then find any survivors and protect them with our own lives."

Shortly after that last broadcast, Gaia telepathically asked her Lady-in-Waiting to come back into her quarters. There, they both watched as their planet's battle fleet landed at the Spaceport near the capital of their world. When at the end of the day the front door opened, Selo rose from her chair and bowed as the Royal Consort and his Captain entered with an enemy leader. The leader also bowed to the Queen.

"May I introduce General Taaak'a, the leader of the enemy star fleet," Amendus stated. "He does not know our language but we can communicate with him and he will understand us by using our telepathic abilities to translate our two languages into words we can all understand."

"My friend," said Gaia, putting out her hand. "Do not bow before me. I am not your queen. You have another royal ruler. Pray tell, how is he?"

"He is dead, Queen Gaia, by his own hand," Taaak'a replied, "just as our home planet and people are also dying. My dead leader was wrong to have once again made war on the Gaian race. He thought we would win but I was certain we would lose. And lose we did."

"Are you certain you have lost your own planet? Is there anything left worth saving?"

Taaak'a looked up at the Royal Queen. "Yes but we will require great amounts of assistance, help and resources for years to come. If we are given that, then we can save our planet."

The Queen looked to her husband. "We must do this thing. It is our mission to save races like this. All we must do is help them to terraform their planet back to what it was many years ago, before they started mistreating it as well as many other people."

"Let us talk in English so that Sally may also understand." Amendus looked at his Captain. "Sally, this leader wants us to help his people by terraforming their planet into a home where they can live yet again. If you were our ruler, what would you do?"

Sally looked at Amendus and Gaia. "I would do it. That is who and what we are, after all. We are peaceful and we live to serve others."

Gaia smiled. "Then you tell this leader. I will think your English so he can understand."

Sally reached out, taking the slender hand of General Taaak'a's in her own. "Sir, I have been asked by my Queen to tell you what we will do. First, we will take you back to your planet. We promise to help the injured and to give all survivors shelter if they need it. One year from now by our time on Gaia, we will have finished terraforming your planet. Then you can start anew. We will give you as many resources as you require to bring your civilization back to its feet. The only thing we insist on is that you never make war on anyone else again. Not now, not ever. Or General," Sally said, looking him in the eye, "we will be forced to destroy all of you using powers that you will never understand nor be able to replicate."

The General began to pull his hand back. His face, monstrous by Sally's experience, had but one eye and was far too thin to support what she knew had to be an immense brain and intellect. But what she thought was a glare was, as she learned later, a way of saying 'thank you' in his native language. His mouth opened and he said something that she couldn't understand.

"Taaak'a says that he is grateful and agrees to all that you have said," Gaia translated. "He thanks us all for our help over the coming many years. He also hopes that we can come to be with them when they elect a new King or Queen to rule their planet."

"Then it's a democracy?" Sally asked of her Queen. "Or is it a monarchy?"

"Right now, the planet is ruled by dictatorship," the Queen smiled. "But now, this General will transform his planet's government into a monarchy and democracy. Much like on our planet." Then she turned to General Taaak'a one more time. "Sir, may I offer you and your troops some refreshment? We will all go back to the Spaceport where we will have a celebration of the ending of this battle and a new peace that has come to us all."

As the General left with Amendus, the Queen turned again to Sally. "My dear, you have made me proud. Soon, you will have a new command. It is an intergalactic spaceship that we are now building. I ask you to take a few weeks off. Then, you must report to your new duty. From now on, you shall be known as Commander Sally Simpson. Kneel, my granddaughter.

"But my Queen and grandmother, I have no real experience…"

"Do you not? What did you do to win this outrageous war, Commander Simpson? Once again, if it had not been for your quick actions, many more would have died. Do you not understand, Sally? You were born to lead and command." The Queen smiled again. "With your new command comes a golden sword." She turned to Selo. "My dear, can you please get my father's sword from our bedroom?"

When Selo came back, the Queen took the sword up in both hands. "This, Sally, was my father's warrior sword. He used it in many great battles and it has been covered by the blood of our enemies. Someday, you and your mother may hold this sword. But for now, I have another one that I give to you."

Gaia pulled back her gown. At her hip rested a golden sword. She took off the belt and scabbard and handed it to her granddaughter. Then she commanded Sally to kneel and placed her father's sword on the new Commander's right shoulder.

"By the fighting sword of my father, I make you a Commander in our space force. May you wear your new sword as a symbol of your growing responsibility, justice and constant humility. Now rise, Commander Simpson."

Sally rose, strapping the sword with its belt around her waist. Then she bowed.

"I thank you again, my Queen. I will work hard and shall do my best to never let you down." Looking up again, she smiled. "Nanny, I meant what I said and now promise. I'll always try my best for you. Now can you tell me about my new orders? Where will I go in my new command?"

"Where do you think you will go, child?" the Queen said and laughed. "It is time for you to go back to your home planet. There, you will visit…"

"Mam and Dad!"

She ran into the Queen's arms, laughing. Gaia looked to Selo who stood again beside them.

"Children, don't you love them?" the Queen whispered. In her arms, Sally was now crying.

"Why does the young one cry, my Queen?" Selo asked. "She goes to see her parents after many years of separation."

"She cries because she loves and misses them, as you say. But soon her happy tears will dry and she will smile again." The Queen pulled Sally's face up by the chin. Looking down on her, the Queen asked, "What will you say when you see them?"

"I won't be able to say anything," Sally replied. "I'll just smile at them."

"Then so it shall be and it is already done. Go now, my Sally. Go forth to help save your planet. Soon, you will understand fully why it needs saving."

Chapter Thirteen

In the new interstellar spacecraft, Sally soon discovered that instead of leading, she had been ordered to rest by her Queen due to stress caused by the most recent war against the enemy race. The new Gaian Space Commander watched from a seat in the Command module as her Captain and second officer controlled the ship. The Captain turned around in her seat and grinned at her senior officer.

"Commander, you're officially on vacation, or so the Queen has ordered. I have a note from Our Royal Queen right here. Would you like to see it?"

The Gaian Captain handed Sally a white envelope. Opening it, she found a single sheet of paper inside. On it the Queen had written in longhand:

My dear Grandchild

It is not time yet time for you to protect your planet with this new Spaceship I've given you to command. I have not yet christened it, so you will have to think of a name for your starship. Instead, I want you to take some time off as we discussed to get to know Doug and Helen again. When you arrive, you will find that they need you. They will need and want your heart, your love and a shoulder for Helen to lean on. Upon descending to their home in a place they call Long Island, you will first appear to them as Commander Sally Simpson with the U.S. Air Force. They will not at first recognize you. But take heart! Over the coming weeks and months, first Helen and then Doug will realize that you are their long-lost daughter Josie, come home again.

Then, and you will know instinctively when it is time, you will take a new disguise as a friend of your grandfather, Bill Richards. We shall supply you with a United Airlines Captain's uniform at that time and transform you completely once again. This way you can be with both of your parents at a time and place when you are needed the most. Commander Simpson, of course, will be hidden from their view for the duration. But when all is well, they will come with you and you can take them home to Gaia where we shall all discuss what must be done to protect our Earth. With all my love to you and my good daughter, Helen, as well as Doug.

Gaia

Helen read the letter a second time and smiled. "Thank you, Captain. It's not what I expected but it will have to do. Can you tell me, how long will it take to get to Earth?"

The officer smiled back at her official passenger. "You know how it works as well as I do. When we fire up the Stardrive, a box in the back of this spacecraft will generate a small black hole. From there, it will create enough energy to propel our vessel at a velocity well beyond the speed of light. For that reason, we will be there yesterday or the day before, Earth time."

The Ensign sitting in the seat to the right of his Captain looked at him, questions in his human eyes. "Ma'am, I'm sorry but I don't quite get it," he said, scratching his day-old growth of beard. "Can you explain that to me? We've started to study those physics and mathematics at flight school but we're not to the end of it yet."

Sally stood up and walked forward to stand beside the Ensign. "Dinny," she said, placing the empty white envelope she no longer needed on the control panel in front of him. "How well do you know Albert Einstein and his theory of relativity?"

Dinny shook his head. "Not well at all, I'm afraid, Commander."

"Give me a pen," she asked him. When he gave her one she wrote a simple equation on the back of the envelope.

$$E = mc^2$$

She pointed to each letter and number and explained the simple formula.

"*E* is energy. Energy is equal to *m* which is mass times *c*, the speed of light, which is what number in seconds, Ensign?"

"One-hundred and eighty thousand miles per second. Then it's squared, is that correct?"

"Correct! Okay, but while Einstein almost had the formula right he made a simple mistake. He treated the speed of light as a constant. But what the physicists and astronomers found on Gaia is that light speed is not a constant."

"No?" Dinny asked. "But it's always been treated as a constant."

"But what if it isn't? What if speed is infinite?"

Dinny looked to his Captain. "If speed is infinite we could go as fast as we wanted to."

"Correct, Ensign. That's how we developed Stardrive. We treated light as a mass, not something ethereal."

"Light has mass?" Dinny asked, scratching his right ear. "But light has no mass."

"Doesn't it?" his Commander replied. "Everything in our Universe has mass. Dinny, give me your cup of coffee." He handed it to her. "Our spaceship has a gravity of about 1 unit of Earth gravity. That's called 'little g' by Earth's physicists. 'Big G', on the other hand, is a constant mass no matter where you are in the Universe if, of course, that cup isn't affected by any kind of gravity like a nearby planet or star."

"So what?" Dinny asked. "How does that affect anything at all?"

Sally tapped the metal cup with her pen. "Let's say we could convert all of the coffee in this cup as well as the cup itself into energy. How much energy would that give you according to Einstein's formula?"

"I'll need to do some calculations. Let's assume that the cup of coffee has a Big G of 500 grams"

Sally handed the pen back to Dinny. He turned over the envelope and started to write.

"I reckon that its energy would be… 1,383,840,000,000,000 in kinetic energy. Now," he said, still writing the equation, "The number of joules using this example would be… 25 joules, assuming that it had a velocity of ten meters per second. Now, one last conversion. Let's say I converted all the joules into electricity. That's the number of Watts that the cup of coffee would have. That's 25 Watts which is the same as the light from an old-fashioned lightbulb."

"That's right, Dinny," Sally said, nodding her head. "Now let's assume that this cup of coffee is a black hole. How many Watts would a black hole develop?"

"An infinite number of Watts," Dinny replied. "It could power the entire known Universe if it were harnessed correctly. A Black Hole, so we've been taught, has no end and no beginning. It constantly eats energy from other stars, black holes and black matter: anything that comes near it. Ma'am, am I correct?"

"Absolutely," Sally replied. "Which means that if you could harness a small Black Hole, and placed it in a Stardrive, how fast could you go?"

"As we've agreed, as fast as you wanted to."

"And if you went faster than the speed of light, what would happen to time?"

Dinny only took a second to answer. "Time would go backwards, not forwards. As we approach lightspeed, time actually stops. Then, when we go faster than lightspeed, time actually moves forward."

"Right again, Ensign. When this trip is over and if you study hard, I'll give you the exam. to make you a Junior Grade Lieutenant. Then, if your Captain agrees, you can help to fly this ship home."

He grinned. "That would be an honor, Ma'am. I promise to study as hard as I can for the examination."

The captain turned to his Commander. "Ma'am, can you take your seat? I'm just about to fire up the Stardrive."

"Will do, Captain. We've just finished our little lesson on Einstein's guess at his theory of relativity. He was almost correct!

And thank the stars he wasn't or it would take generations to get back to our home planet."

Sally patted Dinny on the shoulder then took her seat and buckled herself in. She looked out the porthole. All she could see was the Centauri Galaxy spinning on its eternal axis. As she watched, the titanium doors slid shut, blocking the stars from her view.

"All set?" said the captain. "Ensign, you start the engine when I say 'three'."

"Will do, Captain," Dinny said, looking up at his monitor.

"One, two…three!"

Dinny touched a screen on the command console. Behind him, Sally relaxed in her chair as the force of the Drive pushed her down. She realized that if anyone saw them, they'd look like a meteorite or a small asteroid hurtling through space.

"Ensign, begin the deceleration procedure. On my mark. Mark!"

Again, Dinny touched the screen. Sally felt the barely perceptible pull of gravity as the starship slowed down. When she looked up, the portholes were already open.

"Is that Saturn?" Sally asked the Captain. "It's gorgeous!"

"We're still traveling at one-quarter of the speed of light," the Captain explained. "See your sun over there? Within ten minutes in your Earth's time, we'll be in stationary orbit over your state of New York."

Sally looked out and beheld her sun. Her stomach tightened as she realized that soon, she would see her parents. Within five minutes, they had passed Mars. Then, as Dinny decelerated the ship further, she could see the distant glint of her home planet.

"Ensign, I have command," the Captain ordered. "We'll put the ship on the same orbit as the Moon except we'll be both stationary over Earth and, of course, invisible to any of their radar or telemetry systems Commander, why don't you get ready? Your U.S. Air Force uniform is in your personal locker. You'll see that Gaia has given you the rank of Major General for this special occasion."

Smiling in anticipation, Sally walked from the Command Module into her living quarters. As she began changing into her new uniform, she couldn't help but wonder what her parents were doing. Having changed, she looked out of her quarter's porthole to see the Earth beneath her. Her heart raced when she saw Long Island. It was a perfect day. Sunlight reflected off the blue waters, golden beaches and the windows of neighborhood houses. She moved into the transport room and prepared herself to be flown to the surface.

"Commander Simpson, are you ready to make the leap?"

"Yes, Captain," she called back through the room's transceiver. "I'm ready when you're ready."

"Okay, on my mark. Three. Two. One. Mark!"

Sally heard the transport mechanism hum as it powered up. She crouched on a circle, placing her arms at her sides. Then there was a flash of light. When she woke up, she found herself at the front of a three-story house. It was cold outside, and Sally pulled the uniform jacket as close as she could. Then, trying not to laugh out loud, she walked toward the steps of the house. At the door, she looked up, seeing lights on.

"I don't want anyone to think there's a problem," Sally said to herself. "Like Granny said, I'll say that I knew Doug's father. It's a lie but a white one. All I want to do is see them both."

Then, with her finger at the doorbell she thought again and tapped on the window glass of the front door.

Chapter Fourteen

When the door opened and Doug looked out on to the porch, Sally took a deep breath as she tried not to cry at seeing him. He stood in the light from an outdoor streetlamp and she thought he looked about the same as when she was a child in Ireland, though she expected him to look much older. Then she realized it had only been two or three years since her parent's had met each other. He looked her up and down and, seeing the Air Force uniform, pulled his robe tight around him.

"Is there a problem, Ma'am?" Doug asked. "It's four o'clock in the morning. My fiancée is sleeping upstairs and I don't want to disturb her." When the military officer made no immediate reply, he stepped back a little and studied her face in the shadows. "Maybe you'd better come in. It's cold outside. I fly with United Airlines and have to get ready for a trip in a minute. So if you don't mind, let's make this quick."

He led Sally into the kitchen. Smelling the hot coffee, she took a seat at the table. Her father poured two large cups and, when she took it, warmed her hands by wrapping both of them around the hot mug.

"I'm sorry to disturb you, Mr Masters. My name is Sally Simpson. I've been transferred to New York's JFK Airport as part of a military exercise. I just wanted to stop in to see you. My father knew your dad when they were both based in the Aleutians. Dad was also a radio operator and he taught me how to fly which is why I ended up in the Air Force."

"Good Lord," Doug whispered and stretching out a hand, shook hers. "It's so good to meet you. My father had many friends in the old Army Air Force. What's your dad's name?"

"Toby Dunlap."

"That was my father's best friend! Unfortunately, both of them have passed on."

"Mr Masters, please call me Sally. And yes, I know that both of these good men have flown West. Dad told me about Mr Richards' dementia right before he died. I'm so sorry that he's no longer here for you."

"They both had great careers," Doug replied and smiled. "But call me Doug, okay? Look, I'd love to discuss our fathers some more but I really have to shower and get ready for my trip. I'm flying copilot on a DC-10 to Atlanta, and have to leave soon to beat the traffic to the airport."

Sally started to get up but Doug waved her back. "Don't leave now. Finish your coffee. Helen will be up soon. She's upstairs still sleeping. But she always gets up to see me out the door."

"Thank you, Doug." Sally's heart raced at the thought of seeing her mother. "I don't want to bother anyone. I only wanted to say hello. I can come back later if you want."

"Hah! Are you kidding? Any daughter of my father's best friend is also part of the family. Wait here. I'll be right back."

When Doug went upstairs, Sally took her mug and moved into the living room. A table lamp was on. In the dim light she could make out some framed pictures standing on the mantel of a fireplace. When she looked closer at one she could see three people. She stepped back as she recognized herself.

"But that's not possible," Sally whispered to herself. "The last time I saw Mam, other than in our dreams, I was only a few years old. I could never have been in that photograph."

"But you are," a voice said in her head. "I took that picture when you were fourteen years old yet that was only a few months ago by an Earth calendar. Don't you remember? While I promised your mother that she could always see you in her dreams, we both visited her physically when your parents first moved into their home. You came with me, granddaughter Josie. You sat with them on that couch behind you and I took the picture using your father's camera."

"But weren't they frightened to see us?" Sally asked the silent whisper.

"Not!" she heard her Granny laugh. "They were excited. When we appeared here they had already become used to the fact that you were alive and with me."

Sally heard footsteps coming down the stairs. She turned and saw a woman wearing a full-length blue robe. "Mam," Sally whispered.

"Yes that is Helen and she will soon recognize you. You must not tell her who you really are but she will guess and when she does you must not lie. She misses you terribly. Remember, right now you are Sally Simpson but don't hold tight to that ruse. When she calls you Josie, you must tell her the truth."

Helen stepped into the living room and turned on another light. She looked at the woman in the military uniform and smiled. "Doug told me why you're visiting us. Thank you for taking the time. You've made his day."

"I'm so glad I came, Ms Fox. Doug told me you'd get up to see him off. Is he still upstairs?"

"He's putting on his uniform. Can I get you another cup of coffee? Come into the kitchen. It's warmer in there."

When they both sat at the table with fresh cups of coffee, Sally tried not to squirm in her seat.

"Doug tells me that your father and his dad Bill knew each other."

"That's right, Ms Fox. They knew each other for years."

"Do call me Helen. But can I ask you something? How did you know my last name was Fox? Did Doug tell you?"

Sally hesitated. Taking a sip of coffee, she looked her mother in the eye. "No, Helen, he didn't. I guess I heard my dad talking about your family."

Helen's eyes narrowed. "But Sally. Doug and I met each other only after his father had passed away. He wouldn't have met me much less known my full surname." She gazed at the woman in the military uniform. She took in the red curling hair that hung just above the coat collar. It was just like her own only much shorter. It reminded her of Josie's hair when she had visited her not only at the hospital in Ireland but also in the conversations they had had in her dream. She had also seen Josie as a teenager when she had come to their home with Gaia. It was she who had taken the photo of the three of them that stood on the mantel in the living room.

"You look so much like my daughter and have the same long, auburn curling hair."

"My hair is usually blonde but my grandmother likes my hair auburn so I dyed it and had it curled."

"It's nice that way," Helen replied, again eyeing Sally's long auburn hair. "May I ask how old you are?"

"Thirty-five."

"That's much older than when I had Josie. You're about the same age as I am now."

Doug walked into the kitchen dressed in his airline uniform and carrying a black leather flight kit. "What are you two talking about?" he asked as he poured himself a final cup of coffee. "The good times that my father had with Toby?"

"No, Doug, not that," Helen replied. "We're talking about the relatives we might have in common."

Doug stepped back to study the two women. "You do look similar to each other. Sally, what did you say your last name was?"

"Simpson."

"Which is nothing like Fox!" Doug laughed. "Still, it could be a possibility."

"Sweetie, would you like some eggs and toast for breakfast?"

"No thanks, Helen. I'll get something on the way to the airport. Look, I'll call you before we take off and again when I get into the Atlanta terminal. If you need me, call the crew desk at JFK. They can get a message to me and I'll call you back. Oh, and I left you a note right here," he said, pointing to the kitchen counter.

He gave Helen a kiss on the cheek and she kissed him back. Then, picking up his flight bag again, he walked to the front door. Both women followed him.

"Have a safe flight, sweet," Helen said as she opened the door for him.

"Don't worry. I will. Sally, great to meet you." He shook her hand and then gave her a kiss on the cheek. "That's from my father to you. Your mom and dad sure did make one beautiful woman."

"Thank you, Doug," she said, blushing, because she knew a secret he didn't. "I was always proud of my parents and still am."

Both women started to follow him out the door. "Stay in here. It's really cold outside," he said, turning back. "Helen, I'll be home before you know it." He put a hand to his lips and threw her a kiss. Then the door closed and he was gone. Helen sat down on the couch. She patted the cushion next to her and Sally sat down, too.

"Sally, can I ask you something? A lot of things you told me don't make any sense. I still don't know how you know my name. Too, you look just like my daughter if I could see her at your age." Helen's gaze turned into a knowing look. "Your name isn't Sally, is it?"

Sally looked at her with tears in her eyes. "That's what they call me now. Some people, anyway."

"Do they? And what about your grandmother. What does she call you?"

"One of my grandmother's died but, well, my parents are both alive," Sally said as she turned away at the question. "How do you know I have a grandmother that has outlived my parents?"

"Because I do. Sally, why did you lie about Toby? Honey, you look too much like Josie to be anyone else and you look so much like me though you've lost your freckles on your face. You have the same hair, apple cheeks and eyes as I remember when you were a child and a teenager. Please, sweet. Tell me the truth. Is your grandmother named Gaia?"

Sally could only nod yes.

"Then I'm your mother. And Gaia, she is both my mother and your grandmother, isn't she?"

Sally started to cry. Helen put a hand to her shoulder. "Your real name is Josie, isn't it? Josie Fox."

Sally could only nod again. Then she was in her mother's arms Helen stroked her daughter's hair as she soothed her. "Hey, my daughter, look at me." When she did, Helen started crying, too. "It's been too long since I was able to hold you. It's only a few months since you and my mother were here visiting us but it seems like a lifetime"

Then the woman whose name was Sally to many transformed before Helen's eyes. Once again, she was a three-year-old child. "Mammy, I'm sleepy," she said, and climbed up on Helen's lap, leaning her head against her mother's breast. Helen again stroked her daughter's hair but now it was longer and even more curled.

"So am I," Helen said as she wiped the tears from her eyes. "Why don't we go up to bed for a while? I'm tired, too."

When they were in Helen's bed, Josie snuggled against her side. "This is just like our old home in Ireland but it's bigger, isn't it Mammy? When's Daddy coming back?"

"He'll be home in a few days. Go to sleep now, chicken. When we both wake up, we can have some breakfast. Then you can go out and play."

As Josie slept beside her, Helen looked up at the ceiling of her bedroom and smiled one last time. "Thank you, my mother, for letting my daughter come back to me." Then she yawned and, with Josie at her side, slept.

Three hour later she woke up. Just as had happened so many years ago in the Irish hospital, Josie was no longer curled up at her side. Instead, the woman named Sally Simpson sat on the bed beside her. She was dressed once again in her Air Force uniform.

"Mam, I have to be Sally Simpson for a few more years. But Gaia has promised me that from this point on I'll always be here for you. Wherever we both have to go, we can always keep in touch. You see, Gaia gave me the same gift that you have. I can talk to you from anywhere but no longer in our dreams Instead, all you have to do is whisper for me and I'll hear you and get straight back to you."

Helen reached out, stroking her daughter's face. "Last night, I thanked Gaia for the gift of having sent you home to me, Josie. For now, I'll also call you Sally Simpson if that's what needs to be. But not forever. That's the promise your grandmother has made to both of us and she always keeps her promises."

Sally leaned over and gave her mother a kiss on the cheek. "I have to go back to my command now. But I'm not far away. A Gaian space vehicle is directly above the house. When you and Dad need me, I'll be right here."

The room lit up. Helen watched as Sally knelt and let both arms hang straight down toward the floor. The room grew brighter, so bright it was as if a star were in the bedroom. When Helen again opened her eyes, Sally was gone. All that was left behind was a stuffed rabbit lying on the floor.

Helen got out of bed and picked up the toy. "This was Josie's, the one I'd bought for her when I was getting ready for her birth. I'm sure of it. I thought I'd lost it years ago."

Going downstairs, she placed the rabbit on the mantel next to her daughter's picture. Then she went back to the kitchen. Picking up the note Doug had left on the kitchen countertop, she read his careful handwriting.

Dearest   Helen,

My flight leaves at 10A.M. I'm due into Atlanta about two and half hours after that, depending on weather. I called the crew desk when I got up and they're expecting unusual thunderstorms along our route. Not to worry, though, I'm flying with another great Captain: Bud Himes. He has over 30,000 hours of flying experience and is an ex-Marine fighter pilot. If we're late due to the weather and you get worried, call the JFK crew desk. My flight number is UAL FL38. They'll tell you exactly where I am. But I'm sure we'll get in on time and I'll call you from the Atlanta terminal. All my love. Doug xoxox

Helen glanced up again at the wall clock. It read 9:30A.M. She realized that Doug was already in the cockpit, preparing the plane for departure. For that reason, Helen also knew she couldn't call him nor could he call her.

Later, at 10A.M. exactly, she called the United crew desk at JFK airport. Flight 38 had left early. Talking to Mark Wright, the manager, she found out that Doug's flight would also arrive early.

"Helen, the flight is expected to be into Atlanta an our early due to strong winds blowing in from the north," the crew desk manager told her. "That's giving them a tailwind much faster than we had anticipated before Doug's plane left the airport."

"Thank you, Mark. Doug has taught me a bit about flying. How fast is the aircraft going?"

"I just talked to ATC. They're flying at six hundred and twenty knots. If you have any other questions or concerns, feel free to phone back."

As she hung up, she smiled to herself. "That means Doug will call me an hour earlier than he hoped to."

Helen got on with her day. She drove her car into town, bought some groceries and had her hair done. When she came home, she vacuumed the living room and looked again at the photo of Josie as a teenager. Gazing out the window, she wondered if the woman some called Sally was still high above her.

Two hours later she made herself some lunch. As she was cleaning her plate, the phone rang. It was the United crew desk manager.

"Helen, this is Mark again. Look, we're not sure what's happening but we're just off the phone with Atlanta Approach Control. Captain Hines radioed in when their aircraft was about forty-five minutes from landing. Doug's DC-10 is late now. But as I said before, we expected his flight to be in an hour early."

Her stomach tightened as she gripped the phone. "Mark, do you have any idea where his plane is? Maybe they had to land at a different airport due to those thunderstorms"

"No, Ma'am. We checked with every airport in the area. As far as we know, Doug's flight is still in the air. He could have had an electrical failure in which case the crew wouldn't be able to communicate with anyone in the air or on the ground."

"Okay, Mark. Thank you. Can you phone me back if you hear anything else?"

"Helen, you have my word on that. Don't be too concerned. Electrical failures don't happen that often but when they do, it's usually of no concern. I just wanted you to know in case he didn't phone you when he walked into the terminal."

For another hour, Helen tried to distract herself with housework. Having finished everything she could think of, she sat in the kitchen and stared at the phone. Looking out the window again, she closed her eyes and whispered quietly in her head.

"Josie, if you can hear me, please help your father. They don't know where his jet is and I'm so worried for him. If you already know something I don't, can you please come to be with me?"

She heard a horn blare from outside. Glancing again out the window, she saw a car driving up to the house. As it sped into their driveway and came to a stop, Helen ran to the front door and opened it.

A man she didn't know who was dressed in a United Captain's uniform and wearing a blue airline cap stepped from the car and brushed rain from his long overcoat. Grim-faced, he walked up to her, standing below the front step of her home. When he took off his hat, Helen saw that he had greying red hair.

"What? Is it Doug?" Helen guessed, putting a hand to her head. She looked into the United pilot's blue eyes and knew at once what had happened. "Where did he crash? Did he survive?"

The Captain put a strong hand on her shoulder. "Helen, Doug's all right so don't worry. Half the passengers and crew survived. Doug was one of them. If it hadn't been for Doug and his flying skills, no one would have survived the accident. During the flight, Captain Himes had a heart attack and Doug was left to fly the airplane with the flight engineer. As to where the accident was: they came down in Charlotte, North Carolina."

"But that's not even close to Atlanta, is it, Captain?" she asked and, as her eyes welled up with tears, she read the ID badge that hung from a lanyard around his neck. Printed in black, the dark letters spelled TONY DUNLAP.

"Sir, you can't be Mr Dunlap. Doug told me that Toby, his father's best friend, died a number of years ago."

Helen looked closely at the older man's face. As she did, she noticed his eyes. They had changed from blue and were now hazel in color. She again noticed the closely cropped greying red hair. As she watched, the tips of the hair turned to auburn then blonde.

"You're not Toby Dunlap," she whispered. "You're Josie and Sally."

The man's face remained serious but he nodded and, without opening his mouth, said silently: "Yes, Helen, I am Josie and Sally together with Toby Dunlap. Gaia knew that soon you would need me as well as someone from United. Few working with the airlines now remember Mr Dunlap because he retired many years ago and will not be recognized. But because he is an experienced United Airlines pilot and has personal company identification and a current pilot's license, they will all believe that he is an official representative from the airline. Gaia has allowed him to share my mind so that we can both be with you during this horrible situation."

The man's eyes blinked and his irises turned again to bright blue. He winked at Helen and, when his face turned serious again.

"From this point on, Helen, please call me Toby. If you'll remember, I fly for United, too, and am close friends with Captain Pryde, your late father-in-law Bill Richards as well as the late Captain Himes. Jerry Pryde told me how he loved meeting you when you first met Doug on your flight to New York City. Years ago, I was also a flight manager and ALPA representative. That's the Airline Pilots Association, our union. As you know, I've known Doug for years.

He's a great friend and a fine pilot. He's being taken by ambulance to a hospital near Charlotte, close to the airport."

"Thank you for coming, Captain Dunlap."

"It's Toby, remember?" he said as he climbed up the front steps and squeezed her shoulder. Seeing the tears in her eyes, he said. "I told you, don't worry."

"But I am worried. When can I see him."

"United has already arranged a seat aboard a special flight for you. It leaves in an hour. I've come to take you to the airport. Don't worry about any luggage. We'll buy anything you need. Just bring your handbag. You don't even need money. United has an employee fund for this kind of emergency."

It was then that the news hit Helen hard, as if a tsunami had washed over her. As she collapsed into his arms, Captain Dunlap held on as her entire body shuddered and she broke into a flood of tears. Inside the airline pilot's body, Josie and Sally also shook at the thought that their father had been injured and could die soon. But due to Toby's presence, she soon got hold of herself. Thinking of Gaia, she said a silent prayer for Doug.

"Do not worry," her grandmother's voice answered. "Your father is safe. From now on, let Toby Dunlap take control. Try not to even think. I will tell you when it is time to go back to your spacecraft. Then, later, you will transfer to another intergalactic vehicle to go back to our home planet. As you do so, I with my husband Amendus, will work to prepare your mother and father for what they must do next."

Chapter Fifteen

Captain Dunlap somehow managed to help Helen into his United Airlines car that the company had lent to him. She was still sobbing uncontrollably as he climbed in and closed the door; she was leaning across the gear lever of the two-door Pontiac then fell gently onto his shoulder. He backed out of the driveway and then, seeing that the street was empty, gunned the engine and drove at speed out of the neighborhood. Climbing onto the freeway, he noted that, fortunately, there wasn't much traffic. Half-way through their journey, he looked more closely at this woman who cared so much about his best friend's son who would soon become his wife. Seeing that she was asleep, he decided that he wouldn't wake her until they were almost to their destination.

Weaving between light traffic, he flipped on the windshield wipers as snow started falling. Glancing at his watch, he knew there was a good chance they'd be late to the airport but because he would fly the company's twin-engine Bombardier Challenger down to North Carolina, he knew they had all the time they needed. As they approached a toll booth, the traffic grew heavy with cars and trucks making their way to the airport. Having paid the toll, he pulled over and to show his United Airlines ID to the operator. Explaining the grim situation, he was allowed to use the toll booth phone. When a United manager answered his call, Toby asked about Doug. Having verified Captain Dunlap's identification, the manager said, "He's made it to hospital, thank God, but he's going to be in surgery for several more hours. They think he's going to be OK but he might lose a leg. Is Ms Fox with you? You'd probably better warn her. Phone me again later if you can and I might know some more."

After he had hung up, Toby slouched in his seat staring at the snow now falling in heavy flurries. He knew that losing a leg wouldn't necessarily mean the end of Doug's flying career but certainly his life would become immeasurably more difficult. But he also knew that the UAL family and Helen would take great care of Doug and do whatever they could to help him recover from the horrible accident.

When he at last pulled back into traffic, he glanced at Helen but she was still sleeping. He gave a sigh of relief, glad that he could postpone the moment when he would have to break the grim news. He made up his mind that he wouldn't tell her the full implications of the accident until they were on the company's jet. When at last he could see the New York City skyline, he gently placed his hand on Helen's shoulder, shaking it slightly. As she opened her eyes, she rubbed them then remembered where they were going and why.

"Are we almost there, Toby?" she asked, sitting straight up in her seat. "Have you received any more news on Doug?"

"See, there's the airport, Helen. We're almost there," Toby replied and, having avoided her difficult question, he pointed to the JFK terminal in the near distance. As Helen looked up, she could see an aircraft landing on the runway.

"It's hard to believe that Doug left only a few hours ago. What time is it?"

"It's almost two o'clock. We'll have you to the airplane in fifteen minutes. We're using a private aircraft, a Bombardier, owned by United. Boeing, the manufacturer of the DC-10, have their engineers going down to Charlotte, too, so they'll be joining us on the flight." He glanced over at her, doing his best to mask his worry. "We won't have to go through security so that will save us a lot of time."

When the car arrived at the airport, Toby turned at a sign directing him to the Executive Flight Terminal then drove to the security gate. The woman inside the grey hut looked up then nodded at him as she lifted the gate. He hadn't even been asked to show his ID.

"We heard what happened," the woman said, leaning out the hut's window. "Is that the co-pilot's wife?"

Toby nodded.

The woman stepped out from her small cabin into the snow. As she walked around the car, Helen opened her window. "I'm so glad your husband's OK," the security officer said. "We all heard what happened. If it hadn't been for that brave man, no one would have made it out of the airplane alive."

Helen managed a smile as the woman stepped back. Then Toby sped his car to the hanger. As they rounded the building, Helen saw the waiting jet aircraft.

"Is that our plane? It's so small."

"It's not that small," Toby replied, "and anyway, I'm used to flying small planes. Doug's dad often flew with me in my Stinson Stationwagon. That's a light plane almost like the one Doug learned to fly in. I've also trained to fly small jets so Helen, I promise, you're in safe hands."

They parked and Toby helped her up the small staircase into the waiting plane. Helen was too upset to notice the sumptuous interior as she was led to the aft of the cabin by the flight attendant. She noticed a number of men and women—experts from United and Boeing—who were engaged in a conversation as she passed by. Before she took her seat, she heard a phone ring. She could hear a woman say, "Already? Thank you!"

Then Helen heard the rest of the short conversation. "They've found the Black Box and the Flight Recorder. Now we'll know what caused the accident." For a brief moment, the cabin was filled with spontaneous applause.

✈ ✈ ✈

When the aircraft landed at Charlotte International Airport, it was met by a black limousine. As Toby helped Helen down the aircraft's stairs, he put his hand on the small of her back which reminded her of how Doug did the very same thing when they took walks together. At the bottom of the stairs, she stumbled and Toby caught her by the elbow.

"Helen, are you all right?"

"It's these heels," Helen replied, knowing that what she had said wasn't the truth. Regaining her composure, she said, "They're uncomfortable and make me slip."

"Let's get you some running shoes. After we check you into the hotel, I'll do some shopping for you. What sizes do you take?"

"I take a size thirty long for jeans and trousers. Shoe sizes are usually size six. Blouses and most everything else is a medium."

"I'll get you at least a week of new clothes to wear."

"A week? Will I need enough for an entire week?"

"A week or more," he said. "You're going to the hospital today to see Doug and tomorrow we'll want you to attend the NTSB review here at the airport which could take at least a week. That's the National Transportation Safety Board. They're the organization that conducts investigations of aircraft accidents. They'll ask some personal questions about Doug's character. We'll need you to provide a reference because you're his fiancée and you know him better than anyone."

"What kind of questions?"

Toby took off his sunglasses, looking directly into her eyes. "They'll ask you some important questions. For example, how much alcohol does he consume in a day? Does he use any kinds of drugs or is he addicted to prescription medication? Do you suspect that he has dementia? Has he ever been placed in a psychiatric unit?"

"Would they really question Doug's mental state? Yes, we both drink, but we're only social drinkers. Doug told me all about the eight-hour rule. I know a pilot can't fly if they've taken a drink eight hours before they fly a trip. He hasn't had a drink in over twenty-four hours. He's not an addict and he's certainly not crazy. I know Doug. I know we haven't been living together long but it already seems like a lifetime. This accident wasn't Doug's fault."

"That's why I need to buy you some clothes. You'll want to dress up for the review. Helen, I'm afraid this is going to be like attending court. And it's only the beginning of the investigation. Eventually, we'll have to go to Washington D.C. where Doug will have to join us when he's recovered. You know, he'll have to testify."

"He'll have to testify?"

"Yes. They'll ask him some very serious questions about the accident. When people die as a result of a crash, they do everything they can to get to the truth."

"Will I have to testify too?"

"That's right," Toby nodded. "Not just. Probably a few times. That's why you'll need more than one good outfit. We'll be in Washington, D.C. for at least two weeks."

"Toby, will you remember my sizes?"

Toby smiled. "I still have a good memory and besides, I'm married. I know my wife's sizes by heart. So don't worry. I'll remember. And if you'll think back on what I said, it's all being paid by the United employee fund."

They climbed into the limousine with the other passengers from the aircraft and within minutes they had arrived at their hotel. The reception area was filled with a crowd of newspaper photographers and live TV crews, and a hotel security guard took them through a back door and into a storage area where the airline analysts were introduced to the hotel manager. With a reassuring touch on her arm, the manager led Helen to the freight elevator and then up to the third floor. As she showed Helen into her room and handed over the keys, the manager began reassuring her in a southern drawl.

"We're delighted to have you, Mrs. Martin. I'll make sure no one bothers you. I'm sure you realize we had to bring you through the back and by the freight elevator because reception is just heaving with reporters. A pack of wolves, that's what they are. Did you see all those vans in the back parking lot when you drove in? The ones with satellite dishes? Of course, what they all really want is an interview. Local or national, they all want to be the one to get you for their news slot. We were certain you wouldn't want that."

"I don't want to see anybody," Helen said. She had blushed when the manager had called her Mrs. Martin but she hadn't corrected her. She would marry Doug soon enough.

"Can I get you anything else?"

"Not a thing," Helen replied. "Sometime soon, I'll need my clothes washed and ironed. Is that possible? Other than that, all I want to do is see Doug."

"Sure you do, sweetie. When you have dirty clothes, there's a big bag inside the closet. Put them in the bag and place it outside the door. We'll pick them up, have them washed and ironed within an hour, and returned to you. And no charge at all, of course. Not even to the airline."

"It's free?"

"Honey, it's all free. It's the least we can do. The hotel is full of survivors of the crash. Everything, including drinks and meals, is on the house."

Then the hotel manager stepped toward the room's front door to leave Helen on her own. Before she left the woman put out her arms "Now come on here, honey. Give this woman a big ol' hug."

When she released Helen, the manager smiled.

"Now you take a nap, ya hear? When you're awake, we'll get you something to eat. Then you can visit that husband of yours in the hospital."

Helen laid down on the King-sized double bed. Within seconds she was asleep. For once, she didn't even dream.

Chapter Sixteen

At an altitude of one-hundred and ten thousand feet above the U.S. state of North Carolina, Captain Sally Simpson looked up at a television monitor. Below the invisible Rescue spacecraft all she could see was a sea of white clouds that covered the hospital where her father was recovering and the nearby hotel where her mother was still sleeping.

"Captain, we have two bogeys on our radar," the Gaian Lieutenant sitting next to her stated in a matter-of-fact voice. "It shows two F-4 Phantom jet fighters from the local National Guard taking off from a North Carolina civilian airport. The lead aircraft's backseat communications and fire control officer has picked up our radio signal."

"But that's impossible!" Captain Simpson replied. "We're physically invisible to their radar and our radio traffic is in Gaian code and can't be heard much less interpreted."

"That is true, Ma'am. But those jets are ascending toward us faster than two angry Gaian flying beasts."

Sally looked up at the radar screen. It showed the bogeys now ascending past forty-thousand feet.

"Captain Simpson, the lead fighter has just armed its missiles. They have locked us in and are getting ready to fire."

Captain Simpson ordered the Rescue craft to ascend another eighty-thousand feet. There, the vehicle would be out of range of any missile that the jet fighters had to fire at them. "Our scientists must figure out how to throw a veil around any radio traffic from our spaceships in the future," the Captain said to her Lieutenant.

"Sir, I have intercepted the radio traffic from the lead fighter. The man in the front seat has reported to his superiors that they have detected what appears to be a Russian bomber flying toward Washington, D.C. A Colonel is asking him to confirm his suspicion."

"Understood Lieutenant. Let our Queen know of the situation." Sally looked again at her television monitor. In it, she could see the Phantoms still streaking toward them. As she watched, two missiles were loosed from the lead fighter at their Rescue craft.

"Sir, I have two Sparrow missiles locked onto us. What are your orders?"

"Destroy those rockets now. Then return to our pre-planned altitude. I need to see how my parents are."

"Understood, Captain."

As Sally watched, her second-in-command reached for his screen. But before he could touch it, her TV monitor showed one of the missiles mis-fire. She watched as it cork-screwed and, having lost control, turned toward the other jet fighter. It hit, exploding the Phantom into a million pieces.

"What about the other missile, Lieutenant? Is it still on target or will we destroy it?"

"Working on that now, Ma'am." The man from Gaia touched the screen. On the TV monitor Sally could see the remaining missile explode in mid-air. "Target neutralized."

Sally still watched the monitor. Large pieces of the destroyed American jet drifted toward Earth. Then she saw two men hurtling toward the ground thousands of feet below them.

"Their parachutes have failed due to the severe explosion. Two officers from Earth will die chasing a ghost," she said to the Gaian sitting on her right. "We will not waste two lives. Lieutenant, reach out with your telepathy to activate both parachutes."

Her second-in-command concentrated. When Sally looked up at the monitor again, she could see two white parachutes opening only hundreds of feet above the ground.

"Thank you," Sally said. "You saved two lives. Too, we never compromised our presence here. The two officers of that destroyed jet fighter will think they've been lucky, that's all."

"I agree. What are your orders now?"

"Lieutenant, drop down to five-thousand-feet."

"Yes, Sir." He held his finger to his headset again, listening intently. "I am now picking up radio traffic from the remaining jet fighter stating that both missiles were faulty and that they are returning to base. They also say that the radar in their Phantom is faulty. They have lost the Russian target on their screen."

"Do they ask about their fellow officers?"

The Gaian looked at her. "Yes Ma'am. They are both very relieved that their friends have survived."

Sally smiled as she looked over at him. "Tell me when we're over the hospital. Please get our Queen on the intergalactic telecommunications network. It's completely masked so no one on Earth will hear us."

In another Gaian Rescue vehicle far, far away from the Earth and traveling between galaxies, the Queen and her Royal Consort Amendus stood at the controls. As the radio signal came in from Earth, relayed to them by Space Command on planet Gaia, the Queen looked to her husband.

"It is Sally that is calling," she said to him in their Gaian language. "She tells me that her vehicle has been detected by humans on Earth. My dear, we must be more careful. Humankind is not ready to know that we are with them."

"Do not worry, my wife and Queen. Our scientists have already determined why Sally's rescue vehicle was found on that antiquated fighter's radar. It is simply a matter of inserting another invisibility device into all of our spacecraft computer systems"

The Queen nodded. Looking out the starship's portal, she saw nothing but stars. Studying her reflection on the glass, she noted that her green skin was glowing orange for the two pilots who had almost been killed on Earth. Tears automatically formed at the corners of her large liquid eyes. Wiping them, she looked again out the portal. Below them, a giant red sun was throwing great flares of light into space. "We are lightyears from Earth but soon, that sun will explode, Amendus. When it does, it could kill Sally and Doug and destroy a spacecraft, or so what I sense about their future possibilities tells me. We must wait here for them so that we can save them. Tell Sally what we are doing. She can then plan on our next strategies when that Earth couple who are also our children come to our planet."

Amendus looked at a communications screen. "Space Command, this is the Royal Consort. Do not bother to confirm this message back to us. Simply relay what the Queen just said. Did you understand her meaning?"

They heard a hiss as the radio dish outside their spacecraft locked onto the Space Command antennae located on the planet Gaia.

"We understand, your Lordship. We will let Captain Simpson know immediately."

"Done," Amendus said to his royal wife. "Now, my darling, it is time to sleep. Can I fetch you a cup of tea first?"

"I have already had one with my Lady-in-Waiting. She will help me to change and then I will meet you in our quarters."

When his Queen left the command deck, Amendus waited for five minutes until he was certain that his wife was in bed. Then he looked again at his monitor and, with a silent thought, asked their unseen telescope revolving in an elliptical orbit around Earth to focus on North America. As the continent came into view, Amendus thought of how human beings wasted the most precious gift of all: life.

"All they want to do is make war on each other including unseen and unknown targets that could be their enemies," he said to himself in a deep Gaian voice. "I do not understand why my Queen bothers with these people. There are many other civilizations worth fighting for. But of course, we have two children who are also from Earth. And as my wife continually reminds me, someday their ancestors will help us to create many more Universes and settle new planets with millions of beings from their galaxy and ours."

The Gaian lord placed a hand on his chin, then reached up and scratched the side of his face. "I hope this entire journey is worth the cost in lives to us and to those people who live on Earth, as well as many peoples from this Universe."

At eight o'clock the next morning, Toby picked up Helen at her hotel. Within fifteen minutes they had driven to the hospital under police

escort. Once inside, they again avoided a throng of reporters by using a back entrance. Rushed up to Doug's floor, she was taken immediately to her fiancé's private room. She sat down next to him while Captain Dunlap stood at the door talking to a surgeon.

"What chance does Doug have with that leg? Does he need to have it removed?" Toby asked the doctor, quietly.

"We're still not sure about the leg. In addition to it, he faces a number of other problems," the doctor replied, outside of Helen's earshot. "He has burns to both hands from when he pushed the hot frame of the window out of the cockpit. Then he burned his left arm climbing out. He was carrying the captain's body, of course, which made it really difficult. He's also likely to develop PTSD. Post traumatic stress disorder is common following any traumatic accident. He also has a slight concussion caused by bumping his head against the cockpit's front window. Oh, and quite possibly a punctured lung. The left leg is also broken as well as both ankles. Doug has crushed ribs and some internal bleeding and we've already had to take out his spleen. But in a week or so, he'll start to heal except for the crushed right leg. Try not to worry. We're going to do our best to ensure he can walk again."

"But will he fly again?" Toby asked. "Flying is Doug's life."

"The jury's still out on that one. As I said, there's a good chance he'll walk again but he'll need a lot of therapy and he'll probably need support for most of his life. He'll also have to battle the trauma he experienced. I talked to our hospital specialist. He told me that PTSD can affect physical perceptions and mental acuity. In some ways, it's like dementia. For weeks, possibly the rest of his life, he could have nightmares, sweats, shaking hands, blurred vision, psychotic episodes including delusions and apparitions, and other mental and physical problems. We put Doug on a variety of medications for his pain including sedatives. When he's had surgery, the psychiatrist might put him on medication for his psychiatric issues. Those meds could include an antipsychotic drug. Don't worry," the doctor said, placing a hand on Toby's square shoulder. "We'll fix him as best as we know how. We'll do everything we can to make sure that Doug flies again. But I warn you, it's the end of his career with United. For the rest of his life, he'll be limited to general aviation aircraft."

Toby tried to cover his shock as he glanced over at Helen, still sitting next to her fiancé. As he watched, she reached out, taking Doug's hand. Then Toby motioned to the doctor, knowing that Helen wanted to be alone with Doug and they both left the room.

"Sweetheart, I'm here," Helen whispered, holding on tight. "Doug? Wake up, baby. Open your eyes."

Doug's eyes fluttered then opened, though he only stared at her. Helen wiped the sweat from his forehead with a damp washcloth and looked at the winch that held up his crushed right leg which was now in a full cast. She examined the bandages that protected the burns to both hands and his arm, and lifted the blanket slightly so she could see the cast that covered his other leg. Seeing a thick red pen on the nightstand near the bed, she picked it up and held it in front of him so he could focus on it.

"Let me be the first one to sign your cast," she said as she wrote a special inscription on his right leg's cast. "It's easier to write on the one that's been lifted into the air. Besides, every nurse coming into your room will see it." When she finished, Doug's head swung up to see what she had written. On the white plaster, her cursive writing spelled out clearly:

From your love to my love. I'll love you forever!

Then she signed it HELEN with a flourish and below that XOXOX.

"The nurses here are gorgeous, Doug," she stated, then added a line to her message on his cast. *KEEP YOUR HANDS OFF MY HUSBAND!!!* She also lifted up the blanket and added the same message to his left cast.

"There, done!" she said and put down the pen.

Doug reached up, grabbing the steel bar that helped him to sit up. He took a look and grinned. "How do you know the nurses attending me are gorgeous?" he asked in a groggy voice. "They're pretty plain as I recall."

"You're dreaming again. They're not only gorgeous but belong in a fashion show! One of them I saw looked like a movie star. That's why I wrote what I did," she said, pointing to the last line all spelled out in capital letters.

"But we're not married yet."

"So, don't tell anyone. If you do, I'm going to break both of your arms, too."

"I'm glad you're here, Helen," he said as his eyes finally focused on her. "I had a dream about you."

"What did you dream?" she asked. "I bet I had the same dream as you did. We often have the same dreams"

"I dreamed…" he started to say and tried to pull himself up higher in bed but Helen realized that the pain was excruciating. He flopped back onto the pillow and tried to relax. Helen took his bandaged left hand in her own. Only the fingers were showing. "I dreamed about you but also about a woman I didn't know," he continued, his face looking perplexed.

"What did she look like?"

"Like you, except she was different."

"In what way, different?"

"For one thing, she was wearing a long white dress and a large blue scarf which also acted like a stole that covered her head and reached to the floor."

"You mean like the Virgin Mary?" she asked as she looked into his eyes. She saw that his pupils were enlarged and she began to worry about his mental condition. "Did she look like the statue we have back at our parish Church?"

"Yes, but that's impossible. I never dream of religious things."

"But Doug, this time you did. Did she talk to you?"

"Yeah, but I can't be certain what she said. She was praying. Her hands were clasped together."

"Like this?" Helen asked, placing her two hands together as if in prayer.

"Exactly like that. And she was saying something."

"Go on, Doug. Try to remember what she said."

He thought hard, thinking about the dream and the woman he had never seen before. "She said something like, 'Beware.'"

"She was praying a warning?" Helen asked, now even more concerned. "What did she say?"

"'Beware, all ye who have sinned for your time is coming.'"

"She said that?" Helen said, pulling back in her chair. "What else did she say?"

"She told me *they* were coming."

"What do you think she meant by '*they*'? 'They' could mean many different kinds of people."

"They. She only said *they*, and that's all she said."

They sat in silence together as Doug thought some more about the strange encounter. Helen turned in her chair, thinking to call a nurse. She looked back at Doug's face. It was again covered in sweat.

"As I remember it," Doug continued, "I couldn't exactly hear what words she was praying. She was uttering silently. It's as if she put the words right into my head. But then something even stranger happened. It wasn't what she uttered or the prayer that she was praying. It was how she looked and the music that came from the ceiling and the wings I saw flying above her, as if they were angel wings that stretched to the heavens and beyond. It was as if the ceiling opened up and I saw all the planets. Then, her golden white angel wings flew past the Moon."

"Past the Moon?"

"Past the Moon, Mars, Jupiter, Saturn, Neptune, Uranus, Pluto. It was as if I was flying, too. And you were with me using your own pair of golden white wings."

"*Me?*" Helen replied doubtfully. "Doug, I don't have wings."

"Oh, yes you do. I see them right now." Doug pointed behind her head and up to the ceiling with a shaking finger. "They're brilliant golden white wings and are stretching up, up, up and up some more. Through the ceiling and all the way to the center of our galaxy. It's as if we're both flying with them, first doing a two-step, then a waltz, just like when you taught me how to dance to Irish traditional music."

"But Doug," she said, becoming even more worried for him. "When we dance we stay planted firmly on the ground."

"No we don't. We hop, skip and leap, don't we?"

"Sometimes," she said, hesitating. "But leaping isn't flying past the planets on wings of golden light. What kind of wings were they?"

"Angel wings. Helen, I saw them more than once flying up from your shoulders. In fact, I still see them."

"I'm no angel, Doug. Please, honey, sit back in bed. Do you want me to call a nurse?"

"No. I realize I sound mad, but that's what I see. And Helen, you are an angel. You've always been my angel."

"Did the woman in the blue stole say anything else?" she asked carefully. "Did she give you some sort of message?"

"Yes, and this time it was more important," he said, pushing himself further toward her. "When we flew to the center of the galaxy, we found a Black Hole. You know, the type that's at the center of every galaxy. You and I stepped right into it, dancing up to a shimmering curtain of light. Then we two-stepped right through that—one-two—and found ourselves on another planet."

"Another planet?" she asked, now even more perplexed at what she was certain was the psychosis that she'd heard Doug's doctor mention to Captain Dunlap. "Did the planet have a name?"

"She called it something I didn't understand. I finally heard her praying again, this time it was audible and her voice was clear, as if she was speaking in a foreign language. She used a term I could not understand—it was all Greek to me—but she leaned over and whispered to me that our scientists have named the distant sun Proxima B of the Centauri galaxy, and she called the planet she had mentioned *Gaia*. She told me that Alpha Centauri B, which is what human scientists have called that exoplanet, is not its real name. It's called Gaia—she told me that's what they call it in *their* language."

"Alpha B and the Centauri galaxy?" Helen asked, clearly puzzled. All of a sudden what she thought was Doug's psychosis started to make sense. Helen thought back to a recent ABC News report both of them had read a few weeks ago. "Do you remember, we were reading an article by an astrophysicist from NASA? She said that they'd found a signal—almost like a code—coming from the heart of that galaxy."

"A code from Centauri? I remember that. It also came from the center of the constellation Perseus."

"It did? Then the article stated… I don't remember the rest of what the scientist wrote."

"Well, I do. I remember all of that article," Doug replied. Helen noticed that the sweat on his face had dried up and his hands had stopped shaking.

"At least your head is working even if mine isn't," Helen said, feeling sudden relief because she knew Doug's brain was close to normal even if he'd had a very strange dream. "What did it say?"

"They found it as part of SETI, the scientific organization that looks for alien life throughout the universe. The signal they heard was like a heartbeat, or a symphony composed of three beats then five beats. Three then five, three then five, over and over again. When they slowed the recording of the signal down, it sounded like a strange version of Morse Code."

"You taught me some Morse, remember?" Helen reminded him. "Dah—dah—dat, da—da—da, dah—dah—dat. That's S—O—S."

"That's right. But this cycled back and forth for what seemed like forever to those scientists. It's a longer code than S—O—S yet just as simple."

"Did the lady in the blue stole tell you what it means?" she asked, again referring to Doug's confused dream.

"Oh, it's a code all right. She said that it's the key to life. When interpreted it will tell us how to overcome all illnesses and death. It's a gift they bring. And very, very soon."

"You said 'they' again. Can't you tell me what she meant by 'they', sweetie?"

"Alien life from the stars. That's all I can think that 'they' might mean. Particularly in the context of the code and music they found in the Centauri galaxy." He looked intently at Helen and leaned closer; his eyes opened wide. "The gift of the code can heal so many things. It's better than T-Cell Therapy. It can solve so many puzzles, like Early Onset Alzheimer's, Parkinson's, Down Syndrome, heart disease, strokes, ruptured spleens, ruined livers, acute diabetes, dementia, autism…the list goes on and on. Their cures will even solve the riddle of small pox, Ebola, spina bifida, measles, mumps, and other diseases which use various modern injections, though many parents won't have their children injected because they believe these jabs are a joke and won't have any effect on meningococcal, rubella, whooping cough and ADHD to name only a few of the many threats to humankind."

Then Doug's eyes glazed over and he sat back in bed. Suddenly, he changed subjects and to Helen it sounded again like psychosis.

"Helen, what the Bible says is based on factual evidence. The New Testament has four books, as you know, because we've read it together. But did you realize it's missing one? That's what the lady told me, too."

"A book? Which one? I know the Catholic Church decided not to publish some in the years just after it was established. Are those what you're talking about?"

"No Helen. It's a fifth book written by Jesus Christ himself. It's based solely on the words of *Jesu Kristos*, and it's so very simple. He taught us a prayer after handing out the loaves and fishes that encapsulates that new fifth book of the New Testament. Can you guess which one?"

"Do you mean The Lord's Prayer?"

Doug nodded. "In fact, the mysterious lady told me that I was the man who stood before the huge crowd with some of my apostles. I blessed five fishes and some loaves of bread and then there were hundreds of baskets of food to share with the thousands of people who had gathered to hear my sermon of life and memorize that prayer. Truly, it was a miracle, one of my first."

Helen tried to get out of the chair to call a nurse but Doug stopped her. He began rushing through what he said next, as if someone was telling him what to say.

"You really think I'm crazy, don't you? But Helen, I'm not. Our Lady told me I made many other miracles. I walked on water. I healed the sick. I was able to cure leprosy with a wave of my hand. I cured a sick woman with the touch of her hand upon the hem of my gown. I could raise the dead with a simple thought and the help of a flying dove that held an olive branch in its beak, which we call the Holy Ghost, and bring solace to anyone who has suffered. But rather than being left alone because I was not causing any disruption nor doing anything illegal against Rome, I was punished for what I said—I didn't even know how to write. Like my father, I was a simple carpenter who would have been better off making tables for my parents' home. I was crucified on a cross between two other sinners. Like me, they had denied the One True God and had gone against the laws of Caesar. Then I was hammered to that tree of wood and died. Lightning flashed and there was thunder. Though dead, I looked down and I saw you, Helen. I saw my mother. I saw my wife. You and she are one and the same person, and she is named Mary Magdalene by our common mother. I saw Peter, who had denied me three times. I saw the men who would later take me down and bring me to a tomb. I saw the crowd and beneath me, playing dice, the Roman soldiers who had torn up my gown and sash and were gambling for them.

"Then thunder rumbled again. It caused panic in the town of Jerusalem and upon the hill of Golgotha where I was murdered. God's thunderstorm caused earthquakes, obliterating our Hebrew temple and causing hundreds of Romans to die. But not any of the Jews. Like years before, the plague of dying passed over them. To this day, many celebrate my day of death as Easter or Eostre, the pagan custom of life overcoming eternal night. After I died they took me down from the cross and placed me in the tomb. A day later, I visited Hell and met Satan. I spat on him and took him on a ferry rowed by our Charon across the River Styx. Today, Satan is gone, buried forever and forever and forevermore in the fiery swamp of Hell's great burning Cauldron. The Lady Oracle I dreamed about told me that someday, and unfortunately many years from today, there will be no death, no school shootings or any more wars anywhere on Earth. Instead, there will be nothing but eternal peace. Democrats will be elected in 2024, but maybe not Joe Biden. He'll either pull out of the race, catch Covid again and pass on due to old age, or choose not to run again. Or, he could win. A man named Ex-President Trump together with the former Mayor of New York Rudolph Guliani, and many of their henchmen, will be found guilty of wire fraud, tax evasion, conspiracy to overturn the U.S. Constitution, treason and much more. They will all be sentenced to Federal Penitentiaries, and not even the Supreme Court will be able to stop it. Many federal judges appointed by Trump will uphold the verdicts. Our country will be in turmoil and will approach civil war.

"American police and those working for democratically-elected countries will be allowed to carry guns but no one else. When our Angelic soldiers, our Mother, and the Son of God which is me arrive to this planet on an out-of-this-galaxy spacecraft—and they will, as she has said, within the next forty years—we will outlaw most weapons on Earth. Missiles will not fire. Nuclear weapons will refuse to work because they will not explode. But soon, we're both going somewhere."

"Where are we going, Doug?" she asked, now extremely worried about him but mesmerized by his far-fetched tale. She looked over her shoulder to see if Toby and the doctor were still there to hear her fiancé's rantings but they were gone and she was on her own.

"As I say, I'll tell you later," Doug continued, and now his entire body began to shake. He put out both hands as if he was Christ the Lord preaching on a mountaintop. "I wish now to speak words of great importance to you and all my people. Everything I have said about the fifth book of the New Testament, *The Lord's Prayer* and the other teachings of Our Lord are true. The woman I saw in my dreams is, in one sense, the Virgin Mary but she is also so much more. She promises that the two of use wrote the new book together. Most wonderful of all, and as was foretold, we will both have wings of white gold that will enable us to fly to distant realms of the universe. My wings will be stronger and larger than yours, because mine will be the longer journey and the greater burden. Now, Helen, let us take a leap of faith together."

"Doug, are you serious?" Helen responded, and thought again of calling the doctor to ask for more meds and another sedative. "Doug, look behind you! You don't have wings just like I don't have wings."

Helen rose to her feet, finally deciding to call a nurse. Doug saw her walk toward the door.

"But we both do!" he said emphatically, looking up again. Helen stopped. She turned to him and saw how he stared again at the ceiling as if he could see the clear blue sky appearing through the hospital tiles above him. "I can see all the way to Heaven. I can hear trumpets sound and angels sing. I can see the Gates of Heaven from where I sit. Can't you? You're also an angel, Helen. Why don't you believe what the lady said?"

"But you're not Jesus Christ."

"It's that woman who says I am, not me. And not even I believe it!" He laughed. "Did you hear me? I sound just like a priest reading the Bible or preaching a sermon to his congregation. I was told by the lady that, in fact, we're already married. We've been married since the beginning of time and even before that. It's like a revelation! In a previous life, you were known as Mary Magdalene, my wife and lover. You were a sinner, but you decided to follow

Christ as His most perfect disciple. Even the male disciples took orders from you."

"Doug, that's ridiculous. I'm not a disciple. I'm no Mary Magdalene."

"But you are! Can't you hear the choir singing?"

Helen turned back toward the door, determined to get Doug help.

"Helen, come back! I know I sound deluded. But honestly, I'm not. Just listen and you will be able to hear singing."

She again took her seat, knowing that if she called a nurse or the doctor Doug would become even more upset. "Doug, you're not Jesus Christ. And I don't hear anyone singing."

"Just wait and you will. I know I'm Doug Martin. But something in my head tells me what to say."

Despite her worry for his injuries and obvious delusions, Helen leaned back in her chair. She listened intently but couldn't hear anything. But then, like a rising chorus coming out of nowhere, she could hear the song. Words came into her head as if whispered by a choir and she found herself singing with them a song from *Jesus Christ Superstar*. As she sang and hummed, she calmed down. She would not get worried or upset by Doug or any problems that would confront her in the coming days and weeks. And yes, everything really would be all right. She had to believe that because she had faith in God. But, still listening to the choir singing as if it was in the room, she realised she was also suffering from something that was much more than PTSD. She was worried that she was as mad as Doug. She looked down at her hands and saw them begin to shake.

Then she could hear other voices that sounded like Angels singing in four-part harmony; the song reaching a crescendo. Helen looked at Doug's bedside table. Though no one was near it, a glass of water and the medication resting next to it began to vibrate. A vase of flowers toppled over, the water pouring onto the floor. A pen upon the table began to lift, defying the laws of gravity. As she watched it rotated on its own, then stopped as if something unseen were holding it.

She glanced at Doug. She could swear she could see a white halo around his head, nail holes in his hands, one in each palm, one in each wrist. She looked at his pillow and it was covered in what she thought to be red blood. On his head, she could swear he wore a crown of thorns. Then his hospital sheets turned a brilliant scarlet. From beneath the sheets blood flowed onto the floor like a tidal wave from the Red Sea.

Helen lifted the sheet. Doug was no longer wearing a cast. He no longer wore a hospital gown. Instead, he wore a cloth that swaddled his hips and thighs. She could see that the bleeding came from a deep puncture near his heart. His legs appeared to have been broken. And Helen, who knew her Bible, remembered how during Christ's crucifixion he had been stabbed in the side with a spear. She looked down towards his feet and saw that one foot and one ankle were each pierced and bleeding profusely. It seemed to her that water poured from Doug's side, like an outgoing tide, on to the floor where it mixed with his blood, and to her it seemed like a reminder of the sacrifices Christ had made for all the people of the world.   For reason's she did not understand, Helen reached down and touched the puddle. She brought the red blood to her lips and tasted it. It did not taste like blood but instead like a good red wine. Just like the wine that Doug had ordered when he had proposed to her.

Then from the ceiling, a hand extended down toward her and with it came a face of brilliant white that flooded the room in light. She realised that it was Doug's face yet, when she looked down again, he was still sitting upright in bed, his eyes transfixed to a spot above him. Then the light subsided and she realized who it was. It was the Great Son of Humankind whom many call Jesus Christ. Yet it was not the image of the Holy Son of God that Helen remembered from paintings in her childhood home in Ireland. This face was not that of a white man like most Irish men. Instead, this face was dark like that of a man from Pakistan or India or even Jerusalem. Then Helen was reminded of what she had been taught in Catholic school and remembered that Christ had been born in Bethlehem in Judea; of course he would be darker skinned, as were all natives of hotter and sunnier climates.

Then as she watched, Doug rose from his bed as if he were being levitated and floated toward her on a beam of golden sunlight. He took both of her hands in his and together, they rose effortlessly toward he ceiling. Suddenly, Helen realized that Doug had been speaking the truth: though he definitely wasn't Jesus Christ, he had undergone some kind of transformation into a very different man. His skin was now dark and his body was completely healed.

As they floated beyond the ceiling, Doug took her in his arms "Helen, dance with me."

And they did. They danced all the way through the ceiling, then into the blue of the North Carolina sky. Together, they swept past white clouds and for a moment Helen turned around and looked down on a vast continent that she knew was North America. Upward they kept flying, past the Moon, the planets and much farther than that. Beyond Pluto, to the center of the galaxy. Then, dancing past the glittering dark skirt at the edge of a Black Hole, they sailed past a curtain of gold, then into a swirling ball of light. Held together by their love, the pair emerged from another Black Hole in the center of a rotating constellation of stars. Helen wondered if they could be in the Milky Way but then she remembered seeing pictures of the Centauri galaxy and thought that maybe that was where they had flown: to a galaxy lightyears from their own. As they moved beyond the center of that constellation of stars, Helen could distinctly hear the code that Doug had described earlier. It sounded just like the one she had heard in the ABC News article and on a radio recording that a local New York station had also broadcast. [1]

"Now that you've heard the musical code, come with me to a star and planet much like our own," Doug said as they rotated together in darkness. "The star is called Proxima B in the Centauri

---

[1] (Author's Note: Find the sonification of astronomical data which comes from the centre of Perseus, 'A Universe of Sound', here: https://chandra.si.edu/sound/.

Speed it up about ten times and it sounds like a symphony. And that, this author thinks, is what Doug means by saying he's discovered a code for all humankind.)

galaxy. The planet, about one-and-a-third times as large as our Earth, is called Alpha Centauri B and lies in a place scientists call the Goldilocks region. On that planet, life originally formed just after the original Big Bang which was the first explosion to bring life to our universe."

Helen looked at him and realized he was still dressed in his hospital gown. She knew that if they were in the vacuum of outer space, they could not be breathing. Yet they were. She again wondered if she were mad and was really sitting in the chair by Doug's side. But as she looked at him she realized that she was not mad and neither was he because what he was talking about made sense.

"Original Big Bang?" Helen asked. "You mean there was more than one?"

"Yes, the lady told me there was more than one. There are an infinite number of universal explosions. Each one forms a new universe all functioning at the same time and but in different dimensions than our own. The planet Gaia, also called Centauri B, was the second planet to support life in our Universe. The Earth was the first which is where the Gaian race was born. Like the Earth, Centauri B has carbon, methane, oxygen, hydrogen, helium…all of the basic building blocks necessary for creation."

"Did God really create life? Or is that all a fairy-tale."

"Sort of," Doug said, again thinking back on what the Lady had whispered to him in his head. "Life is formed by an asteroid plunging through the early atmosphere of many planets. As it hits the water, it causes great heat. Most of the oceans are boiled away, forming new continents. Then the tectonic plates shifted, creating any number of volcanoes along the edges of those tilting plates. Within the boiling water, life explodes, too. First it comes as single cell creatures, then small fishes, then animals that are able to crawl onto dry land. Their lungs gave them more energy. Trees spring up so creatures that look much like our own frogs grow wings. They fly into the leaves of those gigantic forests feeding on a wide-variety of insects. Then they evolve into creatures that look like dinosaurs. Many planets including our Earth and the distant planet of Gaia had a full range of vertebrates covering the land. They included mammals like brontosauruses, the tyrannosaurus, the triceratops, stegosaurus and pterodactyls.

The pterodactyl had wings, of course. It evolved further and, when the giant dinosaurs died out, it took over the skies. Then, eventually, apes came along and from that genetic code people were born. By the time human civilization had developed the ability to travel to the stars, a holocaust had taken place and most of humankind had been destroyed. Those that survived left the Earth and moved to

Gaia. Today many of them still look like the people on Earth but others have evolved and look very different. Some of the Earth's survivors even interbred with Gaians. Most of the people living on Gaia have green skins which they have evolved as camouflage in the wooded plains and hills that form their habitat. They are more than nine feet tall because the gravity of Gaia is about one-third that of the gravity on Earth. These humans have also developed wings because, just like bats on Earth, they had to originally forage for insects in the trees so had to fly high to eat. They had…

"The Gaian peoples have wings?" Helen gasped, interrupting. "I guess it's possible. "

"I admit that it's unlikely and you'd only see that in science fiction books and films. But I whispered the same question to the Lady. She nodded and told me: "Of course they have wings. You don't think that human beings were the first creatures to fly, do you? After all, your people need airplanes to fly. But all sorts of creatures take to the wing to catch what they can on the wind. That's what the race of Gaian's had to do to survive."

"So it's true," Helen said. "These alien humanoids have wings."

"That's right," Doug nodded and laughed. "Wouldn't it be fun to float through the skies of Earth together like they do on their planet?"

"So that's what they looked like, these flying people, at least according to the lady's description?" Helen asked. "What else do you know about their planet?"

"Other alien civilizations threaten them today and have in the past. Many Gaian centuries ago, a giant spacecraft appeared in their skies. They came with one-hundred-thousand alien soldiers and machines that the people of Gaia had never seen before. These tyrants rained down hell upon the planet, almost destroying it. But in the end, the soldiers of Gaia prayed to their great God who is also called Gaia for strength and courage. In the end, they beat the invaders and forced them off their planet. A few of the invaders stayed who looked just like human beings from our Earth. They interbred with the people who lived on that planet and that's why, today, many people on their planet look like us but are stronger and have many more powers which seem like magic to us."

'Magic,' Helen thought to herself. "That's the problem with magic. It's never real," she whispered. "I'm breathing, dancing, and talking to Doug. I must be dreaming. We both must be in the hospital room. I want to be anywhere but where I am. right now. Anywhere. Anywhere…"

"Or nowhere," a familiar voice in Helen's head said to her. *"Or everywhere at once."*

Helen looked up. In front of her, her daughter Josie who looked to be in her early twenties, danced on her own under the starry skies of a spinning white galaxy. She smiled.

"Mom, this is real. I promise. What you've experienced may not seem real, and some of it isn't. Yes, you're in outer space and of course you're alive. You're not dreaming at all nor are you crazy. We didn't want to worry you and Dad about the journey you must now take. Gaia lifted you up out of that hospital room and soon you will be wearing spacesuits to protect you and when you're given them, you'll also know that everything you experience is real. For now, try to enjoy what you see. That truly is real, as real as I am and you and Dad are."

Helen blinked. Josie was gone. In her place, Doug floated in the vacuum and was wearing a spacesuit unlike any she had seen before in television footage of space missions. His suit was thin rather than bulky and the helmet was smaller than those of the NASA astronauts and was bright yellow, not white.

"Helen, look down," Doug said and she realized she was listening to a radio. Doing as Doug instructed, she looked down seeing her hands covered in thin gloves. Then she touched her head, feeling the outside of a helmet with her gloved fingers.

"What just happened, Doug? I thought I was dreaming and still in your hospital room."

"Helen, I saw Josie too. Remember what she said? This is real, not a dream."

He reached out, taking her hand again and turned Helen around. In the distance, surrounded by stars, both of them beheld a spinning Black Hole. Quickly floating toward a glowing curtain that looked like sealight, they stepped through the almost transparent sheet that resembled thin glass.

"We're past the event horizon," Doug shouted over his radio to Helen. "That was that curved light we floated through. But we could be in real trouble. Research by physicists has found that all matter entering any Black Hole will fall to its center where it is compressed to a tiny volume with an infinite density. That's called the singularity. If they're right, then we only have moments to live."

As they fell further past the glowing curtain of the event horizon, stars appeared again but this time from everywhere. It was as if they were speeding down a fantastical roller coaster lit by lights that became streaking meteors as the pair fell faster and faster. When they turned a corner, Helen saw a distant star. As they both speeded toward it she could swear that it was a giant rotating spaceship. Then she again heard what sounded like the Code.

"Do you hear that, Helen?" Doug's voice in her helmet asked. "It's coming from there!"

As they moved closer to the silver object, they were buffeted by great solar winds as planets exploded around them. In front of them was the spacecraft. Behind it, a giant red star threw out immense tentacles of light, pushing them ever closer to the craft.

"That's a solar flare!" Doug cried. "We can't be hit by it or it'll kill us. We need to get to that spacecraft and board it."

As the flare increased in strength and brightness, they floated closer to the ship. They could see a familiar hull and lettering that was familiar to them from news reports on Earth. The square black lettering read. USS ST VINCENT.

"Helen, remember that spacecraft?" Doug exclaimed as they drifted closer. He maneuvered himself so that he was directly in front of her and could see her face through the windows of their helmets. "NASA launched it years ago from Cape Kennedy. It was a secret then and only a few people with security clearances, including the President, knew about it.   It was launched into deep space in an attempt to dive deep into the Centauri black hole."

"That was the purpose of its journey?" Helen asked but, not knowing how to work her radio, Doug had to guess what she had asked.

"That's right. To leap into a Black Hole to see where it leads, and to understand the bizarre signals that emanate from it—although that makes no sense because even audio signals should be captured by a black hole's gravity. Scientists are still astounded because those signals sound like some sort of code. They're don't understand why *any kind* of signal escapes."

Looking up, they both saw the red giant flare again. "When we get close to that spacecraft, grab onto its hull!" Then Doug took Helen's hand again, hoping they'd make it to safety.

Chapter Seventeen

As they drifted up to the USS SAINT VINCENT, Doug grabbed an antenna array. Reaching back, he pulled Helen to him. Together, they floated toward a stainless-steel door. Holding onto the hull, Doug noticed a sign with large red letters: ROTATE TO OPEN. He grabbed the circular steel lock and tried to turn it with one hand. 'It's opening,' he thought to himself because the lock began rotating automatically. "Now what?" he said to Helen over the radio. The door still remained shut. To the right of the circular lock, he saw a steel handle and, with no other option available to him, lifted it toward him then pulled on it with all his might. "The handle is stuck. Helen, help me lift this thing, okay?"

Looking behind him, he could see Helen's face through the glass of her helmet but she appeared to be sleeping. Seeing how blue her lips were, Doug realized she was almost out of oxygen. As he grasped her by the helmet, he again looked up. The solar flare from the giant red sun, a long tentacle of bright white light, was heading straight toward them. Now lit by the brilliant flare, he grabbed the handle with both hands and lifted it with every ounce of strength he had. The outer door slid open and a sparkling plume of oxygen vented into the vacuum followed by a variety of detritus including paper, tools and square plastic containers. Pulling Helen inside the spacecraft as fast as he could, he looked around the circular chamber and, punching a red button lettered EMERGENCY OXYGEN, closed and double-locked the outer door. As he did he could hear the rush of gas venting into the room.

Because there was no gravity in the SAINT VINCENT, Doug pulled Helen to him and, floating above the floor, rubbed her arms to wake her up. He took off the helmet and at last heard her take a deep breath. Then her eyes opened wide.

"Oh, God Doug. I can breathe again," she said, coughing as she gulped in the welcome air. She blinked, looking around the strange environment. "How did we get in here? We still have to be dreaming."

"This is no dream. It's a miracle given to us by Our Lady. Remember how we saw your daughter Josie? You're safe now, Helen. We made it into the ship just in time."

"What ship? Where are we?"

"We're on the USS SAINT VINCENT. Remember, we saw the ship and tried to get aboard it. We're safe because we just managed to make it inside this room."

"Room? Where are we? Near Earth?"

He looked at her, realizing that she didn't remember how they had flown across the Universe through the Black Hole. "Don't worry. You'll remember soon when you get over the shock and warm up again."

Doug floated to another steel door on the opposite side of the small room and, pressing a button, it slid open revealing a long dark hallway. "Is anyone aboard?" he shouted. "Can anyone hear me?"

When no one answered, he turned back to Helen. "Let's get to the command deck. All I need to do is access and read the spacecraft's log to understand what went wrong with the ship."

Because the VINCENT had no gravity they had to float toward the command deck, pushing their hands and feet off the bulkheads to move forward. Doug noticed a large yellow lever that read: PULL FOR GRAVITY. When he pulled it down, they could feel the entire cylindrical section of the VINCENT begin to revolve then spin faster. As the spaceship's artificial gravity took hold, materials for repairs, crew supplies and reports including wrenches, hammers, bolts, nuts, water, food, napkins, steel cutlery, paper folders and files fell to the deck as the ship regained gravity. Helen and Doug floated to the floor and landed on both feet.

"I guess we're home but what a home," Helen said. "Doug, we'll be stuck here for years!"

"For now, this is our only home until we can figure out how to be rescued. But Earth is lightyears away."

They spotted a steel ladder at the side of the room, climbed it, and at the top found another door. Doug pushed a button and the entrance to the command deck slid open. Inside, the room was dark. Helen found an exterior light on her spacesuit and flicked its switch.

"Point it over there, toward the control console. We need to turn on the power to the bridge," Doug said. "Then we'll be able to discover what happened."

When she did, Doug found a Master switch and powered up the vehicle. Lights came on throughout the VINCENT. He turned to a computer and saw a CD player. He pushed a button to eject the CD then watched as it slid back in. A small monitor next to it flickered in green, then displayed English writing.

"Over here, Helen! Look, this is the Captain's final report."

As the screen settled down, they read the bold green writing:

EARTH TIME: 1147 ZULU, 24 DECEMBER 1977.

This is the Captain of the USS Saint Vincent. We've encountered numerous problems the hull was breached by something we could not detect with any of our instruments: possibly small grains of rock traveling thousands of miles per hour. I've ordered my crew to take refuge in the sleeping quarters. I'm powering down our vessel but before I do, I'm sending out an emergency signal on our radio array. I recognize that it will take hundreds of centuries or even more to get to NASA mission control, and many more years for them to organize any kind of rescue. We successfully traveled through the black hole and have recorded the phenomena of what sounded to many like morse code. Our analysis indicates that it's not morse but something far stranger. You can find the code recorded on a second disk that I've put in a safe in my quarters. We've done our best to repair the hull and when I'm finished writing this final report I'll order my crew, or what's left of them, to hibernate. We've lost two crew members: Rosco Frasier and Allison Veselly, both excellent team members and mission specialists. They were both biologists and detected some sort of life, possibly bacteria, on the hull of the Vincent before she was breached. They ventured outside when our onboard sensors detected that lifeform on the hull and attempted to take a sample. We were unable to rescue them when both of their spacesuits were punctured by the same rock that breached our hull. Having run out of oxygen, we brought back the remains of the crew members. God speed to them and to our fellow astronauts who will follow us here. If we're not alive understand that we're proud to serve. Signed: CAPTAIN DENNEHEY, US AIR FORCE

When Helen finished reading she looked up at Doug.

"They left some time before 1977? But it's millions of miles to this location, isn't it?"

"Farther than that. The Centauri Constellation is almost five lightyears from Earth. It would have taken the crew literally thousands of years to cross that distance using conventional science and physics. No one will be able to prove exactly how the VINCENT came to be here. Not until someone rescues us which is also thousands of years from now unless they've built a similar spacecraft to the VINCENT. We'll have to leave a report describing what we've found here. There's absolutely no explanation at all for what we've found unless…"

Helen watched as he floated back to the instrument console. There, Doug saw a gauge that he assumed measured the amount of fuel the ship had left onboard. He tapped it and it turned bright red. A warning bell clanged. He turned toward a bank of other instruments over his head. There, he saw a bright sign blinking yellow. WARNING! WARNING!" Below that, he saw another gauge that read 'Nuclear Propulsion'. That gauge was right off the scales.

"My God, Earth's scientists have developed a method of propelling spaceships with nuclear reactors," Doug gasped. "The gauge reads that the propulsion unit's fissionable material could go into meltdown if not properly replaced." He touched the gauge again to silence the warning bell. "The VINCENT got here in a few years, not thousands of years. How the hell did they develop it with no one else on Earth, like the Russian or Chinese military and their satellites, noticing it."

"Maybe they tested it on the dark side of the Moon?" Helen suggested.

"Of course! That's how they did it. They set up a base on the back of the Moon. China have already landed a spacecraft there,

NASA must have done the same thing. Let's find the crew and wake them."

They looked first into the crew quarters but no one was there. All they found were the remains of the two astronauts zipped into body bags. On each bag the name of the deceased astronaut resting inside was printed in large bold letters on a white square of material.

Then they went to the hibernation room. There, they discovered twelve large cylindrical units. Through the clear glass windows, they could see figures clad in white latex body suits. All but two contained astronauts sleeping in deep hibernation. But when Helen looked up at the monitors, she saw that every heartbeat was flatlined. A steady green line showed that there was no sign of life at all.

"Dammit," said Doug, "What the hell happened? These were good people. Why did they all die?"

"Maybe they ran out of oxygen," said Helen. "Perhaps that's why they died."

"But we're breathing oxygen. No, there has to be some other explanation."

"Let's go back to the command deck, Doug. This is creepy."

They walked back along the long tunnel that led to the control room. Then she looked up, startled, seeing a flash of light out of a square glass portal.

"Did you see that? What was it?"

"What? I didn't see anything."

"Out the window." Helen pointed up to it. "I'm sure I saw something. It was like a swarm of fireflies."

Then Doug saw it too: the remains of an asteroid or a comet. "Those are the same thing that breached the VINCENT'S hull."

The entire tunnel shuddered. The lights blinked on and off. Through the window, they could see an explosion: a great ball of fire streaked toward them then struck the aft section of their spacecraft. The floor beneath them shook as if the VINCENT had been caught in a cataclysmic earthquake. Helen looked behind her. Through an open hatch, she could see a wave of fire heading toward them. Through another glass portal, they caught a glimpse of a tumbling boulder as it passed by the window above them.

They ran toward the command module and its command deck. As they crawled up the ladder to the airtight door, they heard metal grinding. The entire vessel shuddered again as the ship's central axel which controlled the vessel's spin disintegrated. Gravity vanished instantly. Again, they were both floating but this time in a severely injured spaceship.

"Grab my hand!" Doug roared as he looked down on Helen. She was holding on to the steel ladder below him. As he reached for her, there was a final explosion. They could both hear metal twisting and grinding as the entire command module shook and parted from the rest of the vessel. As Doug pulled Helen into the command-and-control center, he looked down one final time, seeing only smoke, fire and starlight, as he closed and locked the outer door. Through a circular window in the control room, all he saw was darkness and then he could see the aft section of the VINCENT which included the propulsion unit, oxygen tanks, crew quarters, provisions, and all that was necessary for life, float away into outer space. He knew all that was left was the air-tight globular structure of the command center, and the storage area with the crew hibernation compartment, together with a large hanger and storage area, directly beneath them. He remembered a television reporter covering the development of the VINCENT: a large steel arm was located in the hanger. The crew could open the huge outer double doors and use the arm to launch and recover satellites, repair the outside of the spaceship or conduct research. By sitting at the very end of the arm the crew could even reach the aft exterior and nuclear propulsion units. Doug   also remembered that the antenna array that was used to contact Earth when the VINCENT was in Earth's Solar System was attached to what remained of the command module.

"We're safe again," Doug said as he pulled Helen into his arms "I'm going to check to see what's still working and find any supplies of food and water that might have been stored here."

"Let me help you."

"No. There's not much to do. I'll take the first watch. Try to sleep for a few hours. If I hear anything, I'll wake you instantly."

A few minutes after he had helped Helen remove her helmet and strap herself into a reclining crew seat, he saw that she was asleep. For half an hour he floated around the command deck, taking stock of their situation. The vessel's communications still worked, not that the radio would be this useful so far from Earth, but when he looked into the various drawers and bins he found little food and no water. He was also worried about their supplies of oxygen and how much power their floating lifeboat had without the nuclear-powered propulsion unit. Having taken the inventory, he floated back to his seat and made the decision to take off his spacesuit. Placing that and his helmet in a locker, he looked toward Helen. She was still in her spacesuit and fast asleep. Doug strapped himself in and pulled his seat as close to hers as he could. Then he lay his head against hers and slept, too.

Chapter Eighteen

Waking, Helen felt Doug's head upon her shoulder. Gently, she eased herself up from the second-in-command's seat. Looking down and seeing that he was wearing only his suit's thermal underwear, she remembered that he'd had that major accident in North Carolina what seemed only a few days ago. Yet, like the dream she thought they'd both had in the hospital room, he no longer wore a cast on either leg.

Doug stirred and opened his eyes. "Are you okay? What's wrong?"

"Both of your legs were broken, remember? But now they're completely healed."

He unstrapped himself from his seat, looking her in the eye. "You thought this was all a dream, didn't you? So did I. I know I had two broken legs and surgery. Yet look at me. I really am healed. How could we be in a NASA spaceship in a different galaxy that's over four lightyears from Earth? It still makes no sense."

"We need to believe what our five senses tell us, Doug. What I see right now is you. That's all that matters to me."

Doug told her about the food and water supply. Having had nothing to eat or drink in the over a day, he discussed the situation as Helen helped him to put on his spacesuit again.

"Let's get some water, Helen. We'll have to be careful how much we drink but we don't want to become dehydrated."

Finished dressing, Doug led Helen out of the command module, down the ladder and aft into what remained of the spaceship. Dim light from the emergency power supply still flickered in this part of the destroyed VINCENT and they carefully made their way through a web of electrical wires that still sparked and crackled, consuming what remained of the compartment's oxygen. When they finally reached the hibernation unit, Doug saw that near the cylindrical units of the astronauts that now acted as coffins were twelve spacesuits with oxygen packs that also incorporated thrusters to propel anyone wearing them to their targets. Above them, fixed on hooks, were the spacesuit helmets. Doug realized that when the VINCENT'S oxygen supplies in the command module were fully depleted, or if they had to stay in the stricken vessel for more than a few weeks, they'd be unable to breath. All they'd have left would be the supply of oxygen in the spacesuit packs. Doug helped Helen struggle into a new suit with oxygen tanks. Then he exchanged his old oxygen cylinder for another one as well as a new helmet.

"Putting on a spacesuit is like putting on a wetsuit, isn't it?" Doug said. When he placed the new helmet on her head and rotated it in its steel fitting to make it airtight, he closed her visor, locked it, and switched on the oxygen supply. "Take a deep breath. Can you fill your lungs?" he shouted. When she nodded, Doug pointed to the helmet's chin switch. "It's just like an aircraft radio. Push that with your chin when you want to talk. When you want to listen, let it go."

Helen nodded and tried it. "This is Helen. Doug, can you hear me?!"

"Five by five," he said, putting up a thumb. "Now let's see what's left in the rest of the ship."

Doug flipped down his own helmet visor and locked it. Floating out of the hibernation unit, they made their way to the hanger-like storage area further below decks. Helen waited by the door as Doug floated to a bank of controls. Reading the various labels of over fifty switches, he depressed a large black button to activate the giant titanium and steel arm the VINCENT used to launch and capture satellites. As Helen watched Doug float in the huge compartment, she tested her suit's radio again.

"Doug this is Helen. Can you still hear me?"

"I sure can. Wait here while I check this thing out."

As he floated toward the steel arm, Helen frowned and toggled her chin switch again. "What are you planning to do with that thing?" she said as she watched him take a close look at what looked to her like the dead steel tentacle of a giant octopus.

"I need to go outside to see if the command module skin has been breached. If it has, I need to repair it or we'll run out of oxygen sooner, not later."

As Helen watched, Doug crawled up the arm to the very end and sat in the control seat. She saw him turn sideways, twisting a red handle with his right gloved hand. Above them, the hanger doors opened.

"Doug, are you sure you know what you're doing?"

"No, not yet. But the controls seem simple."

Helen looked up seeing only stars. "That's beautiful!"

He pointed up to the dark universe. "Do you see that red sun? That's the source of the solar flare that hit us. Okay, Helen, stand back as I activate the arm."

Helen grasped a handhold, pulling herself back as Doug used two handgrip controllers, one on each side of his seat, to guide the arm up and out the doors, and then outside the spaceship high above the hanger floor. "Doug, are you still okay?" she asked, worried about him. "You've never done anything like this before. Be careful!"

"Will do," he said, and she saw him make an A-OK circle with his fingers as he grinned down at her. "I'm going to swing myself up toward the outside of the command module now. Stand by."

As Doug sweated with the arm and Helen worried and waited, neither of them could see a metal flange hidden behind the base of the steel arm. Held together by bolts, the flange had split in two as a result of the explosions and had started to part. The single critical connection held together multiple hydraulic lines which powered a number of pistons. In turn, these moved the robotic arm up and out of the hanger bay and through a three-hundred-and-sixty-degree arc.

When the flange had finally ripped apart as a result of the extensive damage to the VINCENT, its sharp edges had started to cut all the lines. Hydraulic fluid had begun to leak out, floating like unseen dark marbles between the steel plates of the bulkhead and the hull. If NASA engineers on Earth had seen it, they would have known that if all the lines were cut this would cause many of the arm's pistons to seize, resulting in fractures to the stainless-steel control rods because of the differential pressure that exceeded the structure's design tolerances. Unfortunately for Doug, now at the end of the steel and titanium arm, he had no such NASA experts aboard the USS SAINT VINCENT.

Still floating near the storage bay floor, Helen watched as Doug slid the arm out further. As the robotic arm extended, he disappeared beyond the edge of the hanger doors and out of sight. Helen had the sudden impulse to try to climb up to the top of the storage hanger to see him but then she heard her radio crackle as Doug said: "Yep, there's a breach, all right. I'm going to repair it."

"I hear you, Doug. Are you sure you can fix it?"

"Yeah, Helen. It should work out fine. There's a tool kit here in a storage compartment and a list says there's some compound in it." She heard only silence for a moment then he said: "Okay, I'm going to start. I'll let you know what I'm doing at every step. First, I'm going to take out that compound."

All she heard was the hiss and crackle from his radio. Then she heard him mutter, "Damned thing won't come out."

"What won't?"

"The compound. The label says it's a tube of glue the crew uses to repair breaches in the hull. I can't get it out. The steal box of the compartment is bent. It must have been damaged during the explosion." Helen heard him grunt again and could imagine Doug as he pulled at the damaged container. "Okay, I've got it. Now I'm onto the next step. I'm leaning down to the hull. There's vapor coming out of the crack. All I have to do is spray the compound on and that should stop it."

Again, she heard only crackling over her radio as Doug.

Then she heard a terrified scream. "Helen! Helen, I'm in trouble!"

"Doug, what is it! Hold on. I'll be right there."

"Stay there! Don't try to come after me."

She pushed herself off the floor and toward the arm, determined to climb it. With both arms on a steel ladder, she suddenly felt the entire structure vibrate. Then she saw dark globules of liquid and watched as a half-dozen rubber hoses whipped past her, all of them spurting more of the liquid. Because the hanger bay was open to the vacuum of space, she didn't hear but rather saw the arm as it fractured. More globules of hydraulic fluid flew past her helmet. Torn tubing whipped at her spacesuit as if trying to puncture it. With the arm fully fractured, a long cylindrical piece that looked like a sharp lance whipsawed past the open doors and almost struck her. Pushing herself sideways, she avoided it, then kept crawling up what remained of the arm. At the top, she could see Doug still strapped in his seat, his arms flailing in panic. As the main part of the steel arm finally broke in two, she watched helplessly as, still sitting in the command seat, he was hurled into the darkness of space.

"Doug!" she screamed. "Doug!"

But all she heard back from him was silence.

Chapter Nineteen

Helen grabbed a steel girder that had broken off when the arm had fractured and again crawled up toward the top of the SAINT VINCENT hanger doors. When she encountered the barn doors of the hanger, she saw that one was torn in two by the destructive force of the hydraulic arm. The other half had been hurled into space together with the piece of arm holding Doug attached to the seat. She had to move carefully because the jagged edges of the door could easily rip her spacesuit which would result in a total loss of oxygen. Negotiating around the sharp edges of metal that glinted in the starlight, Helen crawled out and onto the hull. She looked up. Three hundred feet away she spotted the fractured arm. It had become trapped against the hull, tangled in the radio antenna attached to the globe-like command module.

"Doug, can you hear me?" she said, toggling her chin mic again. "Doug, say something!"

But only silence greeted her attempt to contact him.

Helen glanced at her suit's air supply indicator which was on her spacesuit's right wrist. Seeing that the needle had swung into a red warning triangle, Helen realized that both she and Doug would die of oxygen starvation within minutes.

"Doug told me the oxygen tank was full when he helped me on with this new suit," Helen said to herself. "Do I have a leak somewhere?"

She tried to look her spacesuit over but couldn't see very much. Then she noticed a small tear in the right knee. Reaching down, she found her supply pack. Opening it, she discovered a small red cannister. Taking it out, she pointed the nozzle and pressed the trigger. The thick liquid covered the tear in her suit and only one small bubble remained to remind her that she could have died.

Again, she looked at her suit's oxygen supply indicator. It still read almost empty. Already, she was having trouble breathing. She remembered seeing two smaller space vehicles in the hanger of the

VINCENT, parked in a separate area. Clambering back over the hull and down the girders of what remained of the steel arm, she floated across the storage area and saw another door. She pushed a large green button. The door slid up. As she floated in, she saw a bright yellow sign: EMERGENCY OXYGEN. PULL DOWN. She grabbed a red lever and pulled hard. The door swung shut and she saw venting as the small room filled with gas. When she thought the pressure had equalized, she pulled off her helmet, her long hair floating in the zero-gravity environment.

"I can breathe!" she gasped. Helen grasped a handhold and rested. As she did she looked around the room. In front of two circular outer doors, a pair of black rectangular space vehicles sat, looking to Helen like square shaped insects. The rear door to one of them was open and its lights inside were on. Above the door was stenciled: RESCUE SHIP—ALINA III.

Easing herself from her position, she grabbed her spacesuit helmet and swam through the small hanger to the Rescue vehicle. When she pulled herself inside, the first thing she did was to find a new oxygen tank and replace it with the empty one. Then she looked to the front of the small craft and saw what appeared to be a standard aircraft instrument panel and two steel seats, a configuration that was similar to the DC-10 cockpit that Doug had shown her. The instrument panel had been automatically switched on. Sitting down in the left seat,

Helen strapped herself in. Through the front windshield of the rescue vehicle, she could see the large steel outer hatch. Then she heard a woman's computer voice coming from a black speaker in the exact centre of the instrument panel.

"Hello, Helen. This is Veronica. What can I do for you today?"

Helen stared hard at the speaker as the woman talked in a syncopated voice. Helen cleared her throat and said: "Yes, Veronica. This is Helen. I need to rescue Doug but don't know how to fly this thing. Can you see him and will you help me go get him?"

A television monitor at the top of the panel flickered and lit up. Helen watched as a picture taken by an exterior camera hunted across the hull and found the fractured boom of the arm. Then it tracked higher and Helen could see Doug in his seat. The camera panned even closer and zoomed in. Helen could see that his helmet glass was intact. But inside, Doug had his eyes closed and appeared to be unconscious. She knew there was little time to save him before he ran out of oxygen, or maybe he was already dead.

"Veronica, I need to rescue him as soon as possible."

Helen heard a whir of a pump as the hanger that held the rescue vehicles was vented of its oxygen.

"Opening the outer door, Rescue commander," the computer-generated voice said.

As Helen watched, the outer door opened revealing nothing but stars.

"Helen, sit back and tighten all of your safety straps. Sliding the Alina III out of the hanger door."

Helen did exactly as she was instructed. As the Rescue vehicle slid out into space on a steel ramp, she put on her helmet, clamping it shut but left her visor open. When Alina III was in the vacuum of outer space, the small ship swiveled to the left to face Doug's lifeless form.

"Engaging propulsion system and radar," Veronica stated. Then the Alina III with Helen inside ventured across the hull and toward the white target. As the vehicle approached her future husband, Helen keyed her mic again. "Doug, I'm coming as fast as I can."

As the Alina III approached its target, Helen smelled the strong odor of an electrical fire. In front of her, the glass instrument panel reflected tongues of red and blue flames. Snapping shut her visor and looking to the right, she saw three fire extinguishers. Taking hold of the one marked FOR ELECTRICAL FIRE ONLY: CLASS C EXTINGUISHER, she squeezed the trigger and directed the nozzle behind her seat and toward the small fire that had taken hold in the electrical wires on the back wall. The non-conductive powder dampened down the sparking flames and soon the fire had been put out. As she placed the extinguisher back in its holder, Helen toggled her chin switch. "Veronica, what caused the fire? Was it the result of the destruction of the SAINT VINCENT?"

"Yes, Commander, that's correct. But now that you've put out the fire, we'll take no chances. We'll rescue that astronaut as quickly as possible. Rescue commander, use the front claws of the spacecraft to grasp the transmission antennae as we get close to it."

Helen felt her seat vibrate as Veronica fired the vehicle's small thrusters, slowing the ship. They traveled further down the hull and toward Doug.

"Helen, look up. The antenna array is right above you."

Helen looked up and saw the antenna. She swiveled her seat around and grasped the two handholds of the exterior front claws that hung beside her seat, suspended from the ceiling. Trying them, she saw that they were easy to use. Pulling back on one of the handles caused a claw to retract. Push it the other way and the reverse happened. Close her fist and the claw at the end of the arm shut and then opened. When she looked again at the monitor, she saw that they were hovering just below their target. Helen pushed out the arm then closed the claw. It grasped the antenna. But the hydraulics of the stainless-steel claws proved too strong for the fragile structure and crushed it flat. When that happened, the fractured boom of what remained of the arm broke free from the array and floated into the void of space with Doug still held in his seat.

"Doug!" Helen cried as she watched him grow even smaller in the television monitor. "I'm coming!"

She unstrapped herself from the command chair and, floating through the small compartment, saw a spool of thick steel rescue wire attached to a bulkhead. When she grabbed the stainless-steel clip at the very end of it in her gloved hand, she easily pulled out a twenty-foot length.

"Helen, I know what you're doing," Veronica said. "Remember that your spacesuit's oxygen cylinders are rescue tanks. They only have enough oxygen for thirty minutes. Also, when you vent the ship to leave the spacecraft, there will be almost no air left to get back to the command module. Keep that in mind as you rescue Doug, so make your journey as fast as possible."

"But why is there so little air in this tank? Are there other full tanks of oxygen on the Rescue vehicle? There must be some left!"

"Most of the VINCENT'S remaining air cylinders are almost out of oxygen," the syncopated voice continued. "This is because they were used when the two astronauts were out on a spacewalk to repair the hull, then ran into trouble. The Alina III went out to rescue them, and when that Rescue crew found they were dead, returned to the mother ship with their bodies. This is why your rescue vehicle doesn't have much oxygen left. We also don't have much propellant onboard. You have a choice, Helen. I can get our craft halfway to your target but then our fuel supply will be minimized. You must take the rescue cord and use the propulsion unit of your suit to fly to Doug. Once there, latch the steel wire onto his spacesuit. When you are ready to retrieve him, radio me and I'll pull you both back in. Commander, such a rescue is very risky. Many people have died having attempted a rescue without adequate oxygen. And also remember that your suit's propulsion unit is almost empty."

"I understand," Helen stated. "But it's a risk I need to take."

When she was ready, Helen vented the oxygen in the Alina III into space then opened the outer door. Looking out, she saw that Doug still floated away from the Rescue vehicle and toward the countless stars. "I'm coming right now, Doug," she called over her helmet mic.

She stepped into the void and, holding the rescue wire in her glove and activating the suit's propulsion unit, accelerated toward the target. On her suit's green heads-up display which was reflected in her helmet's visor, she could see the radar of the Rescue vehicle as it was broadcast to her by Veronica. A red target was slowly creeping closer and as it did, she heard a series of 'bleeps' and knew her suit's navigation system had locked onto the fractured arm with Doug still strapped in his seat. As she looked out her visor, she could see the tiny white speck of Doug grow larger. On the heads-up display, two red circles closed in on the primary target, and when she was within fifty feet of him she heard Veronica say, "Helen, your target is reached. Reverse your suit's propulsion unit."

She reversed thrust and reached out with a hand. Grasping Doug firmly by the wrist, she reached around his waist with the other hand to unbuckle the safety belts which tied him to his seat. Pulling him to her with both arms, she attached the rescue wire to his suit.

"Veronica, I've got Doug. Bring us in now."

As Helen turned around with the last few seconds of her suit's propulsion fuel, she felt a hard tug on the rescue wire. Letting go of it, she held onto Doug and now at speed was reeled back to the Alina III. She was blinded by the Rescue craft's front lights as she and Doug came closer to the small spacecraft. Traversing the distance in a matter of seconds, Veronica extended both of the rescue craft's front steel arms

"Place Doug in the arms," Veronica instructed. "I will retract both arms to hold him. Then get into the Rescue vehicle. I'll take us to the command module. Our ship's fuel indicator reads that there is just enough to get back."

The small spacecraft turned around and slowly moved through the vacuum of space toward the command module. Turning in a one-hundred-and-eighty-degree maneuver, the Alina III faced the back door of the VINCENT. Re-extending the arms, Veronica released Doug and slowly retracted the rescue wire. Looking at Doug's face through his helmet visor, Helen saw that his lips were blue and his eyes still closed due to a complete lack of oxygen.

"Veronica, get the crew hibernation room ready. Doug needs oxygen. Please hurry."

"Yes, Helen."

Carrying Doug, Helen floated into the command module then closed the outer door. She hit the red button for Emergency Oxygen and once again heard its welcome rush. Taking off her helmet and then Doug's, she pulled him into the hibernation room. There, she stripped him of his spacesuit and wrapped a large blanket around his body. Then she stripped herself of her own suit. Placing a hand on his cheek then his belly, she realised that he was as cold as ice. Sliding him into the oblong steel and glass cylinder of a hibernation unit, she pushed a green button to shut the long door. When she was certain it was airtight, she looked toward a monitor where Veronica watched her progress.

"Veronica, Doug's inside the hibernation chamber. Please flood the chamber with oxygen."

"Yes, Helen. Right now."

When Helen heard the welcome hiss of gas, she watched as Doug's lips turned from blue to their normal color. She saw him slowly open his eyes. They fluttered then opened wide. Coughing, then hacking loudly, his body bent over and started shaking. Then she keyed the hibernation chamber mic.

"Welcome home, Mr Co-pilot. You sure neglected your future wife when you decided to take that spacewalk. You promised me you'd only be gone a few minutes, remember? What happened? Did you decide not to come home?"

Behind the glass, Doug smiled. "You know I'd never leave Helen home alone, don't you? I feel like I've been gone for a year."

"Put on that other blanket floating near you and strap yourself onto the table. Then try to sleep. When you're awake, I'll have Veronica give you a complete physical check-up and we'll get you something to eat. Are you thirsty, Doug? There's a water bottle at your right hand."

He looked across the cubicle and saw the plastic bottle tied to the floor with a white string. Grasping it from where it floated and placing the tube in his mouth, he drank from the bottle until it was empty. Then he closed his eyes and, in the warmth of the incoming air and pulling his blanket tight, Helen watched as he closed his eyes and slept.

Chapter Twenty

Following three hours of oxygen treatment, and after Doug was extracted from the hibernation unit, the pair moved back up to the command module. The first thing Doug did was look at the VINCENT'S oxygen readings. "We're almost out of O2," he said. "We're going to have to go back into hibernation if we want to survive."

"I don't want to go back there, Doug. Seeing what happened to the NASA astronauts who tried to survive while hibernating was more than enough."

"But Helen, if we don't go to sleep in those units we'll die of oxygen starvation."

"I don't care," Helen replied. "I never want to do that, nor do I ever again want to put on a spacesuit or go out into space. Do you understand?"

"Loud and clear. At least we're together. Let's get comfortable."

They changed into blue coveralls with the SAINT VINCENT logo stitched onto the fabric above their left breasts. When Helen looked into a mirror, she giggled, trying hard to make light of their deadly situation. "Doug, we look like twins."

"That's exactly what I wanted. We could have had twins."

"Don't say 'could have had'. There has to be hope."

"Right now, there is no hope. What are we going to do? Take the VINCENT back through the Black Hole? Even if we had our propulsion unit I wouldn't know where to start."

"Come on. Let's curl up and sleep. Let's dream of the blue planet that's our home. You never know, there could be a rescue."

"There will be no…"

She put a finger against his lips. "Shhhhh. Let's try to sleep for at least an hour."

They strapped themselves into the hammock in the command module and Helen's blonde hair swung freely due to the lack of gravity. As Doug slept beside her, she watched as he began to dream. His hands and legs twitched then, startled, he sat up.

"It's the woman again."

"Who? That woman who looked like the Lady? The one who said she was praying for you?"

"Now she's praying for both of us. This time, it's a prayer of rescue. She wants me to tell you that they'll be here in five minutes in their rescue vehicle. It will be called The Gaia IV."

"How do you know that? That's crazy. No one would ever rescue us this far from Earth."

"Honestly, that's what I heard in my dream. But then she said something that sounded like Morse code again."

Helen thought back to the time she had first visited their Long Island home with Doug. She remembered how he had pointed out his father's license plate which now hung in her husband's tool shed in their new home and how he had taught her some Morse code.

"Did the code you hear really sound like Morse?"

"Yes but no. It varied a great deal and warbled up and down, faster and faster and higher and higher. At times, the numbers added up to eleven or two. I did that in my head though I never had to think about it. It sounded like a welcoming song. Remember when we saw the video of that online article about intergalactic code? It sounded like that, only far more complex. If it's code, it contains an important message."

When five minutes had passed, the radio crackled to life.

"But that's impossible," Doug said. "The outer antenna was destroyed."

First they heard a long *'ping'*. Then, as they listened to the speaker, the 'ping' turned to the sounds of an extraordinary number of dashes and dots. Separated by long silences, the series repeated itself again and again. Helen could see that Doug was listening intently. His lips moved as he counted.

"That's standard Morse, Helen."

"Let me get you a pen. You can't do that in your head."

Helen rummaged around in a drawer of the control console and, taking out a blue marker, handed it to him. "Write it down on that white bulkhead."

Doug backed up to the wall of the command module and as he listened, began scribbling down the letters. When he had finished scrawling, his hand had written twenty feet across the bulkhead, ten lines down.

"What does it say?" Helen asked, not able to read his handwriting. "Go on, read it out loud."

"It says: 'We come in peace, bearing great gifts from the planet near the sun Proxima Centauri B and not far from where you are now located. The code that you hear is the gift of life. We bring them to you to distribute to all of humankind.'"

Helen looked at him, puzzled. "Proxima B? That's the sun we read about. And the planet? That's the one I visit when I dream about Josie."

"I know," Doug whispered. "It's impossible. If the signals do come from a planet near that sun, it's a brand-new transmission never before detected by any of our scientists."

Then a steely voice came to life on the radio transmitter.

"This is Gaia IV Rescue Vessel. In a moment, we will board your command deck and take control of your space vehicle. Do not be afraid. We look different than you. But in spite of that, we have human-like DNA and are, in many ways, the same as you."

The lights dimmed on the command deck. Then the couple heard a *hiss* that grew in volume, as if an organ played a harmonic song that warbled up and down in volume and octaves. In front of them flashed two objects that quickly solidified into strange looking creatures. When the transfer was over and the song had finished, two beings stood in front of them. The ceilings in the command deck were just over ten feet tall. But Doug, measuring them with his eye, whispered to Helen, "They must be over nine feet high."

"I know. The tall woman is … my dear Holy Mother…*it's Gaia!*"

"That's Gaia? That's the woman you dream about?"

"You dreamed about her too, Doug, but you didn't know it."

"But she looks *different*! The Lady I dreamed about had brown skin, not green. She was dressed like the statues of the Virgin Mary that we see in church."

As they both watched, the tall woman stretched her arms straight out, horizontal to the command deck. It was then that Helen first noticed the long wings extending from both shoulders. They flexed as if Gaia wanted to fly, then stretched up to the ceiling.

"Our Rescue craft has much higher ceilings," Gaia said to them in English. "We have a large warehouse that is big enough in which to fly because it is enjoyable and necessary to keep us healthy."

"Gaia, I never knew you had wings," Helen said. "Can you really fly?"

"Of course, we can fly," the tall male said as he extended his own set of wings. "Humans are not the only beings who can fly. We do not always extend our wings. We do so when we fly but when we do not they retract into our shoulders and down into our back."

"Helen, remember that I heard and saw Our Lady in my dreams but I never saw her in the flesh," Doug said. "Who's the male that's with her?"

Helen stared at the tall man then looked at Gaia. Doug did the same thing and felt his stomach turn over. Both beings had skin of light green that shimmered in the overhead lights. When he looked at their eyes, he saw irises that looked human but the corneas were green with flecks of gold and red. They were dressed not in uniforms but in body-length gowns that also shimmered in the dim light. To Doug, it seemed that the gowns were transparent. He could see through them. The woman's breasts were small and upraised.

When he looked at the male he noted the same thing. His gown was also transparent. Just like the female, his genitals were wrapped in some sort of loincloth like the Hindu people wear.

The male extended his hand toward as if he wanted to shake hands. Doug noticed that both beings had six fingers. Their naked feet, which protruded from their gowns, also had six toes and were webbed like those of a salamander. In spite of his dreams and Helen's reassurances, he did not know what to make of these beings. Doug took the male's hand in his own, uncertainly shaking it. "I'm Doug Martin. Thank you for saving us."

"I am Amendus, a General in our planet's Space Command Fleet," the male said in a low, gruff voice. "May I introduce you to Gaia, who is our Queen, Chief Protector and Inter-Galactic Leader. To you, because you are both Catholics, she would be much like your Pope Francis. You have both met her when she came to your home with your only living daughter. However, she looked like humans from Earth not from our planet."

"You know that we're Catholic and you have the ability to transform your bodies?" Doug asked, suddenly scared of the strange visitors. "But how do you know anything about us? We live on Earth, lightyears away."

"Don't be afraid. We've been monitoring your planet, watching the development of humankind, for well over one hundred thousand years. And as for you—we've been watching both of you since you were born, as I assume my Queen and wife has told you. But you know that because Helen's mother shared that with her."

Doug turned to Helen. "That woman? She's your mother?"

"Yes, she is. Wait until she speaks again then you'll know the truth, too."

"But why?" Doug asked, still afraid of the alien beings. "What could be so special about us? We're both average human beings."

Rather than answer Doug's question, the male who had called himself Amendus stepped aside and bowed. As the tall beautiful female walked forward, Helen, still astonished by her sudden appearance, started to curtsy. Gently, the kind lady grasped her arm and pulled her up.

"There is no need to be formal, my daughter Helen. Remember, I am just like you but I look very different now. After all, I gave birth to you."

"You couldn't have," Doug said, his eyes wide at the shocking statement. "Her mother Josephine had Helen. But your voice. It sounds just like…"

"Your dreams?" Gaia answered again in English. The woman smiled and her eyes glinted. Doug saw that they were larger than any human's he had ever seen. Her irises were round and green, glinting with flecks of gold and red. "All will be revealed when we take you to our planet," the Lady said to him.

"Your planet? But how and why? May I ask you: how can you possibly look like you do but also look like the Virgin Mary in my dreams?"

Gaia smiled at Doug for the first time and again, he saw her kindness. "My son, it is easy if you know how. All I do is transform myself when you dream of me."

As Doug watched, the alien being changed before his eyes. As the Virgin Mary walked toward him, he saw that she looked just as she did in his dreams She wore a long white gown and covered her head in a blue stole. In her hand she held a pink and silver rosary. Doug was transfixed as the Virgin Mary leaned toward him to kiss his cheek.

"You see my son," she said in Hebrew which Doug found that he understood, "you need not be afraid of me for I, too, am your mother. Trust us both because we are here not only to rescue you but soon you will understand that my children Helen and Doug were born to save our Earth."

Then the holy woman transformed again and in front of him stood Gaia.

"Do you see, my son, how easy it is? We do this to instill trust in those we have selected to help us. Trust us, my children. Be not afraid of us or anyone from our home planet."

She stepped back and considered Helen's gaunt and worried face. "Daughter, I know you are hungry and thirsty. I know you are almost out of food and water and haven't eaten properly in days."

"That's true," Doug said. "We're also almost out of oxygen."

"But now you won't need to be worried," Gaia replied. "We have brought you plenty of supplies on our mother ship. We transported them into what remains of your storage area to replenish your vessel when we were flown down to your command deck. Come with me. I have a surprise waiting for you both."

"A surprise? Like what kind of surprise?" Doug asked, his voice now strong and unwavering. "You plan to kill us, don't you?"

"Doug, don't," Helen said. "What Gaia says is the truth. She really is my mother as well as yours."

"But what about Josephine and my mom? Aren't they our mothers?"

"Of course, they are. But as Gaia told me, I have two mothers. We also have a child named Josie, remember?"

"Is she with you?" Doug said to the man who called himself Amendus. "If she is, show her to us and I'll believe you."

"No, she is not with us," Gaia stated. "She is now on our home planet. But you will see her when we are ready for you to see her." Then the woman laughed in a wonderfully sing-song tone that moved from one octave to another.

"My friend and son Doug Masters, hear me now. We *never, ever* kill unless it's absolutely necessary. Besides, and as you will soon find out, you are to be protected because the both of you are not only important to our planet as well as your own planet and its Solar System and galaxy, but to the very survival of our existing and future Universes. No, this is a surprise just for you two. Now come. Let me take my daughter's hand."

As the Royal Queen took Helen's hand and led her on, Doug and Amendus floated behind them. All of a sudden Doug noticed he could walk on two feet. Gravity had come back to the VINCENT. "But that's impossible. The ship is…"

"Dead?" remarked Amendus. "It is not dead. We knew what you needed before you did. We have been reading the human mind on your planet going back to when the Neanderthals padded through the forests, and even longer than that. Reading your minds, as well as this ship's computer mind, the artificial consciousness of the VINCENT, was easy."

When they entered what remained of the storage bay, Doug looked around at a brand-new hanger area and a new steel arm. When he looked up, the bay doors were new and closed. They walked through an open door and into a new crew's quarters. The dining room table had been spread with a feast. As Helen looked down on the food, she recognized many things that grew on Earth: squash, melon, cucumber, lettuce, tomatoes, radishes, onions, raspberries, blackberries, blueberries, strawberries, apples and peaches.

In the middle of the table were the main courses. A hot dish looked somewhat like beef but smelled quite different. A variety of fish and seafood looked exactly like that found in Earth's oceans: scallops, mussels, shrimp, crab and lobsters, john dory, flounder, bass, breaded sole and many other fish dishes.

Round cheeses and a variety of different kinds of bread were spread out on large platters, and to the side were cutlery and napkins. Desserts which she was certain looked like chocolate fondue as well as strawberry-honey poured over ice cream. were contained in appropriate dishes, some hot and some freezing, together with a variety of toppings. But other dishes she didn't recognize at all. What looked like pink sorbet was smothered in a green tinted jam. that resembled some kind of mint julip.

At another small table, bottles of beverages that looked and smelled like wine, beer, water, and soft drinks, together with a wide variety of glasses and buckets of ice with tongs, were ready to be poured and drunk.

When Helen looked up from the table, confused, Gaia said:

"Some of the meats are rather like beef, chicken or pork that you eat on Earth. The fish and shellfish are the same, of course. Much like your planet, our home planet of Gaia is almost entirely covered by oceans. I did not show you any of that when we saw each other in your dreams But soon I will show you everything."

"What was the planet's name? Did you say 'Gaia'?" Doug asked as he remembered an article he and Helen had read about how Native American tribes called their planet Gaia, the mother of all beings.

The Lady laughed yet again. "Yes, its name is Gaia. Why they named four of our planets after me was silly. I'm only a simple Gaian, after all."

"How many planets are there in total that orbit around Proxima Centauri B?" Doug asked."

"Four, as my Lady said," explained Amendus. "Those from Earth call them the Proxima Centauri planets. But as we've already explained, we call them the Gaian planets and there are four: A, B, C and D. B and C are in the goldilocks region and are much like Earth in that they're capable of nurturing life. We are currently terraforming A, which is similar to your planet Mars. It is too hot to support any type of life and no longer has much atmosphere. But just like Mars, where the atmosphere is being reconditioned, that planet, too, will soon be transformed."

"Humans are terraforming Mars?" Doug gasped.

"No, we are," explained Gaia. "We are now starting that long process and when we come to visit your planet, we will give you the technology, as well as many other gifts, to completely transform that red planet."

"What kind of gifts?" Helen asked. "You're already given us so many gifts. You give us food, water, oxygen, a new spacecraft, a new life…"

"Let us eat first, child, and when we are finished we will explain everything to you."

Chapter Twenty-One

An hour later Helen, accompanied by Gaia, Doug and Amendus, exited the SAINT VINCENT for the last time. As Doug left the command module, he realized that no other human being would ever again visit the stricken vessel. From now on, this first intergalactic starship created by human beings would be listed as the last resting place of all its crew. As the Queen and her Royal Consort walked past the vehicle's new storage area, Helen paused and entered through the door with Doug. There, she stood by the crew body bags that now contained seven astronauts, not just two.

"We can't leave them like this," Helen said when she had finished praying. "Their bodies just can't be left here."

"No, we'll do what their Captain had planned." Doug once again took a seat in the repaired hydraulic arm. Helen opened the bay doors by pressing an actuator on the arm's giant hinge. When the doors opened revealing a million stars, Doug gasped each bag with a pair of small arms that Gaian engineers had installed on the seat.

"Preparing to extend the hydraulic arm, Helen, and this time I don't need to promise you that I'll be right back. You can stand there and see exactly what I see, and all of humanity will eventually see."

Helen understood what he wanted to be done. She commanded Veronica, the starship's computer, to record the proceedings which would be transmitted to the Gaian Rescue vehicle then directly to Earth. As the camera panned to look straight up, Helen also watched as Doug extended the arm as high as it with go.

"Okay, I'm ready to release them now. Helen, do you have any last words?"

"I guess that Our Lord blesses them and their families and that one day soon, they all see each other in Heaven. Doug, they're going to go where no one has ever gone before. Can you make sure they don't fall into that red sun? I'd rather that their relatives know that their remains have all gone to circle the Centauri Galaxy forever."

"Will do." She watched as Doug let the seven bodies go. They drifted for a moment and then, as the gravity of the nearby galaxy gathered each of the NASA astronauts to it, Helen and Doug observed the white bags fall toward the distant star system.

"If the men and women wake up, maybe they'll think they're on their way home," Helen whispered to the heavens above her. "Be there for them, won't you God? Make sure they get home safe someday."

Finished with this last mission onboard the U.S. starship, Doug retracted the arm. Then, with Helen, they went to find the Royal couple. When they did, the group of four used standard methods to board the Gaia IV. The rescue vehicle was now connected to the NASA craft by an airtight gangway. When the Americans climbed aboard the alien craft they were shocked at how big it was.

"I've never seen anything like this," Doug marveled as he looked around the huge cabin and at the simple instrument panel. "Is this all there is? Where are the directional controls? You must know about the VINCENT's Rescue craft, the Alina III. It has a control system much like most aircraft on Earth. Even Helen and I can use it."

"This vehicle has no controls like you know them," replied Amendus. "We use simple mental telepathy to control the craft. All we do is think and our vehicle does what we command. In our heads, we describe in words, images or emotions what we want the spacecraft to do and it behaves accordingly. For instance, in a drastic situation like you experienced during the emergency landing in North Carolina where you saved many passengers, we would not have to place our hands on the controls. Instead, because we also become frightened, we simply think the commands and the vehicle will take whatever action necessary to avoid an accident, even if the ship was damaged. However, at any time we can activate a manual control system much like you have."

Gaia added to her Royal Consorts explanation. "Usually, we use telepathy as Amendus described and we sing to each other, ship to ship, to keep in a tight formation during military missions or training flights," Gaia said. "It is rather like what dolphin mammals in your seas, rivers and oceans use to navigate. An echolocation that can travel vast distances through time and space. Too, it is somewhat like the code we sent you from our planet."

"That Morse Code came from your home planet?" Helen asked. "But our astronomers thought it was coming from a Black Hole in the Pegasus constellation."

"We made it look like that," Gaia laughed. "We do not want anyone to discover our planet. Not until we are ready. All we did was move the source of the signal to a region just outside our local Black Hole, and then to another Black Hole in the Pegasus system. Then, when we suspect that scientists from Earth know about the source of the code, we will move it back to our own galaxy's Black Hole. In fact, I saw an interview today on CNN…"

"Gaia, you watch television transmitted from Earth?" Doug asked.

"Of course, we do. That and your radio transmissions and someday soon, your Internet communications. It is how we continually monitor the situation on your planet and Solar System. Now, as I was saying: an Earth-based scientist was explaining the possible cause of what he termed 'a strange song'. He said it was caused by vibrating dust that collided just outside the edges of the Black Hole's event horizon located in the Orion nebula, not the Pegasus system. Only days ago, by your timeline, we moved the source of the code again. Confusing, is it not?" she said laughing. "That's exactly what we're trying to do. Mask the source until we want to reveal ourselves."

"You can move it?" Doug marveled again. "How did you move the signal?"

"No," stated Amendus. "We moved the *apparent* source of the signal. That is easy. All we did was retransmit it using telepathy. Also, we can use our satellite system to move the apparent source of the signal. They also use our Stardrive system and can travel through space faster than the speed of light. The one responsible for masking the code for Earth is currently in an elliptical orbit around that Black Hole in Orion. The code confuses humans, am I correct?"

"But Orion, Pegasus and Centauri are lightyears from Earth," Helen stated. "How do humans hear it if it's transmitted from so far away?"

"Again, we use telepathy to speed up those signals," Amendus again explained. "Just as Gaia explained, and how we transmit from our ship to other spaceships or around this Universe, all we do is concentrate and that echolocation sings to your Earth."

"So that's how you do it," Doug said. "No one is sure where the code comes from or what it is. Some think it's a song from aliens. Others think it's hokum and doesn't even exist. Still others think it's part of an elaborate plan, a signal from aliens, to take over Earth, or broadcast by the Russians from a transmitter located on a satellite somewhere beyond Jupiter. And some even think it's a song from God"

"That's right," Helen stated. "Those believers are convinced it's God's song."

"We understand that," Gaia said. "Which is why many will think we are gods when we visit your planet. But we are not. As we have said many times before, in many different ways, in dreams, codes and other signals across your galaxy and Solar System, which includes solar flares from your Sun, many of you will think we are Angels because we can fly. Or reptiles, or other mammals. Some will even think we are Satan. We shall talk about that later but first you must listen to a story I am about to tell, and hear me because it is relevant to you and Doug as well as to all humankind. This is the story of a man who came down from Heaven to save your world. Some called him King but others said he was a fraud because he had betrayed the Hebrews, not only *Jesu Kristos's* people but also your people if you go back far enough.

"Because the Pharisees said in Hebrew, 'You Jesus Christ say you are the Lord on High, the Son of God the Father and you will never die but will rise again? It's a sin what you utter. You have betrayed us. You are no Christ! You are nothing but a betrayer and a fraud and we will have you crucified. Not even Pontius Pilot, our Roman Governor, will be able to save you from certain death. Instead, he will release Barabbas, your first cousin, and will kidnap Mary Magdalene your wife and hold her to ransom! So take up a collection right now for us and our temples or you will never see your Mary, who is only a whore-wife, alive again! Not even Judas, your one true disciple, will be able to save you. We have already paid him with two bags of gold, one of which he has already spent on women, wine and gambling. So die like a pig, you miserable Christ. We will flog you. We will place a crown of thorns on your head. We will drive eight nails into you: two into each of your feet and ankles, one in each of the palms of your hands and one each into your wrists. Then we will hang you on a tree between two thieves. Our Roman soldiers will gamble and cast lots to see who will divide what remains of your clothing, and who will get to violently love your wife,'" Gaia said, "which is not exactly what they meant by the way. What they said in Hebrew was a word that is more terrible. It means 'to make love' but to do so without any passion. In other words, what they meant was 'rape'.

"That is the tale that you read in a Holy Book called the Bible by many, many faiths. But to continue this tale in my words, not those of the Pharisees, your Jesus was killed on a cross of their making, not His. He died as was prophesized to take the sins of all the people of the world away from them, no matter what faith they believe in or what their color or sexual practice or gender. Here, I will give you one hint as to the meaning I say. My son is Doug Martin yet you had a mother who gave birth to her. What is her name?"

"You can't be my mother. My mother's name was Mary Rose," Doug replied. "But what's this got to do with Mom?"

"Everything and nothing. If it had not been for your dead mother and father, you would not be here. Your real mother's name is Mary. Just like Mary Magdalene who is *Jesu Kristos's* wife. But as I said, we will discuss more of this later. What I want you to hear now is about you two, Helen and Doug.

"Helen, I called you my child and you are. You are already a Righteous Woman and a Saint. On Earth in the days of Christ, they called you Mary Magdalene, those people who believe that Christ had a wife. Doug calls you that in his dreams, and at other times Pookus, the lame one. Helen, you love to pray to Saint Padre Pio, do you not, which is why you will name one of your many children after the saint who suffered the wounds of *Kristos* in both his hands, feet and side. You have already risen to Heaven not once but many times and sit at the right hand of our Unknown Father who is sometimes called Ralphus Rex and at other times Tomas Christus, after the doubter Disciple Thomas. He stands right next to you even now. And do not think that he is only Doug because he is not. Instead, he is like a dolphin or a caterpillar or even *Jesu Kristos*. He has room in his heart to love not only you but many, many other people and especially children and older people and people of color and those afflicted by many kinds of diseases, and those who some slander as being gay, lesbian or queer. He is your risen almost husband, is he not Helen?"

As Gaia talked, her sing-song voice had put Helen into a trance. Shaking her head, she woke up enough to answer the question. "I dream about Doug all the time. If what you say is true then you know about all the dreams I have ever had in my life. Exactly which dream do you mean? If it's about Jesus Christ, then I dream about the Son of God all the time, usually right after I say my bedtime prayers, as well as my daughter Josie and you."

"And when you dream about Doug and Jesus, what do you think is the meaning?"

Helen looked away from Doug because she felt embarrassed. Hot blood rushed into her cheeks and she realised she did not want to answer the question Gaia had asked her.

"Well, you see, when I dream, sometimes I dream of Doug and Jesus as if they were in the same body. Or I have waking dreams When Doug was in the hospital, I saw him with his arms stretched out as if he was on a cross. Blood poured from his hands, feet, back, forehead and his side. He rose high up and was then cast against a wall as if he had been nailed there. Then I smelled it: the putrid smell of decaying blood and flesh. I looked up and Doug was dead! His head hung down and from his side blood mixed with water poured out of his side like a tide of the Red Ocean. It filled the room to the top of his bed's mattress and I found myself standing on it, sure that I would drown. But then I smelled wine, like the good red wine that Doug often drinks at dinner. I put my hand into it and tasted it. And Doug," she said, finally turning to him, "it really was wine, remember? Blood still poured out of your hands and feet but it was transformed and I remember rose petals which encircled my head and then glowed. My head was warm to the touch and the room lit up as if I was wearing a halo. Then my hands and feet tingled as if I was walking on warm carpeting, so very soft and reassuring, and then I woke up! That's when I found myself with you, dancing toward the stars." Helen looked at Gaia. "Is that the dream you meant, My Lady?"

"Yes, child, I am Your Lady. You pray to me every night when you say the *Hail Mary*. But I am not that Virgin. Instead, I am one of a triumvirate of people who are responsible for all that we have. They are, in order, John, whom you call the Unknown Father; me, Gaia, which, in my language, means the Eternal Mother; and Pookus whom you call the Holy Ghost. She is the one who is greater than all of us and the mother of the origins of life in all our Universes and we also call this creature that we cannot see the Unknown Quantity and our Maker. This unseen thing which is all about love proceeds us and predates us. It was there before Eternity began. This is what was responsible for all life. Before the Big Bang as your scientists call the very beginning, and there have been many Big Bangs I tell you, the love in its heart became lonely. So it decided to create something which some scientists call the 'knife edge' of life. But this was not just any kind of knife edge. Instead, this was a perfectly formed first universe. In it, as it exploded and expanded at the speed of light, it alone created all the things that were and are still necessary for life. Think of all the elements that are in you, and the molecules and water. All you need is a single spark from that being whom you call God the Father, which is really me, you, and Pookus the Holy Ghost and Unknown Maker put together, and that is the miracle that creates life.

"But Doug is also responsible for life because it takes two people, a male and a female, to create a child. But that is not all of what was said in your dreaming reality. As you might remember, Helen, soon we will be visiting Earth."

"You're really coming to our planet?" Helen said, not able to take in or fathom what Gaia was saying. "When?"

"Soon, but not until we're ready. When we come, as I started to say when we all last ate, we will give your entire planet and all its people and living things eternal gifts which you will call many miracles."

"Can we ask what they are?" Doug said. "When you say 'miracles', what kind of miracles?" Doug thought a moment and laughed. "How about rescuing all the people of planet Earth on some sort of enormous spacecraft? After all, many think we need rescuing from ourselves."

"Of course, we shall do that," Amendus chimed in. "You have already destroyed your planet. You have used up all its resources. In not so many years from now, there will be an intense war in the Ukraine caused by a man named Putin who will kill tens of thousands of people and cause over five million Ukrainians to flee across borders to other countries. Even the United States, the United Kingdom and European countries will accept many Ukrainian refugees, but particularly widows with small children. But that is not the worst of it. With this war once again comes the threat of global annihilation."

"Other factors will try to work to destroy your planet, too," Gaia explained.

"Like what?"

"Some you know about and are trying to deal with but not too effectively. Global warming, for instance. You will soon know that you must lower carbon dioxide gas and will work to restore the ozone layer which is already growing thin. But in lowering carbon emissions you will go in the wrong direction."

"But why?" asked Helen reasonably. "Doug and I have read articles about this, too. By restoring the ozone layer, we can deflect the sunlight that's causing higher temperatures."

"We had the same problem on our planet," Amendus said. "We were emitting too much carbon gas. But instead of decreasing the carbon emissions which were the result of our many manufacturing operations, we simply planted more green living things. The leaves, as you know, absorb carbon dioxide and create more oxygen."

"But the real threat to your many nations is threefold," Gaia explained, holding up a hand and ticking off each point on her long fingers as she explained what would happen. "North Korea is and will continue to be a constant threat. Soon, they will learn to sling their nuclear weapons at Japan, China and the United States. Using Multiple Independent Reentry Vehicles, some of them will be impossible to stop by any western country's nuclear deterrence. The result could be catastrophic. They could kill at least twenty-five million innocent people or more. Much worse than what your strategists in their War Rooms think could happen.

"Two. Putin and a man named Trump who thinks he is successful right now on the east coast of your United States will also become threats to your world. In not quite forty years, both will be presidents of their countries. They are both the same so I will talk about them at the same time. Putin will never be any friend of Trump, as that man will someday think. He will want Trump to play into his hands and that is exactly what will happen. Trump, alone, will almost cause nuclear war as you will someday read in the global press when that imbecile visits the North Korean Prime Minister. Trump will lose his next election but by a hair's breadth. There will be, of course, many, many Trump supporters. They will do their best to steal that next election in two thousand and twenty-four."

"But how?" asked Doug. "Elections are safer than they were in the Kennedy and Nixon presidential fight."

"It is easy to do," shrugged Amendus. "When Trump loses that next election, he will fight it in court. But when at last it makes its way to the U.S. Supreme Court, he will lose despite the fact that the court justices are mostly conservative. They will realize that they must uphold the U.S. Constitution as they did many times before throughout your country's history."

"Now the final catastrophe on your planet," Gaia stated gravely. "Remember, these are not predictions. This is exactly what will happen." She slowly lowered her next finger. "North Korea will strike its many enemies with nuclear weapons. The western nations will have no choice but to reign down fire on North Korea. Seeing an opportunity, the Chinese and Russian War Rooms will respond with a blanket of missiles using hypersonic vehicles. Flying at Mach Five, and jigging and jagging so no radar can pick them up, some will be shot down using Earth's latest laser technologies. But that won't prevent Mutually Assured Destruction.

"Seeing all of their capitals blown to cinders, and with billions of souls now dead, the western countries, including Pakistan, India and Israel, will fire as many nuclear weapons as they have. Some bombs from China and Russia will include cobalt bombs. These will blanket the entire Earth in radiation, and only a few will survive. Those few will live in Australia, New Zealand, the Antarctica and the very southern tip of South America. But when it is finished, the swirling atmospheres of the Northern and Southern halves of your planet will mix. Radiation will finally destroy most of those remaining humans on your planet. The very few who survive will hide in nuclear shelters. But the half-life of uranium, covering your planet in a deep, deep blanket, means that those survivors will not be able to come out of their shelters for over one thousand years. They will die too because they will all run out of food, water and air."

"Isn't there anything you can do?" asked Helen, her eyes opened wide at this woman's horrifying forecasts of what would surely come to pass. "You must do something or the Earth and every creature on it will perish."

"Of course, there is," Amendus stated. "We have been preparing for this situation for thousands of your years. The nature of many human beings is mutually assured destruction. While most want only Peace on Earth, tranquility for all faiths, colors and sexual preferences, and to be left alone to live their own lives, the minority of people are cruel, heartless and exist by fraud, murder and other illegal acts. So here is what we will do. My wife, please continue."

"Remember, we won't let the people on Earth end their lives. After all, you are my children," Gaia said and raised a single index finger. "Have you ever heard of a science fiction writer who wrote how atomic bombs could not detonate?"

Doug nodded. "I read his novel. It's called *The Jesus Factor* by Edwin Corley. It's a great book."

"He was a very insightful, intelligent novelist and predicted what would happen if the evil people tried to destroy the Earth. We planted that seed of an idea on the day that Edwin was conceived in his mother's belly."

"How could you do that?" Helen asked doubtfully. "No one knows what's in a child's head the day it's conceived."

"We do," Amendus said, laughing. "We simply manipulated his parent's DNA. Before that, we changed the DNA in Edwin's parent's ancestors. It wasn't even an experiment. We do it all the time."

"Do you mean like Hitler's Doctor Mengele?" Helen asked, now horrified. "He experimented on hundreds of Jews, killing some, but also harming them by fertilizing twins to see what would happen. Often, they were born with horrific birth defects."

"No, not like that," Amendus frowned. "We do these things only for the greater good."

"But back to the Atomic Factor," Gaia continued. "Edwin had it almost right but not quite. In his book he stated that any nuclear weapon could never go off in flight. It could only go off when it was stationary, like hanging from a tower. What Edwin forgot is this: back in the days when the first atom bomb was tested, the scientists fired five nails into a ball of uranium, using simple bullets, causing a chain reaction with another mass of the same material. Then there would be a chain reaction and the bomb exploded."

"Bullets from a gun?" Helen asked. "It takes only that to make an atom bomb explode?"

"That's right," Doug replied instead of Gaia. "Only bullets from a gun and a few kilos of uranium. I don't understand where you're going, Gaia. Can you explain it further?"

"It is simple," Gaia continued. "We have the ability to stop any nuclear weapon anywhere in the world. But these must have an electronic trigger. If a terrorist group gets their hands on a source of uranium, then uses a simple device like a clock, bullets and nails, it will explode causing widespread destruction."

"But where can they source uranium or plutonium?" Doug asked. "I thought most of these sources were restricted and highly classified as to their location."

"Wrong, Doug," Helen stated. "Don't you remember that the Soviet Union has its primary submersible fleet in a submarine base in Crimea? If I wanted uranium, that's where I'd go to get it."

"I see what you mean," Doug said, thinking. "It doesn't take much to swipe an entire warhead from a sub. All you need is a fake security clearance, a screwdriver and something to remove a few bolts. And rather than lift it out of the boat, because a warhead is Amazingly heavy, I'd simply swipe the plutonium, saunter off the submarine with that material in a bag like a hold-all, and leave the port."

"See how easy it would be to cause mass destruction?" Gaia continued again. "If a group of terrorists coordinated their attacks, they would hit many of the same cities and capital buildings that North Korea, China and the Soviet Union would. Not even we could stop such terrorists from carrying out such a threat to mankind."

"Will all nuclear weapons be disabled, except for these terrorists and their manual way of exploding their bombs?" Doug asked.

"No," said Amendus, decisively. "Some countries in the West will still have nuclear weapons that work. This way, they will continue to police the world."

"Like which countries?" Helen asked. "All Western countries?"

"No, only those who are a part of the Geneva Convention. The United States, England, France, Germany and a few others."

"But let me finish what I started saying a few minutes ago," Gaia said, her voice resonant with knowing. "As I said, Helen, you will dream of your future husband as a reality that is more important yet, in many ways, as far-fetched as the greatest science fiction novel you have ever read or any film based on those novels. Someday, Helen, when you are ready, Doug will point at you with feeling and it will not be a dream or a nightmare, but an integrated reality as you and Doug become one. On that day of Doug's birthday, which is 4 October 2035 you, Helen, will know a greater reality than you have ever known before. You, who will someday also be called Pookus which means The Lame One, will not only come home to all of us but will be better than ever before. You alone will be the bridge between your planet and your Solar System and the distant stars in this galaxy and many, many, many other Universes. On that day of Douglas's birthday or perhaps a few years before or after, the world will know no more war or suffering. Instead, it will only know peace for all eternity. All our gifts we give you freely will come true. We shall come from the stars to all of your many great cities including Washington D.C., Delhi, Moskva, Beijing, Tel Aviv, Jerusalem, and all other cities but in particular those that have nuclear weapons. Night will descend as we put out the sun to prove that your husband, who is also *Jesu Kristos*, will no longer be a human being but will travel from what many call Heaven to be with His children again. He shall call His visit His Unknown Second Coming. At that time, many of you will fear that this is His Second Coming as has been foretold in your Christian Holy Bible. But they will be wrong! This is His *Unknown* Second Coming. No one will recognize Him because he looks like a normal mortal. He shall have a balding grey head; he will have a beard sometimes but sometimes not and perhaps a ponytail. He will be a pilot of aircraft, and will dance with his wife to relax and entertain. One bright day, both of your voices shall announce his Holy Coming and you will be in control of all communication devices and airways, including all television, radio, printed and online news and social media. It shall be broadcast all at once across the globe and in many languages so that all people will know, and his Ancient Commandment of the Golden Rule will be repeated entirely at every hour and then every three hours and then twelve hours and then daily for an entire year on every radio, television and Internet station around the world. And that is when we shall all visit his local Church together to get on our knees and give Eternal Praise to Our God and yours.

"To codify this Fifth Book of the New Testament, He shall guide you to a Holy Mountain in northern India, the second tallest peak in the Himalayas. There, beneath the snow and ice ye shall find not only Noah's great Ark but also the Arc of the Covenant. Inside, having prized open the lid, you and your people shall also find a Golden copy of God's gift to Moses, the complete version of the Ten Commandments which are actually Eleven. But this time they shall be writ in Your God's glorious handwriting. In the ancient past, the tablet upon which our Lord God the Father wrote with his powerful finger all of the Commandments has turned to dust. What was never seen was that, prior to handing that Stone to Moses's people, the stone split in half and one of the Commandments was lost but not forever. This time, the Eleventh Commandment, which is the Golden Rule, will be writ at the top of the tablet in Jesu, which the Hebrews call Yeshua's language, but also in all other languages used on Earth. This will be a sign unto you that the Lord is come to save you again, so very soon. At his last Rising, which is not only his Second Unknown Coming but will also be, at its ending, his Last Coming, trumpets shall sound and Angels shall sing and the Glory of the Lord shall surround all people everywhere. These are the best tidings to a New Jerusalem that the world will ever sing."

Then Helen, whose eyes had glazed over, as if in a trance again or held in a fugue state, took up where Gaia had left off.

"Doug's Second coming," she faltered with words that hesitated then grew stronger, "Doug's Second Coming is some years before His Third Coming which will be my husband's final one. During His Second Unknown coming, Doug and Jesu and you, Gaia, and me too, will write a Fifth Book of the Gospel and it will only be two pages long. It is based on *The Our Father* and *The Sermon on the Mount* and the *Holy Mary* and the *Act of Contrition* and *The Apostles Creed* and many other prayers from our Catholic religion and any religion practiced by people of faith or even agnostics or atheists who believe in The Golden Rule. On that day, and that day alone, we shall bring you a greater peace that you have ever known before. From that day on, our people will rule not only our Earth but also the Solar System. We shall first go back to the Moon and then to the planet Mars with our children and our children's children aided by billionaire owners of many large companies. We shall bond together as one with many other countries like North Korea, China and Russia, too, because they will soon realize that if they do not take such action it is the end of the Earth as we know it. Should they not take actions together, all that will be left is a glowing cinder and a Black Hole where the Earth once stood. But not all is lost because there in County Kerry, Ireland, a tranquil place surrounded by tall forests, the smell of damp rain, and where birds sing in triumph, a Black Hole will soon exist; and at a seaside resort in County Cork Ireland, a Buddhist retreat built in part by our brother the Dahli Lama, we shall witness not only the end of one planet and Solar System but the beginning of a new dimension which shall be hailed by all as the beginning of a new Holy Bible and which shall be entitled: *The World's New Revelation.*

When Helen finished what sounded like a Sermon, she looked at Doug and Gaia with eyes as wide as a startled fawn. "Did I say something? If I did, I don't remember anything at all. My Lady, what happened to me? Please explain it. I'm so cold, I'm shivering."

"When we land at our Space Port, we shall take you to a warm place and let you sleep. But let us wait until we land on our giant continent which is one single country, and which my people also call Gaia. Then we will explain all of this at length. But let me end with this. I read so many books that people from your planet have written. Since humanity has started writing down the written word, I have read literally millions of books in all different languages. One genre in particular has attracted my attention and these are books concerning religion, spirituality and Christ's eventual coming. For instance, in *More Than a Carpenter* by Josh and Sean McDowell which will be published a number of Earth years from now and which will then be sent to Doug at considerable expense by his friend Don Townsend, Josh worked with his son to scientifically prove *Jesu Kristos's* future second coming. Citing many, many authorities who researched the Bible, a few of the authors' chapters of this excellent book caught my attention. For instance, on page forty-two, the author writes: *'Many people hold the opinion that if you can't prove a thing scientifically it can't be true.'* He concludes his book by writing, *'Christianity is not a religion; it's not an ethical idea; it's not a psychological phenomenon. It's a person—Jesus Christ—who is in the business of changing lives'.* What is so very interesting is this: Helen, who do you think I am? I am not just a woman, a scientist and a government leader. Can you guess who I also am—and who Doug is?"

Helen, still recovering from her waking dream, looked from the Lady to Doug then back again. As before, she hesitated for a moment, then said with conviction: "You are Our Lady Gaia and our mother, but we look at you also as The Holy Virgin which Doug and I saw many times in our dreams As for Doug, that's easy and as I said before, he is not only my future husband. Within him rests the Great Lord and Savior, Jesus Christ. He is now strong enough and large enough to carry within Him not only Doug but also our children and our children's children. It is He who will change the world with His vision of peace and a newly written Fifth Book of our Holy Bible that preaches a simple gospel: Do unto others as you would have them do unto you. Is that the answer to your question, Holy Lady?"

Doug then looked from Gaia to Helen and back again. "But I'm not Christ. I'm only Doug, aren't I?"

"Oh, you are much more than that, Doug Martin!" Gaia laughed. "Believe what your future wife has told you. You are our future! If it was not for you and a man called Jesu, and a sixteen billion-to-one lottery which I'll someday explain to you, then your planet will have nothing!"

"Don't worry," Helen said, hugging him. "I'll always be at your side. Believe that."

"And I will always be at your side," he replied, hugging her back. "That's a lot of information to foist on a simple human."

At the front of the vehicle, Amendus was now at the flight controls of the Rescue craft which he had rolled out from behind the Gaia IV's command deck wall.

"Doug, now let us do something simple; something you are used to doing," he said, turning in his seat and beckoning the American to come forward. "Why don't you take the controls? Landing is easy, much easier than a Douglas Aircraft Corporation DC-10. All you have to do is fly it like a small private aircraft. We even have a glass cockpit with an artificial horizon, as well as instruments that help you keep track of your altitude, airspeed, distance from our central Space Port, an artificial horizon to let you know if the craft is banking, yawing, turning, descending and time until landing. Our glass cockpit even has something like a VOR radio. Much like Ham Radio, as you know, it signals in Morse Code then repeats itself. You fly this vehicle around the Space Port, then descend on a glidepath until you are given permission to land. Then you talk to Space Port ground control for permission to taxi to the terminal and disembark all of your passengers and crew."

"Is there that much traffic that it requires a ground controller? How does he communicate?" Doug asked.

"The same way you do. With a radio. Rather than using telepathy, which we often do, I've asked Space Command to talk to you in plain English over the radio."

The Rescue Craft passed the other planets of the Gaian Solar System as Helen looked out the window.

"Look at that, Doug. That planet is bright green and has multi-colored rings. It looks the same as Neptune only rather than blue, that planet has flecks of gold and red in it. And over there! On the surface. What do you think those five giant light blue spirals are?"

"Hurricanes high in the planet's atmosphere, just like your Neptune," Amendus said. "We call that planet 'Neptune Two', named after that planet in your Solar System. Helen, strap yourself in. We're about to make our final approach to the Star Port." He glanced at Doug, winking. "Doug, you know how to fly. Want to make the approach?"

With Amendus in the left seat as the spacecraft's Captain, Doug took the right seat, sitting next to him. He looked in front of him and saw a glass cockpit that could have been the instrument panel for many small aircraft he'd ever flown.

"This looks just like a normal instrument panel on our commercial airliners or private aircraft," Doug said. "Why do you use similar technologies to us when you come from another galaxy with much better scientists?"

"Simple," Gaia said as she took a seat next to Helen behind the two pilots. "We developed the technologies you have first. We planted them in your heads before the dawn of humankind."

Sitting at his station, the Captain of the ship ran through his pre-burn and pre-landing checklist. "Spacedrive. Off. Wings and stabilizers extending." He punched a button and Doug saw a light flash.

"Why is that red light flashing?"

"We've extended our flying wings, vertical stabilizer and horizontal stabilators to control the ship when we enter the atmosphere," Amendus replied, and turned in his seat to face his passengers. "Helen, in a minute you will look up to see flashes of light which command modules like your most recent spaceship, the NASA shuttles, experience when they re-enter Earth's atmosphere."

"So it really does fly like a plane?" Doug asked.

"Yes, it does," Amendus said and struck another button. Their seats slid closer to the control panel as dual control yokes extended from the middle of the panel. "We are not in the atmosphere yet but test the yoke just like you would in one of your aircraft."

Doug tried it. The yoke behaved just like any he had used in any other airplane he had ever flown before. "I'm testing the control surfaces?"

"That is correct. What we both call in English the ailerons and stabilators."

"But where are the rudder pedals?" Doug asked, looking at the floor in front of his seat.

"We do not need them," Gaia explained from behind him. "It is a very, very stable vehicle. It flies through the air like a normal Earth aircraft only it does not require a rudder because it has stabilators."

Amendus ran through the glass instrument panel with Doug, showing him all of it. Doug was surprised that the glass panel was as simple as what he was trained in by his dad: first in an Aeronca 7AC Champ and then in a Cessna 190.

"This is so easy to understand!" Doug exclaimed as his Captain took him through the instruments. "There's the altimeter and airspeed. There's the compass and turn & bank. And right there," Doug said, tapping the panel, "is the rate of descent and climb."

Amendus laughed again. "It is so easy to fly! And, as you know, simple when you know how."

The Rescue Vehicle began its descent into the controlled airspace around Gaia, which to Helen seemed bigger than The Republic of India. "It's Amazing!" she said, looking down on forests, streams, rice paddies and ancient temples. "What's that huge statue down there?"

"That is Buddha, our Lord and Brother. Many on our planet are Buddhists and come here daily to worship him. See how they do it?" Gaia explained. "All they take with them is a candle and a match to light it. Then they say prayers and clap hands once to three times." The Lady bowed her head and prayed in a language that neither Helen or Doug could understand.

"I speak in the Hindi language to say their prayers," Gaia continued. "Some Buddhists here practice the Hindu religion, too, to worship many of their multiple gods."

In the left seat, Amendus keyed a standard microphone. "Mahatma Gandhi approach, this is Rescue One. We are ten miles out and would like a straight in approach."

"Mahatma Gandhi?" Helen asked. "You named your airport after that famous Indian leader?"

"Yes," Gaia said and looked out the window as they approached the space port. "He was a man of peace but he died by violence. It is important to both our entire population as well as yours that we do not forget the teachings that he put into daily practice."

Doug listened as the radio speaker crackled. "Rescue One, this is Gandhi approach. We know that the Royal Queen is onboard. Approach approved. Many are waiting to meet you now that you've returned from your latest mission."

"Doug, you have the aircraft," Amendus commanded as he took his hands off the controls. "I will monitor the instruments and radio. You fly the airplane."

"Airplane?" Doug said with excitement. "This is nothing like an airplane."

"When it is in any type of thick atmosphere, it flies just like any of your standard aircraft," Gaia said, smiling as Doug started to laugh. "Just let the vehicle do the work. Fly it and have fun."

Doug took the controls and tested them. He swung the wheel to the right and the aircraft banked to the right. When he turned the control yoke to the left, it banked accordingly.

Helen watched as out the large window which had been revealed when the Rescue vehicle had extended its wings, she could see them descending through dark clouds. Then the radio crackled to life again.

"Rescue One, this is Gandhi approach. We have thunderstorms in the area. Just follow my instructions as we vector you around the storms Then continue your straight-in approach. Turn left to a heading of two-nine-zero degrees."

At the command, Doug used the compass on the instrument panel to turn to the heading. After two or three minutes, Approach control ordered them to bank to a different heading. After Doug had complied with the instruction, the Gain controller said, "Rescue, you're a mile from the airport. Do you see the runway?"

Through the clouds, Doug saw blinking red lights that marked the end of the runway. Then he made out bright white lights that outlined both sides of the landing strip.

"Roger that, Approach. We got it."

As they neared the runway, Doug could see huge white painted letters which read: 090, the heading of the runway.

"Rescue, altimeter is 1127 hectopascals," the Approach Controller confirmed. "Wind at zero-one-two-one at sixty knots."

"You use standard European barometer settings?" Doug asked as he settled in his seat to prepare for the landing.

"Where do you think the people from Earth learned them?" Gaia said, chuckling again. "That, too, is something we gave to you many years ago."

"You have a right crosswind that is severe due to the thunderstorm, Doug," Amendus warned as he pointed at the bright orange wind sock. "See how the flag is whipping around?"

All Doug did was grin. "When Dad taught me to fly, he told me that in a crosswind as strong as this, all you have to do is this."

Doug crabbed into the wind and, as the aircraft neared the runway, he banked the plane right then pulled the throttles back, pushing down a lever to lower the wheels. He looked at the TV monitors above his head, seeing the landing gear extend. As the four tires neared the concrete landing strip, Doug pulled back on the yoke as far as he could. Rescue One touched down as smooth as silk.

"Not bad for a first landing, was it?" Doug asked. "Was that okay to you, Captain?"

Amendus glared at him and said, "If you did any better, I would be out of a job and you would be the next chief pilot." Then he glanced back at Gaia. "My Lady, should I hand in my resignation? You have a better pilot than me right here."

"If you hand it in I shall tear it in two, husband!" Gaia retorted. "Now I have two Chief Pilots to command at least two Star Fleets."

After touching down, Helen saw two Y-Wing fighters through the window as they screamed past their ship. Doug and Helen watched as the spacecraft did barrel rolls in honour of their Queen returning home, then pulled up to vertical, disappearing into white cumulous clouds.

As Rescue One cleared the runway, they were met by four large ground vehicles with water cannons which drenched their spacecraft in welcome. Then Doug noticed a stubby vehicle with a Follow Me sign written in English on the back and placed there for his benefit which blinked orange on a yellow steel plate. He followed it as it led them to a large hanger. Inside, they could all see a set of risers lining both sides of the massive building. Both stands were filled with citizens of the planet, Gaia explained as they taxied in: farmers, technicians, school teachers and fishermen to name but a few. "See the central set of risers between the two stands?" the Queen continued to explain. "Those are Ambassadors from around our galaxy and Solar System." As Doug taxied slowly toward the open hanger doors, he saw a human woman who behaved like a ramp agent on Earth who met returning aircraft as they taxied up to a terminal. Using two bright orange batons, the woman waved them in. As they taxied, Helen noticed a massive crowd standing on each side of their vehicle. Some held up large signs printed in a language she could not read. Others held huge banners that spelled out WELCOME! in English. Many of the creatures she saw looked like Gaia and Amendus but others looked like normal people from Earth. They all cheered and waved at the spacecraft as it taxied past them.

When the craft had fully entered the hanger, Amendus pointed out the engine shut down control. "Just touch that button," he ordered. Doug touched the button and they could hear the engine wind to a stop.

"Home," they all breathed and, as they opened the door, the vehicle filled with the cheering of an immense crowd and the playing of a large brass band.

Chapter Twenty-Two

As the door to the Rescue vehicle opened, the four passengers were greeted by more cheering and they could all hear a nearby brass band playing a military march.

"What's that song?" Amendus asked. "Gaia, was that created on our planet?"

"Not at all," Helen smiled as she was led down the spaceship's stairs by Doug. "That's a tune that the Glen Miller Marching Band played during World War Two. It's called *The Saint Louis Blues March*." She watched the band as it marched past them and turned to Doug. "Those band members are humans, not creatures from this planet. How did human beings get here?"

"I've no idea. But in your dreams you talk to your daughter, and Gaia has promised you that she's safe and now living here. Maybe those people in the marching band came to this planet the same way. They passed on and Gaia made them live again. When you meet Josie, you can ask her."

Doug and Helen turned again toward the crowd. With the Royal couple, they stood on the steps as the band, all members of the U.S. Army Air Force, finished the number then turned and saluted. Gaia and Amendus returned the salute then walked off the steps of the Gaia IV Rescue vehicle. At the bottom of the stairs, Doug studied the conductor of the band. The tall, thin man was wearing a Major's uniform and wore rimless glasses. He held a baton in his hand and bowed to the planet's Queen as she passed him.

"Helen, look at that guy. Do you know who that is?"

"I don't believe it. That's Glen Miller. But he's dead! He died at the very end of World War Two when the airplane he was flying in got lost on its way to France."

Doug put a hand on her shoulder. "I guess what we talked about a moment ago is true. Here, death seems to mean nothing."

As they walked with Gaia and Amendus toward a tall podium, they were introduced to the Mayor of the Gaian City of Seattle. When

Helen asked the Queen why the city had been named after a leader of a Washington State Native American tribe, she explained that it had been called after the famous warrior for very good reasons. "We honor bravery not only on this planet but throughout our Universe," Gaia explained. "This honorable chief of a Native people gave a speech in your year eighteen fifty-four. He chided the white people for ignoring the environment of their planet and is reported to have laughed in the face of many politicians and business people, behaviour that could have been met by imprisonment or execution. His words will someday be put into action as you people attempt to save your Earth. Courage, as you know, is a commodity that cannot be ignored."

The mayor Seattle walked up and presented them all with medals for heroism. When it came time for Helen to get hers, Gaia took it from the mayor and hung the multi-colored ribbon with the gold medallion over her neck, herself.

"You deserve this and many more medals," Gaia said, her face serious. "You not only saved Doug with your bravery but by rescuing him, you also saved the future of your planet. You want to ask me why but I can only say that someday I will share that secret with you as well as your family."

They all stepped up to a group of microphones. The Gaian Press took pictures and asked millions of questions all at once but Amendus put up his hands. "Please, please, you must ask your questions in English so that all of our visitors and residents from Earth will also understand. But let Our Lady Gaia speak first."

Gaia took the microphone and cleared her throat, speaking in English so that Doug and Helen could also understand. "It is so good to be back to my home," she said but the crowd roared again, drowning her out.

Behind them, she noticed a bearded Hindu scholar walking toward her. His face was sad, his eyes red from crying. Gaia stepped back from the Podium and had a brief word with him.

"What's going on, Amendus?" Helen asked. "Look at the man's face. It has to be bad news."

Then the man walked up to the microphone

"We have just received news from Delhi on Earth that our beloved Prime Minister Indira Gandhi has been assassinated and has passed on into the hands of Shiva, our lord and master. As we all know, she fought the great battle and won. She served our Indian republic for over fifteen years by our Earthly timekeeping. That nation is in mourning as are all of the people from India who have been raised up from Earth to Gaia and are now citizens of this planet."

The entire crowd rose, many crying, as they broke into the Hymn, *God Save the Queen*. When they were finished, the Hindu man said, "Now, let us pray for our dead Prime Minister, Indira Gandhi." The large crowd bowed their heads, praying in many languages. When they were finished, they all started applauding.

"Why did the crowd sing *God Save the Queen*?" Doug asked. "Do they still care about Great Britain and the Queen of England?"

"Of course, they do," Amendus answered. "Here, we have many who have ancestors in England, India and across the British Commonwealth. For them, the throne of Great Britain is their throne, too. They honour a distant Prime Minister and a Queen of England who has served their peoples well. That is why they sing and now cheer."

When the cheers were finished, the scholar was replaced by a middle-aged man dressed as a member of English royalty and wearing a small crown on his head. He bowed to the crowd then said a short prayer. After that, he walked to the row of chairs behind him.

"Doug, is that who I think it is?" Helen asked hesitantly as she watched him take a seat with the rest of the VIP visitors.

"Who do you think it is? It can't be an English King. Queen Elizabeth is still on the throne."

"It can't be," Helen said, her eyes wide. "That King of England died years ago right after World War Two ended."

"Who is it?"

"King George the Sixth. The King who stuttered."

They turned to Gaia who smiled mysteriously and said, "I told you; you are our children. No one who has died since we visited your planet thousands of years ago has truly passed away. They've all been taken to a place many call Heaven and some call Nirvana, which is this planet Gaia or other planets in our Solar System or our galaxy, and are alive. In fact, they'll never die again. Some of course, like Indira Gandhi, choose to stay on Earth for some time as unseen spirits. But eventually, she too will come to me as will all others."

"You've defeated death as you told me when my Josie died?" Helen asked in almost a whisper. "You mean we all live forever?"

"No," explained Amendus. "Not quite. For every life a living being must pay with one death. People die but they re-incarnate almost instantly. They can choose whatever body they want, as long as it's made of living tissue. They cannot come back as a rock or mineral but why would anyone want to be some sort of inorganic material? If you're not yet dead but even terminally ill, then you will be healed with the gift we shall someday bring you."

"As we discussed before," Gaia said, "nature is a funny creature. There are so many diseases that remain untreatable back on your planet. But soon, when we give you our code, every disease in the world will disappear *like that*."

And Amendus snapped his fingers to emphasis his wife's point.

"No more dementia, cancer or other diseases?"

"None," Amendus replied. "But many of your people will die before you will learn to understand our code."

When Helen yawned Gaia took her by the elbow. "Child are you sleepy? You've had a long few days. We were up early and now it's well after midnight."

"Is it really that late?" Doug asked. "Then let's go to bed. Do you have two bedrooms we can use? You see, I promised Helen that we would never sleep together until the day of our wedding."

"We know you are not married yet," Amendus replied. "I'm afraid our guest hotel is almost full due to Gaia's arrival celebration.

We have only one room left which has one bed. But it's so big, wide and soft that you'll both be asleep in an instant."

"When we wake up can I see Josie, My Lady?" Helen asked.

"Yes. But do not be afraid if you do not recognize your own child. She is now much older than when you last met her at your home in Long Island. She is now on a special assignment on this, our planet. When you see her you must continue to call her Sally Simpson. When you meet her you will be as proud of her as I am of my daughter Helen."

"If you tell me Josie is still called Sally, that's what I'll call her, too," Helen said. "If that's your will, mother, then that's what I'll also do. I just so much look forward to seeing her, no matter what she's called."

✈ ✈ ✈

When Helen and Doug were dressed for bed, Doug turned out the lights. He sat by Helen's side, stroking her soft hair as she slept. When her eyelids flickered he knew she was dreaming. He carefully crawled over her and into bed, covering himself and Helen with a warm down blanket. Soon, he too was sleeping while beside him, Helen dreamed that they were in Vermont. A tribute band to Glen Miller played a medley of the famous band leader's compositions.

In her dream, Helen thought she and Doug were married that very night, and it was Christmas Eve. In her nighttime fantasy Mr Miller was on a stage near their wedding bed and introduced Bing Crosby. As an unseen crowd roared the star's welcome, Bing crossed the stage to the microphone. Then, as a band played, he broke into song with _Too Ra Loo Ra Loo Ral_. Helen found herself on a dance floor Among the invited guests, including her mother, father, aunts, uncles and cousins, all of whom had passed away many years ago. She looked up to find herself in Doug's arms A golden wedding band glistened on her ring finger, which she noticed as she placed her hand in Doug's right hand.

"Are we really married? But it can't be Christmas. Not on this foreign planet."

"Don't you remember? At 3P.M. today a Catholic priest married us. Josie was our flower girl. She threw rose petals as we walked down the central aisle of our church in a town not far from here."

"I can't remember. How old is Josie?"

"Four," Doug said, holding up a hand and counting off his fingers. "She was so cute dressed in her white dress. She looked just like her mother and grandmother, except her skin was white as snow."

"Will I see her again?"

"Sure you will. We both will. Josie calls me Daddy now. I guess what I dreamed about you and your family was true. I really am her dad."

Doug gripped Helen's hand tight. Now belly-to-belly, he guided her through the other dancers. As they waltzed around the floor, Doug pointed out his relatives who had come to watch their first wedding dance.

"That's my uncle, Harry but he died twenty years ago," he said, his voiced awed. "That's my sister, Judy."

"I didn't know you had a sister," Helen replied over the music of the band. "When did she die?"

"Judy died of Alzheimer's five years ago, before I met you. You would have loved her just as I do."

With the song finished, Mr Cosby stepped again to the podium. "This is for our wedding couple, Helen and Doug. Now put your hands together and let's all get on the dance floor for a jitterbug with Glen Miller!"

The famous conductor led his band, playing one of Doug's favorites, In the Mood. "Come on, Helen. Let's do it!" He swung her around a dozen times and everyone on the dance floor was laughing. When he twirled her, Helen got dizzy and asked to sit down. "Doug, please! Let me find a chair. There's one over there." She pointed to a table but Doug wouldn't let her stop dancing. As they turned again, brushing shoulders with other couples, he turned his wife around and almost collided with another couple.

"Excuse me," he said, then looked up to see his long-dead parents. "I don't believe it. What are you doing here?"

"Did you think we'd miss your wedding?" his father Bill replied. "Why don't you introduce Helen to your mother and me?"

After drying his eyes, Doug led Helen forward. "Honey, may I introduce you to my mom, Mary Rose."

As the two women shook hands and hugged, his mother looked at her new daughter-in-law with approval.

"You know, Helen, Doug dated many women before he found you. I didn't trust any of them. I thought they'd never be good enough for my son. This time, I am certain he's got things right. Now come here, daughter. You're my favourite because you've married my son."

Taking Helen in her arms, they hugged. When they parted, Mr Miller stepped to the mic. "Folks, we're having a brief intermission as we change the stage to a new setting. Why not have some coffee or a drink? So sit back and relax for just a minute."

The lights flicked on and off once, then onto the stage walked Bing Cosby. This time, the famous crooner sang *I'm Dreaming of a White Christmas,* a song that Helen had loved since childhood. Believing that she was still dreaming, she again found herself held tight in Doug's arms, his hands more real than any dream she could have had. With her hand on his shoulder and his right hand grasping her fingers, the couple danced again. It was only then that Helen looked down at her clothes and realized that she was wearing a bridal gown. She looked again at her ring finger. Next to her diamond engagement ring she still wore a wedding band of solid gold.

"I have to be dreaming!" Helen said to her new husband. "It can't be Christmas, not now."

Suddenly, she found herself back in bed with Doug. Thinking she was still dreaming, for the first time they made love. Doug, a tender lover, touched both of her breasts gently, then her belly and her hair and stroked her ears. Then he moved into her and Helen gasped, "Doug. Remember, this is my first time with you. I don't know what to do to make you happy."

"Well I do, Helen," he said, smiling down at her. "I already know how to make you happy. So just relax, sweetheart, until this wonderful journey is over."

Helen woke up with Doug still sleeping next to her. She then noticed that her nightdress was wet. Getting a towel from off the bottom of the bed, she wiped down her whole body.

"Sweetheart, are you all right?" Doug asked, stretching his arms high. He leaned over, smiling at her. "I had the most wonderful dream last night."

"So did I. I dreamed we were married and then we finally made love."

His eyes went wide. "That's what I dreamed! But it was just a dream, wasn't it?"

She gazed at him and as she did, his eyes traveled down her body to the wet spot on her skin. He touched it. "Helen, it's sticky."

"I know. I felt it too. Doug, do you think we really made love?"

"No, Helen, we're not married yet. You know what we promised each other."

A few minutes later, they heard a knock at the door. When Doug opened it, a tray full of food lay on the floor in the hallway. Picking it up, he also noticed a card. He handed it to Helen and she opened it.

"It's a congratulations card," she whispered. "It's signed by your mom and dad."

"That can't be right." When she handed it to him, he read it as they ate at the hotel table. "That's what it says. And those signatures look very familiar. I dreamed we met Mom and Dad. Is that what you dreamed?"

As she nodded, Helen felt a rumble in her belly and rushed to the bathroom. There, she knelt by the toilet bowl and got sick. Then, knowing that she had eaten nothing that would make her vomit, she dressed quickly and, leaving the bedroom, told Doug what had happened.

"Honey, you stay here. It will only take me a minute to get dressed."

"What happened? Did you get sick?"

"Yes, and I'd like to see a doctor. I may have picked up a bug when we came here. Gaia must have different viruses than those on Earth."

When she left the hotel room, she ran into the small village and did her best to find a doctor who would see her but every office and business was closed. It was then that she ran into Gaia.

"What is wrong, Helen? Why are you frowning? Why is your brow wet and your cheeks white? Is it something you ate?"

"No, Mam. I mean…My Lady."

"That's right, you are my child, so use the word 'Mam.'. Didn't I already tell you multiple times that I'm really your mother? In a simultaneous lifetime, you called me both 'Mam' and 'Josephine'. So go on, my daughter, what were you saying?"

"I think I'm pregnant. I didn't want to tell Doug because he'd think I'm crazy. Mam, we have to make love for me to get pregnant."

Gaia smiled winsomely. "You're not only pregnant, you're pregnant with twins. A girl and a boy."

"Fraternal twins? How do you know?"

"Well, if you don't believe me, try this."

Gaia handed Helen a pregnancy kit, just like the ones she'd seen in the chemists back on Earth.

"Go on, lamb. Go to the toilet. Then, you'll be convinced."

Helen tiptoed back into the bedroom, past Doug who had fallen back to sleep. She went into the bathroom and quietly closed the door. Sitting down on the toilet, she urinated. Putting the small stick into the stream. of urine, she withdrew it, shook the droplets off, waited thirty seconds and looked at it. The small white wand was blue. It was then that she knew for certain that, just as her mother Gaia had said, she was expecting at least one child.

In the morning, she told Doug. On his hand he also wore a golden wedding band.

"Then what we both thought was a dream last night was real," he said to his new wife as they both dressed for the day. "And you're truly pregnant?"

"Look, sweetheart," she answered, pointing at her swollen belly. "Already, I can't fit into my trousers. I have to wear a dress."

"It's a gift that I've wanted for years, Helen," he whispered into her ear as he hugged her. "A child for next Fall. Maybe it will be a girl."

"Or a boy. It makes no difference to me as long as our baby is healthy."

Finished dressing, Doug heard a knock on the door. A Gaian officer stood there and bowed.

"I am sorry to bother you, Mr Masters. The Queen has requested your attendance at the Space Port Command Center."

"Please tell the Queen that we'll be there in just a minute. My wife is getting dressed."

As the door closed, Doug mouthed the word again. 'Wife', he uttered silently. "I never thought I'd love one word so much."

Chapter Twenty-Three

With the celebrations for the Royal homecoming over, the entire planet immediately got down to business. The first thing on Gaia's list concerned the state of the birthplace of the Gaian civilization, planet Earth. While they had transmitted a code that would provide all of humanity with everything they needed that Gaia and Amendus had previously described to Helen and Doug, they needed a detailed DNA analysis of the human race to prevent future diseases. Having given the order to her scientists to visit that planet in human disguise, Gaia decided she had to act again due to the new, dangerous conditions that existed on Earth.

"Admiral of Space Command, come in," Gaia said as she keyed a mic in the Space Port's Command Center. The Admiral immediately came back.

"Cummings here, Ma'am," the Admiral who had been born on Earth replied over a speaker. "Reading you five-by-five."

"Where are you now?"

"We've moved Space Station Chandra as ordered. As you know, Ma'am, the station has been revolving around Betelgeuse in the Orion Constellation for the past fifty Earth years. We have been changing our position occasionally, hoping to receive a reply from Earth's scientists or astronomers. However, while our receivers located on the dark side of Earth's moon have picked up our signal, the human's SETI network has not heard it despite the fact that we're rebroadcasting our code every ten seconds using Gaian transceivers so that anyone on Earth can pick it up in real time. We even started to recycle that broadcast, repeating it in standard Earth Morse Code and in multiple languages every ten second."

"Still nothing comes back from Earth?"

"Not a thing, Ma'am. Those that hear it must think it's background noise from space or interference. As to Morse? Few know how to use it to communicate with it anymore."

Thinking hard, she rekeyed her mic. "Admiral, move the Space Station immediately. Put it in a stationary geocentric orbit over Washington, D.C. but ensure that no one on that planet can see you. Then place broadcast repeaters above every major capital in that world including London, Paris, Seoul, Berlin and Toronto as well as the capitals of every nation with nuclear weapons such as Russia, North Korea, China, India, Israel, Pakistan and any country who side against peace. If Earth-bound scientists can't hear it then, they must all be deaf! Expedite that order immediately."

"Will send that order out ASAP, My Lady. This is Cummings, signing off."

Gaia contemplated her quick action and possible consequences to planet Earth, just as Helen and Doug came into the Space Command Central Control Room. Helen looked as if she was already four months pregnant even though, only moments ago, she thought she was only a month gone. Doug walked toward his now mother-in-law and bowed. When he looked up, he noticed the frown on the Royal Lady's face as she studied a bank of TV monitors.

"What's going on?" Doug asked, as he looked up at four of the screens. "Is that the Turner Broadcasting Network as well as NBC and ABC news? What's that Fox News television? I've never heard of it."

"While you were sleeping, my son, I decided to let you know what time it really is on Earth. It is no longer the decade of the nineteen-eighties on your planet. Now it is the decade of sin, the twenty-twenties."

"But why did you do that, my mother Gaia?" Helen asked. "Why have we lost all those years of life?"

"You didn't, my child. You must remember that you and Doug have traveled at speeds over that of light. Beyond lightspeed, time moves forward slowly or rapidly depending on your speed and distance to any final target. But you are still the age that you were before you left Earth to travel to our galaxy."

"My mother, are you saying that time actually moves forward if a person goes beyond the speed of light?"

"So it does, Douglas. That's the order of physics and astronomy, and the laws that they bring. Someday soon, your Earth scientists will find the same natural secrets that we have."

Amendus had been standing with a Gaian General. Having heard the conversation, he stepped closer.

"We're monitoring all of the broadcast news from Earth," Amendus explained. "The news on any station, including the BBC,

Ukrainian TV, the Journal and Sky News isn't at all good." He glanced at Doug. "My son, you should know that the Turner Network is now known as CNN. Compared to when you left the planet, your Earth now has many, many more transmission stations."

On CNN, a television announcer turned to camera. "This is Chris Wallace reporting. We're sorry to interrupt our regular programming but we've just received this News Flash from the Associated Press. The Ukraine has been invaded by an overpowering army of Russian soldiers protected by columns of tanks, missiles and supersonic jet fighters."

"Russian?" Helen asked. "What happened to the Soviet Union?"

"It is gone," Gaia said. "The strongmen of that fractured country were cowards and drank too much alcohol. A man who is now dead but famous named Gorbachev helped to knock down the walls between his many countries and what you all call the West. But now a new leader, Vladimir Putin, is determined to bring back the old Soviet Union. He will continue to do that with deceit, theft and lies."

On a screen above them, a reporter showed a map of the various battlefields across the Ukraine.

"Crimea was always part of the Ukraine," Doug said as the reporter explained in English how the Russian government were determined to get back what was rightfully theirs. "Has Russia taken control of a peninsula that is rightfully the Ukraine's?"

"No, Doug, listen to the reporter," Helen replied. "Putin annexed it!"

"I don't know who this Putin is, not yet anyway, but this thug has gone too far. The Western world will never stand for it. They'll force his hand with sanctions and the war will stop soon."

"I don't think so, Doug," Helen replied. "Putin has far too much to gain. I read about him when I was growing up in Ireland and many times when we lived in Long Island. All that man wants is power and wealth. And now that he has it he'll never give it up."

"Yes, and he now has far too much to lose to stop the bloodshed," Amendus added. "If he is not careful he will cause wholesale mass annihilation due to nuclear war. This is a turning point on your home planet and why my wife made the decision for you both to see this. Someday soon, we need you to help us stop this murderous human being."

The four of them watched the television monitors for over twelve hours as Putin's Army defeated one battalion of Ukrainian soldiers after another. Then, the president of the Ukraine—President Zelensky—was interviewed by Chris Wallace on a satellite link from Kyiv.

"We will not surrender, we will not lose, we will fight to the end," the president said, wearing his military green T-Shirt and sounding like a young Winston Churchill as he also talked to the British Parliament and United States Senate via the satellite link. "We do not want to lose what we have, what is ours. just the same way as you once didn't want to lose your country when the Nazis started World War Two and you had to fight for the survival of Britain and America."

Wallace broke away from the interview, interjecting: "The President of the United States also spoke of the fifty children 'who could have lived' had they evacuated their city near the Russian boarder but instead were killed by Russian missiles, along with those Ukrainian people dying from dehydration and hypothermia where the population centers had been blockaded by Russian tanks and troops."

"How are you able to watch Earth transmissions from here?" Doug asked. "We're more than four lightyears from Earth."

Gaia just smiled. "That's our secret. One of many which you will receive when your people finally break the code. By the way, Doug. Happy Birthday.

"What day is it? It can't possibly be October the fourth."

"But it is," Gaia replied. "See the date being broadcast on the BBC? Funny how time works in outer space. On Earth, it's the fourth of October. How old are you today, my son?"

"I forget," he added. "What's another year, more or less."

"Well, you're older than I am by eight years and I'm thirty-three," Helen added. "So if I'm thirty-three, you're forty-one. Doug, what do you want for your birthday?"

"I have everything I want right here," he said, again taking her in his arms He showed her his ring finger. On it his wedding band glistened in the overhead lights. "See? I always hoped that we would get married at Christmas, remember? My wish has come true."

"Just like the song that Jiminy Cricket sang in the Disney film *Pinocchio.*"

"Just like that."

And despite the fact that their Gaian parents stood in front of them, watching, they kissed each other. "Helen, you're also giving us a child. What more could I want for my birthday?" He glanced back up at the TV monitors. "When I think of the people who are suffering right now, I know how lucky I am."

The couple were interrupted when this time good news broke. Fox News came on the air with a Special Report.

Neil Cavuto reported this time from the Fox News Times Square studio that the Ukrainians were winning all battles on most fronts. Their armies had kicked the Russians out of the western Ukraine and were now concentrating on the east of the country.

"What the hell happened?" Doug asked as Cavuto kept reporting. "A minute ago, it was the start of the war but now the Ukrainians are winning?"

"That's the miracle of controlling time," Gaia said. "We can dial through time like you dial an analogue radio. We can stop the transmission to view it closer or record audio and video, or go back in history or forward a million years and more. All of this, too, you will receive from our gift of the code."

"Oh my God. Look at the fighting and all of the body bags," Helen yelped as they all watched a live report from the Eastern

Ukraine about the body count and casualties on both sides. Then a retired U.S. Army Officer, Colonel Cedric Leighton, came on air live from CNN studios in New York City.

"The Russian strategy has been to topple the Ukrainian government but they've failed. They want to prevent the U.S. and other supporters to stop providing the Ukrainian fighting forces with additional weaponry. Then, they want to conscript as many Russian men as possible, using them as part of this campaign. It's going to be a very difficult thing for Putin to do. Already, hundreds if not thousands of men have escaped by crossing boarders into other former Soviet Union countries as well as Poland."

"Russia's going to lose, aren't they?" Helen asked.

"It's inevitable."

Amendus placed his hand on his shoulder. "Let us move away from bloodshed and instead to a message of profound hope. This is something both my wife and I want you to watch. It was recorded by the Ukrainian Army only yesterday, as they marched across the Indian Himalayan Mountains to surprise Putin's Generals preparing for battle in Pakistan." Amendus turned to a corpsman in the Command Center. "Soldier, please play the recording I gave you earlier today."

"Yes, sir," the soldier replied. A monitor above them flickered. When the transmission cleared, they could see a man dressed in a snow-white uniform holding a piece of wood.

"The man talks English so all will understand," Amendus explained. "When you hear what he has to say and show you, you will know better the great gifts that we bestow on you as well as those much larger than most of us."

Helen drew closer to Doug as the man on the TV monitor began talking.

"My name is Uri Pavel. I am a soldier in the Ukrainian Army but I am also a lecturer in archeology. I stand on Mount Kamal in the Indian Himalayan mountains. What I hold in my hand is very special." He held up what appeared to be an old piece of parchment. "This is a map of the Himalayan mountains. The inscriptions, which can barely be read, are all in Hebrew. Here, there is an X. It is exactly the position I'm now standing on. Our team. found this in a museum in Kyiv where it had been stored for centuries and never noticed by any of the museum staff. This is the map that led our army here. We will battle Putin's forces in four days but our government asked us to divert eight-hundred kilometers to check this. But if this is special because it is so old, then so is this. Even more special. In fact, I call it unique."

He looked down at a long piece of white wood he held in both hands. To Doug's eyes, it looked practically new, like something he might use to fix a wooden table in their home in New York. "We found this long plank yesterday. It was buried in a deep crevasse. This piece was pushed out by meltwater and is special because no such species of tree has ever grown so high in any mountains of the world. That would be impossible. I have taken the opportunity to have it carbon dated. This piece of pine is well over three-thousand years old. While some people build cabins made of wood in the high mountains, we have determined that this is not from any kind of cabin known to modern humanity."

He turned and, as his cameraman followed, climbed through some rock scrabble before standing at a crevasse. "I cannot take you down because it is too deep. When we found this piece of wood and knowing how old it is, this morning we descended five hundred feet on ropes. With light, we recorded what I show you now. I have had this edited so it is all one video."

The transmission blurred then the archeologist came back on the screen again. This time, he stood against a wall of long white planks. He placed his hand on it, looking up at what seemed to Doug like the side of a large wooden ship. "Humankind has been searching for this wreckage since time immemorial. Some thought they had found it in eastern Turkey. Others say it landed in the high mountains of Africa.

Yet more have speculated that the original Ark could never have existed. That men three-thousand years ago did not have the knowledge or tools to build such a ship."

The camera followed the Army soldier as he walked beside the long length of white wooden planks. "Can you direct more light up here my friend?" The cameraman did as he was asked. Two long cuts in the timber spaced thirty feet apart, obviously a large doorway, ran from the top to the bottom of the camera's field of vision. "Yes, if you guessed, then you guessed right. This is an immense entryway. We do not have room to lower it completely in this small location penned in by rock and ice. I would not call it so much a door but a gangway. We have been inside the ship. In a moment I will add what we have found there."

The TV monitor went black. Doug looked to Helen. "Is that what I think it is?"

"If you mean Noah's Ark, that's impossible! The wood would have all rotted by now."

"Not in a dry environment like a crevasse in a high mountain. It's so cold there's no moisture there. Archeologists have found wooden tools that are hundreds of thousands of years old."

The TV monitor lit up again. This time, the archeologist was pointing at what remained of a large wooden box. "We have removed it and placed it here. As you can see, this container made of pine is approximately 3 meters long. When we used tools to take the top off, we found another wooden box, this time made of acacia wood which is still found in Egypt. When we removed that box, we found this." The camera panned down, focusing on a glittering golden flat surface. Hebrew words had been cut into it. The archeologist placed a palm on it. "This, my friends, is the treasure we have all tried to discover for many, many hundreds of years. This is only the protective top of what was beneath it. The Hebrew inscription reads: *Beware the Finger of God for He alone tells Truth which has been Placed Reverently Inside.* In one moment, I will give you all the Arc of the Covenant. What you will see now, only a few eyes have seen. No human eyes have seen what we now show you for over three-thousand years."

The camera swung. A golden box fitted with two giant eagles, their wings spread, came into view. It also sat on the stone floor. To Doug, the box looked like an ancient Egyptian sarcophagus. As they watched, the archaeologist put his hand into the immense golden artifact. When he withdrew it, he held a fist full of sand.

"Ah-hah! You were thinking that I would hold some sort of ancient treasure? It is only sand, but is it? At the bottom of the Arc, we found a large piece of sandstone. On it was written in Hebrew what we now are certain is the final commandment of God our Father, the Tenth." He walked to a large piece of flat red rock that had been stood up against the wall of Noah's Ark. "In this light you can just make out the Hebrew writing. It says, 'You shall not covet thy neigh…'. Then the stone is broken. But over here, we have yet another piece that we have found." He steps to his right. The camera focuses on it. "I am no scholar in the Talmud nor am I a religious scholar of any kind. I have had a friend of mine also in our Army translate this, too. He has fluent Hebrew because he is Jewish. This is what this piece of an ancient tablet states clearly and in full."

The camera swung down revealing a complete piece of the large tablet. As the archeologist pointed with a finger to each word, he translated the sentence.

"This is my last commandment I give you and it is My Eleventh. Treat other people as you would have them treat you. This shall be known as MY GOLDEN RULE and will be taught to you by my Son who will follow after me whom ye shall call Yesu."

The camera swung back to the archeologist's face. It was filled with awe. "I am with the Ukrainian Orthodox faith. And yes, I believe that this last commandment was written by the finger of our God the Father. I also believe that the golden box I showed you earlier really is the Arc of the Covenant and what we found inside are the remains of the original stone tablet that God gave to Moses. How it ended up on Noah's Ark is beyond me. The Great Flood occurred thousands of years before Moses's birth. So that, too, is a miracle. But I have one more to show you."

Again, the camera moved, following the Army archeologist. This time, he stood in front of what appeared to be a massive rectangle of gold. He again pointed to the floor.

"This is a golden tablet. We estimate that it is the same size as the original stone tablet before the rock crumbled due to time. On this gold are written the original Ten Commandments as well as God's Eleventh Commandment. They too are the work of the finger of God. This one is in English. See?" The camera moved closer. On the screen, Doug and Helen could easily make out the original commandments written in English.

"You shall have no other Gods before me except those whom you believe are as Good and as just as me," Helen read. "But that's different than what we learned in Catholic school, isn't it, Doug?"

"You shall make no idols to replace me such as Golden ones except those that revere and honor your many saints and gods," Doug said as he read out the second commandment. "Again, it's different than what we were taught. How can these be the original commandments?"

They read the other nine as the camera slowly moved over the tablet. They were all the same as they'd been taught in school except the last one. Then, the camera once again showed the archaeologist's face.

"When I read these I thought they were fake. But they are not. We have had all of these tablets dated," he said, pointing to the block of gold. "There are over one hundred tablets each written in a different language. They are all the same age. Over one-hundred-thousand years old."

"That long before Moses?" Doug asked. "But that's crazy! There were no humans on Earth back then. It must be a fraud."

"This is well before the time of the Ancient Hebrews including Moses and the advent of human beings on our planet. But," the archeologist added, "God seems to have added an explanation and perhaps a warning. See? Look to the bottom of the English language tablet." He again pointed to the wording and said out loud: "Woe is he who translates my commandments with vengeance or bigotry. Yes, there are other gods in the many universes we together have created. And yes there are idols but not golden ones like I have writ to you on. And yes, there are many who will misinterpret my Blessed Will and

Written Words. Beware the fraudsters that will come after me. They are here to steal your soul that my Son must sacrifice Himself to save it. I give you peace. May you give me, your Father, peace."

"It is written like a note a father would leave his child except for the ancient way of writing things, isn't it Doug?" asked Helen.

"Agreed."

Then the TV screen went black again. Amendus smiled. "See what great gifts your God gave you so many years ago? A set of rules yet many of you do not follow his warning. Maybe it is not worth having us bother saving your race, after all. Or is it?"

"I hope it is," Helen answered. "Every living thing is worth saving. Isn't that why you'll be giving us the gifts?"

His smile broadened. "Right again, Helen my Princess. You're all worth saving, each and every one of you, no matter how many times you sin. It is a pity that your God the Father had to take time from His other chores to remind you to practice the actions and words that to us Gaians have been obvious from the very beginning of our Universe."

Chapter Twenty-Four

The next day, the 5th of October, the day after Doug's birthday, Helen and Doug watched the global news from the Command Deck of Gaia IV. The broadcasts from Earth all proclaimed both victory but also an ominous warning. While Putin's Russian troops were losing all over the Ukraine, he now threatened the world with nuclear destruction. His advanced technologies, as reported on all news channels, would not only cause massive destruction to Kyiv and a huge loss of life but also, stated one NBC news reporter, "This is no longer a possibility but a fact. If Putin launches his nuclear missiles, we'll have Mutually Assured Destruction of the entire planet."

Time then moved on quickly for Helen and Doug because there was so much to do and plan, just as their Royal Lady had said it would. When nine months had passed on the planet Gaia but over thirty years on Earth due to the fact that the couple had traveled over the speed of light more than one time, and with the war in Ukraine not yet over, Helen gave birth to fraternal twins. For reasons they did not yet understand, and with their children only three months old, the Queen and Amendus ordered the family to return to Earth. When they arrived on a Gaian Starship back to their home in Long Island, New York, Helen and Doug had their children minded by a local nanny in the United States. Under the protection of Gaian soldiers, the couple then journeyed to India, where Doug had always wanted to go. The couple went to Delhi, the capital of that nation, then to Mumbai where they took part in the many festivals to the Hindu gods. Finally, they ventured to the State of Kashmir to see the great Indian and Pakistani Himalayan mountains. As they trekked up narrow passes on horseback, and finally to the a park called The Gates of Paradise, they dismounted and had a cup of sweet tea served by dark men and women from India who smiled and chatted to them in English.

"Doug, is that the great mountain where we saw the interview on the Gaian television monitors?" Helen asked. "Is that where they found the Noah's Ark and the Arc of the Covenant along with the many gold copies of the Holy Bible?"

Doug also turned to gaze at the snow-white mountain. "That's the mountain all right. But have they found it yet? Who knows. I'm not sure if that's already happened or if it's a recording of a future interview that will take place years from now." Then he put a hand to his forehead. "God I hope it's not too many years. The archeologist was a Ukrainian soldier, remember, Helen? He was helping to take supplies to his army in the Ukraine. If it was years in the future, that means that the war will last what will seem like forever."

"Hopefully, the interview has already happened or will happen soon. Let's not even talk about that war lasting forever."

When they were finished touring India, they then traveled to Israel and Palestine to observe at first-hand how peace had not yet come to those two nations. There, they made their way to Bethlehem to visit the stone stable where Christ was born. Then, they decided to take a boat to Galilee and the very beach where Christ had divided five fishes and five loaves of bread into many, many more to feed the masses as he walked high above them and onto a stone altar, then taught them to say *The Lord's Prayer*.

As the Catholic couple from America got off the tramp steamer they had decided to use for their long-awaited trip due to its inexpensive passage to that area, and climbed down onto a small powerboat, a storm came up, whipping the water to foam.

Fortunately, the two adults were the only passengers on that single-engine boat.

"Doug, look up!" Helen exclaimed, suddenly awed by a bright light that shone above them even though the afternoon sun glittered on the stormy waters. "Doesn't it look like a star? See the long points on it, one ascending to Heaven, the other to Earth. It reminds me of the star of Bethlehem."

"It can't be," Doug said, standing up in the boat.

But because of the inclement weather that had suddenly descended on them, and due to the boat's rocking, the single crew member told him to sit down again. That woman, a good friend of Doug's named Julie Aldridge, a painter who had also long wanted to visit Galilee and had worked her passage off by becoming a cook on the steamer that had taken Doug and Helen across the sea, started the engine and drove toward the golden sand of a long, deserted beach, just as the weather abated. It was then that Julie made out what was descending toward them through the fog that surrounded them.

"I'm sure it isn't the Bethlehem star," Doug's friend said. "That's just part of a story in the Bible, and both a fable and a metaphor. Perhaps it's a comet? That's what most astronomers think."

"It's a what?" Helen asked. "A comet?"

"That's no comet, Julie," Doug replied. "It's not leaving a ghost-like trail behind it. It's glowing like starlight, though, isn't it?"

When they all agreed, and as Julie grounded the bow of the craft on the beach, the bright object hovered above a ledge of rock that looked like a long altar. All of them were shocked by this unsettling sighting. As they watched, the starlight diminished.

"That looks like the silhouette of a man," Helen observed as the shadow became a three-dimensional figure. "And look at the wicker basket."

"It's just like the pictures I've seen in the Bible," Doug said, awestruck. "That looks like Jesus getting ready to divide the loaves and fishes."

"That's right," Helen said. "I've seen the same pictures."

"Come on, Doug," Julie replied. "Jesus Christ was only a man! Humans don't make miracles. What you're seeing is a mirage brought on by the heat of the mid-day sun. See?" she said, looking up. "The sun's out again."

Then something miraculous happened. Suddenly, the deserted beach became crowded thousands of people. Though Doug, Helen and Julie were far away from that part of the beach, they could hear a conversation as if two men were in the boat talking to them.

"Is that Simon Peter, Christ's friend and founder of the Catholic Church, and his brother Andrew?" asked Doug.

"Listen!" Julie said, now the one to be awestruck. "I want to hear them."

From across the distance, they could hear the voices that Doug and Helen were now certain were two of Christ's disciples.

"There is a boy here who has gone fishing, and his mother made bread for their family of four," they could hear Andrew say as he pointed toward the crowd. "That ten-year-old son of a fisherman then gave Jesu, Our Lord and Savior, five barley loaves and two small fishes for our dinner. But what of the rest of the crowd? They all need to eat, too. Yet, they are a gathering of at least five-thousand people. How do we feed them if we can barely feed ourselves?" He looked up at his older sibling. "Brother, why have they come, anyway?"

And Peter, who would one day lay the foundation of the Catholic Church, replied, "Because they have come to hear the word of our teacher and theirs, Christ the Lord."

Then Jesus, standing above them on the altar of stone, looked down on the crowd and said to his two disciples: "Make all these people sit down and be quiet so they can hear My Words but first they shall eat."

"My Lord Jesu," said Thomas, who joined them after hearing his fellow disciples talk about the lack of food. "I'm sorry I'm late, Master. I have been resting following the storm. But how can they eat? I've already heard Simon Peter say that we can barely feed ourselves. What's two fishes and five loaves of bread to five-thousand people? If you try to feed them with what you have in that basket, surely they will argue, fight and someone will get killed! Let us eat, my brothers, rather than risk such an ugly massacre."

"You've always doubted me and you will continue to do so," Jesus said. "Even when I die from a terrible crucifixion and rise again, you will doubt what you will see with your own two eyes. Instead, you will demand to thrust your right hand, not your left, into the wound in my side. You will withdraw it and see all of my Holy Blood. How can you forsake me, Thomas, when so many others will believe in that Holy Miracle despite the fact that they will never witness it? Two thousand years from now, many people across this Earth shall sing my praises, trusting My Word and the Word of the many Commandments. Yet, despite the fact that I love you, you will refuse to listen to me."

"Jesus, I love you with all my heart," replied Thomas. "I would never, ever doubt your word."

"But you do."

"I promise you. I never will."

Jesus sighed. "No, you will doubt me only that one time. You will never betray me because you truly are my brother. We are both descended from the same God and Mother, after-all. However, Peter will betray me by denying me thrcc times."

"I will never do that," Peter cried. "I love you, dear brother Jesus, with more words that I can ever say."

"When, on that sad day of unholy murder, and the cock crows a first time, you shall deny me once. When it crows again you shall deny me twice. When it crows again, you shall deny me a third and final time. Then you shall flea the maddening crowd and only be present when I am at last crucified. Don't you believe me, my beloved Peter?"

"I can't, my Master," Pcter said, now in tears. "How could I ever deny you? I've told you I promise you that I'll never, ever leave your side. Please believe me, my Lord. Please…"

Jesu smiled. "Of course, I believe you my son and elder brother. Now, let us all eat."

Now there grew a great deal of grass near the beach. Jesus stepped down from His Altar and took up the basket of bread and fishes. When He had given thanks to his Father and Mother, he distributed the meal first to the three disciples who ate a loaf of bread each as well as one of the fishes. Then he blessed the basket where it sat in the grass, and a miracle took place. Instead of one basket there were one-hundred and thirty-five. Each wicker basket held at least forty loaves of bread and an equal number of fish.

"Now, my friends," Jesus said. "Distribute these baskets to the crowd because they, too, are famished."

When the crowd had eaten their fill, Jesus said to his disciples, "Gather up the fragments that remain, that nothing be lost."

The disciples gathered them together, and filled the one-hundred and more baskets with the fragments of the loaves and fishes which remained, and which all could eat later that day.

"Remember," said Christ to his three brothers, "because you are all blessed, my friends, you will never again run out of food to feed the poor. Someday, one of you will sacrifice yourselves to an angry mob because you testify My Word and the next coming of the Messiah."

"When will that take place?" asked Peter. "Lord, I do not talk about my sacrifice, I might add, which I'm glad to give. But Your coming again?"

"It is foretold in the Bible," Jesus replied. "But that last chapter of My Story in what will one day be called the New Testament shall be called the Book of Revelations and neither are written yet. But I know it by heart including the way it is misinterpreted by what will one day be called the Evangelicals who interpret every word of the Bible literally, even though much of it is a metaphor. They call that day of days in the Book of Revelations the Rapture but it isn't! Some day in the future, a famous dictionary written in a language much different from our Hebrew will define that word, *'rapture'*, as follows: 'A feeling of extreme pleasure and happiness'. Evangelicals, who will also call themselves Christians in My Name, have it backwards. Their thinking is that *'rapture'* is not happiness but rather the end of everything!

"Those who follow me in this so called 'Christian Way' as these misguided Evangelicals define it, will go to Heaven. Those who are made to follow that narrow path, like children and young adults who may disagree with that dishonorable misinterpretation and are the *real* Christians, will be put to shame or even death if they object! Upon the day of what they think is My Second Coming—and Peter, I say this to you for they are wrong!—this young group will be frightened of the hereafter because they fear they will lose everything because they will be condemned to a Hell of these so-called Christian Evangelical's own making. While these young people know they will rise to Heaven they are traumatized because they are told that those who believe in *any another way*, not the Evangelical Way—and I have always said that there are many, many ways to come to me and find the Truth—including friends and family, loved ones, different religions and faiths, different ways of looking at the world, those who define themselves by their various genders or color and those who choose to believe in nothing at all … even loving pets and those of the four-footed variety can find me for I am the Alpha and Omega and love every living thing and those that are not alive anymore and the things that have never lived at all—anyone that chooses to follow what these Evangelical fools *think* is My Way (but it is *not*) are condemned to a Hell of their own making, not mine! But you asked when I am coming again. All I can say to you is this, and this is the short version of a very long Biblical Chapter that will one day be written in stone but will again be misinterpreted by being written thusly: and remember THIS IS WRONG!

"'Behold, there shall be a final coming and Holy Reckoning. And it shall be called The Rapture. On that day, the end of days (which I say to you, *it is not*), Christ the Lord on High will come down to his People through the clouds on a Golden Chariot. Angels shall blow trumpets and sing! And that image the Evangelicals call Jesus will divide those who follow His Way from those who do not. Those who Do Not shall Perish in Fire, while those who Do shall ascend into Heaven.' Which is ridiculous," Jesus finished.

"What's a 'bible'? Do you mean The Torah?"

"That's the Old Testament as practiced from the days of Moses, as you all know," Jesus explained. "After I am gone, some of my chosen people will write what humanity will call the Bible. It will consist of all of my teachings and describe the miracles I make on Earth, and will include a First Part which is the Hebrew Torah, which is mostly history, not metaphor or allegory."

"It will? This new book will even include our Hebrew Torah? And the Book of Revelations is the last book of this new and old Bible?"

"As I say, the last half of the Holy Book shall be called the New Testament. And yes, the last book in that Testament will be called Revelations."

"But why is it all ridiculous, this Evangelical interpretation?" asked Peter. "Isn't that what you taught us and the crux of your teachings? That there is only one way to Heaven and that's through You?"

"Not at all," said Jesus and placed his arm around his brother's shoulder. "Rather than all of those confusing words, some of which will be allegory and is therefore subject to interpretation, all anyone has to do is remember the *Golden Rule* which is, 'Treat others as you would treat yourself'. Then Jesus turned to the crowd that had finished eating. "Come, my brothers. It's time to teach our followers to recite something very special. Soon, they will call in *The Our Father* and in its few words it sums up the Golden Rule."

It was then that Helen, Doug and Julie saw Jesus turn to the crowd, stretch out his arms to get their attention, and say for the first time in the history of humanity, *The Lord's Prayer*.

Then, following Jesus Christ's blessing of the crowd, the vision left them. And when they were all done rubbing their eyes, they looked up again. Dressed just like the dream they all had, except wearing a bright halo of golden light, Jesus Christ the Son of God once again descended onto a nearby stone that looked like another altar.

"Be not afraid," He said, "for if you listen, you will hear no angels trumpet my coming. Nor are there crowds nor loaves and fishes. This time, my unseen, unknown Second Coming, which happens now, not in the future—and let it be known that my last visit to my Earthly Kingdom which will take place in over a thousand years will be my Third Coming—will not be marked by many, many miracles, only by some. This day-of-days is not the time for a Final Reckoning or a time for looking back, only forward. You see, my children, you who are named Helen and Doug, you are the only hope for humankind."

Jesus had been looking at the couple who were closest to Him but, as Julie started to creep away thinking that this stranger's words were not meant for her, He glanced in the woman's direction.

"Child, your name is Julie, is it not?"

"Why, yes, it is," she said, startled that this man who she believed was both a liar and a fraud, knew her name. "But how could you know that? Or did you find me on social media? After all, I'm an Irish-American artist and well known by some people." She marched up to the tall man, ignoring the bright light around his head which she knew was fake and part of his disguise. "For that reasons, not only my family and friends know my name. Complete strangers do, too."

The tall man dressed in white robes laughed. "Julie Aldridge, do you think you are invisible to me? I don't need social media to see you. I see everything in this Universe except on those occasions when you want complete privacy. You, too, are needed because you are an artist, and art inspires frightened people, those who are sick, deaf and blind, and those who have lost their way."

"Artists?" Julie barked to the stranger. "Why do you need artists?"

"Didn't I just explain it? Who do you think painted the Sistine Chapel, one of the most famous paintings on Earth. Didn't that great artist help inspire a European Renaissance?"

"That's easy," she replied, thinking he was making fun of her. "Michelangelo."

"Correct!" Jesus laughed back. "And what was he? A simple painter."

"Come on, whoever you are. He was much more than that. He was a genius."

"Yes, but he had to start from somewhere. How did he learn to paint?"

"By studying and copying those great painters that came before him. He learned by standing on the shoulders of giants."

"As you do," Jesus continued. "He was a genius and so are you. So come with us, please. And bring anyone and everyone you love along with us."

He held out his hand and she tentatively took it. But when he tightened His grip, holding her hand with warm loving fingers, she instinctively tightened her own.

"Now we are complete," Jesus continued. "Now is the time for resting. Then, much later, we shall finish this song *not* with a bang or a whimper. But in a Glorious Song that is greater and louder than any Great Amen."

With that, they heard a far-off trumpet playing three notes that startled the seagulls but that the humans could barely hear.

"Listen!" said Helen. "It sounds like our song, Doug."

"Which one?" Julie replied. "The one they played at your wedding? I had the same dream. I dreamed that you both were married by a strangely-dressed woman as well as a Catholic priest."

"Do you mean a tall woman, a woman nine feet high who appeared to be green?"

Julie nodded. "That's right! Now I remember all of it. You were married and then…the dream ended."

Doug and Helen smiled at each other because they both remembered that, in the dream and after Bing had sung his famous song, they had first made love. And they also realised that just as Jesus had promised, people had moments of complete privacy whenever they wanted it. "Mr Cosby sang *Tura Lura Lura* in our mutual dream, isn't that right?" Doug asked Julie. "That was the first dance at our wedding, too."

Julie could only nod back. "I wish I could have been there. But the dream was enough. I also have had a dream where you had two children. Twins." Then she looked toward the man who had taken her hand. "Doug, is that really Jesus Christ?"

"You're also Catholic," he replied. "Why don't you believe it? Did you see the miracle of the loaves and fishes like we did? Or are you just like Thomas, a doubter, too?"

"Believe what's in your heart, Julie," Helen said, smiling. "This man is Our Lord, the Christ whose Passion cleansed our sins and restores our faith in life."

Julie took the man's hand in her own again and looked deep into his eyes. "You don't seem like a fraud. You know my name but what's yours?"

"Julie Aldridge, you already know my name. You heard my disciples say it many times in the vision I gave to you three. So you tell me. What's my name?"

"Jesus Christ," she whispered. "But, sir, is there any way you can prove it to me?"

"Why is it people of faith still need any proof at all? If you want proof then I give it to you."

The Lord held out a few pages of parchment. "Here. This is the Fifth Book of the New Testament as written by me, one that is in addition to the Books of Matthew, Mark, Luke and John. Mind you, there are other Great Books of the Bible but the Roman Catholic Church refuses to publish them. They tell many secrets about my Next and Final Coming, and my wife who was a whore to make a living. Her name is Mary Magdalene, and she's always been my wife and continues to be. This Last Book of the Bible, and there are Thirteen Books which have now been written, is even simpler to understand than *The Lord's Prayer*. This isn't a Gospel or Psalm or prayer. It's based on a simple teaching, just like the prayer that I taught to the masses. It also includes the central themes of the *Hail Mary*, the *Glory Be*, the *Act of Contrition* and what many call the *Apostle's Creed*, and all other teachings found in all of the world's religious teachings. Read it, my children, and do your best to memorize it, for it is the final salvation of humankind and this planet you call Earth."

He handed it to Julie who unrolled the parchment skin upon the altar made of stone. As they all read it, and Jesus looked over their shoulders, they felt their scalps prickle.

"It really is simple," Helen said as she read the short document. "My Lord Jesus, what do you mean by this?"

"This?" he said, tracing the final line. "*Beneath this altar of stone you will find a map that will lead you to Noah's Ark*'," he read and turned to her. "This is one of my prophesies of what will come to pass in the future. Your future and mine. Already, you know this story but I will tell it to you to remind you what you saw only recently on a new technology that is still foreign to me. Your archaeologists think they have found it somewhere close to us, high up on Mount Ararat. But they are mistaken. One day, someone will find that map, perhaps a geologist or archeologist. When they find it, they will tell you that it is much more than two-thousand years old, much older than my first coming. There, beneath the red X, they will not only find the complete, unblemished Ark that is and was Noah's, they will also find another Arc. It is the Arc of the Covenant, and beneath its golden eagles they will discover not a large stone tablet as they expect to find but instead a Golden Tablet upon which is written not only the Ten Great Commandments but also an Eleventh. You see, the original tablet of stone had broken off at the bottom, destroying that eleventh commandment from what was given to all people by God the Father, who sits high on His Throne in Heaven. When, not if, they discover it on the second highest peak of the Himalayan Mountains in India, they will find that all of the commandments were written in Hebrew. But other Golden Tablets, all created at the same time with the same golden ingots that Noah had on board his Ark, spell out in all of Earth's many languages not only Our Father's Ten Commandments but also my final words on what I wish for all of you, which is the Eleventh Commandment, which He also wrote with his fiery finger.

"Now go. Spread my word to all of humankind. Remember, someday there shall be a Third Coming which people then, a thousand years from now I dearly hope, will interpret as the Second Coming of Christ their Lord. But tell them they are mistaken. It is my Third Coming. I repeat, for all of humankind's benefit, I am the Alpha and the Omega, and have been Among all of you for an eternity and much more."

With that Jesus vanished and left only a whirlwind of dust behind. The parchment again blew open and Julie, Doug and Helen read the Holy Words of *Jesu Kristos* one more time:

The Fifth Book of the Bible, According to Jesus Christ Our Lord and Saviour

Take my words literally. This book is the Word of God's Will as well as Christ's teachings. It shall not be misinterpreted by my so-called Evangelical Ministers or so-called right-leaning peoples who would destroy the US Constitution or other constitutions across the world. Be warned! Or I shall have my Angels take you to a Hell of your Own Making!

When Mark wrote his Book, John the Baptist said:

"I will send my messenger ahead of you,

who will prepare your way"

"a voice of one calling in the wilderness,

'Prepare the way for the Lord,

make straight paths for him.'"

And so I came to earth for the first time.

My message was, and is, simple and is found in God's 'Golden Rule':

Do unto others as you would have them do unto you.

Thus it was and so it shall be forever more.

In this year of Christ the Lord 2023, I write to reveal my revelations and give you warning: To those who warp these *simple words for your own purposes*, there is only oblivion which before was called Hell but which I now bless as a <u>*New Limbo*</u>.

For those who do not believe shall be damned to a prison of *their own making*, not mine, until the day comes that they choose to believe because there is *no alternative*, and out of a conviction that they can make *their own free choice*.

The Revelations of Christ Revealed

As I write these few words on Christmas Day, I set to print what is in my heart and in my head: *Christ's New Revelations*, revealed.

- In my Sermon on the Mount all was previously revealed in the *Lord's Prayer* and still stands today: the Golden Rule is all that matters - treat others the same way you would treat yourself or your friends or relatives. Nothing else matters.

- Many passages in the Old Testament foretold the coming of the Messiah. I tell you, I have come again. The book of Revelations foretold all of this: the 2nd Coming is not only at hand, it is a fact that I set here before your very eyes. You shall hear the sound of angelic trumpets. You shall witness my coming in a spacecraft called *The Enterprise* from a far-off star, Proxima A, my other home. You shall see how your loved ones have risen just like Lazarus. But, no, I shall not judge you as it says in the Bible. Judging one another is up to you and your courts of justice.

- I give you as fact: on 4 July 2035, there shall be a bloodless coup in North Korea and the People's Republic of China. When the people's choice is made clear, existing illegal governments will have no choice but to hold free elections, delivering new freedoms enshrined in constitutional Amendments much like the US Constitution's Bill of Rights. Thus, all men and women will be recognised as being created equal for the first time in history. There shall be no slavery. The colour of one's skin or faith or sexual persuasion or any other so-called 'difference' will no longer matter. It will all be laid down in law.

- For those who struggle, the homeless, the indigent, alcoholics, single parents, those suffering any injustice whatsoever, they shall receive help to ensure fair housing, additional training, college degrees, or whatever they require and choose to make life happier. This shall be paid by *Me*, not any other government or private institution or similar fundraising or giving.

- Should illegal governments object, they will find that they have no choice. This is the Will of God, and Mine. No person or government shall sunder Our Will and New Testament.

- Some governments will balk at these changes. When that happens, and it will, I shall have my soldiers including my General, Saint Michael the Archangel, storm these so-called Citadels of Power. My angel Gabriel shall blow his trumpet of justice until these halls, including State Secret Police buildings, disappear as if they had never existed. Yet, despite the apparent damage, there shall be no collateral damage. I personally shall give thirty minutes warning for all people to clear the area.

- No weapons shall be used. Should these governments somehow conceal armaments and ammunition, including Nuclear Weapons, beyond our reach, they shall find that nothing will fire. It shall be the world's largest, most historic, bloodless coup and shall be considered the Bible's most stunning miracle.

- These so-called walls of power shall continue to fall throughout 2022. However, State geopolitical lines shall remain. Yet, divided countries such as Northern Ireland and the Republic of Ireland, and Israel and Palestine, shall know a new peace, with a significant increase in trade across the world. That factor shall be at a minimum two by two and no less than that.

- Putin shall fall. North Korea's leadership shall fall. The People's Republic of China, that corrupt government, shall be obliterated, struck from history and the face of the earth.

All of the above I promise and give to you on this day, 25 December 2021. This is my message of Revelation given to you just as the Lord God promised Moses in his glittering rainbow and his miracle of dividing a vast sea in two so His people could escape the clutches of an ancient, God-fearing Pharoah.

So it shall be, so will it be, and so it is. Signed this day by my hand, which will always be invisible to you, my children.

Jesus   Christ   the   Lord   your   God
Written at the kitchen table in my village and Irish Home

(The signature above is, to many, what I am—their Lord. But please remember, not everyone believes that so do your best to be tolerant. And I add one more thought—it is easier to find me than placing a thread through a needle. I am much larger than any single hole in a metal or wooden needle, and much longer than any spool of thread in this, your solar system. Think about that! JC.)

Having finished re-reading Christ's Fifth Book of the New Testament, Helen looked to Doug. "It's such a simple book, isn't it?"

"Just like art," Julie replied. "The simpler the better."

"But what does He mean about all wars ending?" Doug asked them. "Wars will never end. That's the nature of humankind."

"If Jesus says they will, then they will," Helen replied. "It's in his *Our Father* anyway. Forgive them their sins, remember? So all wars must end because they are unforgiveable."

Chapter Twenty-Five

Having finished a vacation of discovery and mystery, Doug and Helen again did as Gaia and Amendus ordered them to do. They again journeyed into space. As they took their infants from a NASA Artemis vehicle into Space Station Chandra circling high above the Earth, they looked down on humankind's beautiful green, white, blue and brown jewel of a planet and wondered again what Putin must be thinking.

"The man is mad," Helen said as the space station moved past Russia. "Don't you know what the result of his actions will be? He'll blow our planet back to the very beginning of civilization."

"Not only that," Doug replied as he fed one of the twins, who were now four months old, "he'll ruin the chances of survival, not only for our James and Joanna but for every child that comes after. There will be so much radiation from illegal bombs such as cobalt bombs that their DNA will be tarnished forever. What will you have left? The novel, *The Canticle for Leibowitz* predicts it the best. You'll have humpbacked maimed dwarves with two heads, no homes to go to, and only deserts in which to incubate a new civilization. Like the monks and priests of Ireland before them, only a single Abbey will be left standing to hold what is best in past civilizations. But as the author of that novel, Walter Miller Junior wrote, even then it will be too late. Human survivors will create atomic bombs again and launch them against their perceived enemies, and that, my Helen, will be the absolute end of the human race."

"But you forget what Arthur C. Clarke wrote in *Childhood's End*," Helen reminded him. "It's not the end of everything, it is only the beginning. It has to be."

Doug sighed. "I hope so too, Helen. The last thing we need is a world with no hope at all."

Then below them, through the window showing their picturesque planet, the sun came out at least three times over what Doug thought must be the country of the Ukraine as uranium bombs exploded. He looked up at one of the space station's monitors, then consulted a map, noting that the nuclear blasts were located above Kyiv. "Here we go," Doug said. "Helen, we're seeing the end of Europe and soon my Homeland."

White contrails began to streak above the northern Hemisphere. As the world revolved below them, that hemisphere quickly turned to night. Now beneath them, they could see the brightly burning lights of other huge cities. "That must be Los Angeles," he pointed out. "And to the north, the San Francisco Bay area. Then, farther up, Seattle and in the darkness Puget Sound with its U.S. Naval bases."

Bright burning suns came out everywhere along the west coast of the United States. Soon, as the world continued to turn below the space station, every large city in America had searing nova's of destruction above them, murdering most of the population of America. As they watched, they could make out pinpoints of light streaking high into the atmosphere from America's corn belt region, heading west, bound for Russia, China and North Korea.

"That's it, Doug," Helen cried, holding one of their twins tight. "That's the U.S. counterstrike. Everything that our Commander-in-Chief can throw at them, he will. Only a few million people will survive. Billions and billions of people will never live though this nightmare of mass destruction. Those who live will run into deep caves while those that are rich will have nuclear shelters that they can hide in. The Southern Hemisphere will be safe for now. And the few who are living in the Antarctic, or in homes at the bottom of the sea, will be safe. Doug, did you hear about the lottery that the Queen organized with the United Nations? Seven-hundred thousand people and no more, regardless of race, creed or color, were chosen to journey into outer space. Boarding a number of Gaian spacecraft, they will add to the population already living on Mars, as well as venturing to Europa, one of Jupiter's moons, and Titan, Saturn's largest moon, where they will establish basecamps. NASA, together with all other nations including our enemies, got together trillions of dollars in finance to help with other costs. Earth scientists have spent years studying how to build a city beneath the sea, capable of housing and feeding a million people, which is perfect for both Titan and Europa. Soon, other spacecraft will take off, carrying any survivors of Earth to those distant locations."

"It's not so distant now, Helen," Doug reminded her "Remember, just as they promised, Gaia and Amendus gave the human race their Code because no one could break it, and with it came the gift of their Stardrive. Now it's just a short hop in any sort of space vehicle to any part of our solar system."

"But not into our galaxy, the Milky Way? Surely, there must be other planets Among those millions of stars that can support life."

"Not yet, Helen. Gaia says we're not ready. Humans continue to be a threat to other civilizations living across our galaxy. Looking at what's happening below us, you can understand why our Queen and mother thinks that."

Below them, another explosion destroyed what Doug thought might be Reykjavik, the capital of Iceland which was of strategic value to America, and Helen prayed that it was the final bomb. But then the horizon lit up in a massive conflagration. What seemed to be the entire northern hemisphere was lit in a huge orange light and, as they looked down, seeing the Himalayas in an early morning sunrise, they saw what had to be a number of bombs destroy Delhi, Mumbai and much of the west coast of India. Fires lit up most of the country and as the pair watched, an earthquake ripped India away from the rest of the Asian continent. The fires caused by nuclear explosions were buried beneath a giant tsunami sweeping in from the Indian Sea. Both of them knew that anyone who had survived were now dead.

"I had a dream last night," Doug whispered. "It wasn't a nightmare. Rather, it was full of hope."

"What was it about, Doug?" Helen asked. "I didn't dream at all. For a change, it seems you had a dream all on your own."

"This is what the dream was about. In it, I'm told that I'm the one who wrote the book we both dreamed about before when we first saw the vision of Our Lady, the final book of a frightening, unpublished series of books that someday I'll author. I even remember the title. Do you want to hear it?"

"Go on, Doug. What was it?"

"The Final Resurrection of an Unknown Writer Who is the Son of God."

"That's a long title, isn't it, Doug?" Helen asked, trying to make light of the situation because she could sense that her husband's agitation. "Okay, so that's the title. What was the story about?"

"And it *is* a story. Okay, let me try to tell it. For a change, I remember everything."

Doug got up and, holding his infant son, stepped toward the window and looked down on a Hell he did not want to ever remember.

"The sub-title is *Remembrances of the Unseen*. One day, on an October the Fourth when I'm an untold age, Pookus the Lame One, an unknown entity I remember both of us talking about, will come down from Heaven as perfect as ever before. With a woman named Harsha Thacker, an unknown wife to me and also her daughter Happy, Pookus and Harsha will see my Golden Wings that fly up to Heaven and well beyond it. Then, somehow, we all go back to what's left of Ireland and to a home we've lived in for years but have never seen before." He looked back at Helen. "Which is weird. Ireland will surely be devastated. The population will soon be wiped out by radiation drifting in from Iceland and the Eastern seaboard of the United States. But anyway…" Doug cleared his throat and started again. "I know we've already talked about this with Amendus and Gaia, but it's worth repeating so we both remember. When Pookus sees the old seaside home perched above a lovely bay, her memory will come back and somehow she will be interviewed on every news channel all across the world—even though I don't think there will be anyone left to watch those broadcasts—and spread the news of a Second Unknown Coming of Christ. Some will call it The Day of Rapture and they'll be frightened of Our Lord's coming. But Helen, and that's you my lovely wife, will explain in subsequent news broadcasts that, while yes, this is Christ's Second Coming and it's happening on the day that Pookus broadcasts that Good News to Humankind, He'll come again a thousand years later for a Third Coming. However, the Second Coming of Christ our Lord is a *quiet* Second Coming by an unknow pilot and writer, even though I'm not a writer at all. Then they will all be married, a man with the initials

JC, a writer with the initials of CRJ, as well as Harsha, Pookus and an unknown woman with the initials JA. It is only then that humankind will finally know peace, comfort, family values, and no weapons of any kind at all. They will know this when I again write a Fifth Book of the New Testament which is nothing but a rewrite of *The Lord's Prayer* and the Golden Rule, just like what we read when we beheld the vision of Christ on the Sea of Galilee. Then, when Gaia's spacecraft comes again, it will be a new dawn for humankind, and there will never be an end to the world or the Solar System or our Universe again." Helen saw Doug's eyes glaze over, sweat gathering upon his brow, and his hands began to shake.

"Doug, are you all right?" she asked but he waved her away.

"Let me finish this before I forget." He wiped his face and started to speak again. "Then there will be a great conflagration, and those who are alive will call it a Fourth Coming, but they will have misunderstood. It will be the Third Coming. That Great Day will not be like Hell or Nuclear War. Instead, all of the living and dead will rise up and beat drums and play trumpets. Then Angels will sing a Grand Halleluia. On that day, that day-of-days, humankind as we know it will cease to exist. Like Arthur Clarke wrote in *Childhood's End*, the entire planet will dissolve into a giant, fiery Holy explosion but not before our children's children's children are saved forever in a Heaven not of God's making, but of our own and Gaia's and an unknown father of the many Universes which some still call the Holy Ghost."

He looked back at her, his face relaxing as if something unseen had let go of his mind. "That was the end of the dream. I think I know what it means. Do you?"

"We're saved just as the Book of Revelations in the Holy Bible foretold," Helen replied. "The only difference is that *all* of us will be saved, even those who have sinned or who are inherently evil. Unlike *Childhood's End*, where only innocent children were saved by a being that looked like Satan, and because we are all children in the eyes of God and Gaia, the entire human race will be saved and live together, freed from hatred, and living a life of loving friendship forever."

Then Doug looked out the window at what seemed like a bright star that had lifted off from a dark part of Earth. As it came closer, he realized that a missile streaked toward them, intent on seeking out and destroying their space station. As the weapon went off, a sun brighter than any in their universe lit his field of vision.

"Helen, get down!"

He grabbed her and, with their two children, they ran toward the door. But then the blast outside the observation window was smothered by what seemed to be the dark hand of God. Darkness swept over the space station. Helen thought that they were all grabbed by something she had experienced before. Light beamed through the ceiling and for a moment, darkness descended on them again.

✈ ✈ ✈

Moments later, on a beach somewhere in western Australia, Doug and Helen with their twins looked out to see a new day; a new dawn. Standing on the golden sand, still holding their children, they puzzled over what had happened to them and their space station.

"Gaia and Amendus grabbed us," Doug said. "It's the only way we could have come here. I don't see any wreckage of the space station on the beach or floating detritus in the water. Somehow, our Queen plucked us out of the station and transported us here. Do you remember anything about it?"

"All I remember is you finishing your story and the light from that nuclear explosion. I held one of our kids and you held the other. The rest of it…I can't figure it out at all. Too much took place all at once. The Northern Hemisphere is destroyed, Doug. Gaia and Amendus must have taken us here to make certain our family would be safe. But why are we so special? So many other families have died."

437

"I don't know. It's a question I don't think they'll ever answer. They'll only give us hints. It has something to do with that strange story I told you in the Chandra. I'm sure that soon, they'll pick us up and take us to a safer location with other survivors. While we're waiting, let's rest, okay? I'm really tired."

"So am I, sweetheart," Helen said. As Doug laid down Helen did too, placing the twins between them on the warm sand. "Let's try to get some sleep."

But just as Doug was closing his eyes, he heard a buzzing noise come from high overhead. Jumping up, he waved as Helen also stood up. Above them, an Australian Air Force helicopter banked toward them. As it descended to the beach, Doug shielded their children with his body.

"Cover your face, Helen!" he roared over the chopper's down blast as the huge propeller blades kicked up a storm of sand. A winchman standing in the helicopter's open door put his thumbs up and dropped a wire tied to a chair. On it was a radio mic. When Helen put the headset on, the winchman contacted her.

"We found you right where Queen Gaia said you'd be. Climb in, Helen, with one of the children. We'll get you two onboard, then do the same thing for Doug and your other child."

When the family was aboard the helicopter, it swung toward the south and, picking up speed, left the beach deserted except for tall palm trees that swayed in a soft breeze that would soon be filled with radioactive fallout.

Chapter Twenty-Six

While Helen and Doug with their children slept in a nearby Sydney, Australia, hotel bedroom, Gaia and Amendus discussed the plan to govern the Earth for what might possibly be the next thousand years.

"It could take that long, under our guidance, for *all* of the survivors of the human race to unlearn how to hate each other which is one of our most important objectives," Gaia stated as they stood in the War Room of their Command Starship as it orbited, unseen, above planet Earth. "Many do not hate now. They've already gone through too much. Suffering does that to humans as well as any intelligent being. Most of those who survive will not hate anyone anymore but be grateful for their lives and those of their families who have been spared the great nuclear holocaust."

"But some will still hate, won't they, My Lady?" Amendus replied. "Hate will be worshipped by some who think it's the only emotion that will let them regain power. Some who will have survived Putin's illegal war, and the nuclear destruction that followed, will believe it's the only way for them to rule the world with an iron fist. For that reason, and I agree with you, we must be prepared to stay on their planet for at least a millennium, if not more. But what about the response when we finally take over and govern their planet? Some of us are already on the surface and look as human as they do—brown, black, white, yellow—as a way of becoming part of the Earth's many cultures, understanding these multicultural people better and not being detected. But many of us look nothing like human beings at all. My Lady, what is your opinion?"

"No, my husband. Give me yours first. It will help me form my own."

"When we land, some people will call it an Extra-terrestrial invasion," Amendus opined in his deep barrel-chested voice. "Those who still have nuclear weapons will respond to our presence as if we're a threat to all of humanity. Some nations will launch atomic missiles at our ships. Some will use laser weapons while others will simply instruct their surviving populations to stay in place or go to bomb shelters, such will be their fear of us."

"I agree, husband," Gaia responded. "But it's a risk we have to take. Their weapons pose no threat to us because of our advanced technologies. But what I'm worried about is the fact that despite the J-Factor, many of those retaliations will get through because we do not have the power to stop them all. We cannot possibly track the hundreds of nuclear weapons that are left even with our state-of-the-art detection systems and telepathy. The nuclear explosions that will be caused by terrorist groups, also undetected by us, will wipe out a number of surviving cities including Chicago, Atlanta, Pittsburgh, Liverpool, Hamburg, Saint Petersburg, Belgorod, Rostov, Hong Kong, Shanghai, the Australian capital Sydney, surviving cities in the Indian State of Kashmir, the strategic airports in northeast Canada, as well as other smaller cities. The radioactivity will head again toward Ireland and Europe, and then into Russia, Asia and the North American continent. The only survivors will be in what remains of Australia, New Zealand, the Antarctic and parts of South America but those remnants of that planet's population will soon die, too. Billions will again die needlessly because of the implanted prejudices that some people have about us. As we told Doug and Helen, some will think us to be Satan. Yet others will believe we are Angels fallen from the sky. Yet it matters not because our coming is foretold not only in their Christian Holy Bible but also in our own mythology. For that reason, we must do what we have set out to do because it is the Will of our Unknown God and Mother."

"But if what you predict comes true," Amendus replied for the first time angry with humankind. "If atomic weapons wipe out the entire planet, we must abandon it because there will be nothing left of this Earth, which is home to our original birthplace and our species. We come to save them, not kill them or imprison them. We must convince them that the gifts we bring are here to help, not hurt. Some will believe that we have landed for the better good but you also know that some will not believe that at all. While the odds that our birth-planet Earth will die in what will be a continuation of this horrendous nuclear war, with all of its inhabitants reduced to ash, we must believe that we can succeed despite the odds."

For the rest of the night, Gaia and Amendus planned how they would take their Fleet bearing their shiploads of additional gifts from Gaia to Earth. A holographic sphere of Earth's globe filled a tactical war room in the Space Fleet headquarters on their Command vessel. Together with their military and civilian cabinet, they plotted a way to land across that world without creating mayhem among the population.

"Our Fleet will hide on the backside of their Moon then move one-by-one toward the few remaining cities across the six continents," Admiral Jurdus Coinifusios, commander of the Earth Fleet said, pointing at the glimmering three-dimensional plan of the planet. "By moving in singly, what remains of their military is unlikely to think that we're attacking. Our ships can orbit geocentrically well above the surviving major cities. That way, we will demonstrate no threat to them."

Using voice commands as well as telepathy, the advisors in the war room placed miniature holograms representing each of their large Gaian space freighters over the cities that needed desperate help. As one military surgeon pointed to the globe, he noted that they included all of those metropolitan areas that had been hit by nuclear strikes and laser guided missiles.

"Of course, we will have to leave out the enemy countries like Russia and China," the surgeon stated. "We don't have enough resources to help all of those who were killed or hurt if we add those Red State nations. We'll also have to abandon the entire Middle East."

"Why would we abandon anyone at all?" Gaia interjected. "No, that's not what we believe in. We must not leave out anyone. Generals, add all of Israel and Palestine as well as the entire Middle East to that map. Make sure to place more of our freighters over most American cities as well as North Korean, Chinese, Russian, Ukrainian and all of Southeast Asia because that's where we're needed the most. Billions are now dead, or so our friends on Earth think. But that will be transformed when we arrive *en masse* tomorrow."

"Tomorrow?" Jurdus replied with contempt as he banged on the table with a fist. "We were supposed to hide behind their Moon first, remember? Or has Our Lady forgotten? If we do what you order, and I know that's not just advice but a clear order from our Queen, you'll put the entire fleet in peril! Thousands of our medical teams, construction workers, soldiers, government officials and other specialists, as well as their families, will die. But you don't have enough power in all of our many universes to give renewed life to all of them, do you Royal Highness? That type of grand scale transformation requires the power of so many stars that our physicists state that they do not yet exist."

"Then we'll create more stars, Admiral. Who do you think I am, anyway? I'm not just your Queen. You of all Gaians know I'm much more than that!"

"Your ego is getting the better of you. You'll betray us to our enemies, not only on Earth but to those Alien creatures from distant Galaxies who would destroy us as well as our own planet Gaia and our many universes. Gaia, you are not a lady. Look at the smirk on your face. You are angry because you know I speak the truth. If you have set your mind on *invading* tomorrow, you will destroy all of us!"

"You are a liar, Jurdus. My ego has no part in this. We are here to save lives, not to argue."

"You know what history will say about this? It will tell those that read those many books that *I was the one who is right, not you*!"

"Get out, you scum. Go back to our planet right now! If you do not obey me then I know that it is *you* who would betray me."

"It is not I, a mere Admiral in your fleet who betrays you. It is someone else and his name is Amendus. He works to overthrow you and take power for himself."

"You dare lie to me again? I trust my husband with my entire soul." Gaia turned to her security detail. "Arrest this man! I already know what he has done. I created you, you Judas! That was the disciple who betrayed the human Christ. And so you would betray me to take power for yourself? Do you think your telepathy is more powerful than mine? I heard you whispering in your sleep. Yesterday, as we began our approach to Earth, you reached out to those survivors who control nuclear weapons. You already guessed at what we would plan and how we would save Earth." She strode to the glimmering globe, her finger pointing at it, her entire body shaking with rage. "You knew exactly which cities we would decide to come to first. What you did not know is that you were wrong! Dead wrong. The messages you sent to our enemies did exactly what I wanted them to. They will aim their rockets in the wrong direction and go hurtling harmlessly into space. After that, with no weapons left to fire, we will hunt down those who have betrayed us and arrest them, and have them tried before human courts as well as our own Gaian Supreme Court."

She swung to the Captain of her security detail, turning her back on her Fleet Admiral.

"Captain, arrest that former Admiral for treason against the state. Have him placed on the next spaceship going back to Gaia and imprison him in the brig until I return to our planet." Then she looked one last time at Jurdus. "Do you know what, my friend? I feel so very sorry for you. No matter what happens or where you go after you are sentenced for the highest crime possible against our Royal Government, I will always be your friend. Before you are escorted from this room I give you this. A memory of me until you come home."

Gaia stepped up to her former Admiral. When he tried to bow she stopped him. Then, kissing him gently on each cheek, she took the ring bearing the Royal Seal off her finger and slipped it on his own. "See? It's a perfect fit, my child and most important of disciples. One day, and I hope it will be soon, after you have some time to think about what you have done and the possible consequences of your actions, you will again sit at my table of Royal advisors."

As the prisoner was escorted out of the War Room, Gaia found tears on her cheeks. Wiping them off, she stamped a foot as she got back to business.

"Sally Simpson! Come to me!" A young woman dressed in the uniform of a Vice-Admiral of the Fleet stepped forward. Saluting, she bowed before her Royal Commander.

"Yes, my Queen? What can I do for thee? Give me any command, My Lady, and I will do my best to carry it out to the letter."

"Young woman and my daughter, you are younger than anyone who has ever been given the position of Admiral of the Fleet. I suggest that when we all have time, you get yourself a new uniform with gold braids on each shoulder, and a new hat bearing the Admiral's Golden Leaves on its brim. Kneel, Admiral Simpson." When the woman knelt before her Commander-in-Chief, Gaia laid a hand on each of her shoulders. "By Royal decree, which will be made in a more formal way when we return to our home planet, I declare that Vice Admiral Sally Simpson is now a Full Admiral and henceforth and until her next promotion, shall be the Admiral of our Earth Fleet. Sally, look at me."

The woman looked up, her face full of wonder and shock. "Yes, My Queen and Commander?"

Gaia smiled. "While we're taking care of this necessary business, tell the payroll department that you need a raise in salary commensurate with your new position. In fact, tell them that I order an annual salary of twice what our old Admiral was paid. When we are done with this mission, take a week off so you might visit your parents. Then prepare to go to work again, immediately, because on that day you will be given a new assignment."

"Another one, my Queen?" the new Admiral said, her voice quivering. "I'm still very young. Surely, there are others who are more experienced for this important position."

"I guess you'll just have to do," Gaia replied, smiling. "You'll be in command of a new generation of starships that have been fitted with something more wonderous than Stardrive. You will boldly go where none of us have gone before by Captaining the U.S.S. Enterprise XXI, named after that famous human television series and its interstellar spaceship, to start new universes that are very different than our own.

You will seed them with the energies of many suns that I will send you. But as I say, that's another promotion and another day's work."

Helping the new Admiral to her feet, Gaia kissed her on both cheeks. "I am so proud of you again, my Josie and granddaughter. When you see your mother and father, tell them that I say I love them, too." Then Gaia turned back to her advisors.

"Ladies and gentleman, let's get back to work! Get rid of those miniature freighters on our holographic sphere of Earth and let's start again!"

Jurdus Coinifusios had been promoted to Admiral of the Fleet by Gaia for good reason. He was in many ways just as intelligent and clever as she was. A rising star as an Ensign in the Gaian Navy, he had decided to abandon seagoing vessels and instead worked hard to get his wings in the Gaian Navy's fleet of aircraft carriers and then the planet's Air Force. Having flown just about everything that was available for him to fly, he applied and was accepted into Space Command. He once again excelled at all of the exams and every spaceship that was thrown at him. When he was promoted to Captain of one of the Gaian rescue vehicles, his first operation was to retrieve three NASA Earth astronauts as they experienced difficulties in what that American organization called Apollo XIII.

Thirty Earth years ago, as he descended toward the Moon of that planet, he heard an astronaut call on the Apollo's sideband radio, "Houston, we have a problem", and couldn't help but smile. Working hard to make sure his first rescue was much more than a success but a historic mission, he had spotted the problem with the U.S. spacecraft's oxygen tanks while it was still sitting on the pad in Cape Kennedy, Florida. In fact, it was he who logged the potential accident with Space Command, and when they approved the mission due to the possibility of disaster and loss of human life, he was selected to rescue the three Americans from certain death.

Abord the Sirius V Rescue Vehicle that he commanded, Jurdus led five team. members to do everything they could to bring the men of Apollo XIII back to Earth alive. With all his skill as an aviator and a ship's Ensign he swept over the Moon but realised, as he and his crew watched on the overhead monitor the white plume of oxygen vent into outer space from the NASA spacecraft's Service Module, that they were far too late. Ordered to keep their identity concealed from the humans by his Admiral, Jurdus seethed secretly because he realised that all he had to do was make one radio call, lock onto the target, and fix the wrecked oxygen tanks to make his first rescue mission a success that historians would never forget. Instead, he had to wait.

When at last he saw that what was left of the American craft had attached itself to a spider of a Moon landing vehicle, he radioed Space Command for permission to creep toward that target. Given approval by his Commander, Jurdus ordered the Sirius V to move again toward the Apollo. But just as they were about ready to capture it without the NASA astronauts ever detecting their presence, the spider craft's retro rockets began to fire. Locked together as if in a huge embrace, the pair of coupled space vehicles began to tumble end over end over end. Realizing that their rescue objective would soon be lost in the void of Earth's Solar System, Jurdus telepathically transmitted instructions to the three astronauts. Later, having been plucked from the sea by a helicopter, the pilot of the Apollo spacecraft was reported to say, "It was as if God was in the Command Module. We weren't quite sure what to do or when to fire the retros. We used a small telescope with cross hatches on it to site at the terminator of the Earth. Then, I heard a voice in my head say, "Go!". I counted to one and pulled the trigger to fire our retro rockets."

A few days later, Jurdus and his crew watched from their Rescue craft as that spaceship floated gently into the ocean beneath three orange and white parachutes.

When the Rescue vehicle Sirius VI returned to his home planet, Jurdus and his crew received a commendation medal for their actions. But Jurdus himself was never rewarded for his fast thinking when he reached out with his telepathy to the astronaut. As Gaia later told him, "Young man, we are here to save lives wherever in this or any other universe they're in peril. You don't need a special reward. Few brave soldiers ever receive them. Just be glad you and your crew came home safe." Then she clapped him on the shoulder, telling him, "By the way, your quick thinking deserves some kind of recognition. How about a promotion to Captain of one of the Space Fleet's freighters? Now go on and take a few days off then we'll send you out on your new orders. Congratulations, Captain, you are now a Commander. There is a promotion in it for you and a raise in salary too, for your quick actions and thinking."

When she left him alone in the Chapel of Saint Sirius on their home planet, he asked himself why he had bothered at all with his military career. 'I want more than promotions and a career,' he thought to himself as he sat in a pew. 'I did damn well, I thought, and so my crew told me when they saw what I did. They all believed I should receive some sort of public recognition, perhaps even a small celebration, for my actions. But that will never happen.'

For days he seethed at being overlooked by Gaia. And though she was his Queen and told him that he was one of the smartest and most reliable men in all of their home planet's military services, he knew that it would never be enough for him. 'One of these days I'll have the chance to turn the tables on that Queen Bee', he continued thinking as he walked flat-footed back to the Space Command Center. 'We'll see who is the smarter of the lot. All I need is the right opportunity. Then, I'll turn the tables on her.'

He knew it would take many years for his wish to come true but he was certain that someday soon, it would.

Confined to quarters aboard a ☒☒☒ freighter that was heading back to planet Gaia per the orders of Her Royal Highness, Jurdus paced the small confines of the ship's brig. He smiled to himself, knowing that it was just a matter of time before he had the visit from the vessel's Second-in-Command. When the lights went out and an alarm siren sounded, Jurdus knew his time was at hand. Outside the closed metal door, he heard a yell then an inhuman scream. The door slid open and Rengal, a humanoid from the Orion Belt, sidled into the brig, putting his laser gun back in its holster.

"It is done, Admiral Coinifusios, just as you ordered," the creature said, his scarred face twisted into an ugly grin. "I kept my promise and I know you'll keep yours. The bargain we made said that I'd find a Billion Gaian dollars in my bank account. I just checked, and thank you. You even gave me a bonus of one million Gaian dollars."

Bowing before the Admiral and new Commanding Officer of the spacecraft, he saluted and Jurdus returned the salute. "Well done, Captain Rengal. Is the ship unharmed?"

"Yes, sir. Just over half of the crew agreed to follow you and help me to capture this vessel. The former captain is dead, the coward, and a number of his crew members are both dead and injured. But as you ordered, no prisoners were taken. We threw the injured into the airlock and they are now feeding the stars."

"Good. Just as I ordered. Bring the freighter about and put her on a course back to Earth. There, I am to meet with the government officials who helped to defeat many other governments of that planet. Those survivors are determined that Gaia will never take over Earth because they want to rule it themselves for the betterment of all humankind, and with a fist like steel to ward off all enemies of their planned single global-state. Make sure we are invisible so that the Gaian vessels can't detect us, either on radar or read our thoughts with their telepathy. When we arrive at the dark side of their Moon, wake me up. I'm going to the Captain's quarters and sleep for a few hours. If anything unplanned is encountered, wake me up immediately."

"Yes, sir, Admiral Coinifusios. I'll do as you command, sir."

Then Jurdus accompanied his new Captain to the command deck of his new prize which he had won by betrayal and murder. Opening a bottle of champagne he found in a locked drawer, he poured two glasses and gave one to Rengal.

"Here's to you, Captain," he said, raising his glass. After they both drank the champagne in one long swallow, Jurdus smashed the bottle against the wall.

"I rename this freighter the Star Freighter Rengal, in honour of your courage."

Rengal saluted and watched as his new Admiral walked into the Captain's quarters, slamming shut the steel door.

Chapter Twenty-Seven

"Gaian Command, this is Doug Masters. Can you read me, over?"

Now commanding one of the Gaian star freighters, Doug sat in the left seat of the spaceship's large control room. Next to him in the copilot's seat sat Romero Farthing, a freshly-minted Second Lieutenant just out of the military academy, and also, like Doug, one of the few human beings who Gaia had come to in his dreams Only nineteen years old he too had danced through a Black Hole but only in his dreaming visions.

"You okay, Romero?" Doug asked his second-in-command. "Got the jitters or something?"

"No, sir," Romero replied, swallowing the bile in his mouth. "It must have been something I ate. Everything I eat tastes like cardboard. Do you want me to try to raise Gaian Space Command, Captain?"

When Doug nodded, Romero keyed his mic. "Gaian Space Command this is Starship Freighter One. Do you read, over?"

"Freighter One, this is Command. How many vessels do you have in your task force? Our radar is being interfered with by something on Earth."

"Command, we confirm there are over one-thousand vessels with us. That includes eight hundred supply freighters holding our teams of doctors and specialists, as well as two-hundred fighters with their mother ships to ward off any attack."

"Roger that, One. We'll continue monitoring this frequency. Good luck. Out."

When Romero was finished he glanced at his Captain and Doug saw that the poor kid wanted to throw up.

"Romero, I know exactly how you feel. You already told me that you dreamed of Our Lady. I never told you that I have, too, and continue to. When those dreams started a number of years ago, everything tasted like sawdust or cardboard. Then I got really dizzy and had trouble standing up. It seemed that there was a weight in both of my two thighs as well as a pair of hands pressing down on both of my shoulders. At one point, even a coffee cup seemed too heavy to lift. It was as if I was two people, Doug Masters and someone I still don't recognize, yet there are times I could swear that someone I barely know is whispering to me. Lieutenant, is that happening to you?"

Romero looked away as if too embarrassed to tell his Captain the truth. He swallowed hard then described what was happening to him.

"Yes Captain," he said, "it feels like there are hands on my shoulders and at times, particularly after waking in the morning, I can't get up from the chair I use when having breakfast. Even oatmeal tastes like paper and pancakes on their own seem as hard as concrete. But if I add anything sweet like maple syrup, sugar or jam. to pancakes or French toast then they taste almost normal."

"Almost?" Doug said, trying not to grin. "Don't you know what's happened to you?"

"No sir, all I know is that the evenings can be worse. I don't want to eat anything. All I want to do is go to bed no matter how much I've slept the previous night. Yet when I finally go to bed, I'll often have nightmares. I rarely remember them but they scare the shit out of me. I'll get up at 3 am and can't sleep anymore. I'll pace around my apartment and just want the world to end. What the hell is wrong with me? I wish someone could explain it. Captain, please don't tell anyone but I was so worried about the voices and visions I saw and heard that I went for a private physical and mental health assessment and came out clean on both occasions. I wish *someone* could tell me what was wrong."

"Have you asked Lady Gaia? She knows all about it. She told me what was wrong when I asked her about the dreams and visions I had. Why don't you ask her?"

"If I do, she'll stop me from flying. She'll end my career for good reason. Our Queen will think I'm no longer mentally or physically fit."

"Are you kidding? Kid, you're more fit than I am and I've gone through the same damned things. I also took a couple of physicals and mental health evaluations, and they all came out clean. So I asked Gaia and do you know what she said was wrong?"

"What, Captain. I just can't explain it. If I can't I worry I'll go completely fucking mad."

Doug reached out and put a hand on the man's shoulders. "Okay, let me try to summarize what Gaia told me. She calls it the Sixteen Billion to One longshot. She told me it's a sort of lottery. Many are called but few are chosen. Romero, have you seen the film *Close Encounters of the Third Kind*? Remember how all sorts of people were chosen to follow the call of the aliens but only one got to go with them aboard their spacecraft to visit their home planet. Does any of that make sense or sound familiar?"

"No, sir."

"Romero, we're having a private conversation. Let's pretend that we're not in space but at home having a cold beer. Call me Doug, okay?"

"Will do, sir. I mean Doug. But I don't get it. What's that fraction mean? Sixteen billion to one? Sounds like some sort of bet."

"It was and it still is. Okay, let me try to explain it. Eight billion was the population of the Earth when I was born. Helen was born only a few years later so the population was the same. To meet Helen among all those people on the planet was two times eight billion. So sixteen billion to one. Go figure. Of all the women in all the seven continents, and all the countries in those continents, and the fact that I'd never been to Ireland before, and the fact that Helen had never flown in an aircraft before I met her…now what do you think those odds are? And yet today we're married and have two children. I can't even do the math. I'd need a computer to figure out those long odds."

"But how does that apply to me, Doug? I mean, I'm not married and don't even have a girlfriend. It seems to me that I've got pretty even odds of meeting a woman. There are lots of women my age where I come from on Gaia."

"True but there's only one that's meant for you. And if you're an old-fashioned Mormon there just might be two women who are right. Now think about it. What's the population of Gaia? About eight billion, the same as when I was a kid on Earth. So what are the odds that you and I will be flying a freighter together?"

"Sixteen billion to one."

"Yep, that's right. And that's what Gaia would want you to say. Romero, you and I are both here for a reason that's critical to the survival of humankind and this Solar System. So is Helen. So are our children. And so is the wife you'll have one day and the children who will be born to both of you."

"If I have kids, you mean."

"Oh, you'll have them. Trust me. I never thought I'd have kids but I do. Gaia says that soon, we'll have two more sets of twins so that's six kids in total. I told her to forget it! I'm an old guy now. I don't want any more kids."

"How old are you, Doug?"

"Old enough to be your grandfather, Romero. Can I ask you something? When you dream, what do you see?" Romero opened his mouth then closed it. "Go on, kid. I've been through it. What do you see?"

"Golden light, skipper. It stretches as far as I can see. And in the dream I can see to the next universe and even farther than that."

"What's in the golden light?"

"People I know who died years ago."

"Like your grandparents and other ancestors?"

"I see my mom, Gloria. I was only sixteen when she passed on."

"I lost my parents when I was young, too. So did Helen, at least by modern standards. Did your mom say anything to you?"

"She told me she was proud of her son. In fact, every night she comes to me. She tells me to be careful because she doesn't want to see me yet."

Doug laughed. "That is *exactly* what my parents said to me when I first met them after I started dreaming of them. And you know what?

They were *real*. I even danced with my mom on my wedding night and Helen danced with my Pop. Now, do you have any idea what it means?"

"No, sir, I don't. Do you?"

"Gaia finished her explanation with a short ending. It went like this. 'Doug, there isn't one single person who has been selected in the lottery. There are many. You, of course, were the first. But then, because life became more difficult on Earth, we had to select more to spread our word of the gifts to humankind as well as the Golden Rule. The young men and women who have been selected the most recently, they will be responsible for sending our seed to many other universes. And one day, it will be them and not you who will again populate what will be called a New Earth and its moon to bring happiness to all who live'. That's what she said, Romero," Doug said, slapping the young man on the shoulder. "You've been selected for the greatest adventure that humankind has ever enjoyed. Together with your someday wife, you'll first journey to other universes where you'll have any number of children. Neither they nor you or your wife will ever die. Then, when you get done settling other planets, you'll come back to Earth and there, you'll live a true life of peace and happiness."

Before Romero could reply, the ship's radio sparked to life.

"Freighter One, this is Gaian Command. This is a warning to your entire fleet. We've detected a large force of enemy spaceships hiding behind Earth's moon. You're running into a trap, One. The Queen recommends that you do an immediate one-eighty and fire up your Spacedrive and come home to Gaia. The Queen tells me to pass on her message, 'Doug, tomorrow is another day'.

"Command, tell Our Lady, I'm sorry but we're already committed. The entire fleet has begun its final approach to all the cities we targeted per her orders. It's just too late, One."

"Captain, look at that!" Romero pointed up at his radar. "We have enemy fighters heading right toward the fleet. Looks like a dozen of them, sir. At least that."

Doug keyed his mic. "Earth Fleet, this is Captain Masters. Scramble now! And that's an order. Fighters, intercept those incoming targets before they have a chance to shoot down our freighters."

As the fleet carried out his orders, the starry skies of space held a battle never before seen in Galactic history. Radars still operating from Earth tracked thousands of missiles and lazars with their hot signatures as they moved at thousands of miles per hour toward their targets. In Chicago's Northwestern University, the giant telescope swung straight up, its round housing revolving as it tracked the streaks of light. Then the dark sky above them exploded and, as if the sun had risen far too early, it lit Chicago as if it was late morning, not 3:30AM.

In his freighter, Doug and Romero took evasive action when their telepathy picked up a dozen missiles streaking toward them.

"Romero, fire our laser and interceptor missiles. Use them all or we're dead!"

Romero reached up to the control monitor, pushing all the buttons that showed available missiles. "Firing all of them, Captain. Looks like their all tracking hot and true."

Doug watched the radar as first one, then another, and then all of the enemy missiles were destroyed. "What about the laser? Did we take out any of their fighters?"

"We got five but ten more are on their way in."

"Full power and dive toward Earth. With any luck we'll lose them."

Romero lit up the Spacedrive, pushing their freighter toward Earth. As they hurtled toward the wide blue seas of the Indian Ocean, Doug reached forward and grasped the control column.

"I've got it. All right, you beast. Let's see what you're made of."

He pulled back with all of his strength on the twin sticks. The freighter shook as it experienced excessive G forces and both men thought it might fall apart.

"We're exceeding design parameters, Captain! We're going to break up if you don't do something. Stop pulling back on the yoke!"

"I've been here before, Romero. Back in the day, I made a commercial airliner do just this same thing to save most of our passengers and crew. The people who built our freighters know exactly how to put them together."

Doug pulled back even further. Just as he was flying level within the white clouds over the ocean, an enemy fighter appeared right in front of them.

"We've had it!" Doug yelled. "Get ready to eject!"

Romero reached for the handle beneath his seat but as he did, he glanced over at his Captain. Masters seemed more intent on steering toward the enemy fighter than ejecting.

"Go on, man! Get the fuck out of here!" he ordered Romero.

"I'm staying put if you're not going."

"I told you to eject. Do it now! That's an order."

Romero pulled the handle with both hands. For a moment it didn't move so he pulled again, this time as hard as he could. His seat, with him strapped to it, was thrown from the freighter. As he looked back over his shoulder, and just as his parachute popped open above him, he saw his freighter and the fighter hit each other. Witnessing a massive explosion as he floated toward the sea, he was certain his Captain could never survive.

Chapter Twenty-Eight

In the space freighter, Doug looked up to see five enemy Y-Wing fighters diving on him. They fired all their missiles and Doug, not afraid, fired all the missiles that were left in his turrets then pulled up. As the freighter gained altitude the stress finally proved too much for the design. As he sat watching three of the enemy fighters explode as his Bear Strike Missiles hit them, his spacecraft began to break up. He looked at the monitors above him. His freighter's wings were torn off and tumbled back toward Earth. Then the entire spacecraft began to break up. Knowing he could not possibly survive in what was left of the freighter, he also decided to bail out. As he pulled the handles with both hands and was ejected from the command deck, he looked down on what was left of the freighter as it spiraled toward the seas below him. At an altitude of thirty thousand feet, his parachute automatically deployed. Then he found himself swinging from the parachute lines and his harness. When he was ten feet above the calm sea, he hit the buckle holding the harness to him. As he fell, he looked around him. That's when he saw a Russian helicopter swing toward him.

"Oh Christ, I'm fucked!" he muttered to himself as he hit the sea and began to sink due to the heavy weight of his boots. He deployed his life vest with one hand by pulling on the red handle. As it blew up, surrounding his neck, he bobbed to the surface. Looking up, the Russian chopper was directly over him. The downwash of its rotor blades shook him as two Russian divers jumped from the chopper, landing in the sea right beside him. When they swam to him, one of them pulled a pistol from his diving suit and said in a strong American accent, "You're not going anywhere, my friend, ты сволочь, you bastard! You're our prisoner now: двигаться или я стреляю в тебя."

Doug was forced into a basket and hauled up to the chopper door. There, the winch operator pulled him in. He immediately placed handcuffs on Doug, not even offering him a towel to dry off. It was then, as the Russian helicopter sped to the nearby shore, that Doug realized he was truly fucked. "I'll be held prisoner by these hooligans until Gaia finds out. Then there will be hell to pay."

✈ ✈ ✈

In Gaia IV, Admiral Sally Simpson ran to her Queen's bedroom. She stopped, catching her breath. She looked at the door knowing what she was about to tell Gaia would be hard for Her Highness to accept. But Sally knew it was her duty to deliver not only good news but bad news to her Queen.

Ready, she took a breath and banged hard on the door. When no one answered, she banged on the door again. At last, it opened. Amendus stood before her wearing his robe.

"My granddaughter, don't you know what time it is? It's three o'clock in the morning! Your grandmother is trying to sleep. She's over-tired. Gaia hasn't had any sleep in almost four days."

Sally bowed to the Royal Consort. She pulled herself upright and handed him an envelope. "My Lord, I'm here to deliver this news to my Queen. Can you make sure she reads it when she finally wakes up?"

Amendus took the envelope and considered the new admiral. "Why of course, I will, Admiral Simpson. I'm sorry I was angry. I have not slept much either these past four days. But I'll make sure Gaia reads this. May I ask you, is it urgent?"

"Yes, my Lord. I'm afraid it is."

Again, he considered the Admiral and then noticed her flushed face. There were also tears in her eyes. "May I ask you, does this concern Doug?"

"I'm afraid it does, My Lord," she replied and cleared her throat. "Commodore Masters was shot down. His co-pilot ejected first. My father shot down at least three enemy fighters but then his freighter was destroyed. He also ejected but has been picked up by the Russian navy and has been taken to a base in Crimea where he's being held prisoner."

"Good lord above!" Amendus snapped. He tore open the letter and read it. "It's from Space Command. They say that the Russians will hold him for ransom when they find out who he is. Why did we let him go, anyway? There were other pilots just as qualified."

"My Lord, none of our crews on the mission to Earth carry any identification at all. They only way they'll learn of the Commodore's true identify is if they torture him."

"Which they will. They'll have to kill your father before he utters one word that could be used to identify him. If the Russians discover who he really is, they won't only hold him for financial gain. They'll insist that our entire fleet turn around and go back to our home planet."

"I agree with you, My Lord and grandfather. If we do that, if we give in to their demands, then all of our planning and the crews we've already lost will be worth nothing."

Amendus tightened the belt on his robe and looked her dead in the eye. "Do not worry, Admiral. I'll wake your Queen now. Gaia will want to know of this unfortunate news immediately. We'll come up with another plan that will make the Russians realize that they've no reason to keep fighting. They've lost already. Now it's just a matter of convincing them of that fact."

Amendus turned and re-entered his quarters then closed the door. Sally stood thinking for a moment. She was grateful that she was subordinate to her royal leaders and didn't have their responsibilities. Then she turned, too, and went back to the War Room.

✈ ✈ ✈

In a cold, damp cell in Crimea, Doug screamed as Putin's henchmen tortured him. A general from the Warner Army, part of Putin's hired soldiers, grabbed him by the jaw and wrenched it toward him. Doug looked up, blood dripping from his face, as the Russian army officer grabbed an ear and twisted it. Doug screamed again as the pain caused his entire body to shake in the wooden chair he was tied to.

"You will talk, American! Talk, or we will kill you!" the Russian yelled. "Now who are you and what is your rank? Where are your friends landing? They won't land here. They know we are waiting with nuclear tipped missiles and will destroy them!"

Doug's head tipped up. His blurry vision caught the soldier dressed in forest green military attire smirking down on him. Doug shook his head, sweat flying everywhere. He coughed, spitting blood on the floor. His tongue searched his mouth, finding two broken teeth. She spat them out and, with his vision now clear, began to laugh.

"You fool! Don't you think Gaia knows what you're doing to me? She's not crazy enough to rescue me. She knows you've set a trap. I'm the bait but you're dead, you Сукин сын, you son of a bitch General."

"You know my rank? Oh, but of course you do," the soldier said, glancing at the green epaulets he wore on both shoulders. "Now, you tell me your name and rank."

"I am no one special," Doug replied, "so you don't need my name. As to my rank. I am a private in the Gaian Army."

"Really? Privates do not fly space freighters. Your rank must be at least Ensign but you are too old for that, my friend. As to your name…"

The General turned around. Doug's groggy eyes followed to where he looked. A soldier was dragging a body across the concrete. "Romero," Doug whispered.

"I'm sorry for your loss, Commodore Doug Masters. I'm afraid your friend has a loose tongue when we tortured him."

"What did you do to him, you coward."

"I am no coward, Masters. It is my job to protect my soldiers, just like you. We did nothing special to him. But we told him that if he did not tell us your name and rank, we would kill all of his family when we take over Gaia, your planet now. But in fact, we already have. When I showed him this," the General picked up a black bag from the floor and held up a dark object shaped like a ball, "I also tell him I so very sorry for his loss."

"It's a head, isn't it."

"Yes, is head of the man's brother. He also fly for the Gaian military. I tell him that next we kill his only sister. That, as you say, did the trick. Then he tell me your name, etcetera."

Doug looked back again at the trail of Romero's blood leading to a closed steel door. "You just wait until Gaia finds out what you did to my friend. You're cooked meet, you rotten…"

The General stepped back. "But how could she know what we plan? We're fifty feet below ground. Not even she, with all her powers, can know exactly where you are or what we do to you."

Doug smiled. "Can't she? You are the Сукин сын! Don't you know that she can read minds of every person in the Universe no matter where they are? She knows, idiot. She knows what you did to Romero and his brother. She knows what you will do to me today and for every day until you let me go free."

"I will give you one more chance, Doug Masters. Tell me where they will land or we'll place you against that wall and shoot you."

A Russian soldier with a Kalashnikov rifle stepped up. She checked how many rounds were still left in her weapon. Doug watched as she pushed a lever, placing it on automatic fire. Doug realized that if he didn't give the General what he demanded, he would be cut in two. Defiance settled onto Doug's face and he scowled. "I don't care how much you torture me. I'll never give you what you want."

"It benefits no one for you to keep your mouth shut, Commodore Masters. Let's try one more thing." The General reached into his pocket, extracting a large pair of pliers. He took Doug's right hand in his and, opening the teeth of the tool, grabbed Doug's thumb nail. Then he pulled until the nail came off. As blood fell onto the floor, Doug shrieked with pain.

"Pull them all off! Take my arm off!" he screamed. "I'll never say anything else to you."

His head fell to his breast in unconsciousness. The General shrugged then nodded to his subordinate. The woman put down her rifle and picked up a pail of water. She poured it all over Doug's head. He woke, pain again creasing his face.

"Then it's over, comrade, because you are too weak to tell the truth to me and my fellow Russians," the General said. "I'm sorry to execute such a fine soldier. But that's the way life is. Do you have any last requests? A cigarette perhaps or a drink of water?"

"The least you can do is tell me your name. You know mine, now."

"Zarnoff. Peotr Andreyovich Zarnoff."

Doug's lips turned up in a small smile. "If you're going to give me a last request, General Zarnoff, then I'd like a nice glass of red wine."

"Done! I'll join you. We'll also each have a glass of Vodka as a going away present!"

The General clapped his hands and his orderly appeared. In Russian, he told the soldier to bring wine, a bottle of Vodka and two small glasses. As the orderly hurried off, the General untied Doug's arms and hands.

"Soldier! Bring bandages for my Comrade! I will not have him executed with blood on my hands as well as his. внимание! Attention, do it quick!" As the soldier saluted and hurried away to carry out the General's orders, Doug stood. Suddenly, he bent over, his vomit mixing with his blood on the floor.

"Don't worry, Commodore. We'll have you cleaned up soon. We'll move into another room where my personal medic will attend you. Then we will toast both of us and say Na Zdarovya! На здоровье! To

life! What a wonderful way to look death in the face."

Ten miles west and two hundred and eighty thousand feet above the Crimean prison where Doug was being held, a Gaian space freighter was monitored by the Queen, Amendus and Sally—who stood in the War Room of the Command Ship— slide open its large cargo door.

Five US Navy Seals leaped out in high altitude pressurized jumpsuits, using helmets and oxygen, and dove at high speed toward Earth.

Admiral Simpson looked down from the monitors. "They're off! In fifteen minutes, they're sure to rescue Commodore Masters."

"Do not be so sure about that, Admiral," Amendus replied. "Many bad things can happen. The Russian Wallace Company and its General are nobody's fool. There is a good chance the Seal team. will be spotted before they land. They will be shot to death and die in their parachute harnesses."

"My husband, why are you always such a pessimist?" Gaia interjected, smiling at him. "You know they have just as much of a chance to rescue Doug as they do of dying. We must wait, husband. We have not many minutes to go before we find out what will happen. Until then, we can only pray that the team and our son will come out of this rescue operation safely."

"My Queen, where is my mother?" Sally asked.

"She is gone from here to be with her husband when they rescue him," the Queen answered.

"She's crazy! Doesn't she know she could be injured or killed?"

"My daughter Helen is a mad woman, yes. But she loves your husband so much and she trusts all of us to succeed on this mission. Do not worry for your mother, my granddaughter, my Sally. Be confident."

Sally again looked up at the monitors. The rescue team was plummeting to Earth. As the five team members hit the atmosphere, their suits could be seen glowing with the heat of entry through the

planet's atmosphere. Sally knew that no matter what the temperature, the Seal team would survive due to the new technology of their jumpsuits. They were composed of a modern fabric and titanium steel helmets with Teflon coated visors, the best that money could buy. As she looked again at the glowing trails of the five Seal team members, she crossed her fingers behind her back.

Miles below the plummeting Seal team, Doug and the General sat at a table.

"ты мой большой друг!" the General said, raising a glass of Vodka. "You are my great friend." As Doug watched, his nemesis swallowed the clear drink from its small glass in a single gulp. Doug picked up his own glass of Vodka and smiled.

"I don't know Russian at all except a few words General. But if you say I am your great friend then you are my *best* friend!" Doug also drank in one gulp. "На здоровье!"

"To life!" shouted the General. He poured more Vodka into each glass. Doug eyed the bottle. It was already three-quarters empty. What the General did not know was that Doug never swallowed the strong alcoholic drink. Instead, he swished it around in his mouth and, when the General was not looking, spit it under the table.

He looked down at his right hand. The thumb had been bandaged. The medic had also cleaned up the wounds on his face and lips. Doug knew he had black eyes from the beatings he was given. He gently touched his swollen eyelids then looked back at the General.

"Are you ready, Comrade?" he asked, laughing. "What shall we drink to this time!"

"Let us both drink to President Putin," the General said gravely. "Right now, he hides with his family in a bunker beneath the Kremlin."

"That's interesting," Doug replied. "I thought he'd gone to Saint Petersburg."

The soldier slammed his glass on the table. The Vodka bottle rocked, threatening to fall to the floor but Doug grabbed it, placing it firmly back.

"You fool!" the General continued. "Our president would never leave Moskva. It is too important to him. He can't be seen to be a coward, can he, by fleeing to Saint Petersburg or anywhere else in Russia. Is that not true, my friend?"

"Yes, General. President Putin is no coward and neither are you. Sir, did you say he was beneath the Kremlin?"

The General nodded and Doug could see that the man was dead drunk.

"Directly beneath his family apartment. There is an elevator in the president's bedroom hidden behind twin glass closet doors. Slide them open and you find it. See? It's so easy! Besides, no one has ever entered President Putin's family quarters without his direct permission."

"Is that so, General?" Doug said, also thinking how Gaia, Amendus and Admiral Simpson would love this information if he could get it to them. "Then let us lift our glass to Mr Putin and pray for a long and healthy life."

"Here's to our President! May he live forever!"

The General drank again. His eyes glazed over. Doug poured him another glass and said, "Let us drink together one more time for our president's health!"

The General drank. As Doug watched, the soldier began swaying. Then he toppled to the floor. Doug walked over to the fallen man and searching his pockets, finding a set of keys which he knew would let him out of the jail. Doug reached down, unbuckling the General's gun harness. As he wrapped it around his waist, Doug pulled out the silver revolver. It had been made in America. A Magnum .357. He opened the circular cartridge holder and saw that it was already filled with bullets. Then he looked in the holster's pockets and saw that they too were also filled with cartridges. Doug took them out and counted them. There were four pockets filled with ten rounds of ammunition apiece.

"Forty-seven rounds, including the one already chambered in the Magnum," Doug said to the body passed out on the floor at his feet. "Thank you General. I feel like Dirty Harry. Now, let's drink one more time." Doug poured himself a glass of Vodka and this time tossed it back. He could feel his stomach glow with heat and happiness as the strong alcohol made its way into his system. "You make my day, General. You've given me everything I need to get out of jail for free!"

Chapter Twenty-Nine

Doug unlocked the steel door to the medic's ward room with the General's set of keys. Cocking the silver revolver, he crept out into a long hallway. He could hear soldiers' voices speaking Russian echo toward him. Walking silently up the hall, he came to the prison's cafeteria. There, a group of twelve soldiers, all armed with Kalashnikov rifles, sat around a table drinking tea.

"Comrade," one said in good English, "please pour me another cup of tea and hand me the sugar. Are there no good biscuits in this camp or does Putin insist that we all survive on these horrible rations? Even our General knows that soldiers march on full stomachs!"

The soldiers all muttered their agreements in Russian. Then Doug, with his Magnum raised in front of him, crept into the large room and quietly cocked it.

"Крыса вышла из своей клетки!" one soldier yelled and Doug knew that the woman was saying something like 'the bastard is here!' as she spotted him. He pointed the gun at the nearest Russian and opened fire. The soldiers all picked up their automatic rifles. Machine gun rounds fractured the cement of the hallway all around him as Doug dived for cover. He fired twice. Both rounds hit two separate soldiers in the head. As one hit the ground, the table fell over. The rest of the platoon advanced toward him. But Doug fired again and again until he had no more rounds left in his Magnum. Before he ran back down the hall, he quickly counted the fallen soldiers and reckoned he had killed or maimed at least five of them.

"That's seven to go," Doug said as he stopped and reloaded in a deep alcove beside a locked steel door. Breathing hard, he looked down at his wounded hand. Blood crept out from beneath the bandages. His legs hurt but he ignored both. Finished loading, he slammed shut the metal cylinder that housed six new rounds of ammunition. Then, screaming like an Irish Banshee, he ran back into the cafeteria. The seven surviving soldiers were all crouching behind the table, waiting for him. As Doug ran toward him, avoiding automatic rifle fire by ducking and weaving, he emptied his gun, splintering the wooden table. With nowhere to hide, the Russians turned, running out the opposite door. Doug grabbed a Kalashnikov and three full magazines that were lying on the floor and ran after them.

On the other side of the door, he ran up a set of stairs. Above him, light beamed down. Taking a breath, he sprinted up the next flight. He could hear automatic fire and screaming in Russian and English.

"Get down on your knees right now!" he heard someone with an American accent order.

When Doug reached the top of the stairway, an open door led out to the top of the prison. There, he could see five US Navy Seals holding their rifles on the seven surviving Russians. All of them were on their knees, their hands raised, and they were being blindfolded as Doug walked out into the bright sunlight.

A Seal walked over wearing green military fatigues and saluted. "Sir, are you Commodore Martin?"

"That's right, sailor. I take it you're a Navy Seal Team.?"

"Yes sir. Gaia sent us out on a mission to rescue you."

"And you did it, Captain," Doug replied, seeing the dark green epaulets on the man's shoulders. "When you radio her, tell her I'm in good shape."

"Sir, you're injured aren't you?" the Captain asked, pointing at Doug's bandaged hands.

"It's nothing. When you talk to our Queen, tell her I know where President Putin is hiding. Just say he's hiding beneath his family apartment in the Kremlin. I advise her to have another Seal Team enter that building. Go to that fool's family apartment. There, find a glass closet door. Directly behind it is an elevator. Take it down and you'll find that insane Russian president and I suspect some of his henchmen."

"I'll do that now, Commodore," the Captain said, saluting.

Then Doug heard the sound of helicopter rotor blades. He looked up, seeing a Russian gunship sweep toward them. A Seal raised a launcher to his shoulder, the missile housed in its green canister. "Fire in the hole!" she shouted, then released the projectile. Within seconds, the missile had reached its target. The Russian chopper exploded in flames and smoke, crashing in the prison courtyard below in a ball of fire.

"Commodore, we're going to get you out of here right now!" the Captain yelled over the sound of gasoline exploding from the destroyed chopper. "Rescue two-niner will be here in seconds. I've already radioed Space Command and have told them to relay the message about Putin's location. We'll get him, Sir, you can be sure of that."

Doug heard the sound of rockets. He looked up to see a Rescue Vehicle descending toward the roof of the prison. The Seals and Doug all turned away from the heat and dirt as the vehicle landed. Then the door opened. The first one out was Helen.

"Doug!" she shouted, and then she was in his arms They kissed and she looked up at him. "Your Earth mission days are over, you bastard. Don't you know you scared me to death again?"

He smiled as he held her, feeling Helen's warm body against him. "You got it kid. No more Earth adventures for Doug Martin. Not unless you come with me if it's not as dangerous as this one was."

They kissed again then the Captain grabbed each of them by the arm. They ran toward the open door of Rescue Two-Niner with the Seal Team. After they had entered, the vehicle's outer door closed. Then fire and smoke vented from the bottom of the rescue craft as the vehicle shook then took off. At an altitude of one thousand feet, it hovered above the prison. Doug, knowing that no other prisoners were inside and that it was still occupied by well over a hundred Russian soldiers as well as the drunken General, ordered the prison to be decimated.

As he watched on the Rescue ship's Command Deck television monitors, a group of cluster bombs fell toward the large building. It seemed like a hundred explosions followed, obscuring the prison in a ball of orange and grey dust. When he looked back up at the monitor, Doug could see that nothing was left of the building except a few small fires, smoke, a hole in the ground and piles of rubble.

Chapter Thirty

In the medical ward located near Sydney, Australia, Doug had his injuries tended to by both a Gaian surgeon and a male nurse who worked at a local hospital. When the nurse took off the bloody wrappings that bandaged Doug's hand, the surgeon took a closer look.

"Gangrene has set in," the surgeon said to Doug who was still dazed by his fight in the prison as he made his successful escape. "It has happened rapidly due to the unclean environment of your prison. Even now, on Earth, some surgeons would amputate your hand and wrist. But we have less invasive methods to restore human flesh, bone and blood."

Doug, who was lying flat on his back on a medical table and still dressed in his filthy green overalls that the General had given to him, could smell the putrid condition of his flesh. He expected the Gaian surgeon to ask the nurse to hand him some sort of steel surgical tool. Instead, all the doctor did was close his eyes. Doug watched as the mottled salamander green face relaxed then, as the brow furrowed, the surgeon concentrated in a way Doug had never seen before. The doctor's brow furrowed more. The mottling of the green tinted skin looked as if was revolving. The surgeon's face turned from green to gold, then to blue. His entire body floated off the floor and, as Doug kept watching, the doctor's arms pointed down at him.

"Commander, think of nothing at all," the nurse told Doug. "Close your eyes too. All you'll feel is tingling. I'll tell you when to open them again which is when the procedure is finished."

Doug did as he was told. He closed his eyes. At first all that he could see was darkness. Then, as if in the center of his forehead, he saw a flash of light and someone whispered to him.

"Do not be afraid, Doug Masters. You think I am Gaia, your mother, but I am not. I am much more than she will ever be. She is watching me as I do what it is my gift to give to you. You and your wife and children are important to the survival of humankind, just as you have been told. As for me? I am the Unknown Spirit who is responsible for shepherding all that have survived from Earth's many catastrophes. It is my mission to ensure the regeneration of humankind, not on this planet but elsewhere. To accomplish your objective, Doug Masters, you must be whole. Be still now. This will not hurt you, not one little bit."

The voice in Doug's head receded from his consciousness. Then he heard music that he could not at first identify but then realized it was the four notes of the Code that he had heard so many times before. He felt his entire body tingle with a sensation that was like being placed in the warm waves of a far-off sea. He remembered how he and Helen would swim together in the ocean off the Indian coast or in the tranquil lagoons in the Grenadine Islands. Then Helen was part of his consciousness and though his eyes were still closed he could see her as she bent toward him.

"It's almost over, sweetheart. When you're finished they'll call me and I'll come to see you."

Then his body trembled. He felt that he was being lifted off the table. The darkness in his mind flashed with a great light.

"Commander, don't open your eyes yet. Now I want you to clench your hand into a fist. Can you do that?"

Doug did as he was instructed. He could feel his fingers touch his palm.

"Good. Now use your tongue to feel the new teeth in your mouth."

Again, Doug did as he was ordered. His tongue searched for the holes in his gums where teeth had been knocked out by the fists of the Russian soldiers. Yet all he could feel were a complete line of teeth.

"You replaced my teeth?" Doug asked.

"No talking yet," said the nurse. "The surgeon is almost finished."

Doug's entire body shook again. He felt sweat on his face and then he was so cold he thought he had been buried in a ton of snow. When those feelings of extreme temperature passed, his body felt once again normal.

"You can open your eyes now."

When Doug opened his eyes, the first thing he saw was Helen. She ran toward him, falling on top of him. He pulled her warm body on top of his chest and her long blonde hair covered his face.

"You're back, sweetheart," Helen said and started to cry. "I thought I was going to lose you forever."

He smiled up at his wife, wiping tears from her face. "But you didn't, did you? I promised you I'd be back."

"Can I please test his new hand, Mrs. Masters?" the surgeon asked. He took Doug's hand in his own. Doug looked down, astonished. He no longer had four fingers and a thumb on his hand. Instead, he had five fingers as well as a thumb.

"I have a Gaian hand," Doug whispered.

"Now, I want you to take my hand," the surgeon ordered. "Squeeze it as hard as you can."

When Doug did so, he saw the doctor's face turn red. "That's enough, Commander! It works just as I hoped it would."

Helen took Doug's new hand in her own. "Five fingers rather than four," she marveled. "And stronger than you've ever been."

"The woman who whispered to me when my hand was being replaced never mentioned more strength." He sat up, now holding Helen tight to him. "We'll test it later. Helen, I feel like I've been gone for over a year. Can we go to bed, please?"

His wife giggled. "I thought you'd never ask."

But gazing at her, Doug saw his wife's eyes go wide.

"Nurse, can you please hand me a mirror?" she asked. As the medical professional went to find a mirror, Doug took his wife's hand. "Why a mirror? Am I that old and ugly?"

"Wait until you see yourself. You're not going to believe it."

When the nurse handed Helen the mirror, she turned it toward Doug. He looked at his reflection then took it from Helen to look even closer. His hair had grown back and was now as long as his shoulders: brown and wavy, not grey. All the wrinkles on his face had disappeared. The black eyes where the soldiers had punched him were completely healed as were the scratches on his face.

"Look at me," he said with wonder. "I look like I did in high school."

Helen smiled. "Soon, I will too. All human survivors on Earth have to get a treatment just like yours. We'll all be super-human."

Doug smiled. "When I'm with you, I always feel super-human. Now can we go to bed?"

She took his hand and led him out of the medical department and toward their private quarters.

卐 卐 卐

On the bridge of the Space Command vehicle which still hid behind Earth's moon, Gaia received a typed message that her radio operator had just received. Glancing at it, she smiled.

"I see that President Putin is exactly where Doug said he would be. The Navy Seal Team is engaged in a bloody firefight with the troops who are protecting him. It's only time before that traitor is captured together with the surviving members of his family."

Amendus, standing next to her, took the message and glanced at it.

"What's done is done," he said, reading it again. "But he is not the only traitor that still lives on Earth. I have had reports that some of his henchmen have stolen Putin's nuclear codes. We have been monitoring their radio traffic though they do not know it. Even now, they are arming the remaining missiles that still lie hiding in their silos all across the vast Russian continent." He looked to his wife. "My Lady, you look tired again. You're not sleeping well, are you?"

She laughed and shrugged her broad shoulders. "You mean I look older, don't you husband? I've lost count of how many years I've been alive. Is it one thousand? Or is it more?"

"Much more, my love. You were five hundred years old by Earth standards when we first met. Don't you remember?"

"I was so beautiful then," she said with tears in her eyes. "The years have passed so quickly."

"You will always be beautiful to me, no matter what your age is. Admiral Simpson will soon be on the bridge. Why don't you get some sleep?"

She placed her hand on his strong arm and Amendus covered it with his own. "For a change I will do what my husband advises. Wake me in an hour, will you?"

She turned, starting to walk toward their quarters.

"Gaia, will you follow one more piece of advice?" her husband asked her. "Let the ship's medic examine you. I don't want you to worry but you look far more than tired. Last night, when we were sleeping, I felt a lump on your breast."

She turned, smiling back at him. "I found that lump a month ago. But I was too absorbed in our situation to do anything about it. You're right, husband. I'll go to our bed. But tell the medic to come right in. I'll be expecting her."

✲ ✲ ✲

In a secret bomb shelter below the Kremlin, the Navy Seal Team commander, Captain Jina Causkey, a woman of Irish descent, ducked as automatic fire cut down one of the members of her small squad. Pulling Lieutenant James Sawyer toward her by grasping what remained of his uniform, she protected his head as a grenade exploded near them, scattering the ground with hot steel shrapnel.

"Get down!" she yelled to the other five US Seal Team soldiers. Then she cradled James's head in her arms "You're going to be fine, Jimsy. It's almost over. I counted twenty-five Russian soldiers when we entered the shelter from the elevator. Now I think they're down to five or six. We still have seven. Get on your feet, hear me? We need you!"

She lifted James by pulling him up by the shirt but then noticed he was missing almost all of his right arm. Jina set him back down on the cold concrete now covered with his blood and searched the floor near him. She saw his forearm still wrapped in his green and black uniform jacket.

"Jina, your Jimsy doesn't want to die," he said, smiling, his face streaked with blood. "We're getting married next month, remember?"

"Don't you die on my, Jim. Your Jina won't be able to stand it."

"Yes you will, darlin'. You'll be fine." As he closed his eyes and stopped breathing, Jina began beating his chest with both fists, hoping to restart his heart. But after sixty seconds she realized she'd lost the man that was the most important person in her life.

"Jim, don't leave me. Jimmy?" But she realized he was gone.

A Seal Team squad member scrambled to her side, his body close to the concrete as bullets continued to scream overhead.

"Captain, we've got the Russians pinned down. They must be almost out of ammunition for their Kalashnikovs. But they have plenty of grenades left. We also saw them making Molotov cocktails. There's a strong smell of gasoline coming from where they've concealed themselves."

"Where's Putin?"

"Hiding somewhere behind them. We think he's close by and, with what remains of his family and friends, is helping to make those cocktails."

Captain Causkey again glanced down at Jimsy. "Enough of this! Jim died trying to capture that bastard. I'm not going to lose one more Seal to that thug or his soldiers." She waved an arm and the rest of the Seal Team ran up as they covered each other with automatic fire from their weapons. They crouched around her in a circle. "Okay, you guys. Here's what we're going to do. Fuck trying to save this murderer. If we kill Putin, we kill him. I'll do the explaining to the Admiral and President Biden when we get back. We'll charge them two-by-two, okay? Save your ammunition until you get a clean shot. Shoot for their stomachs. It'll hurt more but kill them just the same. Got it?"

The seven soldiers all gave her a thump's up.

"Right. When I say 'Go', do it!"

Captain Causkey crept forward under a hail of automatic fire. She saw a boy, not more than ten-years-old, point his weapon at her. She took out her Colt 45 that Jimsy had given to her last Christmas, and aimed for the kid's stomach. Not wanting to make him suffer, and changing her mind, she pulled the weapon up and aimed for the head. Then she cocked it and pulled the trigger. The kid fell back, blood bleeding from his forward, his rifle discharging uselessly at the floor.

"All right Team. Go!"

Two-by-two, the Team ran forward, all firing when they had a clear shot. Two more Russians fell. As her squad grappled hand-to-hand with the survivors, the Captain saw Putin running toward the back of the room accompanied by a woman in a business suit.

"Kill them all!" she shouted. "No prisoners this time. They killed Jimsy so they all deserve it."

The Captain fired her revolver at Putin as he fled with the woman but the bullets only bounced harmlessly off a cement pillar. When the chambers were empty she put it in its holster then drew her knife. As she ran toward her target she stumbled over three dead bodies. Looking down, she saw that they were all young women dressed in fashionable pantsuits and heels. Automatic weapons were held in their mutilated hands.

"They must be Putin's daughters. The bastard made them fight and die needlessly. Look. They committed suicide," the Captain said to herself as she saw one woman clutching an unexploded hand grenade.

Looking back, she saw that her team was engaged with the remaining enemy soldiers. Turning back, she again saw Putin. Running as fast as she could, she tackled him. The two fell, Jina on top. Knowing he was a retired KGB agent and trained in hand-to-hand combat, she pulled him closer realizing that this way he would be unable to reach for any weapon he might have on him. As they struggled, Putin's knee thrust toward her crotch. As it struck its target, she grinned down on him.

"Men have balls, you shithead. Women don't. Didn't you know that?"

As the point of her knife moved toward his throat, Putin punched her twice in the face. Her eyes full of involuntary tears because he had struck her nose, she relinquished her grip on his jacket. Pushing the Captain off of him, the Russian president rolled to his feet. When Jina stood, again pointing the knife at him, Putin turned and ran back toward the woman who the Captain had not yet recognized. Running after him, she trapped the Russian president against a concrete wall. He turned, grabbing the woman who stood next to him. He drew a revolver and pointed the gun at his captive.

"Mr President, I'm gonna give you one last chance," Jina said, her breath coming in gasps. "Release the woman now and put up your hands or suffer the same fate as the Seal your soldiers killed."

Putin only grinned and held the woman closer. She screamed in fear, struggling in his grasp. The Russian president held the pistol to her head.

"You think you will capture me, comrade?" Putin asked in perfect English. "If you don't put down that knife I will shoot this poor woman."

"You coward! Let her go and I'll spare your life."

"So you can use me as a hostage, dear Captain? And yes, I've seen pictures of you, Miss Causkey. It's said that someday because you are so brave you will make Commander. I congratulate you! But I will never leave Mother Russia so, you cunt, you can go to hell."

The Russian woman still struggled in Putin's grasp; his gun still held to her temple. As Jina watched, the president cocked it and put his finger on the trigger.

"What's it to be, Captain? Do I go free or does this innocent woman die?"

"No, Vladimir! Please do not kill me!" the woman screamed in English then turned to the Seal Team Captain. "He is my father's best friend. Why would he want to kill me?"

"Putin, that's your best friend's daughter?" Jina asked, finally recognizing the woman. "We knew her reported death was a Maskorova, a lying ruse, meant to instill fear and outrage in the Russian people. Are you such a fucking demon that you'd kill her?"

Putin only grinned back. Realizing she had no option at that point, Gina lowered the arm holding the knife. Then she looked at the woman and smiled. "You are beautiful, do you know that, Miss Dugina? As I remember, your first name is Darya, is that right? I'm told you're very smart. Can you guess what it means if I count to three?"

Darya smiled back and nodded. She looked over her shoulder at the gun held to her head. "Please, my President Putin, don't kill me. Surrender."

"No!" roared the president. "I sacrifice you in the name of all things that are Russian!"

"One," Gina said, her eyes glued on the woman. "Two..."

"Don't!" Putin shouted. "You don't have a chance. You're unarmed!"

"Am I?" Gina asked and took a step toward Miss Dugina. "Three!"

Darya pushed hard against Putin then she fell to the floor. Gina, finally with a clear target, threw the knife as hard as she could. Putin stared at her then when blood dripped into his eyes, and dropped his gun. With two hands he pulled the knife out of his forehead.

"I…am…the…Russian…President."

"You're a pig! Now die like one."

Gina picked up the knife from off the floor then thrust it into his throat. Pulling it out, she stabbed her quarry in the chest and stomach over and over again. The president fell to his knees. His hands held his stomach. He turned his head, blood pouring from it, his hate-filled eyes staring at her.

"You really should be made a Colonel, you bitch."

Then he rolled over onto his side. Gina walked up. She felt for a pulse in his throat and wrists but there was no sign of life. Then she walked to the woman and helped her up off the floor.

"I'm not sorry you lost your president," she said. "But too many people have died in this war including my own fiancé."

"You were right when you called him a pig," she hissed. "I was trying to seek asylum in America. My father, Alexander, that man's best friend, found out. He worked with Putin who had his agents track my movements in Moskva and ordered my car to be destroyed and me murdered but he was unsuccessful. My father who is also a traitor, together with this…cutthroat hooligan…put it out to the press that I was dead. For over a year I've had to live in this concrete shelter. Captain, you did the world a favor by killing that traitor to our country."

Behind her, Gina could hear yelling and a final blast of automatic fire. Her second in command ran up.

"Sir, we did as you ordered. We've taken no prisoners." Then he saw Putin lying on the floor in pools of blood. "Is that the Russian president?"

"Sure is. The guy wouldn't listen so I'm afraid I had to slaughter him just like I killed pigs back in Tennessee when I was a kid."

The soldier grinned back at her. "What are you going to tell the Commander-in-Chief?"

"That's easy. I'll tell him the truth. That treasonous pig was holding his best friend's daughter hostage. President Biden will know that I didn't have any other option but to kill the bastard."

"What'll we do with his body?"

"Wrap it in aluminum foil and serve it to the birds, for all I care," she replied, grinning at him. "Seriously? Find a blanket with a presidential seal. Clean him up and wrap him in it. God knows why but the Russians will want to give their boss a national funeral."

When Putin was cleaned up and wrapped in the blanket all that was left exposed was his head. Together with the body of Jimsy, the Seal Team re-entered the elevator with Darya Dugina and ascended up to Putin's Kremlin apartment. When the doors opened and they stepped out, lights flashed as if they were in a tremendous lightning storm.

"What the hell is going on?" Gina asked.

"It is Russian press as well as international television cameras," Darya replied. "Now the world will know what you have done here and how well you have served the Russian people and all of humanity."

Chapter Thirty-One

"The cutthroats!" the newly appointed General of the Wagner Army hissed in English to his staff.

He threw his cellphone down on a wooden workbench, having watched the U.S. Navy thugs take the body of their fallen leader, Vladimir Putin, out into the chill night air through the front doors of the Kremlin. He looked around at his comrades. Their faces were pasty from spending little time outdoors. Instead, they hid in a Crimean nuclear bunker buried in the hills surrounding the harbour where the last Russian and Ukrainian submarines were based. He slammed a fist onto the steel table then turned to his adjutant.

"Bring Vodka. We must toast our fallen President. We will only have one glass each. Then, we must work to repay the West for what they have done to our Motherland!"

When they had finished toasting Putin, they all threw their glasses to the ground and shouted, "Да здравствует матушка россия! Long live Mother Russia!"

"Good," the General said. "Nickolai, come here. What is the status of the Admiral Lenin?"

A Russian Naval Captain stepped forward and saluted. "The submarine is fully provisioned and the crew has reported for duty, General Zelnakoff. We have also tested the firing mechanisms of the missiles. In this," he continued, handing the General a red colored envelope, "are the nuclear codes that our late president gave to me."

"That is good, Captain. How many missiles does the sub carry?"

"Twelve active missiles each carrying twelve MIRV warheads."

"Twelve multiple reentry vehicles? So it's twelve times twelve? That's one-hundred and forty-four warheads. Enough to take out all surviving Western cities. What power do they each have?"

"The warheads, General Kelnakoff? Each warhead is of one-hundred and twenty megatons. Enough to destroy entirely each city they strike. These are our latest nuclear warheads. Their yield is much bigger than anything used to date."

"That is also very good! Captain, when will you put to sea?"

"American satellites pass overhead in an hour. I'd like your permission to put out to sea one hour after that."

"Then you are so ordered. Does each missile have the range to strike their various targets?"

"Sir, these are the latest submarine missiles our past president ordered to be developed. They each have a range of fifty-thousand miles. They no longer track as old missiles did. Instead, each MIRV warhead is powered by a small rocket. They zig and zag like hypersonic rockets to avoid being caught by anti-ballistic missiles."

"Or Gaia and her Earth defense weapons!" the General said and grinned. "Even her telepathic powers and those of her comrades will not be able to destroy all of these superior warheads. Go now, Comrade. Our fleet will escort you into the Atlantic with our guided missile cruisers. We have already broadcast to the West that we conduct naval exercises that are peaceful and not meant to be in any way provocative. When we are well out to sea, you will turn south until you reach the meridian of our planet. Then you will approach the surface and we will radio Headquarter for a final briefing. At that point it will make no difference if Gaia, her Space Command and the Western nations hear our broadcasts. You will fire upon my command and then submerge back to a safe depth. Then we will make our way home, comrade. In a few days it will all be over. Then we will be in command of the entire Earth."

"You say 'we' General Kelnakoff? You are coming with us?"

"I will not stay in a bunker when there is so much at stake. Should we be unable to raise our Headquarters for final instructions and an analysis of where the American fleet is, I will be with you with these!" The General waved the red envelop his Captain had given to him. "This way, there will be no possibility of error. I take it that the two firing keys are also in here?"

"Yes, sir. But what of Gaia and her spaceships? Aren't you worried that they will attack our Headquarters? If so, we will be unable to get any update from our own satellites. As you know, all Russian spy satellite signals come here so our staff can keep a close watch on any new Western military deployments."

The General smirked, his eyes gloating. "Our comrades and their equipment are so deeply buried in the ground that not even

Gaian powers have been able to detect us. She knows nothing about this place."

The Captain started to speak again, his eyes filled with concern. But the General raised his hand. "Nickolai, you worry too much. If we had been detected in this bomb shelter, Gaia and her war cabinet would know what we are up to. We've already told them that we have destroyed every warhead we have. It is part of Putin's great Маскарова. His well-constructed mask of lies makes us look innocent. But you and I know that we have other plans." He gave his Captain a bear hug. "Now go, Nickolai. It is time for us to get to your submarine. I will be with you in moments."

The naval officer saluted then walked out then the General turned to his staff. "It is a great day for Mother Russia, comrades. It is a day that will go down in history! When it's finished, our Army as well as the armies of China and North Korea will control the Earth. We will establish one nation divided not by the West's so-called liberty but united by Communism. Democracy and the free capitalist market have been proven to be a joke! Look what has happened to our planet after the Gaian spacecraft descended and took control? Only one bloody war after another." He saw that there were still two full bottles of Vodka on the table and more glasses. "Fill your glasses again, comrades! Hurry now because we have more important work to do!" When everyone had full glasses, the General picked up his.

Holding it tight, he hoisted it up, putting out his pinky finger as was the tradition in Russia. "A toast! To the great unified Russian Earth. From now on, and like our old USSR, we shall call it from this day forward the UGRP. The United Great Russian Planet! Drink! And I will do my duty by risking my neck just like the Captain and his crew will soon do. In twenty minutes send the official orders to the Admiral Lenin over our coded transmission system. Then we will be ready to leave our port, bound for the inevitable glory of our Motherland!"

In the War Room on Gaia's Space Command vessel, Admiral Simpson listened intently to a radio operator as she decoded the ciphered orders then translated them from Russian to English. Sally bent closer to the operator as she also transcribed the broadcast into the ship's central computer. As the last two sentences were broadcasted and the operator, Chief Cindi McCormick, transcribed those using her keyboard, she looked up at her commanding officer.

"Admiral Simpson, does this mean what I think it does?"

"Read those last two sentences again, Chief."

Looking at her computer screen, the Chief began to read. "Admiral Lenin, you are hereby ordered to proceed due west. When you reach the predetermined launching site we will share with you the position of all Western military assets. When the General gives you the authentication code and orders you to, you will fire." Again, the Chief looked up. "Code? Does this mean the Gaian code?"

"No, it means launch codes."

Sally turned to the rest of her war cabinet. "That crazy Wagner General will fire all of that sub's missiles within a few hours. Get the American Commander-in-Chief on the red phone. The United States is the only country with an effective anti-ballistic missile system left on Earth. I'll talk to our Queen and Amendus. They'll know exactly how much firepower the Admiral Lenin has. Then, we'll come up with a plan to stop them."

The Admiral rushed from the room, hurrying through the main corridor. As she stopped at the door to the Royal Couple's apartment, she saw Amendus standing at the door. His shoulders were hunched. When he turned to her, she realized that he had been crying. Reaching up, she touched his face, feeling tears on the tips of her fingers.

"My Lord, why are you crying? Is Her Royal Highness ill?"

He looked down at her. Tears again fell from his shut eyes and he began sobbing again.

"Sally, I have bad news for all of us," he said. "They say that every good life also owes a single death. So it is for every one of us." The tall husband of their Queen reached down, placing both of his hands on her shoulders. "The medic has seen her. She tells me that Our Lady is dying. She has only hours to live. Not even Gaian medicine can help her because, as I say, she owes her life one death and this is my wife's."

An involuntary sob escaped from Sally's mouth. Looking down at the floor, she cleared her throat then looked back up at the Royal Consort. "My Lord, who will be Queen after Our Lady Gaia is gone from us? Will you be King in her stead?"

"No. I am but a Royal Consort and your father by marriage to our Queen. In our planet's constitution it states plainly that only a female of our species can serve as the head of our government. Therefore, soon after my wife is dead, she will choose someone to replace her."

Sally's face registered no surprise at first but then his words registered. "But Gaia will be dead! How can she choose someone if she's gone from our sight and hearing? Those who have passed on can't talk to us."

He smiled down on her. "Can't they, Sally? We've long told all of you humans that no one really dies. When you pass on we literally catch you. How is it that you could talk to your mother, Helen, after Josie died? Having found death, you are instantly alive again, as you have discovered. You can then choose to be whomever you want to be as long as it is a living creature. Then you can have a new life filled with happiness but this time no heartbreak. So it is with Gaia's life. She will live forever, just like all of us. Isn't that what we taught you? But to do that, I'm afraid first she must die."

"Yes, sire, you did teach us that," Sally uttered as tears fell from her cheeks. "But I already miss my mother."

"You don't need to. She's unconscious now. The medic gave her a sedative. She was in great pain but never said that to anyone, not even me, her husband. She will remain unconscious until she dies. One thing you must do is this. You must locate Helen and Doug. Just before she fell asleep due to the sedative, she told me that her death and eventual resurrection has everything to do with that couple for reasons I don't yet understand. All I know is that they must be here as soon as it can be organized. Do you understand me, my child? Locate them now and bring them to me."

The Admiral saluted. "I will do your bidding, my Lord. But before I do I must also give you bad news. The Wagner Army has a Russian submarine that is sailing to a position a few thousand miles off the coast of Australia. I just heard their Headquarters order them to get ready to open fire with their nuclear missiles."

"Again?" Amendus shouted, pounding his hand against the steel wall. "Will humans never learn? We swore that if humans make nuclear war on each other again that shall be the last straw. We shall turn our back on you and abandon Earth for all of eternity." The Royal Consort took a deep breath and Sally watched as he regained control. "I'm sorry, Admiral. Too much is happening right now. What can I do to help you?"

"Sire, we need to know first if you can stop the missiles. We estimate that the Russian sub will fire over one-hundred nuclear warheads. Second, assuming that they strike major cities, how can we help the survivors this time? I've checked with my crew. We now have well over one-hundred space freighters that can be restocked to save those injured people. We're also starting to reposition our military assets to try to stop those warheads from hitting their multiple targets. And third: what about the radiation? How do we stop it this time?"

"Woman, you ask too much of me this time," he said, sliding to the floor and now looking up at her. Wiping the tears from his face he considered the new situation. "I wish Gaia could answer your questions. I am nothing without my wife."

As Sally watched, Amendus began to cry again, this time breaking down like she'd never seen him do before. His body toppled over and now lying on the floor, his knees came up to his stomach in a fetal position. She knelt beside him and when he reached for her, she put her arms around his broad neck. After a few minutes he stopped crying. She took his hand, helping him to his feet.

"I'm sorry, Admiral. I can't help it."

"My Lord, you may not be human but you have human emotions. I understand. Did I ever tell you how much I grieved when I thought my father, Doug, was dead?"

"No, Sally, you did not," Amendus replied. "We all grieve for those whom we love."

"Dad is a brave man. But I do know that if he had died, he would be immediately given new life."

Amendus stood up and began pacing the corridor. "Then, to your questions. If there are over one-hundred warheads, the Western governments will be able to intercept less than a third of them with their remaining anti-ballistic missiles as well as your naval fleets. Our Gaian defense assets can stop about eighty percent of the rest. But that still leaves enough warheads to wipe out what remains of your civilization. As to your other points: Sally, this time there will be few survivors. The Earth's magnetic core keeps shifting causing many climate aberrations, as you know. When the nuclear warheads strike, the core will shift yet again. This will disrupt the troposphere and change the magnetic poles. When, not if, that happens, and due to more solar winds due to the sun's current activity and large storms across your planet, it will be impossible to stop the fall-out from spreading across the entire planet. Those that do survive will have nothing to go home to. They could live for hundreds of years beneath the Earth's surface but it will be for nothing. When their children's-children's-children come out of hiding, there will be nothing left. Not one single organism can survive the radiation this time. Nuclear holocaust has happened too many times before and like my wife Gaia, whom your planet Earth is named after by native tribes as well as our own, she and your planet have run out of time."

"Is there no hope, Amendus?"

He smiled. "There is always hope. That is what my wife taught me. Where there is hope, there is a source of life. We will evacuate any survivors of this final nuclear war before the radiation kills all of your people. This time we won't take those survivors to live on Mars. Instead, we will take them far beyond your solar system. We shall stop on Mars, of course, to see if anyone wants to come with us. Many will. You and your kind will seed many new Universe's with life, but not life as you now know it. From now on, most of you will be half human and half Gaian, just as Doug is and Helen will be so very soon." Amendus bent, kissing his Admiral on the cheek. Sally looked up into his large liquid eyes, his tears just below the surface, and saw how distraught he was. She reached up, pulling his head down to her and gently kissed him on his dark lips.

"That's from me and Gaia, my Lord. It's from the two of us."

"I know she won't mind," Amendus replied, his arms moving around Sally's waist. "We talked about something like this. We both agreed that if one of us died, as I will too someday, the survivor would take another partner for the rest of their natural lives. Perhaps someday I will find someone just like my Admiral Simpson."

"I hope you do, my Lord. I hope…"

Sally couldn't say what was in her heart. As she let go of him and rushed back to the War Room, Amendus's eyes followed her.

"I never imaged that a human woman could be so much like my wife. Maybe someday we will be together but it is far too early to tell." He watched until she turned the corner then he walked back to the front door of his quarters. He started entering his apartment then leaned against the hallway wall as he thought about his new reality. "From now on I sleep alone and eat alone and read alone and listen to music alone and meditate alone. Such is the fate that this bittersweet life has assigned to me. Unless someone like Sally comes into my life, I will always be alone."

His eyes darted to find her even though he knew that she had gone. "But it is impossible. No Gaian has ever married a human. And as far as Sally is concerned, I'm her step-father. Besides, I'm much too old for her. And yet…" He paused, thinking. "No, now is not the time for another partner. First I must watch my wife depart and I must bury her in a Royal ceremony. Then, and only then, will I let myself think about my own future. Besides, someday my only wife, my Gaia, will come back to me. That's the promise, after all. And if I am married to someone like Sally?" He smiled to himself. "Well, then I will be the Royal Consort to two wives, not only one. One from Earth and one from our home planet." He shook himself from his grief and laughed. "Amendus, stop worrying, for Gaia's sake. Our universe will hold nothing but happiness someday. For now, look to the present and stop thinking about the future just as my good wife always advised."

On the front lawn of a Sydney hospital, a Rescue spaceship sent by Admiral Simpson landed. The door opened and a Gaian soldier ran out. He made his way across the grass and up the steps of the hospital. Ignoring the receptionist, he ran down a hall. Finding the private quarters for hospital staff, he located apartment twenty-one and knocked on the door.

"You are ordered by our late Queen Gaia as well as Admiral Simpson to return at once to the Space Command ship," he stated when Helen opened the door. "That goes not only for you but also for Commodore Martin. You must comply urgently with the order. Australia and the rest of the Western countries of your planet will soon be under nuclear attack."

Doug walked up to his wife's shoulder. Hearing the words of the Gaian soldier, he grasped Helen's hand. "What do you mean by late Queen? Are you telling me that Gaia is dead?"

"Yes, Commodore," the soldier replied. "She left this life only moments ago, so said Admiral Simpson in her last transmission. But the orders are succinct. You must come with me now. Our vehicle is waiting for you."

Helen turned to Doug, her face melting with grief. "She can't be dead. She told me that Gaian's never die."

"I guess they do, Helen," Doug replied as he held her. "There's no time for that now. Forget anything in our quarters. Let's get out of here."

Doug waited as Helen ran into the apartment then to the bedroom. She grabbed her engagement and wedding rings and slipped them back on her finger. As she ran back out the front door, she could hear sirens wail in the near distance.

"What's that? Is that the warning?"

"You are right, Mrs. Masters," the soldier stated. "The threat is now real. I have heard via our telepathy that warheads will be falling on Sydney within ten minutes. Run! We must evacuate now or we will be incinerated."

Doug took Helen's hand and, running to keep up with their military escort, bolted through the reception area. Nurses, doctors, patients and visitors were panic stricken, screaming because they knew what was coming.

"Hurry, Helen!" Doug shouted as the siren kept wailing. Then they were out on the front steps of the hospital. With Helen following, Doug tried to make his way through a throng of screaming patients but was held back by the mob. He could see the Rescue vehicle waiting for them on the lawn, its engines already firing. Their military escort, already at the door, waved to them to hurry. As Doug pushed his way through the crowd, leading Helen toward their Rescue vehicle, a bright light filled the sky.

"Down!" he shouted as he pushed his wife onto the concrete parking lot. The siren stopped wailing. For a moment there was complete silence as the crowd looked toward the horizon. Then an explosion rocked their world as if the area was suffering an earthquake far off the Richter scale. Doug, still on top of Helen, looked up. From the south, he could see a mushroom cloud. Lightning flashed through it as it ballooned toward the heavens. Then a wind as strong as a hurricane, filled with dust and smelling like concrete and death, blew over them. Looking over his shoulder, he watched as the hospital went up in flames. Doug lowered his head again, feeling the extreme temperature on his skin. Yet he already knew that he wasn't injured. The Gaian treatment had also transformed his skin into something resembling leather. Looking at his hand covering Helen's head, he saw that the five fingers and thumb already had a green tint.

Again, he looked back to the hospital. As he watched, patients were being incinerated. One woman, her clothing on fire, staggered down onto the steps then fell over and kept burning. A child of five screamed for her mother, the girl's hair on fire. She turned, running back into the hospital, and Doug hoped she would have a quick death.

"Doug?" Helen said from beneath him. Grabbing her arm, he pulled her up and together they started running again. The Gaian soldier still stood at the open door waiting for them.

"Hurry, Commodore. There is another missile on its way!"

When Helen ran up to the Rescue vehicle, the soldier lifted her with one arm, taking her into the craft. As Doug followed them inside, he turned back, seeing the blinding light of another explosion as a nuclear warhead again struck Sydney. The hospital was already rubble. Dead bodies still smoldered, littering the lawn, the steps and the entrance to the building. Doug hit a large red button and the vehicle's outer door closed. As he staggered into the cockpit, he saw Helen seated behind the two pilots. The smooth deck tilted as the Rescue spaceship lifted off. Through the observation windows, they all looked down on what was left of Sydney.

"The city is gone! Look. The Opera House isn't there anymore. And where's the Sydney bridge or the harbor? What happened to all the people?" Helen cried. "It's the end of civilization, isn't it?"

Doug decided not to say a word. As the Rescue craft gained altitude, he saw other warheads strike distant targets on what he was certain was New Zealand. Then he saw Australian missiles streaking skyward and military aircraft lifting off from the barren territories north of Sydney. He realized that the fighters and bombers were going to destroy the source of the attack, which he suspected was a submarine. The missiles were on their way to Russia, China and North Korea.

"It's going to escalate again," he finally said to his wife. "When all countries use up their missiles, there won't be anything left of life on Earth."

Doug felt their vehicle accelerate and, as they hurtled into space, he looked down on his planet. Once again, he could see missiles seeking their targets across the world, their red rockets turning to white contrails as the warheads fell back into the atmosphere to bomb what was left of Earth's survivors.

"Amendus was right," Doug muttered to himself. "The Earth isn't worth their attention anymore. Soon, nothing will be left on our planet at all. Not one living creature."

With the vehicle's windows closed, Doug looked up at the monitors. There, the Moon filled half of screen. He realized that

within minutes, he would be seeing the body of his Queen and mother for what he knew would be the last time.

Five hundred feet below the South Atlantic Ocean, General Kelnakoff turned to the Captain of the Admiral Lenin.

"Good shooting, Captain. Our late president would be proud of you this day. For that reason, I will recommend that you be made an Admiral and you and your crew shall all receive the Order of Lenin, the highest honor I have to bestow on you."

The General turned, gazing at the boat's crew. "You should all be proud! Good work, comrades! Now all we have to do is to return to our Motherland."

The radar operator turned in his seat. "Captain," he said, looking at the radar monitor. "We have enemy targets coming in. I spot five fighters and two bombers. There is also a destroyer on our port side, range five-thousand meters. I am sure they will soon launch sonar buoys to find us."

"Gentleman, get back to your stations!" the Captain ordered. "Take her down as deep as you can. Depth, one-thousand five hundred meters."

"But Captain, that's not possible," the General said in a shaky voice. "That's almost five-thousand feet! The sub won't take the pressure."

The Captain turned to his General and smiled. "Do not worry, my General. They know how to make submarines in Mother Russia. We will hide in a marine trench directly below us." Then the Captain winked at his General and said in a low voice, "Or so the crew and our enemies think. Wait and see what will happen."

As the deck slanted steeply due to the emergency nature of their dive, the General held on to the plotting table. Metal teacups, pencils and maps fell onto the floor. He looked over at the depth gauge. It already read over two-thousand feet deep. Already, he could hear the steel and titanium hull of their vessel groan and pop under the pressure.

"Isn't this deep enough, Captain?"

"No. Deeper. They must not be able to find us." He turned to the sailor controlling the bow planes. "More angel on the bow! Everyone, take action stations! Chief of the boat, sound the attack alarm throughout the Lenin!"

As the siren wailed, the Captain ordered a reverse of course. "Course, two-seven-zero, Prepare to surface!" he shouted, then grabbed the microphone. "Forward torpedo room, prepare to fire four torpedoes spread across a thirty-degree angle. I'll give you the bearings when we raise the periscope. Missile room! Prepare to fire your remaining missiles. We will divert the aircraft and if they have lowered any sonar buoys, the water will be so disturbed by our quick actions that they'll lose us in the turbulence!"

Again, the General felt the deck tilt and once more he held onto the plotting table. He looked to his Captain. 'The man has balls of steel,' he thought to himself as the sub made its way to the surface. He saw the Captain pull a lever and in the middle of the control room, the silver tube of the periscope went up. Putting his eyes to the lenses, the Captain frowned.

"The destroyer has seen us! She is coming right at us. Narrow the angle on the torpedoes. Fire them all at once! Shoot!"

The General could feel the decrease in pressure as the torpedoes fired.

"Missile room. Aim your remaining nuclear missiles on New Zealand. That will keep their military occupied and they'll forget about us. Shoot!"

The deck shook as the remaining missiles fired. Then the Captain again turned to the periscope.

"Hit! We did it, comrades. We sunk the Australian destroyer!"

The crew cheered as the Captain turned to the General. "With your permission, we shall now head home."

"Good," replied the General, wiping his sweating forehead with the back of his hand. "I congratulate you for killing the Australian enemy and for our surprising get-away."

"Not at all," the Captain replied, bowing slightly. "It is an honor to serve my country."

Then the sonar operator shouted from his cubicle, "Torpedo in the water! Bearing, two-five-five."

"Where?" the Captain said. "But that's impossible! The enemy aircraft were heading back to Australia when I looked and the destroyer was split in two."

Then the radar operator shouted, "It's the Americans! I have an aircraft carrier on that bearing! We now have ten incoming torpedoes headed right at us."

The General looked to his Captain and saw how pale the man's face was. He knew that while they had won they had also lost. "It has been an honor to serve with you, Captain, as well as your crew. We snatched victory from the mouth of defeat when we bombed Australia, New Zealand, and North and South America. Their cities are now all rubble."

The Captain took the General's hand and shook it. "There is no time for a glass of Vodka. All I can say to you and my crew is до свидания!"

Then the room filled with the shrill sound of incoming torpedoes. "Left full rudder!" the Captain shouted, making one last desperate attempt to escape. But they all knew that it was too late. The shrilling sounds came even closer. Finally, General Kelnakoff looked to the ceiling of the Admiral Lenin.

"My President Putin and comrade Lenin! I'm on my way to join you!"

Then the torpedoes hit

⚜ ⚜ ⚜

Directly above the stricken Admiral Lenin, the pilot of an American F-83 Titan jet fighter looked down as the water turned white then spouted high into the sky. He toggled his mic, radioing his aircraft carrier.

"Titan One to base. That's a kill, Admiral Rogers. You can notify the Commander-in-Chief and Space Command that we've destroyed the Russian sub."

"Come on home, Titan One. We're turning the carrier into the wind."

The American attack aircraft turned north, joining the other fighters in its squadron. As he completed the turn, the pilot looked back over his shoulder at the wreckage of the sub that had floated to the surface.

"Bastards," he muttered to no one. "You didn't accomplish anything, comrades, except to destroy the human race."

Chapter Thirty-Two

In the Space Command War Room, Admiral Simpson stood behind her radar operator. They had placed a Gaian satellite in a geocentric orbit about Earth's Moon so she would be able to communicate with her Rescue Team at any time.

As she looked down on the bright yellow line of the radar signal, the operator turned to her.

"Ma'am, that's the Rescue Team. coming back with Commodore and Mrs. Martin. Their ETA is thirty-one minutes."

"Good. Let the Royal Consort know at once! Inevitably, the couple will want to visit Her Royal Highness's remains before we send them back to her home planet."

The radar operator turned to a signal corpsman. "You heard the Admiral, didn't you, sailor? Take her message to His Lordship. Be smart about it."

The corpsman saluted his Admiral then, turning, jogged out of the room.

Admiral Simpson leaned in closer to the radar operator. She pointed toward the glowing screen.

"What are those incoming targets right there?"

"Those are nuclear missiles that China fired. We intercepted their radio transmissions and decoded them. The Chinese government is targeting the Rescue ship, hoping for a strategic kill. They're taking advantage of the Western Government's reaction to the destruction of the Russian submarine, hoping that those governments will be blamed or even Russia, not the Chinese."

Sally smiled. "Good. Just as we thought they would. When do you estimate impact on the Rescue vehicle?"

He looked at the stopwatch in his hand. The second hand ticked down toward zero. "Fourteen seconds, Admiral."

Sally turned to face a missile defense team expert. "Lieutenant, when you're ready, order Gaian officers to use their telepathy to turn the missiles around. Send them back to where they came from. You are not authorized to explode the weapons over any city that still has survivors. But you are authorized to destroy any remaining missile siloes with nuclear weapons still in them."

The British Lieutenant saluted. "It will be a pleasure, Admiral. Blimey, we'll cook those Chinese bastards to a temperature so hot they'll never fire a missile again."

As Sally watched, the British officer gave the command to a Gaian sailor. Sally saw the tall woman concentrate. When she looked back at the radarscope, the missiles had already begun to turn.

"What's the ETA to the Chinese targets?"

"Two-minutes ten seconds, Admiral "

Sally turned her attention to a monitor just above her. An American spy satellite was showing images of a Chines nuclear missile base. As she watched, she could see men and women fleeing from their underground quarters. Then, she saw the blast of rocket, smoke and fire ejecting from beneath them.

"Those are anti-ballistic missiles?"

"Yes, Ma'am. All that China has left. But they'll be useless."

The camera of the spy satellite panned left to follow the rockets. When they were over a series of deserted hills, they all exploded. The screen went white.

"Were those nuclear-tipped ABM's? Are you sure that's all they have?"

"So Gaian Earth defense says. They've been monitoring China's military for years. That's all of them, Ma'am."

She turned to her adjutant. "Gene, I'm going to go get something to eat and try to sleep for an hour. Doug and Helen will be here in a few minutes. Let them go see our Queen's remains then, when they're finished, come get me. I need to talk to the Commodore about what we do next with Earth and our strategy to finish this war."

"Yes, Ma'am," her adjutant replied. "Eat something and get some rest. It's been days since you did so. You need to be fresh for when you meet your mom and dad."

As Sally left the War Room, she looked up at a monitor near the door. There, she could see the Rescue Vehicle carrying her friends land in a fortified hanger. As she watched, the bay doors closed. She knew that it would take a few minutes to pressurize the hanger. By that time, she hoped she would be fast asleep.

As Admiral Simpson slept, Helen and Doug took off their spacesuits,

had a shower and were then tested for radioactivity. Given the all-clear, Helen put on her best black dress and hat together with dark grey high heels. As she applied some lipstick, she looked into the mirror and saw Doug standing behind her dressed in his officer's uniform.

"I won't and I can't believe she's gone," Helen said. "She promised she would live forever."

"Maybe she was just trying to make us feel better. Even Gaians have to die, Helen."

"But who will be Queen now? That planet has had one Queen for all eternity."

"I don't know," Doug said, wiping tears from his eyes. "She was our mother. She always had everything planned to a 'T'. When you're ready, let's go see Amendus. He'll know what Gaia had planned. Helen, I've decided to wear my Commodore uniform. Do you think it's appropriate?"

She turned to him. "You look so handsome," she said, brushing lint from his lapel. "Gaia is proud of you, you can be sure of that."

"I hope so. I did absolutely everything I could to help the people on Earth. But there's more I can do." Taking her hand, he smiled up at her, looking her in the eye. "You've grown so tall. With your heels on, you're taller than I am now. Did you have the Gaian treatment, too?"

"No. I was going to have it when you were recovering from your prison injuries. I talked to the surgeons. They told me I no longer need it."

"You've spent too much time on planet Gaia, that's why," he said, holding her naked arm. "Your skin is becoming the same color as mine, and just as textured."

"Is it too hard?"

"No. It's soft. Just as lovely as when I first met you. Hon, I'm going to go talk to Sally for a few minutes. I'll meet you in the Queen's apartments."

"That's fine. I'll see you soon."

Then Doug kissed her cheek and, with his hand on the small of her back, walked her out the door.

✈ ✈ ✈

When Helen entered the Queen's apartment, the first thing she saw was Amendus talking to a War Room General. The Royal Consort's eyes were narrow, his face red.

"I do not care what you say, General. We are leaving this planet as soon as I finalize arrangements for my wife's funeral. You are ordered to immediately evacuate all of our remaining troops from your planet."

"But your Lordship. What of the survivor's on Earth?"

"There are no survivors other than our military and what remains of that planets armies!" Amendus raged. "They've murdered their civilization because of their stupidity and are not worth saving. Now get out, General. Get out now and leave me in peace!"

When the General marched past her, Helen turned to Amendus.

"Father, it serves no one to be angry. You know there are still survivors on Earth."

He turned to her, rage still in his face. "Did you not hear what I told that stupid General? No one on your planet is worth saving. Besides, what remains is only military and some government officials. They caused this war!"

"You know that's not true," she said. When she walked up to him, he could see how tall she had grown in only a few days' time.

"You are Gaian!" he hissed, stepping back. "How does that happen? I know you did not yet get your treatment.

"My mother came to me in a dream," she replied, taking his hand. "She told me that I am already Gaian because she also gave birth to me, as well as my Earth-born mother. What you see now is the result of my ancestry. Would you kill your grandchildren, Father? Don't you remember that my children and grandchildren are still on Earth? Doug and I made certain they were safe in a bunker before the bombs fell."

Amendus's face grew still. He walked to a couch, sitting down. When he motioned to her, Helen sat down beside him.

"My wife came to you in a dream? What else did she say."

"Nothing yet. She told me to come here to see you. She knew you would behave this way. She told you to be at peace, and now you are: at least for this single moment."

He placed his hand to a chin, thinking. "She was right to send you, my daughter. When you see her again would you please tell her how much I miss her?"

Helen laughed and Amendus thought it sounded just like his dead wife. "You will see her in a moment so tell her yourself. You of all people should know that even now, she's with us. Now, Father, let me go to see my mother. I must pray for her soul."

"Of course, my child. She's in her bedroom."

Helen left him and entered the bedroom. When she did, she could smell roses, her mother's favorite flower. Looking toward the bed, she found Gaia laid out wearing her best Royal Gown. Her hands were folded across her chest. Kneeling down on the floor beside her, Helen crossed herself and started to pray the *Our Father* but found herself uttering a different prayer in a different language she did not at first understand.

"Ga na me na Mama, lee nay softe nesis go fatha in so nee cum de deo, Kristos Jesu. Amen."

She realized it was a combination of Latin and ancient Gaian. Crossing herself again, she thought about what she had prayed and then realized, "I did not pray for my mother. Instead, I prayed for all of humankind and our futures, as well as the Gaian race."

Sitting on the bed beside her dead mother, Helen looked up to see a face reflected in a full-length mirror. What she saw was not Helen Martin, nor even the Gaian version of her, but rather someone else. Someone that looked much younger and that had long dark brown hair not blonde hair. Having studied all of the saints in Heaven, she knew immediately who it was.

"Mary Magdalene," she whispered in awe. Looking down at her chest, she saw that she was wearing a peasant's dress from days of yore. Her breasts were as full as if she was pregnant again. "Nothing is impossible, now or ever," she said to herself.

"Nor will it ever be, not ever again."

Helen looked up. Standing before her was her Royal Mother.

"My Mother! You're dead!"

"Am I daughter? I know what I know and I am not dead but have risen as you someday will."

Helen rose to her feet. Slowly, she walked to Gaia. Gently, she touched her face. "Your face is warm!"

"Of course, it is child. I told you. I am no longer dead. Look behind you."

Helen looked. Gaia's body still lay on the bed.

"But how can you be both?"

"Dead and living at the same time? I've always told you. It's easy if you know how. Now, child. Let us sit down and talk for a while. Soon, my husband will also want to see me to tell me how much he misses me. What I am about to say to you and also to Amendus will have great import not only to your race but to all the races of the many Universes."

Helen heard the door to her Queen's bedroom open. Amendus walked in, his head bowed. He moved to what used to be their bed and looked down on his deceased wife. Sitting down beside her, he kissed her.

"Her lips are cold!" he cried. "Will you not rise up, my Gaia, as you told me you would?"

"But I am risen," a familiar voice said.

Turning, Amendus looked up to see his wife standing with Helen. He rose, staggering toward her, his face filled with disbelief. Helen could see that his pupils were dilated. His hands shook as did his arms Amendus came toward his wife. As she did, she opened her arms wide, beckoning him to her.

"Hug me, my loving husband," she commanded. He bowed first, then took her in his arms

"You're alive."

"Isn't that what we always said to our children? We will die because we owe one death if we live. But now I have risen from death and never again will I die."

"But you are dead!" her husband cried, pointing to the dead body of his wife. "How can you be alive and dead at the same time."

"I asked the same question," Helen said. "Our Queen only said, 'It's easy if you know how'".

"And you know how," Amendus replied to Gaia. "Will you stay with me now and forever my dear wife and partner?"

"You already know the answer to that, my husband and Lord. The answer, of course, must be no. I have other subjects to tend to now in a new Universe far, far away."

"But who will be Queen in your stead, Royal wife? No one can ever take your place."

"Husband, I think you already know the answer to that question."

They both looked at Helen. She stepped away from the couple, uncertain what her Queen meant.

"You want me to be the new Queen? But I'm human! No Queen of the planet Gaia has ever been human."

"Are you certain my dear?" asked Gaia. "Look at yourself in the mirror again."

When Helen looked in the full-length mirror, she was naked. Her skin was as green as Gaia's and just as textured. On both hands, she now had five fingers and a thumb.

"Look at your breasts, Helen."

Gaia looked. She had three breasts instead of two. The middle one was smaller than the other two.

"Touch it," Gaia commanded.

When Helen did, the third breast disappeared into her chest.

"You see?" her Royal mother said. "You'll only need it if, someday, you and Doug have triplets."

"Triplets?" Helen cried. "But I've stopped ovulating. I can't have children anymore."

"You can now," Gaia laughed. "Gaian's have children for hundreds and hundreds of years. Now look at your feet."

Helen looked down. She saw how she had six toes on each foot rather than five. Lifting one of them up, she saw green webbing between each toe. She looked at her mother, unsure what to say.

"That's to help you swim on our planet, which is now yours to rule, as well as any other watery world. See my feet? They're webbed, too."

Helen looked at her mother's naked feet and realized what her Queen said was correct.

"You truly want me to be the next Queen, my mother?"

"Yes. In a moment we shall have a small celebration as I hand you my Royal sword and golden crown. But first, I must tell you both something. Please. Take a seat on the couch in the living room. When I am ready, I shall speak with you both."

As Amendus led Helen out of the bedroom, he glanced at a television screen. It had been tuned in to view the War Room. He could see Doug arguing with their Admiral.

"What's your husband up to now, Helen? As if I couldn't guess."

"He wants Sally to send in the Space Fleet to take Earth's survivor's away from our planet. He is now certain you will abandon Earth."

"Do you agree with him?"

"Of course, I do. Every living being deserves another chance. Why waste even one life when they're so precious. Father, you know you believe that too."

Amendus led her into the living room and sat on the couch as Gaia and his daughter stood above him.

"What is done is done," Amendus said to Helen, finally giving up his anger. "You are right, my Princess. Command Sally to send the Space Fleet to rescue those who have survived this last war. Then we shall abandon it."

"Not quite abandon it, husband."

They turned. Gaia was standing at the open door. She had changed her clothing. Once again, she wore her Royal stole. On her head was the Royal crown and in her right hand she held her Sword, the same one her Father had given to her when he had lost the battle to save the Milky Way Galaxy.

"As I hand these few tokens to you, Helen, I shall talk to you both about what to do next. As part of this short speech which shall be filmed and broadcast throughout our Universe, I shall share with you all one final secret and gift that I am handing you from a far-away creature. A friend, not a foe. A person much like us. We call it the Unnamed Ghost but it is not. Its name is not anything that we have heard before. Its voice came to me as I lay dying. So now, my Princess Helen, please kneel before me."

"What do you mean you won't send the freighters? Admiral, you know there are people still alive on Earth!"

"Commodore, stop shouting. That is the royal command by the Royal Consort."

"But Amendus is grieving. He's not in his right mind. You know that Gaia would give the right order if she was still alive."

"Unfortunately, she's not, is she Dad?"

Doug, still dressed in his Commodore's uniform, stalked to the table. He swept the surface of it with an arm. Reports, pens, rulers and various official papers fell to the floor. Around the table, which was full, sat human Ambassadors who had managed to survive that final war and also surviving government officials. At the top of the table, the Ambassador from Gaia to Earth waited for Doug to calm down.

"You know the Admiral is correct," the Ambassador said. "If Amendus ordered that we leave your Earth now, then we must."

"Ambassador, would you abandon your planet?" shouted Doug, his voice even higher. "I don't think so!"

"Commodore, if you don't calm down, I'll have an armed guard escort you back to your quarters," Sally stated tersely. "I don't care if you're my father. I told you to knock it off!"

He looked at her, nodding, and sat in a chair. As he did, all of the overhead monitors flickered at once. Then Gaia appeared. She turned to them, her face smiling.

"Ladies and gentlemen, I assure you this is not a recording," she said. "I talk to you live from my own quarters. See? My husband and Helen are also with me. They can vouch for my new living existence."

The camera panned revealing the two people. Then it swung back to their Queen. In the War Room, Sally saw that most of them were in shock. One stood up and raised both arms in triumph.

"Long live our Queen!" the Ambassador from New Zealand shouted. "You have defeated death!"

"No, I am no longer your Queen," Gaia replied. "I can never be your Queen again. Instead, you have a new Queen and her name is Helen Gaia Martin. From this day forward, you will swear your fealty to her and obey her. Do you all understand me?"

The Ambassadors all rose as one. "Yes, our Queen."

"From this day on, you may call me Queen Mother Gaia because that's what I am. I am the mother of all of you, as is Helen and Doug."

Helen, who had risen to greet the War Room staff on the monitor looked to her Royal mother.

"Princess Helen, kneel again."

Helen did as she was bid. Then the Queen held out the Royal Sword.

"With this sword I command you to protect all that is living and all that will soon be living, now and forevermore. Will you accept that challenge and responsibility?"

"I will, my Queen and mother," Helen whispered.

Gaia tapped her three times on each shoulder and once on the head with the Royal weapon.

"Now, Helen, rise to say the solemn oath to your people."

When Helen did, Gaia asked Amendus to take off her crown. As he did, Gaia said, "Place it on our daughter's head. Now repeat after me, Princess Helen."

As Amendus lowered the crown onto Helen, the Queen said: "In the name of all that is Holy, I shall accept the challenge that this crown and Sword give to me."

"In the name of all that is Holy…" Helen repeated and when she finished the sentence Gaia continued the swearing in ceremony.

"I shall bring peace to all lands which my Royal Mother and I now share with you in this secret from an Unknown Ghost who is also a spirit."

Helen repeated the words.

"You shall never die, as has already been promised. Instead, you will all have multiple lives. You will be one mind and spirit and heart, but you shall share different bodies of different sexes and races. In this way you shall populate not only a new Earth and Moon, but also the planets in your Solar System and also the Milky Way. You shall even be welcome to populate this Universe."

Helen again repeated what the Royal Mother had said.

"Now finally, here is my only warning. Do NOT go to the Tycho crater on your Moon. There, we shall soon create new life. A new species which will not look or act like you at all. Instead, this being shall be a new Living God. This thing, which you who find it and believe in it, shall be called the *Jesu Incomparable*. He which is also a she, shall fill you with holy fire so that one day you shall be just as Incomparable as Jesu is. Is that clear?"

Gaia looked at the War Room personnel as Helen finished the ceremony.

"Ladies and gentlemen of Earth and Gaia. Is that clear?" the Royal Mother asked again.

In hushed voices, they all said at once: "It is clear, my Royal Mother Gaia."

"Then so be it! Now there is one thing left to do. Doug Martin, my son, kneel."

Doug, caught unawares, knelt by the table.

"Admiral Sally Simpson, use your sword and repeat the words I say to you."

Sally drew her sword from its scabbard. She placed it on Doug's right shoulder.

"From this day forth," continued Gaia, "you shall be a Knight of my new Order of the Rose. From now on, those who salute you must address you as Sir Doug Martin."

Sally repeated the words then moved her sword to Doug's left shoulder.

"You and Helen are already married," Gaia again continued. "But from this day on you shall also be her Royal Consort."

Sally again repeated the words then said, "Rise, Sir Commodore Martin."

As he did, Gaia moved toward the camera in her quarters.

"Now my last point of business before I leave you. My husband come to me and take my hand." When he did, she again looked at the camera. "Sally, hold out your left hand." When Sally did, she saw that an enormous emerald bearing the royal crest was on her ring finger as well as a golden wedding band. "My husband," Gaia said, turning to Amendus. "You know what we promised each other. If one of us died, we would never be alone. Therefore, from this day on you and Sally shall be lawfully wed under my law. From this day on, Sally shall be Princess Sally Amendus Gaia. Should anything happen to the present Queen, Sally shall become the next Queen. When Doug and Helen have more children, they shall be the next in line to the throne. The last thing I did before I died was to change our constitution. From this day on, any Royal member who is in line to the throne, male or female, may become King or Queen. Is that also clear?

"Now, when Sally and Amendus have children, they shall be next in line to the throne after the Queen's children. Sally, please come up to our quarters so you may kiss your Royal Husband in my presence."

As the Admiral began to leave the room, the Queen turned to the camera one final time.

"Sir Doug, who is also my only living son, you now have command of the entire fleet in this Universe. Sally will be appointed to a new post, boldly flying where no one has dared to go before. With Amendus, she shall populate many new Universes, as you and your Queen will someday, too, when you finish this current assignment."

Then the Queen Mother sat, her breathing heavy. "Now I too must move on, my subjects. I wish you well. I wish you all goodness and joy and laugher forevermore. I also wish you love."

Gaia's image on the camera began to fade. As Sally made her way out of the War Room, she stood for a moment and watched on the monitor as her Queen faded completely away. Then the TV monitor had no one in its field of view until Queen Helen stepped into frame.

"I hold the sword my mother has given to me and wear her crown," she said. "I only hope I can be as just and as deserving of your love as was our Queen Gaia. She has gone, my good people, on a mission upon which we can never follow. But someday, we will know here presence again. And do remember, we shall always feel her thoughts and her loving countenance because she is also a Holy Ghost." Then the monitor went dead.

Sally, still standing in the War Room, tried hard not to cry. "I never even had a chance to say goodbye to my mom," Sally said to no one.

"Oh, yes you did," Sally heard in her head, and her Queen Mother Gaia laughed. "Don't you understand my dear? Nothing has really changed at all and I'll always be with you. All you have to do is call to me and I'll listen and advise you. Do you understand my Admiral and granddaughter Josie?"

"Yes, my Queen," Sally uttered. "You'll always be there for me."

"As you will be for me."

Then, with Doug following, Sally marched from the War Room. As they moved out the door, the Commodore turned to a General.

"General Douglas?"

The General turned, saluting. "Yes, Sir Martin."

"Contact Space Command. Send the Star Fleet to Earth right now. As many as possible. I want you to comb the planet for survivors and get them out of here before we must abandon it."

"I hear you loud and clear, Sir. However, and I'm not sure if you've heard the news, but Earth's magnetic gravity is changing poles due to the final nuclear missile strikes. Our geologists fear that the entire core of the planet will soon explode, obliterating our planet."

"Then hurry, General. Get on the radio right now! Have someone in my command break out my spacesuit. I'll join one of the Starships going to Earth as soon as I see my wife and Queen."

Then Doug marched out and the General mopped his brow.

"He was bad enough as a Commodore," the General said to his adjutant. But now, as Sir Martin? Good Lord, he'll make all of our lives absolutely impossible."

Chapter Thirty-Three

"This is Harold Mason, The BBC New Zealand, with a live report on all remaining global news channels."

As the camera turned to him, the middle-aged news anchor staggered.

"That's the fifth strong earthquake we've experienced in New Zealand's capital, Wellington. I'm standing at the top of the Majestic Center, the tallest building in the city."

As the BBC news reporter kept talking, the camera swung around to reveal the harbour. "I've just heard from our news room that the last quake had a magnitude of 9.9, the strongest earthquake in history. The epicenter was only one mile off the coast. We expect a Tsunami of unknown height to wash ashore in less than five minutes. We had a helicopter in that area but we can no longer contact it. We're guessing that it's been brought down by a local waterspout that is the result of tremendous changes in temperatures: as much as twenty degrees in both directions, or so confirms the New Zealand Met Office. We've reports from what remains of that Service that yet another hurricane is making its way ashore with winds that have never before been recorded."

As the camera looked down on the harbour, huge passenger ships began to rock in the sea that was now a lake of white water.

"I've just been told that the Tsunami has hit the beach just north of us. Oh my God! Look at that!"

As Doug watched on the television monitor from his gigantic starship, he saw the camera swing again. A wave as tall as most buildings in Wellington swept in from the sea. When it hit the steel and glass structures, they began to crumble, falling like spillikins. One crashed into another. Gaining momentum, the huge wave swept over the city. Doug knew that any survivors in Wellington except a few like the reporter and his crew, had already drowned.

"There's another earthquake! My God, it has to be off the Richter Scale!"

The camera swung back to the news anchor. As Doug watched, the picture changed: it seemed to shake then for a moment pointed to the sky. The camera was obviously on the ground, the television picture now horizontal, only showing the BBC reporter's legs. They ran toward the camera, lifting it. The anchorman's face was now in close up.

"My reporter, Jane Putney, has been struck by a piece of steel. It's gone through her leg. She's okay. Let me help her to some sort of shelter."

The camera was again put down on the ground as the reporter helped his camera operator. Then it was picked up again and the man's face came into view. "She's safe, friends. We'll report to you as long as we can."

Doug turned in his seat. "Where are the other starships?"

"Sir, they've made it to all of the remaining cities," his second-in-command, Cheryl Tigh, said. "They've done a complete search for signs of life. All human survivors as well as many animals have been rescued. All that's left are the survivors in Wellington."

"Which won't be many," Doug said, then toggled his spacesuit mic.

"Space Command this is Doug Martin. We're over Wellington. We already have aboard a few people we found in what remains of Australia, those who survived the radioactive fallout. We also took with us as many animal species as we could especially those threatened with extinction, as well as species that are already extinct. We've loaded one of the spacecraft's bays with saltwater and taken as many mammals and fish as we could haul onboard. That included a Blue Whale and a Giant Squid which we found locked in battle. They're now in separate compartments. I've also ordered our microbiologists to take as many multi-celled and single-celled creatures as they can fit in their lab compartments. Do you have further orders before I rescue the last survivors in New Zealand?"

"Roger that, Sir Doug. This is Space Command. I have orders from our Queen Helen for you. She tells you do not, I repeat, do not take any more survivors on board your spacecraft. You and the other Gaian spacecraft are ordered to return all, I repeat, all survivors of any species to Earth."

Doug looked at his second in command. "Did you hear that? That can't be right."

The Ensign just shrugged as Doug again keyed his mic. "Space Command can you please repeat that?"

The controller at the other end of the transmission laughed. "Doug, your wife told me to expect that reaction from you. Just follow her orders, got it? She told me to say, 'We already got their backs', you'll know what she means."

"Roger that, Space Command. Will comply with the Queen's orders."

He looked at Ensign Tigh again. "Okay, better do what she says or man will she get mad. Tell the crew to get ready to land. We'll release all survivors here."

As the spacecraft settled toward Earth, Doug looked up again at the monitor. The reporter was again in view and the camera was obviously being held by the cameraman.

"This is your reporter! A miracle has occurred. Look! The sun has come out again!"

The camera panned back toward the city. What remained was washed by a noon day sun. Then it panned up. Huge white cumulous clouds were rolling in toward the city.

"Viewers, that's the most unusual squall line I've ever seen," the reporter broadcast. "It's almost golden white! And look at that!"

As Doug and his second-in-command watched, lightning lit the clouds. Then, the reporter heard something. He turned to the camera; his face awed. "I swear to God! I hear a choir singing!"

"Turn up the volume, Cheryl."

"Yes, sir."

Over the speaker, Doug could barely hear a choir. "They're singing something I know! It's like a song from Handel's *Messiah*."

"The *Halleluia Choir*?" she guessed. "No, not that one."

"It's *The Trumpets Shall Sound*. I used to try to sing in when I was in college. But that's an entire choir singing it, not just one voice. Can you turn it up more?"

"No, sir. That's max volume."

Suddenly, the music stopped. As the camera panned again toward the nearby clouds, they parted in a flash of light. What seemed to be a woman's head appeared between the cumulous clouds which had grown even taller and brighter. Then shoulders appeared. On each shoulder a human boy and girl sat, playing with the giant woman's long golden hair. The huge creature in the clouds opened her mouth and laughed.

"I am not whom you expected, am I, those of you who are Christian." She paused, taking both children off her shoulders with golden hands. She stood them on the clouds where they sat smiling up at her. "My name is Shabbatha. I am the only God of your Universe. Yes, there are many other Gods but me. More than I can say. And those of you who are Christian, if you were expecting Him, the man Jesus, to be here for the final coming, you will have to wait forever. For you see, there is no final coming, only me. And I'm not here to judge you. I'm here to save all of you, even those of you who have died since the creation of this planet. For you are the Holy ones, not me. You are the immortal ones, just as I am. And for now, we must leave this planet on wings of angels. So come all you who are children, come to me. For in my eyes, and even if you are aged, you are all children to me."

The camera swung back to the reporter. His mouth was wide open as he gawped up above him. "I don't believe it. And yet it has to be true! Wait, hold on, people. I feel it again. Another earthquake."

This time, both the reporter and the cameraman fell to the ground. As they both got to their feet, Doug could hear the great God Shabbatha say: "Hurry, before it's too late! This Earth is giving up its life but soon there will be a new planet here to replace what you have lost."

"Sir, I'd better get us down on the ground. Look at that!"

The other monitors all showed the same picture. Below them, they could see a volcano rising in the middle of Wellington.

"You got it, Ensign. I'm going back to help the crew get rid of those survivors."

The ensign gave Doug a thumbs up. Doug went to the back compartments and helped the crew to open the immense cargo bay doors. As they did, the seawater with its many creatures poured back into the ocean below them. Doug held onto a handrail and looked down. One large public park remained in the city. Even as he watched, he could see what he was sure was the Earth's core rising through it. The green grass was burning; smoke rising. To Doug, it seemed as if the very ground was turning into a bright red cauldron of light.

'Hell no,' he thought to himself. 'I'm sure Helen's right but I'm not releasing our human survivors into this'. He toggled his mic. "Ensign, abort the landing. Get us the hell out of here."

As he gave the order, he turned around seeing an older couple. They had their border collie with them. "Is this still Australia?" the old man asked. "We'd like to get out now, sir."

"Pops, get back to your seats and strap yourself back in. This isn't Australia. We're getting the hell out of here before the entire planet gives up the ghost."

But the old woman only pointed out the bay door and to the ground below. "Sir, if you please, we have a train to catch right now! It will pick us all up at Wellington Station. That's in the center of the city."

"Ma'am, please! Just do…"

"Doug, you better get up here right now!" he heard his ensign say through his headset.

"Just do as your instructed, okay, Ma'am?" Doug asked as he strode back to the command module. There, he found his ensign gawking at the TV monitor.

"Look at him. Just look!" Jackson whispered.

Doug looked. The BBC news anchor had risen a few feet off the ground.

"If you're watching anywhere across the world, you're probably experiencing the same thing as I am. The Earth is losing its power of gravity. Its rotational speed is slowing down. Which is why I'm now floating."

As Doug watched, the camera angle changed and Doug realized that the cameraman was also floating above the ground. Yet, the camera remained steady on the reporter. Winds whipped at the man's coat.

"The wind is picking up," the reporter continued. "That's a sign that the atmosphere is escaping from our planet. In a few moments I won't be able to breath. But it's been a historic day of reporting and this is one of, if not the, final broadcast from Earth. If you're watching from space or Gaia, all I can say is thank you. It's been a privilege to report from Wellington, New Zealand, on this final day of our planet."

Then thunder boomed above him as he turned to look at the heavens and clouds.

"My Children!" the God Shabbatha called. "I promised that I will save you and now is the time. Come to me now, into my arms and then into my heart, and I will carry you off so you will not die! Come to me too, those who have already died, for it is time for your final resurrection. Do not be afraid. Come to me now! Right now, this solar system will gain a new home planet."

The camera was still steady on the reporter. As Doug and his ensign watched, the man's face began to glow.

"I feel warm!" the reporter said as he mopped his brow. "And look at my hand. I'm crazy because I think I can see through it. And look at Jane," he yelled, pointing at the camera woman "You're nothing but a bright light now. And it's as if you're wearing wings on your shoulders. By God Almighty. I can see right through you!"

The television monitor filled with light. As Doug watched, it was if the camera, too, was floating uncontrolled by any cameraman. It was rotating. First a few pictures of what remained of Wellington appeared. As they all watched, the ground beneath the city shook. Then, molten rock began to push through the cracks.

"Ensign, get us the fuck out of here! I want to be outside the orbit of the Moon in exactly ten seconds. Got that Mr?"

"Starting the Stardrive now, sir. On my mark. Two. One. Ignition."

The spaceship shook as Doug continued to watch the monitor. Now it looked straight up. Streaks of white, as if starlight or meteors, raced toward the Cloud God who had her arms stretched wide. As he watched, they plummeted into her breasts.

"What the fuck…"

The spacecraft shook again.

"What the hell was that?"

"Sir, look at the rear monitor."

As Doug did, he could see millions of white-hot meteors ascending from the Earth toward the figure of God Shabbatha who still had her arms stretched wide. Then, over the radio, they heard a final broadcast.

"Hear ye all my Children! I do not come to judge anyone. It is not my place to judge you for your actions or behaviour or beliefs. Now you all have a new chance to create a new life with me here, there, and everywhere you hear my voice. Do you understand me?"

Then it was as if Doug could hear millions of voices, including those of animals, all shouting: "We do!" in various languages.

"Sir, we have a report from one of the rear bays. You know all those people that we saved. They're gone!"

"Yeah, and I know where they're going."

From a side monitor, streaks of light headed from the rear starship bays toward the Cloud God. Then as they watched on all the monitors, the Earth gave up her core. The explosion was like nothing Doug had ever seen before. White hot magma shot out from the center of the planet. Then it collapsed inward again. Within seconds, what remained began to spiral around a new center of gravity that Earth had formed when it destroyed itself.

"Take a note, Ensign. That's a new planet beginning to form."

"Sir, look at the radar. The Moon's orbit is changing."

"As to be expected. Change the mass of the Earth by reducing it significantly, and the Moon will orbit good old Sol. Looks like that cloud God was right. This solar system has a new planet."

"Maybe three, Sir, if you include the Moon. See how other material is falling into what used to be Earth's core? Depending on the gravitational forces, that thing could be split into two planets, not just one."

As they watched, white hot gasses began pouring from the direction of the North Star into what remained of Earth. As it did, Doug noted how the mass of what remained of Earth was becoming larger and larger. The rotational speed of the entire glowing new planet was faster than he'd ever seen before.

"Looks like you're right, Ensign. That's enough to make two planets. Add the Moon, which will be whipped out of orbit around the old Earth within days, and that makes three. Doug smiled. "You know what? That's Gaia's doing. She can't stand to be retired. She's going to build us all another planet before she takes off to go to a new Universe." As he finished talking, the Ensign again pointed to the Moon.

"Sir, see that crater? Is that Tyco? Why does it center seem to be glittering in gold?"

"Damned if I know. Take us in closer. Don't land on the damned thing. Remember the warning about anyone setting foot on Tyco. But let's see what's causing it."

Within seconds their spaceship was hovering directly over Tyco. From the TV monitor Doug could make out what seemed to be an immense block of gold. "You know, Cheryl. A few years ago, Helen and I watched a video created by an archeologist in the Ukrainian Army. He had discovered not only Noah's Ark but also the Arc of the Covenant and the remains of the original Eleven Commandments that had been written on a giant stone tablet. He also recorded his finding of a towering block of gold composed of over one hundred similar tablets. These were the Eleven Commandments written in gold. Since that report, I understand that his finding has been verified by many different universities. Even the Gaian University for Archaeology."

"Come on, Sir. Are you saying that that block of gold is God's Ten Commandments?"

"Why not? God would want to save his rules and so would my wife and Gaia. We gotta have some kind of rules to follow if we're going to succeed in the future, don't we? And what better rules than those one? Besides, it's not ten commandments, kid. It's eleven, remember?" Then Doug chuckled and looked again at his Ensign. "Okay, Tigh. Take us home."

"But where, Sir? We don't have a home to go back to. Earth's been destroyed."

"Oh, yes we do. For now, our home planet is Gaia. But when we're ready, we'll soon be able to come back to two new planets: Earth One and Earth Two. And if Helen's right, we'll bring our children."

"Roger that, Skipper. Ramping up the Stardrive."

"Put some music on, will you Ensign? Oh, and you might as well start calling yourself Lieutenant Tigh. And yes, there's a promotion waiting for you when we get home. Any music tracks will do."

"Sir, how about *Homeward Bound* by Simon and Garfunkle?"

"Perfect. They're popular again, aren't they?"

As the spaceship hurtled past the Moon, which was now a new planet, the captivating harmonies of the legendary songwriters came over the speaker system.

"Homeward bound," Doug sang softly. "You're damned right I'm homeward bound. And I ain't goin' nowhere for a long, long time except into my wife, children's and grandchildren's arms"

PART FIVE:

THE FINAL RECKONING OF REMEMBRANCES UNWRITTEN

Chapter Thirty-Four

Once again orbiting high above what was now called New Earth One, and floating in the command center of the Space Station which had been christened only a year ago, the *Helen Gaia Fox*, Doug Martin looked down on his renewed home planet. As he viewed the shimmering dawn of a new day flashing over the curvature of the new Earth, a fantastic sunrise that lit the Western continents in the brightness of a dawn, he looked up and over that beautiful horizon. There, he saw twin planets circling New Earth as if this was a small solar system.

"That's our old Moon," Doug said to the stars, "And that planet that's a little larger than the Moon? That's New Earth Two."

Looking across at the two planets, he beheld lights on their dark continents and blue seas where the sun lit them. "It's only been a few hundred years since they finished terraforming the Moon. And as for New Earth Two and my own planet Earth One? Look how quickly the seas and continents have formed to give life to a wonderful new generation of humans. That's Helen's doing, not our Queen Mother, Gaia. I wonder what my good wife is doing right now?"

With nothing else to do, he took stock of the memories he had of Helen, who had died only a few years ago on 20 May 3074. He was not sad because Helen lived until she was one-thousand, one hundred and eleven years old, and her remains were buried in a wicker coffin in her hometown of New Trim Ireland. Her funeral had been attended by her ancestors but, unfortunately, not him because he'd been confined to the Space Station due to heart disease and cancer of the prostate gland, for which he required special treatment, occasional zero gravity and special medication not yet available on Earth.

Yet her death did not bother him. Often, she still came to him in his dreams and would talk to him. For that reason he knew that somewhere in this Universe or another one, she was still alive. She had died because she had lived. And now, having given up one life, Helen would never die again.

Because his birthday was ten days ago, on the fourth of October, Doug had received old-fashioned paper birthday cards from his ancestral grandchildren, wishing him well on this, his one thousandth, one hundredth and thirty ninth birthday. Helen was eight years younger than he was, and he'd always thought that he would pass on first. But her death was God's will, not his. He remembered what his mother Gaia had taught him: 'For every life we all owe one death. But having died, we will never die again'. Still, he couldn't help tears running from both eyes and onto his ruddy-red cheeks, thinking of all that happened to them and the wonderful life they had lived together.

"I bet'cha Helen's a nurse now, not a Queen," Doug mused as he floated above his new home planet. "She always wanted to be a nurse. Mind you, she could have become anything at all! I well remember," he continued whispering to himself as he gazed toward the new single island of the United Kingdom and Ireland which was just coming into view because it was lit by the bright light of a new day, "how I had always told her that she could do anything, anything at all. And by the Lord in Heaven above, she did all that and more!"

As he finished remembering all the couple had done together, and how much the Universe's civilizations had accomplished in the past thousand years, he looked down on New Earth and saw its clean horizon, no longer in thick haze due to air pollution. He well remembered how, over a thousand years ago, Gaia and Amendus had made good on their many promises. He also remembered the California license plate that was his fathers, which he wished was still hanging in the bedroom in their home in Long Island, and how it spelled in red letters WD6J. He recounted how Gaia had told him that it was a code, if he could put together the pieces. His children had given him a copy of that old plate but had the letters printed backwards. "It read J6DW but it made up the same code," Doug said to himself. "I can almost remember what Gaia told us about the code that is in the letters of my father's old California license plate. She told both Helen and I, at least I think she did, that all you have to do is count the letters of the alphabet and the numbers to see what it really means."

He swept up an old pen and paper from where it floated in front of him and started counting.

"*W*, that's equal to…" he started counting on his fingers to get the right number, "…that's the twenty-first letter of the English alphabet." Then it came back to him of how Helen had done this very thing, by counting it off on her fingers.

"*D* is four," he remembered her saying. "The number six is easy because it's *six*. If you add it all up at this point, the total is *twenty-eight*. And two and eight equals ten. Which, if you add them together, is the number *one*!" he could hear his dead but living wife exclaim. "Then after that is *J*, which is easy, because that's ten, which is also one! So the total is Amazing! One plus one is equal to two! Two is one of my favourite numbers. It's lucky in my family and always has been."

"Two is lucky in my family, too, Helen," Doug recalled himself saying. "Two is equal to twins. My father had twins and so will we, someday, too."

Then Doug recalled how Helen had had multiple twins who, when they grew up, had helped humankind reach the planet Mars and far beyond it. And how their ancestors had more sets of twins, triplets, quadruplets and octuplets. Many of these female and male family members had gone on to conquer the Solar System and were now settled on planets in many different Universes. Even now, as Doug floated above his new home planet, he recalled how one birthday card had been written by his great-great-great granddaughter over eight-hundred years ago in her flowing cursive handwriting:

Dear Grandpapa: Someday, I want to be an astronaut and go where no person has gone before! I want to be one of the first people of the Human Race to venture beyond the Solar System and fly toward the centre of our galaxy: to explore the dark regions of space and set up a new Space Station which I hope will be named the HSS Helen and Doug Martin. Love you so very much and yours forever and ever. Helen (P.S. Not your wife but your Ancestral granddaughter.)

Doug picked up the birthday card which he had kept safe all this time and again examined the handwriting. It was so much like his wife Helen's he couldn't help but smile.

Then he again looked down on New Earth and saw the city, town and village lights shining in the darkness beyond the sun's line of demarcation, and how those same glowing beacons, which had been completely rebuilt following the creation of their new planet, were the cradle of a new civilization. As he gazed at this brand-new chapter of humankind, he remembered what Gaia had promised. Humanity was no longer a threat to any far-flung civilization in the Solar System or their galaxy. Because of that, and making good on her ancient promise, Doug was certain that this new planet Earth would now receive the gift of the latest version of Stardrive and, as his great-great-great grandchild Helen had written, would go where no human had gone before: in fact, he knew that even now and just like his Queen, they were creating yet more Universes and Black Holes.

Finished musing about his memories, Doug looked at the wall clock and saw that it read 2030 Zulu, and time for him to go to bed. But remembering that he had not broken his fast that day, he decided to order in a substantial meal from the Space Station's computer system. Selecting only an entrée of roast beef, he left the weightlessness of the command center and, as he moved toward his bedroom, felt the tug of gravity again. Floating down toward the floor, his feet touched the soft ground. Then he stepped toward his bedroom, looking forward to his meal for one. But on this day, having thought of Helen, he fervently wished that his meal for one was a meal for both of them.

Now horribly lonely for the first time in years, he changed into his nightgown, robe and slippers, and ate at the round bedroom table which also acted as the Station's only dinner table. Served by a member of the Space Station crew, Doug placed a napkin on his lap and began to eat, once again alone.

"I sure wish my Helen was here," he said to the empty room. "What I'd do for a glass of red wine and a bottle of Champagne just like what we had when I kissed her for the first time."

Suddenly, the room filled with light. At his right hand a full glass of red wine appeared. In the middle of the table was a bucket filled with ice and an opened bottle of Dom Perignon.

"Oh God, I'm hallucinating again due to all the meds I've been told to take," Doug said, cradling his chin in his palm. "But I tell you what. This is one great hallucination."

He tried the red wine and it was as perfect as it had ever been. Then he noticed that two empty glass flutes had appeared on the table. Both had been filled with champagne.

"Now all I need is Helen and this would indeed be a perfect meal."

Light filled the room again. When Doug opened his eyes, his wife was sitting across the table from him.

"How now, Doug Masters? I see your older than you were before I left you."

He stared at her. "Are you real?"

"Of course I'm real."

"No you're not."

"Yes I am."

"I said you're not!"

"Oh, yes I am!"

Then they both started to laugh and Helen got up from her chair and came over to him. She kissed him like she always had before. Doug also stood up and then they both hugged.

"Where are you now?" he asked his wife. "You look as young as the first day I met you on the United flight to New York."

"Where am I? I'm here, you stupid twit! And as for young, yes, Gaia tells me that I look younger every day. I can stop getting younger, though, anytime I want. Honey," she said, looking at his face, "you look far too old for my liking. How are you feeling?"

"Old," Doug replied. "So old. To be honest with you, and without my Helen with me, all I want to do is die."

"But you'll never die, Doug. That's my promise."

He laughed. "But what's Gaia's lesson? We all owe a life…"

"One death. But Doug, I died for both of us. You died many times for the salvation of all humankind. It's the least I can do to repay my husband and my best friend. Now let's eat."

Doug looked down and his meal of beef had been replaced by a Filet Mignon with potatoes and vegetables. But when he looked up expecting to see his wife, she was gone.

"One thing's for sure, that was no dream. Look at that meat! I haven't had that since I was a young man in the old United States."

After he finished his dinner, Doug decided to take a shower and then, wearing fresh pajamas, looked at himself in the bathroom mirror. What he saw astonished him.

"Oh my lord of clouds and stars. Look at me! I'm young again."

As he gazed at his reflection, he heard a knock on the front door. Doug turned around as it opened. "Senator, do you need anything else before you retire?"

"No, Captain, I don't but thank you. Sir, can you come here?"

When the crew member walked up to him, Doug asked, "Sir, do I look different than when you saw me the last time?"

"Different?" asked the Gaian Captain. "Sir, why yes. You look younger, that's all. But you're still New United States Senator Doug Martin, no matter what anyone else tells you."

"I guess age really is a number."

"Yes, sir. That's what our Queen told me before she left."

"So she really was here?"

"Yes, sir. She wishes you further success in your next election for the Senate. She told me to tell you that because you are now so much younger, you should plan a run for the presidency of the New U.S.A."

"She really told you that?"

"Yes, sir, Senator. Now if you'll excuse me…"

The Gaian officer turned back to the door then turned toward Doug again. "Sir I forgot to give you this small gift that your wife and Queen left behind."

He extended a large hand and in it was a small bunch of daffodils already in a glass vase filled with water.

"It's almost Spring in New North America. Thank you, Captain. Now I can go to bed happy."

When the Gaian officer had at least left him, Doug crawled into his single bed. As he fell asleep, he dreamed that he and Helen were again in a paradise of their own making. He dreamt that they were living on Proxima B and that he was dictating to his great-great-great granddaughter, Helen—which he knew was impossible even as he dreamed because he knew that the lovely woman was somewhere in new Universe working as an English teacher.

"Hey, granddaughter Helen. Are you ready to help me? I have a new book I want to write. Its title is *The Remembrance of Things I Want to Remember*."

"Can you repeat that, grandpapa?" she asked him in his dream as she held a long notebook and a pencil. "Please say that one more time so I can write it down with a few squiggles. The title is too long anyway."

"Just like your Grandmama, always criticizing my writing. You're taking old fashioned shorthand at school?" Doug replied, grinning. "If you're ready, I'll start."

When Helen had finished taking dictation, she typed out what he had said just as her Grandpapa had instructed. When she was finished and had printed it, it came to only one full standard English A4 page. Telling his granddaughter Helen to sit down, and donning his thick reading glasses, Doug read out-loud what she had printed.

"The new title is The Promises of Queen Helen Revealed," Doug started, glancing up at his granddaughter, then reading out loud again. "They are not promises that were ever revealed before. Instead, they are brand new promises given to all of Humankind as Helen promised you many years ago. Beware, for as *Jesu Kristos* wrote in ancient times, these promises are not for the faint-hearted. Live well, my people, the time is now! Put your trust not in Humankind but in the gifts you are now given. Beware of history repeating itself because it will if you are not careful! Here is what you have already been given but even more will be revealed. In another thousand years, when Humanity is again ready, you will receive a brand-new code from Goddess Gaia, your Queen Mother, as well as one from me, your Queen Helen. It will come not from Proxima B or the Centauri Galaxy, or any other source far away but will, instead, come from a place much nearer to New Earth. In fact, it is already with you, if you listen carefully. That's what we begged you to do before! If you do not interpret that new code correctly, it will mean the end of everything and, this time, we mean everything! You will soon be invaded by creatures from another galaxy, not a far-off one but one much closer, only just over ten stellar lightyears away. That's close by any standard! As we say, read carefully because these ancient gifts still form the foundation of what will save you. Prepare ye the way for the Lord has already come! It is Jesus Christ, Himself, as well as one other who is already among you and has been among you for some time which is the Holy Ghost and the Cloud God. So, go count it off on your ten fingers as you have been taught by the prophet and his wife! Go, our children. Count quickly, before you run out of everlasting time!

"Soon, the new gifts and promises in our new code will be revealed to you through Doug Masters and his many ancestors and new children. We have already given you many gifts, but these are gifts for the taking if you shall want to survive the blasts of interstellar pirates. Go in peace to love each other and know that we shall always protect you. Your Queen in Spirit and Knowledge. Helen."

The next day, when he had woken, Doug again looked out the space station window. What he saw again astonished him. In a new dawn light, two small children, both sleeping in each other's arms, guarded his home planet of New Earth. As he watched, he could see missiles streaking toward the Space Station.

"So it starts all over again, doesn't it?" Doug said to no one.

"No, my husband," a silent voice said in his head. "Even now, we work to destroy what is still evil in this Universe. Does it start again? Well, not like the last time. This time, humanity will protect each other as you and I work to also protect them, and as do our new children.

Then a blast of light filled Doug's room. When he looked out, all he could see were stars, the three planets, and two children smiling as they orbited above New Earth.

"See?" Helen continued. "They know no fear at all. They are always sleeping yet their minds fill the universe with a Universal Warning. 'Do not kill our species.' It is a simple warning, much like the Eleven Commandments, don't you think?"

"Then it does start over again," Doug said and lay back down in bed. "When will you come home, honey?"

"Soon, my baby. So very soon. Or you'll come to me."

As Doug started to fall asleep again, two new voices came silently into his head. Later, when he woke, he remembered exactly what the voices had said.

"This is a final warning to all who would kill humankind or our ancestors or living creatures of any kind. Obey us. Your lives are like ours and do not have to be the same as they have been for an eternity and more. Take the best parts of your civilization and humanity and throw away the rest. Just like our parents Queen Helen and Douglas masters have done and continue to do to this day. There appears to be no ending to this story of happiness and bloodshed. Instead, there is only a prayer and an eternal blessing from us."

When Doug woke an hour later, he mouthed the words of the twins because, in his sleep, he had memorized them. He then had another glass of wine from the bottle that had been left on the table and, still not ready to go back to sleep, thought again of Helen and her visit to him.

"Helen," he prayed to himself, "I want to die. Don't you see that? Please let me pass on so I can be with you. Then I'll never have to die again."

But all Doug heard back was silence. "She's not listening again," he said to the empty room, then grinned. "But what else is new? She never listens to her husband."

His quarters again filled with bright light. When he looked out the porthole of the Space Station, all he saw was the sun and four planets. "That's not New Earth!" he said. "We have three planets in our new solar system. And where are the twin children?"

"We are here, father. We are everywhere."

"Then where is Helen?"

"She is with us. It is now time, Our Lord and Douglas, for you to be rejoined with her to help make more living creatures for many other Universes."

Doug found himself floating above the planet Gaia together with Helen. She reached out, taking his hand. "I told you, my husband, that you'd be with me soon. And so you are."

"Truly, I am blessed. We are all blessed."

She smiled at him. "So said our twins as they circled above the Earth. You've memorized their words. Tell me again what they said."

"They said, 'There appears to be no ending to this story of happiness and bloodshed. Instead, there is only a prayer and an eternal blessing from us." He smiled back at his wife. "And that appears to be true, doesn't it wife? All it needs is a final blessing to all those we know on New Earth, our Solar System, the many

Galaxies, the many Universes that you have created and will soon create and a blessing to all who practice the Golden Rule."

"Why should I give a blessing, Doug. It seems to me that you've already said the blessings. All it needs now, as we begin a new chapter for all living things, is:

— A NEW AMEN —

Acknowledgements

Dedicated to my lifelong partner Carmel Murray; Cindy Randazzo Willis; Gerry Pryde, a life-long pilot and retired Captain at United Airlines as well as his wife, Phyllis Pryde. Blue skies, Gerry. You've 'Gone West', as pilots always say to each other when a fellow pilot passes on. To fellow Captain Toby Dunlap, my father's best friend. Blue Skies too, Toby! To Nicole Jussek, my former editor at Poolbeg Press, Dublin, Ireland. Nicole's experience and wisdom helped me to write an Irish Times young adult bestseller, not bad for my first novel. To Rolling Meadows High School friend, magician and minister, Don Townsend and his wife Debbie. Thank you so much for your support. To Steve Bullock, Chicago buddy and best friend and to the memories you gave me. And to Steve Overton from Sun City, Florida. Your wise counsel has always provided me guidance. To Lourda: a surname isn't necessary. Your lifelong friendship and support did more for me than most people. To Harsha Ganatra, my loving friend from Mumbai, India, and her family. I'll never forget what you've done for me. To Larry Wilson for writing the poem at the beginning of this Novel. And to Rosco Frasier, my great friend from Illinois Wesleyan University. We'll miss your fantastic stories and Hollywood history on Facebook. Rest easy, Ross. Somewhere up there, you just won an Academy Award for your dramatic and comic rolls on Earth and Heaven.

Many authors create their novels and other works by standing on the shoulders of Giants who have come before them. Therefore, to Arthur C. Clarke, SyFy writer extraordinaire and author of *A Childhood's End* (cited often by this writer) as well as Ray Bradbury, and his amazing *Fahrenheit 451*. Your novels were at my side as I wrote this. To the author of *The Jesus Factor*, Mr Edwin Corley; to the author of *The Canticle for Leibowitz*, Mr Walter Miller Junior; to Mr Frank Herbert and his enormous novel *Dune*: to all of them: you created entire futuristic planets and universes populated by what readers believe are real people. You amazed us by predicting future technologies and events. To all of the above men and all of the women who now join them by writing amazing SyFy. And to the men and women who are venturing into space, and will soon travel to Mars: these people deserve our support. Finally, to the children who will one day populate our Moon, Mars, many of the moons of Saturn and Jupiter, and will help to explore our Universe: Good luck to you all. We need you and more like you to accomplish our many missions.

May I also thank Jin Alonzo, my special consultant, now based in Manila. Thank you, Jinny, for your constant support. Written by this Author, who wrote this novel without his loving Partner Carm. Don't worry, sweetheart, we'll get you home so very soon.

And for those of you who want to know: yes, I really was born on 4 October 1955. Or was that 5 October, 1776? I'm not counting and hope you aren't either. Bless you all from my new home planet Gaia and to the crew of my Space Station, THE JOHN GLEN. From here, just above the Earth's troposphere, I can see the glittering lights of our Home Planet. TJR.

Thomas J Richards

Eyeries, Beara, Bantry, County Cork, Ireland

4 October 2023 (the author's 68th Birthday)